KLARA'S BROTHER

& The Woman He Loved

KLARA'S BROTHER

& *The Woman He Loved*

A Novel

Ben G. Frank

Amazon/Kindle Direct Publishing

To my late, lovely wife, Riva, of blessed memory.
She helped me pursue a dream and see it come true.

ACKNOWLEDGMENTS

I am beholden to the following who were there for me with suggestions, editing as well as encouragement to complete The Klara Trilogy with the novel, Klara's Brother & The Woman He Loved: Kathy Fallon, Martin Frank, Martin Hochberg, MD; Scott Michaels, Chrystal Rambarath, Matthew Sarmiento, David Sebso, Robert Reeves, Philip Stein, and Sy Waldman.

BOOKS BY BEN G. FRANK.

A TRAVEL GUIDE TO JEWISH EUROPE. *(FOUR EDITIONS)*

A TRAVEL GUIDE TO JEWISH RUSSIA AND UKRAINE.

A TRAVEL GUIDE TO THE JEWISH CARIBBEAN AND SOUTH AMERICA.

THE SCATTERED TRIBE: TRAVELING THE DIASPORA FROM
CUBA TO INDIA TO TAHITI & BEYOND.

THE KLARA TRILOGY:

KLARA'S JOURNEY.

KLARA'S WAR.

KLARA'S BROTHER & THE WOMAN HE LOVED.

"LET NO ONE FORGET; LET NOTHING BE FORGOTTEN"
— *Olga Bergholz, Russian poet.*

PART 1
"The Beginning."

Chapter 1. Odessa, 1919.
Mischa and Basya.
"They Meet."

•

Our love story begins in the midst of the brutal Russian Civil War. The year is 1919. The Czar has been dethroned. The democratic government which succeeded it, has been deposed by the revolutionary Bolsheviks, commonly known as Reds. Opposing them are the Whites, former Czarist army officers and Cossacks. Mischa Rasputnis, a Bolshevik, starts out as a member of the Communist Red Guard, becomes a Chekist, the new secret police; and is soon promoted to Commissar.

•

Stunned for a minute from a pounding headache and a bruised knee, Mischa Rasputnis can't figure out at first why he's lying prostrate on the Odessa train station floor. Then he realizes, he's in the midst of an angry, surging mob whose members' faces are distorted, their eyes bulging, their arms flaying hysterically as if drowning. Their voices shout in unison: "Let us on the train! Let us on the train!"

Fearing he'll get trampled again and this time crushed, he turns over, sits up and raises his hands, hoping someone will take hold of them and lift him up. In seconds, his arms are grabbed, and his body pulled upward by the strong, but soft hands of a young woman.

"Looks like this crowd flattened you." Seeing he's grimacing as he rubs his knee, she asks, "Are you okay?"

"Yes. Thanks. I'm okay," he replies to the girl before him who, at first glance, is very good looking. He stares at her, she at him. Being an avid reader, especially of Fyodor Dostoyevsky, he recalls a passage in Brothers Karamazov, which noted of the character, Grushenka: "She was very good looking with that Russian beauty so passionately loved by many men."

Both are pleased at what they see. Both try to figure out if they know each other.

"I'm sure I know her. Where from? Come on. Where?" he says to himself, trying to dislodge his stuck memory.

"Of course. She was in my sister's class in School No 1. Klara always talked about her. Basya. Basya Abramskaya. That's her name. Smiled at me once in the school hallway. I was surprised. Barely smiled back. Just a puny kid then."

"We better get out of the way of this rabble," he says, his voice fraught with tension. "Let's go over there. By the wall. We can see everything and be safe."

•

Moments before Mischa urged Basya to move to a safer place, an announcement by a Cossack officer had sparked the stampede that felled him and caused him to limp slightly.

"Attention. Passengers holding tickets on the Odessa train, No.101, to Kiev. The boarding of this train has been suspended. Return tomorrow." The words had trumpeted a death blow to the waiting masses. He gave no timetable for future trains. "Come back tomorrow."

Standing erect, his feet slightly apart, his arms crossed on his puffed-up chest, the Cossack presented himself as an impassable brick wall.

Now desperate, the passengers - exiled Romanians, Greeks, Jews, and Tatars - again prepared to rush the gates. Having heard rumors that sent shockwaves through the dark, Black Sea port city of Odessa that the Bolsheviks were coming back, these refugees wanted no part of the Red horde. They were so frightened that they didn't believe the Czarist commander who ordered them to leave. They began to form a new line which now surged forward, like a raging bull charging *a matador de toros.*

This time, however, they shudder when they observe the Cossacks raising their rifles. The crowd, knowing the troops will shoot to kill, halts in its tracks.

Mischa and Basya observe all this as they wait on the side of the hall near a wall.

"Put away your ticket. It won't help you," Mischa tells Basya who has a high forehead on a long thin face. She reminds him of a Modigliani painting that he saw at an art gallery located near his hometown of Odessa. Modigliani was known for portraits characterized by elongation of faces and figures just like the young lady before him.

Mischa's tone is gentlemanly, unlike the rowdies around him. The words coming out of their mouths are the biting curses in which the Russian language excels.

"I can see the doors leading to the train platforms have been shut!" he exclaims.

"Is there a train waiting to go out?" Basya asks raising her head so she, too, can observe the tracks beyond the gate. "Won't lurking Red guerrillas in the city shoot at the station? They've done that before to create confusion."

"I doubt it," he replies, looking her over again and taking in more of what he sees,

If she was in Klara's class, she's about my age, eighteen. Maybe a little older. Look, she's got long legs, strong arms and long fingers, and nice firm breasts.

The sight of this beautiful young girl reduces the angst in his eyes.

"God," she moans, "What am I going to do? The morning train apparently is the only one out of here today and now, it's not going."

"Correct," replies Mischa. "By the way, I know who you are. You're Basya Abramskaya. You know my sister, Klara. You were in her class. You two were friends. I'm Mischa."

"Yes. I know her," she smiles back approvingly. "Nice girl, your sister. I love her." she adds, though in her own mind, she recalls that Klara Rasputnis, at times, was rather pushy. But now, she doesn't want to risk losing a possible favor from Klara's tall brother who was standing before her. Besides, her wandering, brown eyes drank in his young, handsome face topped with dark brown hair parted down the middle.

"I must get out of here because...." her voice trails off as she says in a pleading voice, hoping the young man before her will take pity on her and help her. She notices would-be travelers are again quietly repositioning. An unaccounted-for stillness settles into the raucous crowd, a silence as if a king is entering his palace and his minions are on their knees bowing before him. Men, women, and children, who a moment ago were grabbing people by their coat collars and shoving them aside so they themselves could advance toward the station tracks, now cower, lower their hands to their sides, and transform themselves into cadres lining up in silent, military-style formation.

Just then, however, the travelers hear the heavy, stamping sounds of more soldiers' boots moving into the station hall. The noise forces them to look half-way up the walls where they see additional soldiers positioning themselves on a plank above the crowd. The troops' cold eyes pierce the soul of each traveler whose skin turns sallow, whose eyes narrow, and whose brow exhibits beads of sweat.

"Will the soldiers fire on us?"

The same Cossack commander again raises the baton he's holding in his right hand. He points it to the street-exits and waves to the pedestrians to move out. He senses that most missed his previous signal. This time, in a harsher voice, he firmly orders, "Come back tomorrow."

"I'm out of here," whispers Mischa, not realizing he's voicing his thoughts to the young lady who has just latched onto him. He doesn't really know her, although again looking out of the corner of his eye, his first impression remains very positive. He hasn't been with a woman like this since his young wife, Olga, died a year ago.

"She's beautiful," he sighs silently.

She catches him looking at her with a steady, incisive stare.

"I'm going to try and get to Deribasovka, the next station up the line. This train's obviously delayed and those soldiers are trying to clear the station. Please. Let me go with you," she pleads.

"Come on. Let's go before the crowd resists and again tries to rush the gate leading to the tracks. They're convinced a train is waiting there. This could get bloody."

Mischa takes her hand and guides her out of the station. She doesn't resist. His hand is warm. Her hand is warm. As they walk down the circular driveway at the station's entrance, Basya is pleased at the sight of this lanky teenager who boasts an upper torso that exudes strength and leads up to a short neck and an unshaven boyish face with a full moustache that makes him look several years older.

He grabs her cardboard suitcase with his other hand.

"I'm Mischa," he says nonchalantly, forgetting that he gave her his name already.

"Yes. I'm Basya, your sister's schoolmate. Nice to meet you."

•

They walk slowly because he limps a little. Mischa notices across the street, an empty, parked four-door touring car, with a peasant standing next to it holding a sign. It reads, "Taxi for hire."

Trying not to be too aggressive, Mischa speaks to him for a minute, takes out a pile of hundred ruble notes from his pocket, and hands them to the driver. He gets into the back of the car and motions to his newly-found, female friend to climb into the back seat with him.

Meanwhile, the crowd appears to be exiting the station.

"Good we got this cab," he whispers. "Got here just in time. If we'd have come later, somebody would have grabbed it."

•

Off they head toward the nearby town of Deribasovka. The car speeds along the road through harsh woodlands. Neither talk. Aware that the driver whose demeanor at first seemed friendly, has turned sullen, they warily look out at the fly-by-scenery. As the driver guides the vehicle along the silent, dirt road, he keeps glancing at the couple through his rear-view mirror. Nearing the town, the driver stops, checks his watch and the surrounding area, and steps on the accelerator. The car bolts ahead.

"Got to get back," says this entrepreneurial driver. "I have a scheduled pickup back at the Odessa station. More money than you can pay me. Made a big mistake taking you."

"Slow down, driver, please," pleads Mischa, sensing the reckless speed of the vehicle.

"Hell no! Can't afford to waste time," he says loudly as he presses ahead.

Coming into view is a razor-sharp bend in the road which causes Mischa to yell again, "Slow down! Damn it! Slow down!"

But it is too late. The shaken driver panics and loses control of the vehicle as he attempts to stay on the road.

"Duck!" shouts Mischa.

The car swerves and heads toward a roadside tree.

"Hold on!" Mischa yells again, while at the same time, he notices the driver opens the front door to escape the oncoming crash. Turning his head to Basya, Mischa doesn't see the almost movie-like sequence of the vehicle slamming into a huge tree. The impact flings the driver head first from the car right into a huge boulder which bursts his head open and splatters the contents of his skull onto the coarse stone.

•

Mischa and Basya, who had braced themselves for the crash, sit for a few minutes in the back seat as a huge cloud of stream of scalding water erupts from under the vehicle's hood. Luckily, the car has not turned over. Extricating themselves from the wreck, they stare at the crushed front end of the vehicle and then at the lifeless body of their driver. They're speechless.

"God must be with us," mutters Basya who mumbles in Yiddish something like a prayer. She knows Mischa's instructions saved her.

"He's silent," she says to herself. *"He doesn't pray. Must be a Bolshevik. They don't believe in religion. Marx and Lenin taught them that 'religion is the opium of the people.'"*

"Are you okay," Mischa asks, though at the same time he stares at his pants ripped around his kneecap from when he fell back at the station. Now he has a torn sleeve on his black winter jacket which covers a turtleneck woolen sweater. He's wearing his mariner's cap, the ones worn by Communist leaders, like Lenin and Trotsky. Fortunately, the rest of his body is unscathed. His knee doesn't hurt anymore.

He can see she's shivering. Her teary eyes beseech him.

"Hold me," she says in a shaky voice. "You saved my life."

He moves closer, embraces her, and in seconds, he can feel that her fear leaves her body.

"I'm okay now," she says in a calmer voice, gazing at the smoke coming from the engine.

"I feel better too," he says affectionately out loud. Silently, however, he mulls over their situation. *"Both of us are unhurt. That's a good omen."*

They realize they can walk, and climb the slight embankment with some struggle. She is embarrassed. Her coat and blouse had caught on the car door and ripped, now exposing her muscular shoulders.

They look at each other, shrug and smile, silently agreeing, "At this point, who cares?"

Walking down the town road toward the station on this cool autumn day, Mischa takes her hand, this time entwining his fingers in hers.

The two - giving each other keen looks - are deep in their own thoughts.

"That was close. It's like that every day for a Cheka agent like me. One thing after another. Spying on the White Army enemy. Thank goodness my instructions came through. Have to get to Petrovirivka. Imagine. I meet a pretty girl. I wonder if she's a Red Guard. Better not ask. I'd give away that I'm a Chekist secret policeman."

Mischa ponders his busy thoughts. He looks at Basya, whom he notices remains quiet. *I wonder what she's thinking? She looks puzzled.*

Mischa's correct. She's indeed challenged at the moment.

"I've got to meet up again with Lev in Tomashpil. Almost forgot about him. Don't tell Mischa. He protected me. His sister once told me that he too hated the Czar. He trained with the political group, the Cadets. I wonder where he's going?"

•

The two reach the Deribasovka railway station. It was empty. Silent. *"I'm tense like an arrow ready to be released from a bow,"* says Basya to herself. *"If no one's in the waiting room, it's unlikely that the train to Deribasovka will stop."*

Bruised and hungry, Mischa tells Basya to sit for a while in the station while he checks out the area. He notices a small tree-lined park just behind the one-room wooden building.

"We have plenty of time," he says, returning to the forlorn-looking young girl. "Let's sit in the park over there. See the bench. If we have to get back to the station, it's close by. It's not too cold today. We're lucky. Warm for this time of year."

"Okay," she says anxiously.

Not a soul in the town park. Reaching the bench behind a grove of trees, he chews down a chunk of black bread and cold beef that he carried in his rucksack. She has cold golubtsy, stuffed cabbage leaves, and some pelmeni, Russian meat dumplings which she has carried in a small, canvas bag.

Satiated and relaxed somewhat, he inches closer to her. She, too, moves toward him. They stare at each other, their eyes meet. They don't talk until he asks:

"Can I kiss you?"

"Yes," she answers, smiling.

They embrace and he kisses her twice. He puts his arm around her neck. She knows he might try and feel her inviting breasts. He does. She lets him. They get excited. She pulls back.

Maybe he guesses her thoughts. Maybe he figures something's good here, and stops while he's ahead. *"Besides, this isn't the place. Out in the open like that."*

"This won't be the last time I'll see you, will it?" she asks, her gazing eyes wide open.

He doesn't answer her. He only kisses her again firmly on her lips.

Later standing by the bench, he asks, "Where are you going?"

"Tomashpil, about six hours from here. I was just visiting my mother in Odessa. I'm taking care of my cousins' house. They moved to Moscow."

"Good. By the way, do you work?"

"Can't tell you," she smiles, trying to play coy. "And you?"

"Can't tell you either," he teases, adding his destination isn't Tomashpil. "I'm going to Petrovirivka, about two hours from here."

"I understand.," she answers. "You work for the 'Revolution?"

Avoiding the question, he replies, "If I can get away from work, I'd like to visit you."

"Please. You'll find me in Tomashpil. My house is on Pushkin Street, Number Seven, near the old, stone church with the huge cross which can be seen from anywhere in town."

They wait. They listen for the sounds of the train. They talk until the shrill whistle of a locomotive chugging into the station interrupts their conversation. A conductor steps down onto the platform. Waving their tickets above their head, the two have them punched by the official. They board and take their seats.

As the long line of carriages rumble out of Deribasovka, the couple is happy to be out of harm's way for the moment.

"You look exhausted," he says.

"I am," she replies, adding, "Please wake me up when we get to Petrovirivka."

A few hours later, he kisses her goodbye and grabs his rucksack. He blows a second kiss to his back-to-sleep-beauty, and puts a note on her lap. It says that he is so happy he met her.

Yet, he thinks of his first wife as he leaves the train.

"Olga. We were together in the Cheka a short time. We even had a child. Your loss haunts me. But it was war. It's still war. Maybe I have the chance to love again. I'm happy for the first time in a long time. I'm going to pursue her. Don't worry. I'm not getting married."

•

Chapter 2. Tomashpil, 1919.
MISCHA.
"A Revolutionary Like Me."

•

A week or so after the excitement of meeting the beautiful young lady in the Odessa rail station, Mischa boards the train in Petrovirivka at around noon on a wintry day in early February, 1919. He carries a perfectly forged passport and a fake White Army pass. Naturally, he hopes his train traveling through White-held territory will not be boarded by security officers.

As it turns out, it's his lucky day. Not one search party gets on. Because of ripped-up tracks, however, it takes nine hours instead of about five to reach Tomashpil, the home of Basya Abramskaya.

Officially, he's carrying out the orders of Commander Andrei.

Mischa's to report to Bolshevik underground forces in Vinnitsa, north of Tomashpil, so he can join his comrades in harassing the enemy. The Commander trusts Mischa. He knows he won't desert to the Whites. Mischa's a Jew and Jews don't go over to the Cossacks or other Ukrainian nationalists who stir up pogroms.

Comrade Andrei has read reports that most residents of Tomashpil have left the White-held town. Knowing it's on the way to Vinnitsa, he asks Mischa to check out that report. Mischa eagerly accepts the assignment.

•

While sitting in the cold, crowded passenger car, Mischa observes that most of the riders have their eyes closed in despair. Their lips are pursed in anger, their nervousness caused by fear of a Red Army ambush. If one of those disgruntled riders observed Mischa, they would see that he had his eyes wide open. He's hopeful that he'll find Basya.

•

Arriving late at night in Tomashpil's deserted rail station, he is greeted by the loud howls of grey wolves hiding in the forests around the village. "No wonder they call it "Wolves' Hollow," Mischa says to himself as he trembles and his heart pounds in fear as he hears the repeated siren-sounding cries of the beasts. Sweat beads form on his brow. He knows they're watching him, especially now that it's close to midnight.

The full moon shines down on the long shadows of those dangerous creatures atop a nearby hill. Mischa quivers from fright. He has heard about maulings by wolves. Residents are frightened, especially in winter when these animals roam the fields at night.

Inside the one-room wooden station, with four windows and a door facing the silvery rail tracks, an elderly flower vendor sits on a bench in the waiting room. She fixes her sad eyes on him. He buys a few winter flowers from the woman and has them wrapped and carefully placed into his knapsack so they don't get crushed. It's for Basya. He tries to concentrate on his work, but instead thinks of her.

"I've become emotional about this Basya. She's got all the attributes, beauty and a gorgeous body-those tits and wide hips - that's what we Russian men want. I'm falling for her," he thinks as he scans the room with thoughts of where he will sleep for the night.

"She reminds me of Olga. Almost a look-alike, with some of the same traits. Not bashful, but intelligent and bright. Let's see what happens. But it's nice

to be around someone like that, especially in war. Dumb me. Why didn't I tell her that as a Communist revolutionary and a dedicated follower of Lenin, I had a duty to fulfill. That's why I had to leave her. Then again, everything with us Chekists is secret. We don't chatter."

The thought makes him smile.

"Wait! What if it turns out she's a revolutionary like me. That'd be great! I'm a Bolshevik. Power to the Soviets!" he utters as he imagines himself marching in the ranks of the victorious Red Army through Red Square in Moscow.

"I love this work. Its dangers don't stop me. And I'm good at writing reports. So, they've also made me a correspondent for Pravda, (the official newspaper of the Communist Party). I'm obliged to write a feature article for the paper every once in a while. I have to keep my eyes open for good stories."

After the flower lady leaves the station, Mischa sits down on a bench in the waiting room and munches on some honey cakes he had placed in his rucksack. As he licks his lips, he remembers the maps disclosing the layout of the area around him. The town sits in the center of a surrounding forest. He knows it's a hike to Basya's house at the far edge of the village. He's going to have to skirt around the settlement not only to find Basya's home, but also to observe any White Army concentrations. He'll have to weave in between huts and dart around trees.

In a shed in the back of the station, he finds several grain bags. Dragging and placing them on the wooden floor, he lies down, keeping his pistol tight in his hand. He dozes off and awakens before sunrise. A cold drizzling rain is just tapering off. Departing, he knows that he's on dangerous ground, not only from wolves, but possible White stragglers left behind.

Soon, small, sunlit bright spots descend on the town this frosty February morning. He has heard that if you love someone, that person, too, can see the same sun that you're walking under. Or was it the moon. "It doesn't really matter, does it," he thinks to himself. The temperature has dropped. He shivers inside his greatcoat.

"Hope I make it," he says haltingly as he continues to slink through the greyness of early morning. As a city boy, he trained every day during his younger years with his high school Cadet unit back in Odessa to be prepared for any event. He no longer hears wolves, only hungry barking dogs whose bite can also be deadly. As he rambles along the muddy road, he observes small clusters of birches and lone pine trees looking forlorn and forgotten.

In Tomashpil, huge trees, some of them several hundred years old, dot the land. Many are acacia trees. Looking at the acacias which cover the surrounding green hills, he is overcome with homesickness. The acacias bring back precious childhood memories that inspire love for Odessa.

Mischa knows that a streak of superstition is embedded in his brain. When he left his house to attend his Cadet military exercises, he felt these strong trees protected him and were literally good luck charms. He would walk between two tall acacias at 11 Primorsky Boulevard, near the Londonskaya Hotel, to bring him good luck for exams that he was taking that day in school. Even in bad weather, he turned down rides in carriages or autos, so he could pass between those very same trees on the way to class.

In late afternoons, the courtyard where he lived, bisected by a communal clothes line strung across the yard, was filled with his friends, running, jumping, shouting, fighting. Short-lived fist fights were broken up. Friendships made and cemented. A tree, on the side of the square, stood as home base for hide-and-seek-games. From it, he hunted down his prey. "Got you," he'd shout as he captured a foe.

Mischa now reaches a cobblestone street. He's fretful and senses danger in this small village the Jews call a shtetl. He screws up his eyes, but sees nothing. "Obviously, most of the inhabitants have fled," he figures, hearing morning bird noises. There are a few residents moving about. He hears their whispers, footsteps, as well as the sounds of an axe chopping wood. And always, there are the sounds of dogs barking, horses neighing, and cocks crowing in the early morning.

Plodding along, he locates the street which lies near the banks of the Rusava River. This road features the main synagogue. More and more, the town appears to be empty. The Jews fearing a White pogrom, probably left. Most dwelling houses are two-story structures with weather-tainted log and board walls. The older log-hewn houses are a story high. The wooden buildings contain elaborately carved scrollwork, dripping from the eaves, and their low windowless attics are often as large as the ground floor. Overlooking this town of several thousand, stands the omnipotent, Russian Orthodox Church, which, the peasants believe, sees all.

Basya had told him the house where she lives stands as a one-story log cabin which resembles all the others on Pushkin Street. He'll be able to recognize hers because it's the cottage with the dull, green moss on the roof.

Meanwhile, he's convinced he's being followed. Maybe that's why he's hurrying. He hopes he's not a target for some crazed sniper.

"Welcome to Tomashpil," mutters Mischa as he scrambles up the slope alongside overgrown hedges. His keen eyes focus on what could be her house. But no smoke is coming from the chimney. There is no glare from candles in the frosted window. The sun is up with not a cloud in the sky. He notices that the houses near hers' have been leveled to heaps of wood. A sudden feeling of fear overtakes him. Something's wrong. At that very moment, a shot rings out.

Without pause, without a quick glance, without thinking about a move, he draws his revolver in the holster hanging at his hip. In one quick motion, he disengages the safety, spins fast, crouches low to reduce his size as a further target, spreads his feet, raises the weapon, and fires at a human's shadow.

Turn and shoot. By now, he's good at it.

Out of the corner of his eye, he sees his assailant - a tall man, clad in a muddy, olive great coat, wearing a tall, visor-less Cossack fur hat. The man who fired the shot knows he missed, so he's seeking shelter.

"Thank goodness he misfired. He had a perfect bead on me," Mischa utters as he fires again. But he, too, is wide of the mark.

Quickly, the assailant pivots around and shoots. The bullet strikes a nearby tree. "I'm not ready to die," shouts the White soldier.

But Mischa is faster. He targets his victim and pulls the trigger. The enemy's head explodes. He slinks to the ground.

Mischa doesn't wait around. He assumes more killers lurk nearby. He runs to her house. There is total silence. Adjusting his eyes, he creeps up to the front door of the wooden cabin and opens it, peeks inside and enters. A stove is located in a corner of the room. Several coals lie near the dormant fire box. He's sure someone has just left the cabin. A freshly lit candle flickers and a large iron pot, still hot, keeps a cabbage soup warm. A pan of pierogies (dumplings) simmers. Unbroken eggs rest in a dish on the counter. His nostrils follow the fresh scent of stale tobacco. His eyes fix on smoke coming from underneath the door in the next room. The door is locked. He kicks it open. A fire smolders in a wicker basket. Ripping off the blanket from a bed, he smothers the flames. On a night-table, he picks up a crumpled, blue blouse and immediately recognizes the smoke-smelling garment. It is the one Basya wore when he met her. A glance back at the table reveals a small photo of Basya in a simple frame which he puts in his pocket.

Moving from room to room, he whispers in a weary, but anxious voice, "This is Number Seven, Pushkin Street. But she's gone. 'Basya,'" he shouts tremulously. "You can't be very far away."

Entering the last room, he sees the floor is covered with ferns. The bed, stripped of its blankets, is overturned. A closet is empty, a night table broken into pieces. Anger and fear overwhelm him. "Time to get out of here," he says to himself.

Running out of the cabin, he's about twenty yards away when he hears a whining sound in the air. A shell is heading his way. Someone pushes him to the ground. His face is down. He awaits death. When the shell hits the house, he turns his face to the explosion. Darkness.

•

Waking up in a nearby Red guerrilla, make-shift infirmary later that day, he's at first blinded by the lights. He blinks and has two immediate thoughts. The first is, "How did he get here?" He quickly dismisses it because the next thought reminds him that hours ago a shell hit the house he fled. The last thing he believes he felt was someone pushing him. He thought he saw Basya's wavy dark brown hair which he had caressed, touched, and kissed that day in Deribasovka. "I'm sure it was her," he tells the nurse.

"If there was a woman in that house, we found no trace of her. Maybe she vanished after she dragged you to safety?" responded the female aide who's wearing a Red armband on her arm. "Our people weren't there. You were unconscious when they brought you to our little hideaway here. You're okay. You suffered only superficial wounds. Rest this morning. You can go at lunchtime."

•

She saved my life. I'll search for her. But will I find her? Closing his eyes, he vows, I'll find Basya Abramskaya, if it takes me a lifetime.

•

And where is Basya Abramskaya this February, 1919?"

Having fled Tomashpil, Basya waits in Vinnitsa for her boyfriend, Lev Kuznetsov. She and Lev have been on the run for months - at times, separately. They parted a few weeks ago, as Basya was being watched. They planned to meet at the Savoy Hotel in Vinnitsa, a few hours away from Tomashpil. But Lev hasn't showed up. "Will Lev

appear this time?" she asks herself without too much concern. She
has learned how to be tough if need be, to push worry away, even in
this case, when both the Whites and Reds seem to be after the elusive
Lev. He has antagonized both by working as a civilian conductor on
each side's train routes.

•

Anxious from being holed up in a hotel room, Basya makes an
impulsive decision. "I've got to get out," she murmurs. She thinks she
can walk safely in Vinnitsa, because she dresses like a native. It is a
skill she's acquired from two years of moving from place to place. She
believes she's relatively safe. She puts on a peasant blouse, flowery
skirt, and high boots and leaves her room in the fully-booked hotel. It
is mostly filled with refugees who had fled Odessa and were on their
way to Kiev. Despite her fidelity to Lev, who's older than Mischa, she
thinks of the young man she met at the station. She compares him
to her coarse Lev. *"Still, I can't desert Lev. He's my love. I must remain
loyal."* she says to herself as his absence becomes a nightmare.

She heads to the market and strolls through it. In normal times,
she loves shopping, despite the disdain of the Communist Party
toward this bourgeois activity. She's not a member of the Party, but
she knows its philosophy. Some things she likes, some she doesn't.

She gazes at the products in the outdoor market: used clothing,
souvenirs, farm produce, chickens hanging from wire strings. She
engages sellers. She's beginning to enjoy her stroll when an accoster
roughly grabs her left arm.

•

"Come here, you bitch," whispers a small woman dressed in a
black skirt, white peasant blouse and a greatcoat with a White Army
insignia on it. "Make a sound and I'll kill you."

"Let me go. What do you want?" challenges Basya who notices
the woman is unaccompanied. This is good for Basya because the
population is anti-White and they might come to her aid if they know
she is being kidnapped.

"Come with me," demands the intruder, in a loud voice. Without
a police companion, she realizes she has to make the pinch alone.
"We're on to you. We know who you are and whom you're to meet.
We've got a photo of you and your boyfriend, Lev Kuznetsov."

"I see," says Basya in a compliant tone which causes the assailant
to relax her hold. "Bad move, you bastard" swears Basya under her
breath. With her free arm, she hammers the woman in her ribcage,

causing her to grovel breathless on the ground.

Knowing the crowd might be on her side, Basya further kicks the assailant in the leg and runs down the cobblestone street. She heads back to her hotel, a safe house for Communists.

"'Stop her!" shouts the agent, getting up slowly. "Police! Stop her!"

Nobody lifts a finger.

Basya reaches the hotel entrance. Once inside, she begins to climb the long flight of winding, marble stairs to her room, just as the agent reaches the front door and begins chasing Basya up the steps. The agent, right behind her, finally grabs her arm at the top of the stairs.

"I got you now!" she says breathlessly.

Just then, Basya's boyfriend, Lev, who finally showed up, hastens out of a nearby room and untangles the pair. Pushing Basya away and hesitating for a moment to ascertain exactly what is going on, he hears Basya shout:

"She's trying to take us in. She's an agent!"

Lev jumps the policewoman and forces her to the floor. She fights back, pushes him off, and tries to get up. Seeing that she's unbalanced, he pushes her hard toward the steps. With her hands flailing as she falls backwards, she bursts out with a loud shriek heard throughout the hotel, as she tumbles down the stairs, and crashes into the floor below.

Moments later, the hotel staff, Red sympathizers, pick up the nearly lifeless body; dump it into a grain sack, carry it through the back door and onto a small truck. A half hour later, the White police agent is lying dead at the bottom of the Southern Bug River.

•

Chapter 3. Zhitomir, 1919.
BASYA.
"Tragic Travels and the Abandonment of her Child."

•

Basya would never forget the high-pitched piercing sound of terror that emanated from the police agent's mouth as she fell to the bottom of the hotel steps. It was not the first time she heard a person's last-doomed desperate cry.

Two years earlier, Basya had visited her Uncle Menachem and Aunt Malke in White-occupied Zhitomer. She joined protesters demonstrating against the Whites, who began to round up so-called troublemakers. Basya was among the arrested, and was at first thrown into a dusty, black-wall-lined storage room of a furniture warehouse in the center of town.

That night, sitting among the prisoners, she heard the fearful scream of oncoming death by one of the captured women who was dragged to her doom by the Cossacks. The woman fought like a bloodied animal and even bit one of the soldiers. A Czarist brute silenced her by hammering her head with his rifle. Basya was getting up to help her, but her fellow inmates quickly pulled her down.

"Don't do it," they whispered, as they restrained her. "They're going to kill her. They'll kill you too if you interfere."

The woman who screamed was the organizer of the demonstration. She knew what was in store for her. Her captors were going to murder her. They did.

Basya stayed down. But the incident made her think about joining the Bolsheviks who had overthrown the legitimate government in St. Petersburg and ignited a cruel civil war.

An hour before the Cossacks hauled the woman away, however, she gave Basya her sealskin coat. The coat alone, however, couldn't give Basya a reprieve. It was the determination of her boyfriend Lev, whom she loved, who saved her. Upon hearing from the underground network that Basya was being held by the Whites in an abandoned warehouse in Zhitomir, Lev left Odessa and arrived in town the next afternoon. He had no trouble locating the temporary prison. Slinking around the single-story building, he noticed only two guards, one of whom was outside at the warehouse entrance. He could see the other soldier through a side window. He was sitting in an empty office, with a bottle of vodka and a pack of cigarettes on the table.

Circling the building again, Lev stopped at another side window through which he spied a small group of female prisoners in a large hall. Moving to the back of the building, he spotted Basya, who had been moved, sitting alone on a wooden box in a room.

"Not a good sign. She's singled out for special treatment," he thought to himself. "I must break the glass and get her out." He hastened back to one of the many Communist safe houses in the town. There, he picked up a steel glass cutter that could quietly remove a pane of glass. He returned to the building and etched the glass window looking onto Basya's room. He slowly removed it in one piece. The night air flowing through the empty space woke Basya who was sleeping now on a worn, smelly mattress. Stunned, she watched Lev ease his body feet first through the empty window and easily jump down to the cement floor.

"My prince in shining armor," she whispered nervously. She hugged him and planted a touching kiss on his cheek. "I love you. Let's get out of here."

Scrutinizing the room, he grabbed the wooden box which could be used in their escape through the window, about six feet off the floor. Looking around the room, he stared toward the door.

"The guard just passed a short while ago. I've been monitoring him all evening. He'll be around again in about forty-five minutes."

"Good. Let's go."

Dragging over the box to just below the window, Lev goes first so he can be in position to reach down and lift Basya if need be. Suddenly, loud voices can be heard from the front office. The guard is chatting with the sentry. The couple waits. Finally, silence.

"Here I go" says Lev, stepping on the box. He easily slips through the open window onto the ground. Basya follows him as Lev helps her up. Now on their feet, they embrace.

•

"The Whites will be looking for us. I've got money," he says. "We can take the back streets to avoid their patrols and get to the railroad station.'"

Lev is correct. They make it to the station, but White guards surround the building. Instead, they head to a safe house where they reside for a couple of weeks. He grows a beard. She dyes her hair "blonde. The two finally go to the rail station. After a day's wait, a train comes through.

"Bad," says Basya. "It's heading to Siberia."

"'Why not go there,' says Lev impulsively. "At least we'll get away from the war.'"

"But Siberia?" she questions.

After a quick discussion, she gives in to Lev. *After all, he did rescue me from certain death.*

•

But war, that ghastly destroyer, sometimes doesn't respect plans of high-ranking officers, or refugees. This Russian civil war follows the couple. The pair only get into a deeper mess when they arrive in Yekaterinburg, during a bitter winter lasting into March, 1918.

The Reds hold the city by then and are looking to recruit men as laborers and soldiers. Walking from the station to the city center, Basya and Lev are picked up by the police. They're shoved into a work camp. The local central committee needs workers. Lev, an electrician by trade, is assigned to a telephone repair crew and told to climb up telephone poles and clear away thick blobs of frozen ice on the wires. They give him thin gloves which, he's soon to learn, are not suitable for the Siberian frost. The subzero weather completely freezes his fingers on both hands. Because he can't move them at all, she does things she never imagined she'd have to do. When he goes to the bathroom, she has to hold his penis and wipes his ass.

•

Lev recovers. They survive because she uses her charm and good looks with local officials who get them out of difficult situations. One day, Red Army recruiters came around and threaten to haul Lev away to a training camp. While Lev pleads his case by showing them his documents and engages in long discourse, Basya runs to the Party chairman's office and gets a deferment for Lev. The intruders leave scratching their heads. Nobody ever pulls rank on them.

Other officials and bureaucrats take a liking to her. Even Communist bureaucrats admire a beautiful woman, even though she's not a member of the Party, nor of the Red Guard, nor in the Cheka. She winks at them and they give her more rations. She doesn't need an appointment to get into a special food store, even though these establishments are overwhelmed and crowded.

•

One day, Lev returns home from the Yekaterinburg city square. He's wearing a railway conductor's uniform, and says: "Basya, I got a job on the railway. How do I look?" He continues, "Now the police won't bother me. I can even get you on the trains where I work."

Lev settles Basya in far-off Harbin, Manchuria. It's safer there. He comes home often. On one trip, he divulges that on a train near Yekaterinburg which he served as a conductor, trouble came in an unexpected way. He had a confrontation with a young Chekist agent. He doesn't tell her much about what happened, but apparently the agent didn't identify himself and attacked Lev who's so enraged that someone questioned his authority, that he fought the assailant. Rounding a sharp curve, the agent fell out and was assumed dead. Lev testified at an inquest in Chelyabinsk. Even though he was exonerated, he remained under a cloud of suspicion. But he managed to continue working. There's a shortage of trained conductors.

•

And then, on one of his leaves from the railroad, Basya tells him she's pregnant. He professes happiness, but worries that Basya, being with child, will hamper their survival in case they have to change places in a hurry.

"You should go and stay with your Aunt Malke and Uncle Menachem in Zhitomir," he advises.

Basya listens and arrives in Zhitomir in the late spring of 1919. Her aunt and uncle take care that no one knows she's back in the town where she was imprisoned. She has her child in late summer. Her aunt and uncle, who are childless, are in their glory to become a mother and father to her while she convalesces after a tough delivery. Unfortunately, the baby is born small and frail and doesn't seem to be thriving. Maybe it's because of a lack of nutrition in her milk, or maybe it's stress, or both. Her aunt has a neighbor who volunteers to be a wet nurse.

Shortly thereafter, Lev, in disguise, finally gets to Basya's relatives' house. Like all new fathers, he's now excited to meet infant Zosia. He decides to remain for a while in Zhitomir even though he, too, is a hunted man, running from the Whites. The family realizes it's only a matter of time until the local White police catch them.

"We must get out of here, or else," he says to Basya one day.

•

Meanwhile Basya's uncle and aunt devise a plan. Uncle Menachem explains it to Lev:

"I want to get my niece out of this swamp. I want her to go to America. It's not safe here." He adds, "I can get safe passage for you to Romania, via Odessa, and then to Germany." Seeing Lev's concerned expression, Uncle Menachem presses on. "My aide, Menashe Goldberg, will drive and protect you till Timisoara in Romania. From there, I have a cousin who will travel with you to the port in Bremen. You'll have proper documents. You'll travel as husband and wife. Once you get to America, you'll be safe."

"But we're not married," declares Lev.

"You'll be by week's end. I have cousins in America. We stick together. You'll contact them. You'll be part of the family. They'll take care of you."

"'Thanks. We'll do it. Anything to get out of Russia. It's bad here."

"Good. You'll leave next week for America," says Uncle Menachem.

"One more thing, baby Zosia must stay with us until you get there. Then we'll come over with the child." He continues despite Lev's alarm. "You can't drag a newborn with a wet nurse through half of Europe and then onto an ocean liner. You'll write us from New York when you arrive and get settled. By then, the baby will be older."

"Basya's not going to go for this. No mother would, even if her child has a problem," Lev protests.

"She will," replies Uncle Menachem. "The three of us will convince her. She'll agree."

For the next few weeks, uncle, aunt, and Lev persuade Basya that it's better for the baby to remain behind, until she's older. "Let's say six months to a year. We'll tend to the newborn as if she's our own. Then we'll all come to America," says Uncle Menachem.

Basya listens to Lev as she has done all her short life.

"I trust my aunt and uncle," she says. "But what if something happens to the baby?"

•

Lev and Basya say goodbye and leave for Odessa in late September, 1919, without the baby. The first few days go well. Then the rains turn the roads into rivers of black mud. They join a convoy of four trucks. After they arrive in Odessa, they head west through Kishinev toward Timisoara in Romania, where they're ambushed by bandits preying on refugees. Goldberg, the driver, is killed, but Lev manages to get them to safety by fleeing into a nearby forest. They are joined by refugees who hate the Bolsheviks. That night, their new group makes camp and lights a fire. Bundled together and wrapped in blankets, they try to soak up the warmth of the bonfire. They haven't eaten for hours. Stranded with little food and water, they share a few crusts of bread to keep away the hunger that almost strangles them.

Exhaustion weighs on them as they wait for the morning. A wild wind lashes their weather-beaten, wrinkled faces. Members of the group drag logs to the small fire they had managed to light to keep everyone warm and frighten off animals. At the same time, they realize the flames could be a beacon to bandits roaming the area, looking for refugees to rob.

"We'll die of starvation," says one of the stranded group as the flames die out and he shivers in the freezing air. "I can't sleep."

"Neither can I," shouts another.

A bearded soldier, whose ripped jacket and patched pants fail to hide his festering wounds, reveals he hates the Army and just wants to get home. "I didn't fall for that Communist rot. They're no better than the bourgeois. Liars, cheats, and thieves like the rest of them. Fooling the people and dragging us into permanent slavery."

"'What have you got to say, lady,'" says the lice-scratching soldier, pointing to a young girl next to Basya. The girl had told Basya her life story. Basya wonders how the young one can tell the group she's the victim of an abusive husband who beats her. How can she explain he carouses around town, then returns home and smacks her. But she does.

Next, an old woman whose husband was shot by the Bolsheviks for hoarding food, discusses the days before the war. "The Czar protected us. We had peace. We raised families. We went to church. We prayed every day. Then came the Bolsheviks, the betrayers of Christ. They brought us death. My whole family is gone," she concludes and crosses herself.

"My goodness. It's my turn," Basya whispers, as she nudges Lev and makes a loop with her eyes urging him with unspoken words, "Let's get out of here. I can't take it anymore.'

Basya rises and runs from the clearing. Lev races after her.

A shell wheezes in and hits the campfire.

"I want to help the wounded," thinks Basya. "But I can't run back. The bandits will murder us. Lev, give me that ok, so I can clear my conscience." As if he heard her plea, Lev shouts, "Keep running, Basya. For baby Zosia's sake."

She obeys. She runs fast. Bullets whiz past. "I don't know if Lev's behind me."

Minutes later, she turns and doesn't see or hear him. Darkness. Silence in the forest. Then, she hears his last gasp, "Keep running."

•

Chapter 4. Zhitomir, 1919.
BASYA.
"Basya Mourns the Loss of her Family."

•

Basya finally made it back alone to Zhitomir in the early fall of 1919. There, she discovered that along with several dozen others, Aunt Malke, Uncle Menachem, and her infant, Zosia, were murdered in a White army pogrom.

The whole town heard Basya's screams, her howls of despair, penetrating their minds and hearts. She doesn't know it, but she is administering scream therapy: relieving guilt caused by leaving her child. "I shouldn't have left her behind." she yells. "It's my fault. My fault. Maybe she would have survived the campfire shooting."

She remains in her aunt and uncle's deserted house in Zhitomir for a month, crying, wailing, barely eating or sleeping. She doesn't bathe nor change her clothes. Her hair is disheveled. She talks to no one. She has no one, except an elderly neighbor who comes every day with some hot soup. The old woman doesn't get near her because of Basya's unpleasant body odor. The neighbor notices a few empty vodka bottles in a corner of the kitchen floor.

•

Sitting in this house of the dead, staring at the bare walls, her mind wanders to the one safe place in her short life, her childhood. Born in 1901 in Kosice, then moved to Hungary, Basya Abramskaya was the only child of Sandor and Ludmilla Abramsky. The family spoke Slovak, Czech, and Hungarian in equal parlance. They knew all three fluently. The city was a gateway between the east and west. Her parents, intellectuals that they were, looked to Prague, at that time one of the leading cities of the Austro-Hungarian Empire, for cultural stimulation, including speaking the Czech language at home without a trace of an accent.

When Basya was eleven years old, the family moved to Odessa. Her father had heard of a physician who was retiring after having built up a prosperous practice. He was selling his business and was offering a reasonable price for it. Basya's father bought the practice and the operation thrived. Basya's mother, a graduate nurse, served as his assistant.

In Odessa, the Abramsky family, who had relatives in the port and in nearby towns, enrolled their daughter in a Russian school. As it turned out, one of the pupils in that school, and a neighbor, was Lev Kuznetsov. In and out of school, the two became inseparable, though he was three years older. Sometimes they would meet after class, but never alone, a parent, a maid, a relative, someone always accompanied the two.

Everything was perfect in her life and peace reigned in the city. Being an only child, Basya was the recipient of much love. She was happy. The only negative was that she had a hard time making decisions, and relied on her parents and Lev to make her decisions. She so respected Lev, even when they were teenagers, that she went along with everything he said and did. That led to her agreeing to a spur-of-the-moment secret meeting with him, the night before he was set to leave for the front with the Czarist army, now engaged in the first days of World War I.

That balmy summer August night in 1914, she misled her parents. She said she had to pick up her forgotten exam book at school, which was open because of rehearsals. They allowed her to go. "Come back soon." With minutes counting down till he had to depart, she met Lev. They retreated to a nearby park bench.

"Basya," said Lev determinedly, happy he had invited her to come out and glad she was in front of him. "I want you to be my girl and wait for me."

"I will," were the only two words she could muster, not moving at all. But then, getting up her nerve and standing, she said, "You can give me one kiss." As she said this, she closed her eyes, pushed her lips forward, took a deep breath and waited. He stood up, kissed her soft, warm lips, and whispered, "It's our secret."

"Agreed," she answered smiling. It was as if their friendship was sealed in a pact, like those lovers in the romance novels she was reading.

"I have to get home." she said, planting a kiss on his cheek. Not waiting for him, Baysa waved as she ran off. In front of her house, she stopped, composed herself, picked up the book she had hidden underneath a broken front porch step. Basya walked into her house where the windows had been left open. The house was cool. Her parents were having tea and cake in the dining room. When they asked her to join them, Basya declined "I have a test tomorrow and need to study".

"Good night." they said.

When she was sprawled out on her bed in her room, she looked at the soccer team pin that Lev had put into her hand after their kiss. She smiled, put the love token under her pillow, placed the book on her desk, undressed, got under a single cover, closed her eyes, and fell asleep. She did not think about the test at school, which, anyway, was scheduled for next week.

•

Lev went off to war the next day and within a few weeks was captured at the Battle of Tannenberg, in Prussia, where Russia suffered a disastrous defeat. Sent deep into Germany to a prison camp which housed enemy combatants, Lev quickly found himself in the last throes of death. He looked like a skeleton. He weighed ninety-four pounds. Emaciated, he could barely walk and was only kept alive with extra provisions by his fellow inmates.

During the war, Basya never heard from Lev. At first, she waited every day at the mailbox. When the mailman arrived, he usually tried to give her hope. "Maybe tomorrow."

The hunger to know if he was alive consumed her. She couldn't eat or sleep. Basya missed him terribly. She became inspired by her mother who longed for her husband, Sandor, too, had been called up to serve in the Russian army. From her mother, Basya learned what loneliness and waiting for "her man," entailed - mind control, patience, keeping busy. Her mother told her, "If you are patient enough, you can have it all." She never forgot those words.

Basya and her mother constantly suffered from hunger, but managed to live off the savings that her father had squirreled away during his years as a physician. As the war progressed, and with it the lack of male figures in her life, she began to make decisions on her own, such as choice of classes, friends, and clothes. In school, she became close to some of the girls in her grade. She learned how to make alliances. With Lev not around, Basya became popular among her peers. They were no longer jealous of her because she had a boyfriend in the army. On the contrary, Lev became a patriotic figure to these hero-worshiping young ladies.

Energized, she waited for Lev Kuznetsov. When Russia pulled out of the war in March, 1918, Lev, after nearly four years a POW and weak on his feet, managed, with the aid of a cane, to walk out of the gates of the Kaiser's prison in Germany.

Basya was at the Odessa station when Lev arrived home.

•

Two years later, Basya found herself abandoned in a run-down, empty house, deserted by life and deposited in the town as the mother of a dead child and a niece of a murdered aunt and uncle. Finally, as if seeing a spiritual light, she got up from the floor one morning and shouted in a loud voice to the empty walls of her abode.

"They're bastards: The Czars and the White supporters who follow them. May they burn in hell!" Her rage continued. "They say Jews are different and disloyal. We're the pariahs. The stiff-necked enemies of Christ. They attack us, inflicting blow after blow: Harassment, forced conversion, humiliation, accusations of ritual blood murder and killing-pogroms." Basya unleashed her hurt even more before making a vow. "From childbirth, Russians and Poles and others sucked anti-Semitic milk from their mother's breast. I'm joining the Reds."

She then heads to the town's Jewish cemetery. A mass grave site is located in a barren field. There are no headstones. The bodies were deposited into a huge ditch. A temporary wooden marker was in front of the field. Standing in front of the grave, she carefully cries out:

"Somewhere below here is my aunt and uncle, and my beloved Zosia. May you and Lev rest in peace. Who knows where he's buried? One day, maybe when the war is over, they'll put up a proper monument with the story of who and why they, the innocents, were murdered. They died only because they were Jews."

"I'll avenge all of you," she yells loudly, her words floating over the flowerless field.

A half-hour later, she returns home. Basya washes, puts on fresh clothes, and leaves the house, never to return. She goes to Bolshevik Party headquarters in the woods. She joins the Party with revenge in her heart. Basya silently pledges allegiance to the Red banner. "I am a good Communist." she says with determination, purpose and blind faith.

•

Chapter 5. Kiev, 1919.
MISCHA and DIMITRI.
"Two Comrades Meet."

•

In the winter of 1919, nine months after his sojourn to Tomashpil, eighteen-year-old Mischa Rasputnis takes the train from Vinnitsa to Kiev, a journey of about five hours. He has heard that people like to call Kiev the mother of Russian cities. He also is aware that the city boasts that Ukrainian girls are very pretty, mostly blonde, and with fine womanly figures.

On his first day in the city he keeps seeing Basya's face in the morning crowd as he proceeds down Kiev's Kreschatik, the capital's main thoroughfare. He's sure she's going to appear and they'll hug and kiss in the middle of the broad avenue.

Kiev is no stranger to him. He's been here several times. But the city has changed. Gone are the days when civilians strolled down crowded streets lined with frequented brightly-lit shops and chatted with friends and neighbors. The pale face Kievans today are flushed with anxiety. Their frightened eyes dart hither and yon to avoid being spotted by White Army spies out in full force. Fearful of bandits and escaped prisoners, residents shun local parks.

At any given time, armed peasant armies, such as the Greens, the Whites, and the Reds, move in and out and occupy the metropolis. No one knows who's in charge. Kiev has changed hands more than a dozen times this second year of the civil war which has turned everything in Russia upside down.

For the moment, however, Mischa's thoughts are not on the war. They're on Basya Abramskaya. *It seems she's vanished into vast Russia. Cheka can't locate her. Somebody must know where she is. I'm sure I saw her in Tomashpil, even if it was for an instant.*

Although he feels the biting, icy air cutting through him, he recognizes that it's not as harsh as it was in Siberia last winter when his guerrilla unit attacked the newly-formed, White Army installations along the Trans-Siberian railway. He shudders at the possibility of being sent back to that frozen land, the wildest part of Russia.

On this bleak, early November day, Mischa's on his way to meet 'Comrade 'D.'

I'm sure this 'Comrade 'D' is my comrade, Dimitri Abramovich Dudin, who worked with me a couple of times last year on the trains. Great comrade-in-arms, although I always worried about him. He couldn't stay away from drinking.

Mischa recalled how in the early days of the war, Dimitri got into a fight with a conductor who pushed him off a moving train. Mischa looked for Dimitri, but was called away after a limited search. Later, Mischa was told that a peasant woman found Dimitri in a deep gully and nursed him back to health. Afterwards, he surfaced in Siberia where he located Mischa.

"He liked my sister, Klara." Mischa thought to himself: *"I hated her. She was picked over me to find father who was somewhere in America. Dimitri tried to bring us together -as brother and sister - one more time before she left Russia on her journey. He set up a meeting. It was the last time I saw the bitch. I think he thought I should have put in a good word for him with Klara. I didn't. He shouldn't have interfered. Despite that, I like him."*

•

Moments later, a cautious voice from behind interrupts his thinking:

"Don't be alarmed. Keep walking."

Startled, Mischa keeps moving.

"Comrade Mischa, it's your comrade, Dimitri, the one and only."

"So, you're 'Comrade D,'" Mischa laughs as he whispers into the man's ear. "I knew it was you the whole time."

The two hug each other as Russians do when greeting friends and relatives. They would have raised their fists in a revolutionary salute, but they dare not. Kiev is now occupied by Cossacks and White Army groups loyal to the late Czar. Although incognito in Kiev, the two may be the first Chekists in the city.

"I was on my way to meet you at the safe house here in Kiev. They told me where you were." Mischa continues, "We're going to work together again."

"We have to be careful," mutters Dimitri, looking around without moving his head, as if he had "razor-cutting eyes" back there. I'm glad we didn't meet at the railway station, nor the safe house. Too many White spies lurking about."

Again, the two men don't have to pretend as if they're old-time, friends, smiling, laughing, slapping each other on the back.

"Anyone watching us by now, surely thinks we're brothers," says Dimitri.

"From this moment on, we truly are again," says Mischa. Admiring his greeter, his mind slowly conjures up what he remembers of the agent facing him. He hasn't changed much since Mischa last met him in Siberia: Short and stocky with long hair combed back in the Polish style.

"You're growing a beard, too," Mischa says, adding: "Proceed comrade. Tell me my new orders."

"We're to take the train to Moscow. We're going to ride the Trans-Siberian railway as special agents. Our job is to prevent the Whites, the enemies of the Revolution, from wresting control of the vital line. We hold it now since we routed their forces this past fall. But we have to stop bandit raids." Dimitri adds, "I'm in charge, with you as my deputy. But we'll work together."

"Where's our base?" asks Mischa.

Yekaterinburg," replies Dimitri. "You've heard of it, I'm sure. The city has received increased notoriety recently. That's where, I'm told, we executed the Tsar and his family, a year ago, July."

"When do we leave?" asks Mischa, staying on subject, but aware that the move to Moscow and Siberia with the Red Army will extend the distance between him and Basya.

He thinks, *I'm a devoted Communist and the Party definitely comes ahead of Basya. My wife is Russia. Never will I cease following Marx and Lenin."* Another thought occurs to him. *"On the other hand, maybe I can also have a mistress, like in French novels? Long live the Communist Party, as well as lovely Basya!"*

"We depart tomorrow morning. Be at the station at seven o'clock." he hears Dimitri say, bringing back his focus.

Good. I'll meet you there," answers Mischa who shows a picture of Basya to Dimitri who waxes favorably over the lady whom he calls beautiful.

With a hearty handshake, they resume their friendship, at least for now.

•

Mischa and Dimitri depart Kiev and head to Moscow. The journey takes a few days longer because the Whites search for Soviet spies and halt trains to find them. Safe in Moscow, they board the Trans-Siberian railway for Yekaterinburg, an industrial city east of the Urals and a major stop on that rail line.

"It's going to be all fun and games," Dimitri tells Mischa, as they get off the train in their new home in a base in Yekaterinburg. The outpost trains Red Army agents in guerrilla warfare.

"Don't be so sure about fun and games," replies Mischa, skeptically. "You'll give it a curse"

"There you go again, Comrade Mischa. That bourgeois superstition of yours. I ought to report you for counter-revolutionary thinking," he says, smiling.

•

Chapter 6. Yekaterinburg, 1920.
MISCHA and DIMITRI.
"The Train War"

•

"Some fun and games," Mischa mutters as he fires away at White bandits attacking the armored train he and Dimitri are guarding. In this attack, the guerrillas are defeated and the pair chalk up another victory for the Red Army in this strange train war along the Trans-Siberian railway. Battles are fought on the railroad tracks as opposing armored cars move up and down the line, often colliding in battle.

A few days after beating back the Whites, Mischa's train, composed of armed carriages, is attacked from the roadside. Once again, he and his men manage to repulse enemy forces. This time, however, Mischa and Dimitri and their team of a dozen cavalry, crossed with belts of bullets, retrieve their horses from a rail car, and begin chasing the Whites into the thick taiga forest. Just as they reach a large grassy circle at the bottom of a knoll, bullets from White forces, entrenched at the top of a hill rain down on them. The Reds barely have time to set up a perimeter. The attackers, who vastly outnumber Mischa's band, continue their heavy fire. In twenty minutes, five Red soldiers are killed

"We're losing men," Mischa shouts over to Dimitri. "Back in Kiev you called this 'fun and games' on the railroad?"

Dimitri doesn't answer.

For a few moments, the enemy holds its fire. Silence. Mischa surveys the scene and remembers that when the shooting started, his unit's horses panicked and raced into the woods. Chances of escape for his troops who survived are thin. *"This can't be the end for me. I'll never see Basya again. Good while it lasted. Too bad it was only for one day."*

His thoughts are interrupted by neighing from the enemy's horses in the woods. He scans the area again. No movement. He's sure they're preparing to charge the camp site. It's the quiet before the storm.

"My goodness, it stinks," he thinks, sniffing the acrid smell of gunpowder hanging in the air, and at the same time, looking down at his shaking hands. *"They're going to hit us any minute. I've got to be ready. Snap out of it, Mischa,"* he tells himself. *"Thinking you're down on your luck is not going to help you. Being frightened is even worse. Wind yourself up again. Fight!"*

Noticing his ammo is almost gone, Mischa's sharp eyes scout the scene. His open nostrils breathe in the smell of enemy horses. His ears perk up to capture any noise, such as an enemy soldier's foot stepping on a twig jutting out from the Siberian permafrost soil.

Seconds later, shots ring out. He and Dimitri fire back. Saliva oozes from Mischa's mouth as he pulls the trigger on his rifle and sees a White soldier fall. Mischa screams: "This is for Comrade Alexei whom you just murdered. And this is for Comrade Vladimir whose life you just cut short. If I'm going to die, I'm taking you with me."

"Here they come," exclaims Dimitri, noticing Mischa' standing to get a better shot. "He's a dead duck. I must warn him."

Dimitri tells the other Soviet soldiers to fire only when the enemy gets closer. To Mischa, he yells, "get down."

Fortuitously, after uttering the warning, Dimitri hears shouts of 'hoorah' from a whooping Red Army cavalry group from the train charging into the edges of the open circle. Having heard gunfire they hurtled to the site. Whirling their sabers through the air, they cut down the marauders. Mischa sighs. Wanting to cry, his eyes become moist. *"I dare not weep with joy. That's weakness and I'm a commissar. I have to be tough!"*

"The skirmish is over. We must bury the dead here," Dimitri, tells the rescuing team. "These comrades fought bravely for the

Revolution." He bows his head.

"Yes. You should bury them for sure. But I'm going after the bastards who got away," Mischa yells out as he moves toward the nearby clump of trees. But the troops from the rescue squad, noticing his shaky hands and a forlorn look on his face, restrain him. Suddenly, he breaks loose and goes after Dimitri, whom he feels has betrayed him with his lie of 'fun and games.'

"Fun and games, is it?" he shouts, raising his fists to strike Dimitri. Again, men from the rescue team grab him before he can land a punch.

"Let me go," Mischa says, cooling down. Dimitri, who Mischa recognizes is fearless in battle, and who, in fact, seems to enjoy killing, hands him a shot of vodka which he squirreled away in a small canteen. The drink calms Mischa and the two angrily stare at each other. Dimitri senses Mischa's traumatized by the battle, a trauma which, unknowingly, would last for a while and influence his thinking. Normally, an army might send a stressed-out soldier back of the lines for needed rest.

But this is Siberia, in the middle of a brutal civil war, and the Red Army needs trained commissars like Mischa. Besides, no Red soldier would dare pull rank on Mischa to take him to a doctor. The men love and understand him. Mischa has shown he cares for them. He inspires them by being on the front line in combat. He chips in doing menial work. Mischa talks to them like brothers. The word among the troops is he married young and his wife died shortly afterwards. He never fully recovered. How could he, living the life of a soldier? Boredom, contempt, hostility, and fear. No one will tell on Mischa for going after Dimitri. The men don't have the same feelings for Dimitri who resents Mischa's popularity.

As they march back to the train under a bright blue sky, their tired eyes dart to both sides of the road checking to see if any White stragglers appear. The quiet is soon broken with sounds of distant explosions ringing in their ears.

Approaching their train whose engines are revving up to move down the line, Mischa realizes that his fear is gone. *"Luck or God, saved me,"* he admits to himself. *"I'm okay now,"* he tells his unit. He drifts over to Dimitri and extends his hand. After shaking hands, they hug each other, as good comrades do. Still, Dimitri says to himself, "I better watch him, he's weakening. I'll never forgive him for embarrassing me before the men."

•

Mischa is not the only one suffering battle stress. Dimitri, himself, is another, though he puts up a good front. A year before his recent encounter with Mischa, Dimitri was assigned to a specific mission with another comrade, as Mischa was summoned to headquarters in Yekaterinburg. Later that day, a train, under Dimitri's command, moved out. Not long into the journey, a torn-up track halted their progress. Getting off, Dimitri spotted a young soldier who had been checking the perimeter for saboteurs. He asked the trooper to fetch ammo from a nearby depot.

"Yes, comrade officer," mumbled the trooper. "I'll do it."

Dimitri, who had been drinking, noticed the lad walking in the wrong direction. He saw the man shrugging his shoulders, as if dismissing his order. When he returned, Dimitri said:

"You said you'd bring the ammo and you didn't?"

Again, ignoring Dimitri, the soldier walks away.

Dimitri, his face distorted with rage, grabs a fellow officer, and angrily says:

"That soldier. That one walking away. The one with the beard. He disobeyed an order. He must be punished," he says in a commanding voice. There's no misunderstanding what the officer must do.

"I'll take care of it myself, comrade commissar."

A few minutes later, Dimitri hears a single shot. He smiles.

•

After the skirmish in the woods, Mischa is ushered into the office of his Cheka commander in Yekaterinburg and told that Soviet victories in Siberia have the Whites on the run back toward the Pacific Ocean. The officer adds that the enemy, aided by the Japanese and the Allies, will make a stand in the Russian Far East.

"Your assignment is to conduct guerrilla warfare in eastern Siberia. After your training mission here, deploy to Vladivostok. Good luck. Dismissed," says Mischa's commander.

Walking back to his small cabin, Mischa's flustered. He says to himself:

"That commander is changing my life. Now that I'm being assigned to eastern Siberia, thousands of miles away, I'll be farther away than ever from Basya. Oh my. If I could just hold her in my arms again and kiss her as I did at the station outside of Odessa. Or feel her warm body next to mine as on the train to Petrovirivka, I'd be happy."

Rehashing what he had just said, he concludes: *"But I must be disciplined. I'm in the Communist movement. Revolution and Party come first."*

•

Mischa keeps busy on the base, learning tactics to be used behind enemy lines, such as assassinating White officers. He handles his loneliness by pushing Basya out of his mind when he's training. He often dreams of her. It's summer. Winter's emptiness has blossomed into verdant fields splashed with strawberry bushes. In one dream, his keen eyes spot a *droshky* (carriage) entering the palaces' long, circular driveway. A beautiful woman steps down from the conveyance and elegantly walks up to the gilded entrance. It's Basya returning to him. Her hand touches his fingers. He gently squeezes her soft-skinned palm. He kisses her lips, as he did the first time at the Deribasovka railway station. Waking up, he realizes the room is empty.

One week, later on a spring night - and this is real - he's helping Basya take off her sealskin coat in his requisitioned log cabin. He pinches himself. It's true. She's in front of him. He slowly removes the red beret from her dark brown hair and puts her coat and hat on a nearby chair. He notices she's thinner. But then again, everyone's slim in Russia in these civil war days.

That night, they don't talk much. She doesn't explain how she found him. Her pale face tells him fatigue has overcome her. He puts some hot stew and bread in front of her. She quickly devours it. She does admit that she came from Moscow. When he asks her how long it took, he notices she falls into a deep sleep in the chair. He wakes her. Guiding her to the only bed in the room, he places her under the covers, kisses her on the forehead, and blows out the candle. He beds down on the torn couch for the night.

•

Chapter 7. Yekaterinburg, 1920.
MISCHA and BASYA.
"A Turning Point."

•

"Mischa, I'm a Party member," Basya begins. "A clerk in a counter-intelligence unit in the Red Army."

"Unbelievable," he answers, as a look of astonishment comes over his tired face.

"Seeing his surprise," she continues, "I'm such a good student that they send me out once in a while on assignment. That's why they wouldn't give me a leave until now."

"Imagine that," Mischa says at last. "The two of us joined together in ideology and work. I was hoping for that ever since we met."

"Oh, how I've wanted to see you," Basya says excitedly. "I'm all yours for several weeks."

With a quick move, he hugs and kisses her hard on the lips.

"I thought you forgot me," she says, gently freeing herself from his embrace.

"How could I? I think of you all the time. I went looking for you in Tomashpil."

"I know. We were lucky. I saved you." She pauses seeing his confusion. "Before the shell hit, I pushed you down. You fainted. I dragged you away from the scene."

Mischa was stunned. "Oh my! I knew it was you who pulled me away from the burning house, even though the Red Army nurse said they didn't have anyone in the region."

"I acted alone," she says, smiling affectionately. Finishing her glass of vodka, she asks for another. He obliges. He has many questions, and Basya continues to explain.

"The bandits probably spotted you earlier in the woods and thought you were someone else. Tipped off, I left in time before they came. At least, I was able to prevent them from picking you up, even though I couldn't stay."

"I can't get over it. We're together in the revolution," he repeats exuberantly. He doesn't seem to be interested in any further explanation. He begins smothering her with kisses, as he draws her to the room's double-bed. This time, they make love.

•

Finally, around lunch time, he says "Let's get some air."

"There's a talk by a professor to Communist youth students at the new Ural State University on Western imperialism," says Mischa as he dons his Red Army uniform. She dresses, having washed up with water from the pump outside and heated on the stove.

"It's a good idea if we go. To further our Party education," he says in a serious tone.

What she doesn't tell him is that in wanting to please him, she feels she must improve her knowledge of the war that Communism is waging. *I need every piece of information I can get to catch up with Mischa.*

"We have a common interest, the Revolution," he repeats as he gazes at her and his desire for her builds up again. He approaches her.

"Now you're bothering me," she says, smiling as she starts to undress again.

•

Later, they walk to the communal eating hall.

Mischa can sense the soldiers watching them as they saunter through the camp. He's happy. The love he has for her strengthens him. Not only does he recognize beauty in her face, but other people do also, he believes, a thought which boosts his ego and self-esteem. What man does not feel good walking down the street with an attractive lady holding onto his arm.

After a hearty lunch in the canteen, Mischa suggests they go straight over to the university. On their walk, they hold hands. They join the circle of young people. This is their new entertainment. This is what young Communists do. At the end of the political discussion, he leads the shout-out with a raised fist salute: "Hooray, for Lenin and Trotsky."

•

That evening, Mischa and Basya are silent. They stare at each other. He rises from his chair, approaches her and plants a kiss on her forehead and another on her wavy brown hair. He's about to kiss her on her lips, when banging on the door halts his romantic intentio ns.

"Damn it. Who's that?" he asks, as he lifts the strap on the gun holster on his belt.

"Who's there?"

"It's me. Comrade Krymov."

Mischa breathes a sigh of relief, but frowns at the same time. He's about to make love to Basya and this intruder, though a friend, ruined it. Mischa opens the door and in struts Leonid Krymov who removes his beaver coat, which he had stolen from a dead Cossack. He's wearing a black military tunic, cavalry pants, and black boots.

"Oh!" says Leonid. "Sorry to interrupt. You must be Basya. Heard a lot about you." He pauses to study Basya before going on. "Only good things, including what a good-looking young lady you are. I now see it's true," he says speaking in an ingratiating manner. Leonid then proceeds to prance around the room with an air of superiority, including the perception that he's got a way with women. He smiles at Basya.

Basya blushes. "You're too kind," she says. Turning to Mischa, she raises her eyebrows, and signals to Mischa to make the introductions.

"Basya, meet Comrade Leonid Krymov," Mischa says apologetically. He nods to the young man who possesses broad shoulders, a small head and deceptive eyes.

"Please to meet you," she says smiling at the newcomer. She's flattered by his comments, though his reptilian eyes frighten her for the moment. Leonid's smile causes Mischa to frown again. Picking up an empty glass, Mischa pours a drink for Leonid, and a refill for Basya and him. All three raise their glasses and drain the power drink down in a single gulp.

Meanwhile, Leonid sees the hidden message flashed by Mischa with pleading eyes and pursed lips, "Stay a while, of course, but not too long. I haven't seen my girlfriend in a long while." A half-hour later, Leonid departs, reminding Mischa of a forthcoming meeting.

•

"I thought he'd never leave," says Mischa as his hand roams over her naked body underneath quilted blankets.

"What's your hurry," she says, with a snicker on her lips, as she moves closer and hugs his hot body, and the mattress springs reverberate as his breathing gets heavier and her sighs louder. "Not in a hurry, love. Just need to consume you," he groans as pleasure stirs his body.

In the days that follow, he feels he's as light as a feather. His colleagues on the training field notice a new Mischa. His skills improve, he's eager to please his commander; and the minute he's dismissed and off-duty, he hastens to his room. His infatuation rises. He begins to hum a ditty that proclaims: *"If you have a beautiful girlfriend, you don't need anything else."*

Meanwhile, Basya spends her days reading and tidying up the room. Unlike other female revolutionaries, she has become a *balaboosta,* an endearing term in Yiddish meaning perfect homemaker. For as long as she can remember, her mother taught her, it's important to please her husband. Though not married yet, she wants to charm Mischa. "I love him," she often repeats to herself.

•

One day, a week after her arrival, Mischa is ordered to drive to the city of Chelyabinsk, about two hours away and close to the Urals. He's to be briefed by a Cheka officer who has just returned from the Russian Far East where Mischa is likely to be assigned. Military command has no objection to Mischa taking Basya on the trip. She's now in a counter-intelligence unit with security clearance.

"Basya," Mischa starts, "There's a change of plans. I'm going to Chelyabinsk." Seeing her alarm, he urges quickly, "Come with me. It's a daytrip. A different scenery will be good for us." Seeing her small smile, Mischa seals the deal. "We can ride in the back of the truck. We leave at five in the morning."

The trip to Chelyabinsk is uneventful. Sitting outside in the back of the vehicle brings them fresh air. It's not too uncomfortable outside. It's late spring and even at the tip of the Urals, the weather is no problem this time of year.

While Mischa is briefed by the Cheka, Basya walks the main streets, eyeing the shops. But displays of dresses and lingerie are sparse and available goods even less. Russia is at war.

The truck heads back to Yekaterinburg late afternoon. An hour into their journey, Micha is standing up when up ahead he notices a roadblock with bandits poised to fire. The driver slows down about a few hundred feet away. Mischa yells down to him to drive right through the barrier. As the vehicle picks up speed, the shooting begins from both the truck and the bandits and Mischa shouts to Basya to lie flat on the truck floor. She obeys. With bullets whizzing by him, Mischa jumps up and fires at the bandits behind the roadblock as the driver crashes the truck through the barrier at full speed. The battle is over within minutes.

Mischa slides down to the floor of the truck, yelling, "Basya, are you okay? Are you hit?"

"No," she answers, as he picks her up and holds her in his arms and smothers her with kisses. She's shaking. "You're alive, thank goodness."

They sit down, their backs to the wooden boards of the back of the truck attached to the cabin of the vehicle. They are silent, except that from time to time, he utters the Yiddish word, *'bashert.'* He feels the two of them are predestined.

She thinks, "He's my protector, I love him so. Nothing can come between us."

•

After work one afternoon, Mischa quickly walks back to his large, single-room cabin. His residence consists of a large room with a double-bed, a small couch, a desk, a black walnut armchair, and two old chairs at the kitchen table. A large map of Siberia graces one wall, and pictures of Lenin and Trotsky, another. He's lucky to have a small wood stove. He's blessed that he is not billeted with other soldiers.

On this day in question, Mischa tells Basya he needs to get some air outside of their charcoal-scented room. The couple heads out on a stroll. Conversing, they stop every so often in the street, for a long kiss.

"After we parted outside Odessa, I looked everywhere. Believe me, I tried to find you," he tells Basya.

"I believe you. So how come you couldn't find me."

"Like I said, you disappeared."

"With a little research, I found you," she says with a touch of sarcasm. She doesn't have to spell it out to him that as a Party member, it wasn't difficult to obtain his location. But why wasn't he able to locate her, she wondered.

"This time, don't leave me," he says in a determined voice which causes her to react and ponder: He protects me. If this relationship is going to continue, I have to be honest and tell him I was married and I had a child.

She pauses and purses her lips to steel herself. "Here goes."

"Mischa, love. You don't know it, but I was married." She doesn't look at him and rushes on. "He was my teenage sweetheart. He rescued me from jail," she says, not yet disclosing that they had a child.

"You were lucky. When did you escape?"

"The night after the Whites arrested me for protesting in Zhitomir where my uncle and aunt lived. At the end of nineteen seventeen."

"Wow! How did you get out?"

"At that time, my husband was my boyfriend. Sometime after he rescued me. Later, he was killed," she says. "His name was Lev."

"I'm sorry," Mischa replies, ushering in a few moments of silence.

Mischa is surprised she discloses part of her past, and his thoughts race through his mind. *Strange. Only our second meeting and already she's divulging everything. So, she's been married.*

Mischa continues to digest what Basya has told him. Basya waits.

I don't want to probe, he thinks. *Maybe some other men want to know about their girlfriend's ex-husband. For now, she's mine. Despite that, I do have to at least tell her that I was married.*

"I figured you had a boyfriend. I, too, was married," he reveals. "My wife, a Chekist, was killed by a terrorist." He pauses to collect himself. "We were separated at the time. I was serving in Siberia. Before she was murdered, she had given birth to our child. I wasn't there."

He stops to look at Basya. "She placed the baby, whose name was Klara, with a peasant woman. I knew she was pregnant, but I only discovered afterwards that she gave away our daughter before she died." Basya interrupted to ask about the baby's whereabouts.

"I found my daughter, got her back; and gave her to a Jewish couple who adopted her. Unable to contain his emotions, he finished, "I made the new parents promise that they'd never tell the child the identity of her real father. I couldn't take care of her. I feel terrible, but the child has a safe home."

Hearing this, Basya takes his hand. "How sad. War is criminal. But I must tell you, Mischa, there's one more thing." He looks at her questioningly. "My husband and I also had a child. The infant was killed by the Whites in the pogrom in Zhitomir along with my uncle and aunt," she says with difficulty. "How I suffer. That's the main reason I joined the Party. The killers of my family, all of them, must pay for their crimes. I want revenge and I'll get it."

"I'm sure you will," he says, hugging her tightly. She's shaking again. With a soft touch, he rubs her back. "We're bound together," he sighs.

"Mischa. I need a drink. It'll calm me," she tells him, not wanting to explain that mentally, she's in pain especially from the loss of her daughter, and she must numb it.

"Sure, we'll both have one," he agrees. He takes a quick swallow of a single shot from the bottle he carries in his rucksack before handing it to Basya. Custom says you have a second shot of vodka immediately after the first. They do.

"I've got to be her knight in shining armor," he thinks, smiling at her.

"Listen, Basya, we've suffered. Let's enjoy life while we can, if that's possible these days. Let's get some dinner at the *Karl Marx* canteen. Already, I'm tasting the *blini*."

That night their melancholy is gone. Time is suspended. They start a love fest which lasts several days, including a few love-in-the-afternoon sessions.

One day, when he returns from maneuvers, he notices she is slightly inebriated. *"I shouldn't have left the vodka bottles in the pantry,"* he thinks. *"I guess she's a drinker. But then again, who doesn't imbibe in Russia,"* he reasons.

He hides the one unused bottle in the back of his bookcase. But the next day, needing a drink, she searches the house and finds it.

Though he has a sense of foreboding, Mischa says nothing. He's reluctant to cut the thread of love that weaves through their bodies as they make love over and over again. With so much pleasure, one doesn't ask questions. At least Mischa doesn't.

And then something happened that changed everything.

•

A few nights later, they go to a tavern where many of Mischa's comrades congregate. In this rowdy, dark inn, the drinking starts in earnest. One shot glass after another is downed, with only tiny breaks between gulps of the fiery liquid. Even though mayonnaise salads are served to reduce alcohol intake, it doesn't take long for the crowd to begin a Czar-Peter-the-Great-tradition of breaking drinkware against the wall after important toasts to bring luck and happiness. Basya joins others in hurling her empty glass, although she refrains from shouting with joy.

"Stop it" announces the tavern owner in a loud voice. "If not, I'll have to charge you more for a drink," he shouts over the crowd's noise which sounds like breaking-thunder roaring across the vast steppes of Russia.

"Who said the Red Army is disciplined.," thinks Mischa, holding back somewhat in his drinking, despite the fact that he, too, not to be a loner, goes along with the glass throwing. By midnight, the crowd is so intoxicated that the proprietor, despite the loss of money from the broken glasses, is raking in hundreds of rubles. Now he sends a few accordion players onto the floor to rouse the audience to drink even more. *"Why kill the golden goose,"* he philosophizes.

Basya becomes emotional and irrational. Drinking does that. It loosens her tongue in a silent message: *It's okay to lose control, as long as it drowns my family sorrows.*

Standing nearby is Comrade Leonid Krymov who senses Basya's vulnerability. She's drunk. Envious of Mischa, he whispers in Basya's ear, "Dance for us."

Staring at him and realizing that Mischa left the room for the outhouse, she grabs Leonid's hand to boost her from a chair onto the table. She begins wildly dancing in place to the accordion tunes, waving her hands over her head, like a Bukharan woman in the bazaar, her arms flaying like a gypsy in a cabaret, her pelvis area rocking as a Greek belly dancer acting out a lascivious act. She loves the attention, especially the mob's encouragement when she slips her peasant blouse up over her head and removes her bra. Nothing arouses these sex-starved soldiers more than exposed, firm breasts, and so they unabashedly shout, "More. More."

At that moment, a pistol shot is heard. Most patrons duck down. Some fall to the floor and crawl under the tables. Mischa enters. His eyes are blazing. He walks up to the table. Waving his revolver in the air, he motions the gun barrel toward the door. "Everyone out," he commands sternly. Noticing his calm, powerful face, the crowd obeys and disperses. Placing his hands on her hips, he brings Basya down off the table. She doesn't resist. Pulling herself together, she gazes around the room and dresses. A hired droshky driver helps him get her into the carriage, and then, into Mischa's room at the army base. He again sleeps on the couch.

Before he falls asleep, he thinks. *What is she, a whore? A slut dancer? The next thing that could have happened last night would be that those drunkards would have grabbed her, laid her down on a rug on the floor and one by one gang-raped her. That's what drunk soldiers do. Do I need this kind of woman?"*

•

Whatever Basya thought or remembered, she didn't reveal it the next morning. Later that day, Mischa and Basya go to the camp canteen where Mischa orders pierogies for both of them. He doesn't order vodka. She insists. He argues. She threatens to leave the table. He acquiesces. He pours her vodka. She stares at him defiantly.

His stomach hurts. He's got the runs. He gets up from the table to go to the bathroom. While he's gone, the food comes.

Basya's angry with herself for last night. She knows she got drunk. She orders a vodka from the waiter and gulps it down. She ignores Mischa's absence and wolfs down her pierogies.

Meanwhile, Mischa's food gets cold. When he comes back and sees that she's almost finished, he leans right into her face, almost touching her mouth. He can't control himself anymore, and screams for all to hear: "Couldn't you wait? And if not, at least tell the comrade to keep my food on the stove! You know I love pierogies hot!"

"I can't take it anymore," she shouts back, unconcerned that the crowd in the canteen has stopped eating and is staring at them. "I'm leaving," she says as she gets up and storms out.

He chases her into the street.

"How dare you insult me like that in front of everyone," he hollers, his mouth revealing what his heart feels, not for the cold food, but for the way she acted last night. "Exposing your tits to drunks," he swears, "was an act of debauchery, the likes of which I have never seen."

Walking back to the cabin, he notices that she wobbles. He stops shouting, calms down, and holds her gently by the arm. Tears are forming in her eyes, as he adds: "Basya, I love you. We had it so good these last days."

"Leave me alone. Nobody can help me," she says, pushing his arm away. But he continues walking alongside her. Silence. Arriving at his residence, she goes in, lies down on the bed and submerges her head in the pillow.

Mischa can sense his nerves are taut, like the day in the battle in the forest when he totally lost control and went after Dimitri. *"I better get out of here,"* he thinks.

"I'm going out for a walk. I'll be back in a while," he declares, making sure she hears.

"I won't be here when you get back. I never want to see you again," she replies angrily. She stares at him, shifts her body on the bed and quickly turns her back on him. Though she has said and done horrible things to him, showing her back signifies rejection, which he can't stand.

"Yeah. You're not going anywhere. You'll be here," he says sarcastically. Opening the door, he steps out and slams the door so hard that she shouts: "Don't come back."

Basya realizes she's made an idle threat. She has nowhere to go. She can't return to Moscow. Her train reservation is for next week and in wartime they refuse to alter tickets.

Walking on the road, Mischa's furious. *"How could a couple who love each other with such passion end up like this?"* he asks himself. *"Just a few days ago, I'm madly in love with her and ....it's crazy. I can't even look at her face, it's distorted, not pretty anymore."*

Though despondent and angry, the cold weather outside lessens his mental temperature. As a trained soldier, he remembers to be aware of his surroundings. *"Thickets on each side of the road can conceal White terrorists,"* he thinks. *"Better not go too far and I'd better make sure my gun is fully loaded."* He takes out the revolver, opens the chamber and notices that there's one less bullet, a bullet he used in the tavern which reminds him again of Basya's wild scene there. Suddenly, a new thought enters his brain.

"The tavern. That's it. It's not me. It's not her. She can't help it. She's be-come a drunk. I saw it like every Russian sees it, but ignores it. There's a doc-tor in town. I'll take her to him. He'll help us. Unheard of in Russia, bringing a lover to a doctor to settle an argument. Most men just beat their wives. I can't do that. I'll apologize. I've got to keep her. I love her."

In the meantime, having dozed off, Basya wakes with a start. Her head aches. The room is swirling. She puts her head back in the pil-low, waits a bit, and now cautiously lifts herself up.

I can't stay here. He's like everyone else, even if he's not a Cossack. I'll leave and go to the station before he gets back. I'll use my charm on a conductor.

Meanwhile, Mischa's sprints to the cabin. He's too late. "She's gone." He hurries to the train station. "Departed," says the station sign. Running to the camp office, he badgers Party officials to lo-cate her. Nobody knows where she is. Nobody wants to talk about her. "Why are the authorities reluctant to say anything about her," he questions. "Damn. I miss her already."

•

Basya, endures a several-day journey to Moscow. *"Only a few drinks now,"* she warns herself. I don't want to get thrown off the train. Re-hashing the time with Mischa. *"Maybe I'm lying to myself. Maybe it was my fault."*

Basya arrives at Moscow's Yaroslavskiy railway terminal on Ka-lanchyovskaya Square. She's weary, especially when she discovers snow is falling in large flakes. She exits and walks a few blocks when a black car pulls up alongside this pretty lady with a suitcase. It's the Cheka secret police. They've been looking for new agents and they believe she has personality and intelligence. She'll defend 'Mother Russia.' They've investigated her. They know she drinks. They'll fix that problem with treatment and therapy. She'll only imbibe on the job.

A man in a black suit jumps out of the vehicle and says, "Good morning, Gospoja Abramskaya. The Cheka has a new assignment for you. You're going to Intelligence School at the Lubyanka. Don't tell a soul, not even your boyfriend, Mischa Rasputnis. In fact," he pauses to make sure she understands his next order, "Let me make it clear, Gospoja Abramskaya, you are not to contact him. And if he tries to reach out to you, you're obliged to report it to us."

"Oh, don't worry about that. I wouldn't ever contact him" she replies firmly, though to herself, she thinks as she enters the car. *"This new job is a turning point for me. I've got something to latch onto. As an intelligence agent, I'm going to be somebody. I better sober up. Wonder if Mischa will ever try to find me?"*

•

Chapter 8. Nakhodka, 1920.
MISCHA.
"Escape to Misha's Past."

•

In the 1904, Russo-Japanese War, the Empire of Japan dealt Russia a stunning defeat and gained prestige, spheres of influence in Asia, and occupied half of Sakhalin Island in the Pacific. From that moment on, Tokyo, always a thorn in Russia's side, had designs on obtaining more land and resources in Siberia. When Bolshevik Russia deserted the Allies in World War I, and signed a separate peace deal with Germany at Brest Litovsk, in March, 1918, Great Britain, France, the United States, and Japan sent massive arms shipments to White Army forces. At first, the arms were to be guarded by troops from each Allied country, so they wouldn't fall into the hands of the Germans. After Germany surrendered on November 11, 1918, ending World War I, some Allied troops began to leave Russia. By early 1920, only Japan maintained large numbers of troops in Siberia to interfere in the Russian Civil War on the side of the Whites in their battle with the Red Army and its guerrilla forces of which Mischa Rasputnis was one.

As for Mischa and Basya, after the bar scene in Yekaterinburg, they both changed.

•

"Ah Nakhodka.
Sand and sky,
Curse and vodka
This is our dear Nakhodka."

A little over a month after his breakup with Basya, Mischa finds himself behind White lines in the Primorsky krai region in the Russian Far East, five thousand miles from Yekaterinburg. His head is filled with anguish. He can't face his feelings of loss of Basya, especially because he believes he caused it. He fights despair by proclaiming to himself over and over again that he must try and find her and win her back. He shudders when he remembers how Dimitri, who had seen a picture of her many times and even met her once, told him: "You must never let someone as beautiful as that get away."

Days following the breakup, Mischa never told Dimitri or Leonid that after an argument, she left him. He only related, "she was called back to Moscow."

In a way, he felt his arrival in the Nakhodka area could not have come at a better time. At least he was away from Yekaterinburg where his fight with Basya occurred. Besides, his work kept him so busy, he didn't have much time for self-pity regarding his loss of Basya. He even stopped humming, *"If you have a beautiful girlfriend, you don't need anything else."*

Fortified by his recent army training, his first task is to map counter-revolutionary installations along the bay and the village of Nakhodka, about a hundred miles by car, southeast of Vladivostok.

•

One clear February morning, Mischa stands on the railing of a small Red naval patrol vessel, about to leave a dock on a routine mission. He's to enter the Nakhodka Bay waters of the Sea of Japan. A wide smile is on his face as he tells two comrades accompanying him, "Just like those days in Odessa, when I went sailing on the Black Sea. I love it," he says in a chirpy voice.

"But don't forget Comrade Rasputnis, this is wartime," notes Pyotr, one of the two comrades who are with him.

"Agreed. To be back on water, on my first assignment here, however, is a treat," he counters, as the boat he's just boarded, readies to go out onto the waters of the Bay of *Amerika,* as it was first known. Being on this craft is significant, because he read that back in 1859, a Russian vessel, named, Amerika, seeking shelter from a storm, discovered the bay.

"Get this, comrades. Did you know that this bay is the only place on the Russian Pacific coast where the sea never freezes," Mischa says excitedly. His explanation is delivered in a tone as if he's leading a weather expedition, instead of a battle mission.

As they listen, the crew casts off the lines and the boat slips away from the dock."

•

For the first twenty minutes, the vessel hugs the shoreline. As Mischa's viewing the coast with his binoculars, a White artillery battery, not on his intelligence map, opens fire on their vessel. The shell, which hits close to their ship, sends a huge geyser of turbulent water and steam upward into the air and panics the crew. Mischa realizes that being bombed on water seems more frightening than being shelled on land. He's trying to decide what to do first when he's confronted by the sight of a sailor trying to sneak away to his cabin.

"Remain at your post," he yells out to the man who was manning the gun.

"Come back. I'm warning you," he adds, pulling out the revolver from his holster. He realizes that his subordinates are watching to see what he'll do next as this sailor continues to slink away. He shoots and kills him. "Pick him up and throw him into the sea," Mischa orders, displaying a toughness that is expected from a Soviet commissar.

At that moment, the ship's captain tries a life-saving, zig-zag maneuver and it works for a few minutes. But the remaining gun crew, obviously in shock, fumbles on positioning the cannon to strike back at the shore batteries.

The craft moves painfully slow. *Maybe something's wrong with the engine,* Mischa thinks. *It's like shooting ducks in a barrel.*

Officially, he's not under the command of the boat's captain since he's on a special assignment. His secret orders do not oblige him to defend the ship. After taking a few minutes to decide whether he and his two men should stay on board, he yells, "Jump!" There's no hesitation. All three leap into the water and swim for their lives.

Moments later, a shell lands in the middle of the vessel, just above the boiler. The ship wobbles. And then, more bursts, one shell after another, again and again. There's so many that the constant barrage breaks the ship apart, splattering the ocean with debris.

Having distanced themselves in the water, Mischa and his compatriots turn, eye the explosion, and realize all aboard are surely gone. And so, with all their energy, they plow toward shore, ending up nearly unconscious on the beach at Nakhodka. Ironically, in the Russian language, the name means a lucky find or eureka. To these shipwrecked agents, however, it signifies isolation, agony, and possible death.

"On our backs, we were. At first, we were panting so much, we thought we'd die on the spot or be shot by the Whites who might find us," Mischa tells Red rescuers who arrive on the scene later that day. "Slowly, we came back to life. Damn it! It's my first assignment here," he says angrily, but thinks, "At least I'm happy that in the battle I didn't feel afraid and acted decisively."

A few of the rescuing soldiers, who themselves fought their way out of a White Army ambush, take Mischa's two comrades with them. Mischa's assigned to a safe house, run by Pavel and Lena Konstantina Sherer, leaders of Red guerrillas in Nakhodka.

Greeted by the couple, Pavel makes it clear that Mischa will have to stay in an abandoned *izba,* (Russian log cabin) behind the main house.

"Fortunately, the Whites rarely come to this area, but you never know. If they do, they'll probably search our house first, so we'll have time to warn you and you can hide in the forest," says Pavel. The couple's small one-story, wooden house consists of several rooms, a porch surrounded by a few paved-stones and a surrounding garden. In summer, the childless couple cultivate full-grown strawberries which they sell to anyone who'll pay for this prized fruit.

"I have to keep you out of sight for a few weeks, until we hear from Moscow. As an intelligence agent sent here to arouse the masses to throw off the White yoke, you're very valuable to the Party," cautions Pavel, adding, "We'll bring you meals, although most of the time, you can eat dinner with us in the house."

•

Exhausted, Mischa sleeps most of his first day in the deserted cabin which has a modified oil heater that doesn't work all the time. The hair on his head still itches, even though Pavel has shaved his head to avoid lice.

On the second day, he repeatedly hears what he's sure is Pavel's wife rendering in a loud voice, a song, whose title is, *"This is Our Dear Nakhodka".*

The voice and tune begin to annoy him, so much so that he finally yells out:

"Stop already!"

Nobody hears him. He's frustrated. As a guest, he can't complain to Pavel about his wife.

He thinks, *All day, she's humming that blasted ditty and it's driving me to tears. I can't stand her belting out those dumb words,* which he mouths in a mocking voice:

"Ah Nakhodka.
Sand and sky,
Curse and vodka
This is our dear Nakhodka."

•

"This woman with a craggy face is not a singer," Mischa thinks unkindly. "She's like a boxer taking a fall in the first round," he mumbles as he sits in the insect-ridden izba.

•

The days go by, January into February. Isolated, cold, and angry, Mischa manages to read books given to him by Pavel, sometimes even the same book twice, such as *Mother*, by Maxim Gorky. He's sure that if he didn't have books, he'd go mad. He writes down ideas for proposed articles in Pravda.

At night, before dinner, he walks with Pavel around a field close to the house.

"My wife and I were picked up by the Czarist police before the Revolution came to Moscow," Pavel explains. "They called us troublemakers for participating in attempts to overthrow the Czar. We were exiled to Nakhodka. The trip here was under conditions worse than transporting cattle. Arriving in the Russian Far East, we adjusted. To survive, we hunted and fished, an avocation turned vocation."

"By the way, Mischa, we are near the area where the great Amur tigers lurk, roam, and range. This is their last stronghold, the Primorsky krai. With the outbreak of the Revolution, those yellow beasts with their narrow black traverse stripes become fair game for both White and Red troops. These mad poachers are going to drive them to extinction."

Mischa agrees. But he can't keep the Amur tiger on his mind. He focuses on his life.

•

Never in my wildest dreams did I believe I'd be so far away from home when I joined the Reds," reflected Mischa one night. I thought I'd be fighting along the Volga, at best. That's where the action is. A week ago, I was out on the water. That adventure didn't turn out too well, did it? A disaster. Now, it's early spring and I'm a resident in this God-forsaken hole.

•

"It hasn't been a bad life out here," Pavel told Mischa one morning. "With its southerly location, oceanic influences, the area turns out to be one of the mildest climates in Russia. It just rains a lot. Ha-ha-ha."

That comment makes sense to Mischa. He can't easily get some air during the chilly days when he's in the hut. At night, he goes indoors to the kitchen where he eats a hearty meal of pelmeni. Fried potatoes are added to the delicious fare. He savors every morsel, smiling and closing his eyes as his taste buds, long dormant, are revived, causing him pleasure. Like most Russians, he knows that the country's food is heavy, fatty and greasy. People lose weight because it's so cold, so they need heavy food for sustenance.

One night, during a meal of chicken, kasha, and vegetables, the three stalwarts offer up many toasts to Lenin and Trotsky.

"We have to be careful," Pavel warns afterwards, "we're surrounded by enemies, the interventionists. A dozen foreign flags are on our land. Americans, British, French, and the worst, the Japanese. All showing up in eastern Siberia to crush our glorious Revolution. Makes you mad."

•

Mischa, who's a captive, even if it's his comrades holding him, has to think of something to keep his sanity and divert his attention from Lena with her ditty, *"our Nakhodka."*

He feels he's helpless to combat the loneliness that's getting to him. He remembers many of his friends back in Odessa and the good times they had, in spite of involvement in revolutionary activities. *"If only I can fight this aimless dreaming,"* he tells himself.

In his short life, he also has adopted the trait known as blaming others and situations for his misfortune. In some cases, women, some of whom have caused him trouble, especially those whom he believes have deserted him, wronged him and disrupted his life.

Basya is high on that list. She rejected him, though he realizes he drove her away and because of that, he beats himself up mentally. I shouldn't have yelled at her. What happened to me? Even with those thoughts of self-blame, he continues to vacillate. Ambivalence often intruded into his thinking.

On the one hand, I could catch up to her and love her again. On the other hand, why would I do that? She turned her back on me. Am I a fool to beg her?"

And yet, he realized that the little time they spent together before what he calls the crash, was happy. She was beautiful and satisfying, and they had common interests, including the Party. Maybe that's why he can't get her out of his mind. He recalls that on the way to Nakhodka, he and his men stopped and took a break in a small village. There, he thought he saw her in a deep embrace with a Red Army officer. How could he love her when someone else was kissing her. When he went looking for her at the spot, she was gone, an apparition. *Maybe it wasn't her. Imagination. Jealousy. She haunts me.*

Back and forth he went. He feels he has to reduce those reminders of Basya. But that's not so easy. So, more and more, thoughts filter to his late wife Olga. She's gone and he can't bring her back. And then, out there somewhere, he has a daughter, his very own flesh and blood, whom he gave up. All these thoughts depress him and he needs a target to vent. His favorite adversary remained his sister, Klara. He's obsessed with her because she was chosen over him in 1917, to find their father, Gershon, who went to Canada before the war, and left the family stranded. Shamed by the slight, Mischa ran away. His departure put the family in dire financial straits. Yet, despite his dislike of Klara, he followed her and at times aided her in her journey through Siberia until he lost track of her. He didn't know if she made it to America, or was murdered on the way.

Finally, he's upset with his poor mother, Zlota, whom he loves, but whom it's hard to forgive because she was the one who picked Klara over him. Mischa's guilt was not assuaged when he sent money to her and his other sisters at the end of the world war. While he dreams a lot about Olga, he rarely recalls his parents in his slumber. They weren't there for me.

Bitterness, grief, and loves' lost are thrust upon him, as he attempts to make something of his life. He needs something strong to latch onto. And that brings him stubbornly right back to Bolshevism and the Communist Party.

•

One rainy afternoon, Pavel brings Mischa some *chai* (tea) and *pechen'ye* (biscuit). "Guess what. You've been re-assigned to Suchan to fight with the partisans. From there, you'll get further orders. You leave in a few days. Meanwhile, let's enjoy this snack while we talk."

"Wait! Did you say Suchan?"

"Yes."

"That's where my late wife lived. Olga Baratz."

"You mean, Comrade Olga Baratz?" says Pavel in a quizzical voice.

"Yes. That was my wife."

"What a small world. My wife and I know all about Comrade Olga Baratz and we know her sisters. Rina and Nina. But we didn't connect her or her sisters to you.

"You know I don't talk about my late wife too much. It's better that way. Too much emotion. It was horrible the way she died at the hands of a terrorist prisoner."

"We heard. She's regarded as a Hero of the Revolution. Sorry for your loss."

"Thanks. Now I remember," exclaims Mischa. "She did tell me she lived in Suchan with her two sisters before she joined the Party."

"Correct," declares Pavel. "One of the sisters, Rina, is a member of the Party. They're both trustworthy. As I understand it, the three sisters accompanied their father when he first came to Primorsky krai years ago, to work in the local coal mines. Unfortunately, he passed away before the outbreak of the Great War. The two youngest stayed. Olga ran away to Moscow and later married, we were told. That's all that we knew. Now I know it's you she married."

Pavel's information causes Mischa to shudder inwardly. To hear someone else utter the name of his wife, Olga, strikes him as a punch to his gut.

Pavel notices Mischa's discomfort. But he feels he has a duty to keep going and tell him about the town where Mischa's been assigned.

"Suchan once served as our Red headquarters, from which we conducted a partisan struggle. At first, we controlled the mines and prevented the Allies, including the Americans, from accomplishing their duties in the region. We knew they wanted to stop a Soviet victory. Even though our cause was just, we lost the mines to the Whites."

"Since last September, the Americans have intervened against us. They have eight thousand troops and are known as the American Expeditionary Force, Siberia, headed by Major William Graves. While supposedly guarding Allied arms, they're really watching the treacherous Japanese whom they also don't trust. At the same time, the Yanks took the coal out of our hands. In case you didn't know it, coal's the region's main product, 300,000 tons per year."

"What happened?"

"Those Yanks are damn good fighters. Even though outnumbered at Romanovka, they stood their ground against Comrade Sergei Lazo's men when the latter attacked them. Can you imagine an encounter between America and Russia? No one will ever believe it."

•

"Before Olga died, she told me," Mischa remembered, 'If ever you return to the Far East, stop in and say hello to my sisters.' She had been away, so she wasn't sure if they became Bolsheviks. 'But they're my flesh and blood and I love them,'" he recalled her saying.

Later, Mischa reminded himself that Olga also informed him, "'One of my sisters is lame. The healthy sister takes care of the disabled one.' She mentioned that many in their countryside love literature, and that Rina and Nina are no exception: 'They read short stories, poems, and the classics and they paint, write, and work in their little garden.' "

"I'm glad I'm going to be in the same town as they are," thinks Mischa. *"I'm going to look them up. Maybe one of them looks like Olga,"* he speculates, not realizing, like so many others who suffer from a serious relationship that ends badly, he's on the rebound. He needs a woman.

At the same time, though slightly ashamed, he's beginning to have sexual thoughts about the good-looking sister even before he meets her. He realizes his mind's full of what some might call black thoughts.

On the evening of his departure, Mischa leaves his hiding space, goes into the house to eat, and inhales the pungent smells of pelmeni. He says goodbye, picks up his few belongings, including a revolver and a map of the area, and waits for the car to get him out of that godforsaken place.

•

The car, stolen from the interventionist Italian army, soon makes its way through the golden hills of Primorsky krai. The vehicle sports an Italian flag as it speeds along the pot-holed, winding road to Suchan, one hundred ten miles east of Vladivostok. The driver and occupants, two Red Army soldiers and Mischa, remain on the lookout for Whites.

Like the hills of Montana in the United States, the area between Nakhodka and Suchan continues to be forested. In the summer, the foliage is bursting with envious green. The hills and mountains are afire with mature, deep red strawberry vines.

Unhampered, the vehicle drives on roads skirting the countryside, Mischa uses the time and opportunity to review his current orders. Once the vehicle reaches the town center, he will get out and walk to the sisters' house. Reports indicate there are no Whites in town, so that's a good place to stay if the Center in Moscow will allow it. Still, security precautions demanded he not inform the ladies beforehand. *Why give them a chance to refuse.*

He's also trying not to think of Olga or Basya. *With me being so far away from Moscow, it doesn't seem like I'll ever see Basya again?*

Regarding his ex-wife, he remembers that he heard that some men marry their brother's widow. Does that mean, he asks himself, that some widowers marry their deceased wife's sister?" Just as he was regurgitating his situation, a shot rang out. And then a second. And a third. In seconds, everything changed.

Mischa's comrades fire back randomly as their car speeds away through narrow streets.

"Shut off the headlights," yells one guard. "Comrade Rasputnis' hit, a bullet to his right shoulder blade. He's bleeding," he adds. He tries to lift Mischa's head to rest on his shoulder.

"He's unconscious. He needs help. I stopped the bleeding by giving him a temporary bandage. We've got to get him to a doctor."

"We'll have to chance it and head directly to the house of those two ladies where he's supposed to stay," says the other guard. "Luckily, Comrade Rasputnis gave us the address."

"It's getting dark. Go in a different direction, so you can skirt the downtown area."

"Hopefully they can take care of him," states the driver

"I don't see why not. One of 'em's a nurse, I was told. She'll be able to get a doctor."

Mischa is brought unconscious into the house where the nurse, Rina, orders the soldiers to take the injured man to the small room which had been used as an art room by her sister, Nina. When the war erupted, that part of the house became a sick ward.

As she begins to dress Mischa's shoulder wound, a nurturing feeling runs through her body. "I'm saving a life," she utters as she instructs her sister to summon the doctor who on arrival extracts the bullet which missed his jugular vein and spine by a fraction of an inch.

A half hour later during the patient's recovery period, a comrade of Mischa's tells Dr. Kahn, "This wounded comrade was coming here to visit. His name is Mischa Rasputnis."

Rina is shocked: "Oh my God. He's our brother-in-law. My sister Olga's married name was Rasputnis. We never saw a photograph of him, but we never forget that name. "

At that moment, Mischa wakes up and opens his weary eyes which focus on Rina. He musters enough strength to utter: "Olga, is that you?"

•

Chapter 9. Suchan, 1920.
MISCHA.
"One is Physically Fit. The Other is Not."

•

A week after his calamitous arrival in Suchan, Mischa slides in and out of consciousness. When he's awake, he often writhes in agony.

When Dr. Kahn returns to check on Mischa, he praises Rina's nursing ability and leaves a medley of pills for the infection. "If the fever rises, contact me," he informs her. "You're doing a good job, comrade nurse. Patient's in good hands. Only a matter of time until he heals."

But being the women that they are, especially in taking care of a relative, they hover over him like mother hens and care for his every need, including giving him his medications and changing his bandage.

One morning when he finally recognizes his surroundings, he murmurs to himself.

"Unusual. I thought one person was taking care of me. But it seems like two. And are they ever different in appearance. One is gorgeous. One is ugly as a witch."

The beautiful face that most often stares into his eyes and employs an inviting smile that lifts his spirits, belongs to nurse Rina Baratz. After a while her looks and the shape of her body conquer his thoughts: "She's just the kind of woman I like. She reminds me of Olga and yes, even a little of Basya." It is true:

Rina is tall, with a narrow face, an inviting, sensuous mouth with soft lips, shiny brown eyes, large and white teeth which show when she flashes a wide smile.

Whenever Rina walks into the room, I melt with desire. I stare at her round breasts, her long neck, beautiful face. Would I love to...

•

He recalls he was told by Pavel that while Rina is often ogled by suitors, she never gets serious. She feels bound to care for her sister. Yet, often with beauty and intellect, however, comes personality quirks. Rina has a short temper. Not being able to suffer fools easily, she has a biting comment for those who cross her or her sister. While she likes to read, she leaves writing, especially poetry, to Nina.

Nina's childhood polio causes her left leg to be lame. With the aid of crutches, she overcomes her disability, so that she can tend the garden and prepare some meals for the two of them. Their sparse home is spotless.

While beauty is in the eyes of the beholder, no one mistakes Nina Baratz as being attractive. No one! She stands out as short and pudgy, a large head on a small body. Her physical condition has left her bereft of exercise or movement and this gives her a disproportionate body. She bares a crooked nose. She is left with bulging, sad, green eyes, a large mouth, small breasts and a stomach pouch, even though she is only in her late teens.

Cursed with a physical challenge is one thing. To be sad and consigned to a doomed life of solitude and hardship, depending on the degree of daily suffering, is another. Nevertheless, Nina possesses a positive attribute - a calm, soothing voice, expressing kindness that goes with a temperament that never divulges that psychologically, she aches from her injury. Nina comforts everyone, including her beautiful sister, Rina, and now, wounded soldier, Mischa. He begins to convalesce. He realizes he is better off here than in a hospital. There, the Whites could kidnap, even kill him, in a raid. He is safer here, in his own room, in an unsuspecting house.

One day, late in February, 1920, as Rina's changing Mischa's bandages she informs him that the White Army has been defeated in Western Siberia. "They're in full retreat and their commander, Admiral Kolchak, has been executed in Irkutsk."

"Great. Can't be long now. Our Bolshevik cause is winning. Obviously, this area, the Russian Far East, will be the last to be captured by us," Mischa responds, adding, "See that?" He continues, "I've been defending the Revolution. Shot at in Tomashpil, almost drowned in the Sea of Japan, and now this, wounded in Suchan. I'm getting hit from all sides, but my injuries aren't in vain."

"You'll get a couple of medals."

"Yes. We should celebrate. You think you can get me a shot of vodka."

"Not yet, Mischa. Maybe tomorrow." She pauses to place her hand on his forehead. "Your fever's down and you are making progress. Now I must go."

Rina gives him a kiss on the forehead. He immediately puts his hand on the back of her neck and leans her into him and he kisses her on her inviting lips. She does not resist, only utters, "I've got to get to a meeting of the local Soviet."

Rina leaves the room.

Days pass and Mischa woos her. A touch on her arm. She doesn't resist. A gentle grasp of her hand for a few seconds. She doesn't resist. Then a longer hold. She doesn't resist. He looks into her eyes. She doesn't turn away. He whispers sweet nothings into her ear and she almost cries when he thanks her for saving him. In Rina's face, he sees his former wife, Olga. Or was it Basya? He's never sure. Slowly, the lovemaking begins.

•

As all this was happening, did Nina hear the sexual acts on the other side of the wall? Heavy breathing, murmurs and giggles in the night, smiles next morning, yawns, warm glances, blushes, tell-tale signs recognized by those who live under one roof?

Sisters fighting over the same man? It happens. No discrimination in love and jealousy. The two sisters unconsciously begin to show their fangs over their older sister's widowed husband. Both are determined to possess him, if not permanently, at least temporarily. But are they prepared to break up their relationship as sisters? Though Rina moved first, Nina watches, like a cat in heat.

•

One evening, when Rina is out attending a Communist meeting, Nina's eyes widen as she smiles, waiting for the right moment.

Mischa's reclining in the only comfortable chair in the house. The women defer to him since he's the injured one.

Called to the table for dinner, Mischa enjoys the hot meal of pierogi served up by Nina who loves dotting on the guest.

On this night, the two, Mischa and Nina, imbibe with a few shot glasses of vodka. Satiated, Mischa retires to the comfortable chair in front of the fire. The heavy meal makes him drowsy. He dozes off as the sun descends.

Awakening with a start, he realizes Nina's leaning over him and kissing his forehead. She then holds his head. Like a mother cuddling her child, she smothers him with kisses.

"Mischa, I love you. "

"Nina, what are you doing?"

"Please Mischa," she says as she puts her hand on his crotch.

"Nina, stop. Are you crazy? Rina will be home soon." "We have a few hours," she giggles, unbuttoning the front of his pants. "Rina's at a Party meeting. Shh. How's that," she whispers.

"Oh. Oh. Keep going," he sighs and closes his bulging eyes.

Later they creep back to their own beds. They're not awake when

Rina returns.

Rina suspects nothing. Her sister's a cripple. *"Besides, she'd never do a thing like that to me. I'm like a mother to her. Who could believe she and Mischa would…."*

A few evenings later, Rina leaves the house. Waiting until she is sure Rina is gone and won't come back saying she forgot something, Nina coos to herself and approaches Mischa. But she's startled to see him waving his hand at her to stop and declaring in a determined, loud voice.

"No."

She frowns.

"What's wrong," she asks. "What did I do?"

"Nothing," he says convincingly. But he nudges her away, thinking to himself: *"How could I have sex with someone so unattractive. Even pity for her won't work."*

Nina cowers back into her room.

What did I get myself into? A different one every night. I wonder if Olga sees I'm in the saddle with both her sisters. It's nice having women fight over me.

Then he had another thought: *But what if one tells the other? What if we made it a three-some. I've heard of such things. Weird. I've got to get out of here.*

•

The next day, a Red Army teenage messenger arrives at the Baratz home. The lad tells Mischa he must leave. "The Japanese are moving into Suchan. You're to join up with Comrade Sergei Geogriyevich Lazo, who's fighting them and the enemies of the Revolution in the area."

"I'm ready," replies Mischa.

Leaving the house, he fakes goodbyes to Rina and Nina. Rina suspects nothing, especially after he walks with her, arm in arm, to the awaiting car. "You're safe. My men will watch over you."

A soldier, standing nearby observes the young couple hug and kiss, like a husband and wife separating for what could be forever. He can't hear every word they utter, only a few.

"Come back soon,"

"I will," he says.

He lies.

•

Chapter 10. Suchan, 1920.
MISCHA.
"We Shall Avenge You."

•

In the months to follow, Mischa Rasputnis will serve with Sergei Geogriyevich Lazo, the brave Red leader of the October Revolution and the civil war that followed in the Russian Far East. His reputation as a Red guerrilla chief has spread far and wide. Lazo had served as a cadet at the Imperial Russian military academy before joining the Bolshevik forces. Lazo, a true Communist, enjoys enormous authority among the working masses. At the age of twenty-four, this legendary hero is worshiped for organizing partisans in the area to harass the Whites, the Allies, and the Japanese. Mischa is proud to be assigned to his unit.

•

On April 1, 1920, the day that Mischa arrives at headquarters of guerrilla leader, Sergei Lazo, the last contingent of the American Expeditionary Force, Siberia, led by General Graves, exits Vladivostok. But Japanese forces remain. Tokyo seeks to grab more parts of Siberia. For now, the Japanese will remain in Primorsky krai, the Russian maritime province.

Lazo's headquarters is spread out in an area of abandoned coal mine shafts on the top of a hill hidden by the forest outside of Suchan. Mischa, having given exemplary service himself to the Red cause since the 1917 Bolshevik Revolution, is welcomed by Lazo as a commissar and an officer, and as such, joins his general staff.

In the first briefing that Mischa attends, Lazo tells the group that a large Japanese interventionist force may be moving back into the Vladivostok area and reasserting their authority now that the American interventionists pulled out of eastern Siberia. With that move, Lazo asserts he and his Red partisans may be threatened, though up to now they have been able to hide in the Primorsky krai's deciduous woods which cover hills and European-looking meadows filled with Friesian cows and willow trees.

"We have to know exactly where the Japs are located. We can't rely on rumors." He pauses before continuing, "We have to do this before a hot and wet summer settles in. Nearest Soviet headquarters is far away, near Lake Baikal, so we have nowhere to hide." He looks at his men. "I'm going to take a small unit of a dozen fighters and go out and find them," explains Lazo, who is recognizable by his dark black hair being parted down the middle, and a large forehead giving off strength, assuredness, and intelligence.

Mischa wants to object to the unit departing camp with so few soldiers. But being a newcomer, he holds his tongue. Besides, Lazo orders him to stay behind in the camp which gives Mischa time to begin his duties as commissar. He is charged with keeping a close eye on various units for any sign of betrayal, including officers, as well as educating recruits to Bolshevik principles.

•

The day after the staff meeting, Lazo, and two of his officers, Alexey Lutsky and Vsevolod Sibirtsev, accompanied by a squad of guards, head to inspect fortifications in the area around Vladivostok and Suchan. The region will be tough going for them since it consists of highlands which cover eighty percent of the land.

For the first few hours of the day, everything goes smoothly. But as they approach an abandoned, wooden house near the railway tracks at a provincial train stop, shots are fired at the group from a large combined Japanese-Cossack infantry unit which captures the Red soldiers and their officers, including Lazo. The Japanese turn them over to the Whites.   •

A day later, when no word is heard from Lazo, Mischa becomes concerned. He decides to organize a group of fifty partisans and heads out to the countryside to find the missing Red commander. The first citizens they meet outside Suchan, point to the house where the group was last seen and where the Japanese corralled them.

"The Japs said they were taking the prisoners to a railway station nearby. They had some Cossacks with them," residents told Mischa's men, adding that the Japanese had at least several hundred men.

Reaching that station, Mischa's unit finds that both the Japanese and Whites have disappeared from the scene.

"The Cossacks beat their captives and forced them on the train," declares the trainmaster. "We also heard shots from behind the station. Looking out the back window, I could see bodies on the ground. They weren't dead yet," he stammers. "But they weren't being treated for their wounds. The Whites, it seemed, didn't care if they lived or died." He became more emotional and stopped. "I was powerless to do anything. Then, the train left. Heading toward Muravyevo-Amurskaya station, it was. "

Mischa, walking around the house, bows his head as he gazes at the dead. He declares in a loud voice, "We shall avenge you!"

Commandeering several trucks, Mischa instructs his men: "Let's go. We've got to get to the Muravyevo-Amurskaya rail station. We'll follow the road that runs along the train tracks." Having issued his order, his mind races. "I can't believe Comrade Lazo's a prisoner. All these months, he successfully fended off their seizing him. It's the Japanese interventionists and their allies who have turned against Russia and threaten our Revolution."

Like a bird frantically circling the sky in search of her just kidnapped newborn from their nest, Mischa and his comrades drive on, through a rainstorm, stopping to refuel in hamlets along the way, getting water from the wells of peasant's timber-made homes, changing drivers, all in the pursuit of the freeing their beloved leader.

Next morning, at dawn, just outside of Muravyevo-Amurskaya, Mischa's group spot a lone, wounded soldier lying near the railroad tracks. He barely has the strength to wave his hand to them. When Mischa's driver stops their vehicle, Mischa and a comrade leap from the car and race to the nearly dead Red soldier.

"What's your name Comrade?"

"Comrade Igor Koppel," says the wounded man tearfully, adding, "They're dead. Our comrades. All of them."

"What happened?"

"Don't believe it myself," says the trooper, his cracked voice emanating from parched lips, so much so, that he stops, and whispers, "water, water."

Mischa bends down and gives the wounded man a few sips of water from a canteen. Then in a calm, but beseeching voice, Mischa prods the disoriented soldier. "What happened? Tell us."

After struggling to get out a few words, Igor continues slowly:

"Bound and gagged, I was. They put a few of us in the car behind the engine. Why they kept me in a separate car, I'll never know. A few other prisoners must have been scattered throughout the train. Some of our group had been shot back at the station, I'm sure. Looking out of the train window I saw villages flit past. Then we stopped at a station."

Wearing from recounting the grim details, he stops, closing his eyes. Then he starts again.

"Muravyevo-Amurskaya, station," explains the trooper who breaks out in a coughing spell. Mischa waits patiently, saying only, "And then?"

"At that point, six soldiers burst into our car. Each of the two soldiers hold up a single burlap bag containing..." - and here he stops to catch his breath, "my God, a body. I swear I could hear murmurs coming from each sack." The soldier breaks down. "I could see a lifeless hand from one of the bags. Oh, it was terrible. My guard pulled me up by the collar and dragged me over to the window-space of the door between the cars." The soldier again haltingly says, "he told me, 'Watch what's going to happen to your beloved Bolshevik comrades now.'"

Mischa and those with him were silent.

Trying to save his breath, Igor struggles to get out the next words: "They threw the sacks with the bodies into the engine's fire box."

A murmur sweeps through the partisans gathered around their dying comrade.

"Bastards," mumbles a soldier.

Igor continues: "I swear I imagined their souls screaming out, 'Save us. Save us.' Here I am and I can't help them," he whispers in a raspy voice. "Moments later, a few Whites came out of the engine car, laughing and saying, 'That's the end of them. They got what they deserved.'"

"I can't tell you more. I can't," mumbles Igor, breathing heavily, and managing with all his available strength to cross himself.

Mischa and the few partisans around him close their sad eyes. They know Igor is going fast. He takes a deep breath and exhales. In seconds, he's gone.

With his death goes the only Red witness to the murder of three comrades, including that of Comrade Lazo.

Returning with Igor's body to the station, they quickly bury him.

Word reaches the unit that the Japanese have occupied much of Primorsky krai. Mischa and his partisans take cover, since all Russian troops are being disarmed by the Japanese.

•

In hiding in village after village, Mischa realizes his Communist task calls for dispensing information to the Party. He is obliged, therefore, to tell the world what happened to Comrade Lazo. Working secretly with an undercover agent in a small-town telegraph office, Mischa sends a dispatch to headquarters and one to his newspaper, Pravda, about the killing of Lazo.

Despite the fact that the partisans did not catch up to the train that carried the Red leaders, and that nobody came forward to corroborate the story of Igor, Mischa's sources are convinced that the Japanese and Whites burned Sergey Lazo, Alexey Lutsky, and Vsevolod Sibirtsev in the locomotive. Mischa knows he has a "big story" and in his Pravda article he plays it up with fervor for the Bolshevik cause. A month later, Pravda runs Mischa's story. It reads in part:

"Our comrades in arms had been beaten by the Whites or Japanese, then hustled onto a train and burned alive in the firebox of a steam engine in Muravyevo-Amurskaya, which was named after the late explorer-governor of Eastern Siberia, Count Nikolai Muravyev-Amursky."

Mischa's story on the barbaric murder of Lazo by the enemy spreads across the world. The young lad from Odessa's first published piece draws acclaim from his superiors.

•

Whatever the Whites or the Japanese thought they would achieve in terms of frightening the Russian people with Lazo's murder, it backfired. The cruel killing of Lazo unites Russians in Siberia and beyond to the Bolshevik cause. Lazo becomes a Soviet hero. The Japanese deny the Pravda version. "A fabrication," claims Tokyo. "The provocateur who wrote that tale is a charlatan with no living witnesses to the alleged murder."

Other commentators said the partisans were shot shortly after capture. But the exact details of the execution never surfaced.

True or not, the Kremlin was pleased with a good story for the masses and Mischa earns a reputation as a reporter who can spot a big story when he sees one.

"Maybe they'll teach me languages and send me abroad as a foreign correspondent or spy," he thinks. *"Maybe I can find Basya. Maybe we can be together again, if she forgives me."*

But his bosses in Moscow have other ideas. They assign him to serve in the Vladivostok port, where the burgeoning Soviet Pacific fleet is berthed. It is a daunting task as ships must be protected, installations guarded, and warehouses secured. That's the reason the functionaries keep Mischa Rasputnis in the Pacific area. They need good people who can't be corrupted, who root out enemies of the people, and who keep an eye on the always-menacing Empire of Japan sitting on Russia's doorstep.

•

Vladivostok may be isolated, but Mischa doesn't have to say a word to strike fear in the minds and hearts of port workers. His swagger and stare marked his demeanor. He wore a black leather cap, a belted long shirt, and knee-high boots in the style of Bolshevik commissars.

Even though unhappy where the Party has placed him, he remains dedicated to the Communist cause, and resolutely decides to make the best of it. He even believes his own propaganda. He remembers lines from a Bolshevik drama: *I'm helping build the new Russia and it's for the good of the Party."*

Often walking in the port area, he concludes, *I'm a good Communist. I can't do anything about the fact that Basya has disappeared. Every inquiry I made about her comes back negative. Oh my! What if she's dead. No! That can't be. She's working for the Party. I've got to get on with my life until we meet again. That's what Soviet patriots do. Who knows what tomorrow will bring.*

•

Lost in the bureaucracy, the months and years grind by. Mischa is bored in his job of stamping papers in Vladivostok, Russia's window to the Pacific. Every time he puts in for a transfer, a clerk in Moscow instructs him to remain in what Mischa calls, the city on the moon.

•

Finally, in 1932, a dozen years later, working at the port, helping grow the city, somewhat active in the community, politically and socially, the end of a generally monotonous life comes for Mischa. The OGPU, (Joint State Political Directorate), successor to the Cheka, is sending him to his birthplace, Odessa.

"It's only because I can run a port," he surmises.

Next day, Commissar Mischa Rasputnis boards the Trans-Siberian railway to Moscow, with a transfer to train No. 92 for Odessa. As the engine and passenger cars lurch forward, he watches the station lights go on as darkness descends and the Vladivostok railyards recede.

"My, how trains and terminals remind me of Basya," he says as the wheels of the locomotive speed down the tracks of the Trans-Siberian to cover six thousand miles through the endless Russian steppe, through two continents, fourteen regions and ninety cities to Odessa.

•

Chapter 11. Prague, 1932.
BASYA.
"Basya Smuggled into Czechoslovakia."

•

About the same time that Mischa Rasputnis is embarking on his long journey from Vladivostok to Odessa, three dark-clothed figures, one of them, Basya Abramskaya, are hurrying through an open field in Ukraine toward the Czechoslovakian border. Suddenly, they find themselves holed up in a nearby pine-wood forest. The Czechs have picked this night to test their border security by lighting up the boundary between the two nations. They launch flares to explode above the trio's path of entry. *"They may call it testing,"* she thinks, "but *if they keep up with the flares, we're dead."*

Basya's challenge at this bleak moment is to get through the border fence looming ahead.

Silence. Maybe her bosses in the OGPU made a mistake in risking this illegal crossing, instead of having her go by train and car to a border station as a normal traveler would. But then again, Basya's not your usual tourist. She's a Russian spy about to enter Czechoslovakia. The OGPU wants to ensure that once she's in that country, the Czechs can never trace her back to the Soviet Union. By crossing at an official post, she would have left a paper trail by showing documents, such as a passport and visa. Her entry there would have been recorded. Now, by traveling via horse-and-carriage along back roads and highways to the Czech border, she and her comrades could secretly get across.

Thus, there is no record of her ever having left Czechoslovakia since her birth in Kosice in 1901. How could there be. Her name is now Tatiana Kovacova.

As she steels herself to move across the frontier, she thinks, *"We'll know soon enough if the OGPU plan works."* With that, the three hunched down and move toward the border fence. A wet snow begins to fall. Her comrades, armed with two pairs of wire cutters, open a large hole for her to wiggle her way onto Czech soil. She slinks through the opening and then runs to a nearby road. There, a young couple awaits her. They provide her with food and a bed.

Early the next morning, possessing a Czech identity card identifying her as Tatiana Kovacova, along with a birth certificate and a letter of admission to Charles University, she rises. She eats a slice of bread with honey, catches a bus on the main road, and heads to Prague. The year is 1928. She is twenty-seven years old.

A week after her arrival, she initiates her well-thought out plan to enter the Czech foreign ministry. She recalls her instructor in spy school telling her, "You're a beautiful woman. You have power. You can get secrets out of a man."

My body is my weapon, an espionage tool.

The next day, displaying her fake graduation diploma from the University of Bratislava, she enters the graduate program at Prague's Charles University. No one questions her. The school administration never dreams that she's anything but a Czech or Slovak. Besides, she's a gifted student, better than most. Quickly joining a debating society, she urges her classmates to take up the matter of Czechoslovak recognition of the USSR. This position flies in the face of fellow students because the Czechs disavowed the Bolsheviks during the Russian civil war.

"What's the use of debating, unless we take on unpopular views?" she argues. Being an excellent debater, she catches the fancy of a history professor with ties to the foreign office. It doesn't take her long to seduce him. He puts in an application for her, but it goes nowhere.

Years of formal training in Moscow taught her how to reel in a married official caught in his hotel room with a prostitute-which Basya hired-while he's attending a conference away from home. Next day, she gives him a knowing look and uses a subtle approach. "How was your night with the lady?" He'd give her a look back, that of a kid caught with his hand in the cookie jar. That's when she'd show him the pictures of him naked. "We'll protect you. Nobody will know."

Years later, she'd remember there was one foreign office official she admired. His name was Alois. He was married. *We'd meet in hotel rooms around the city. He landed me a position in the foreign office without a background check. I didn't break up with him for a while; it wouldn't have looked good.*

From then on, she's successful in her work. She gets promoted, moving up in the diplomatic ladder, starting as a typist, then an assistant, and finally, a diplomat. Often in her rise to the vaunted position she sought, she forced herself to disregard the sordid life she led, sleeping around and bribing officials. "If that's what I have to do to help to defend my country, I'm going to do it," and she would quickly snap out of her depression.

Since her break with Mischa, she rarely calls him to mind. Occasionally, she wonders what happened to him. But as she advances in her work, her thoughts about him, fade. *Everything's now about my life in Prague. I'm a new person with a new name. I can't ask for anything more.*

Her apartment is located in Uvoz Street, in the up-scale neighborhood of Mala Strana, known as The Lesser Town. It's near Czernin Palace, home of the foreign office. A drawing room, a small library, and a bedroom with a sitting room and a small kitchen, overlook the medieval streets with steeples, belfries, and turrets. She believes she's mystically touching the spires of the Old Town below. It's from this apartment that she passes on valuable information to Moscow via her radio transmitter in a kitchen cabinet.

By 1932, Tatiana is ensconced in the foreign office. Both the Russian Embassy in Prague and the OGPU are happy with her work. Indeed, she's about to snare an asset so valuable that she'll earn a medal and promotion to rank of captain in the Soviet secret service.

•

Chapter 12. Prague, 1932.
BASYA.
"Basya's First Case. She Snares a Japanese Asset."

•

One early Monday morning in the summer of 1933, the sun rises in the east over the peaceful city of Prague, the city on the swift moving Moldau River.

It's a day like any other day when Tatiana Kovacova, a member of the Czechoslovakian foreign office, arrives at her desk. She begins pouring over secret transcripts of exchanges between the Japanese embassy in Prague and its headquarters in Tokyo. Quickly scanning page after page, her brown, restless eyes become fixated on a familiar name: Akira Yamagata, listed as a member of the press department of the Embassy of Japan.

"That's him. The Japanese diplomat. I'm sure of it," she says, realizing that her discovery conjures up the memory of Mischa Rasputnis, her old boyfriend, whom she hasn't seen for a dozen years now.

Writing the name, Akira Yamagata, onto a clean page in her three-by-five-inch notebook she always carries in her purse, she remembers what Mischa told her back in Yekaterinburg. He had befriended a Japanese journalist during the civil war who told him, "The 'Rising Sun' of Japan will spread its rays over the Russian Far East, and Russia again, as in 1904, won't be able to lift a finger to stop it."

Realizing she's on to something, Tatiana makes sure she's invited to a diplomatic reception at the Japanese Embassy to be held in a few days. *"It'll probably be the usual boring party,"* she assures herself. *"But at least I'll be able to satisfy my recently acquired taste of Japanese food."* She enjoys miso soup with tofu, sushi rolls, pork and cabbage dumplings, and ramen fried rice, and more. "Ah, the benefits of being in the diplomatic corps!"

Entering the hall which boasts colorful pastel paintings of Mt. Fuji, she spots Yamagata. He's short in stature, has narrow eyes, a small face, and is muscular, especially his arms. She knows he's an avid golfer. At the moment, he's engaging in a toast with a few men from the German Embassy. They're drinking the alcoholic beverage, sake.

Focusing her eyes on Yamagata, she notices that he's also staring at her, as if he recognizes her. By blinking her eyes in an inviting manner, she invites the Japanese diplomat to approach her. He does. Exchanging pleasantries, as diplomats do at these functions, each one sniffing the air for news tidbits like hunting dogs sniffing hiding grouses in bushes in the field.

Tatiana gets the feeling he wants to talk, but not at the party. *Maybe he thinks he's being watched.* He bows. She nods. They exchange pleasantries and before they part, he whispers, "Meet me in Stromovka Park, in the Bubene district. There are benches near the gazebo in the center of the park. See you at eight o'clock, Sunday morning. Come alone."

•

"I know who you are. You're Tatiana Kovacova. But you're not who you say you are." He gives her a hard look. "You're a Soviet operative working within the Czech foreign service," he says sharply at the meeting in the park. The words from his sneering mouth, shock her.

"I have nothing to do with Russia. You're mistaken." She continues, "You can't expose me. No one would believe you. Documents and friends will attest to that. I was born and raised in Kosice and I've never been out of the country." "

"I can prove otherwise."

"He's bluffing," Tatiana thinks.

She counters, "You don't have anything on me. Let me tell you what I have on you, Mr. Yamagata." It is her turn to give him a hard stare. "It seems that you once met in the 1920's, a certain Mischa Rasputnis in Vladivostok. He was a Russian intelligence agent and you told him you had proof that Japan might one day attack Russia.

You passed him a secret Japanese memorandum. Apparently, you needed a lot of money. He gave you many rubles for it."

"You can't prove that."

"Wrong. We have evidence of the transaction," she bluffed with a straight face. She leans forward and says in a dramatic tone of voice: "The updated Siberian Dossier, we want it." Dumbfounded, he remains silent. He gets up. "Let's meet here again at eight o'clock in the morning, next Sunday," he says. "I must go."

They part. She knows he's frightened. She'll intimidate him further.

•

When they meet the following Sunday, she verbally accosts him. "By the way, how are your wife and three daughters? I wish I had such a beautiful family."

Her words obviously cause him deep pain. "How cruel. Leave them out of it. They're not involved," he reacts in a bitter voice.

"Nothing will happen to them, if you cooperate," she says in an almost masculine voice.

Yamagata gets the message. "I can't get the dossier that fast. Give me time," he answers.

Tatiana, knowing he can be an asset in her work, says: "Okay. But I can't wait forever."

They part, and as she walks away, she thinks, "I'll have to put the pressure on him, just like I learned to do in the Lubyanka."

The next day in his embassy office in the Mala Strana neighborhood, Yamagata receives a call from his wife.

"'A man's following me," she says. "'What should I do?"

"Nothing. Go home," he says calmly. "Everything will be okay," he adds, putting down the phone and feeling the trepidation that comes to a man whose family is in danger.

•

A few days later, Tatiana starts following Yamagata from his apartment near Czernin Palace to his embassy in the Turba Palace, and from the embassy back home in the evening. It's the same half-hour walk every day. She does this for several days. One afternoon, he sends a maid from his house to drop off a note at Tatiana's apartment to meet him at noon the next day in the middle of the historic, five-hundred-year old Charles Bridge which crosses the Moldau River.

"How dare you threaten my family!" he challenges Tatiana when they meet on the bridge on a gloomy day which deters the sightseers.

They are alone and Yamagata feels free to raise his voice.

"Calm down Mr. Yamagata. I'm not going to dump you or your family in the river."

He's quiet now and stares in the distance, as he stands at the railing of the medieval stone-arch bridge replete with religious statues.

"Listen, Tatiana, I'm not going to blow your cover. My people don't know about you. But since each one of us has something on the other, we can make a deal."

"I'm all ears."

"I don't want any money. I'm against my military's imperialist plans, not only to conquer lands in Siberia, but to move into Northeast Asia, to dominate China. I'm against this strategy which will lead to bloodshed between our two countries. All I want is to warn your government. I'm what they call in America, a 'whistle-blower.'"

"All well and good. There must be another reason, however, that motivates you to do this."

"Yes. There is. A Russian soldier saved my father's life on the battlefield in Manchuria in the Russo-Japanese War. I'm here today because of that man. My father's alive and he's also opposed to the militarism of the Japanese Navy. I can't go to your embassy. But I can come to you to pass on to warn them. War is on the horizon."

"Okay," I understand. But how long till I get the dossier," she asks.

"Less than a week."

"Okay."

They part.

•

A few days later, Tatiana, shopping in Wenceslas Square, is handed new instructions from Yamagata by his maid. "Meet me in Stromovka Park on Sunday. Here are directions."

That next Sunday morning, Tatiana finds herself sitting on a park bench exactly where Yamagata designated. A few cyclists and runners pass by on the wide path.

Obviously not in her usual civil service garb, Tatiana wears leisure walking clothes, including tennis shoes. She dons a green cap. Leaving her apartment early that morning, she had placed two women's caps, one, red, and one, green, in her gym bag, the latter signifying to a contact person that she has not been followed.

At eight o'clock, she gets up and begins to walk on the path. In a few minutes, a cyclist approaches her from the opposite direction. He's also wearing a green cap. She stops. Now alongside her, he slows down and hands her an envelope and continues biking. She resumes her walk, this time at a faster pace until she exits the park.

•

Tatiana conveys Yamagata's dossier to the Russian Embassy at a lunch with Soviet press- attaché, Anatoly Abramov. It's not unusual for Czech and Soviet officials to meet. Prague and Moscow are drawing closer diplomatically, much of it due to her influence. The two don't meet that often even though Anatoly is her secret Russian official handler. The Kremlin doesn't want to blow her cover as a spy who has burrowed deep in the Czech government's foreign office.

"Comrade Kovacova. How did you do this? We've been trying for months to get information out of the Japanese Embassy on their policy regarding our Russian Far East."

"You're too kind, Comrade Abramov. It wasn't easy." After she explains the espionage adventure, the two diplomats leave. Anatoly, the Siberian dossier in hand, takes a taxi back to the Soviet Embassy. He, the Russian Embassy and the OGPU are happy with her work.

•

In the months to follow, Tatiana often takes a tram from her neighborhood to peaceful Stromovka Park on Sunday mornings. The visits remind her of Akira Yamagata. Shortly after Yamagata handed over the records, he was transferred to the foreign office in Tokyo. Unbeknownst to him, a Soviet embassy photographer snapped a picture of the exchange in the Prague park. With the photo, the Soviets blackmail him. He cooperates with Soviet master spy, Richard Sorge. With information supplied to the Russians by Yamagata in 1941, Serge warns Stalin of the impending German invasion which the dictator disregards.

Later, that year, Stalin receives messages from Sorge that Japan will not attack Russia in the east. Stalin accepts this dispatch and frees up crucial Soviet reserves in Siberia to fight the Nazis in the west. Serge is discovered in 1941 by the Japanese as a Soviet spy and later executed. As for Yamagata, he's caught by his own intelligence department for supplying diplomatic secrets to Serge and immediately beheaded, a victim for getting involved with Tatiana Kovacova.

•

Chapter 13. Odessa, 1932.
MISCHA.
"Mischa Trains to Odessa."

•

Mischa's transfer from Vladivostok to Odessa in 1932 took several weeks due to train disruption in the Ukraine. Stalin had initiated a policy to replace Ukraine's small farms with state-run collectives and punish independence-minded Ukrainians who posed a threat to his totalitarian authority. When the peasants refused to turn over their grain to officials to feed the growing urban areas, the Communist regime not only confiscated the peasants' grain, but all their available food. In some cases, the peasants hid or burnt the crops rather than surrender them to the police. The result of Stalin's policies was the Great Famine (Holodomor) of 1932–33 - a man-made demographic catastrophe. The richer, land-owning peasants were labeled "kulaks" and were portrayed by the Bolsheviks as class enemies. This policy culminated in a Soviet campaign of political repression, including arrests, deportations to Siberia, as well as executions of large numbers of the better-off peasants and their families. Deprived of food, several million Soviet citizens perished in the famine.

•

After hours and days of delay, Mischa Rasputnis' train pulls into Kiev, the final stop on his journey before reaching his assignment in Odessa. Weary and wan-looking, he gets off the train and strolls into the main waiting room of the newly-rebuilt, Kiev-Pasazhyrsky railway station. Eager to board the Kiev-Odessa express, he heads to the gate where he spots a woman being accosted by a policeman. Her stony face, wolf-like eyes, and frail body startle him. He notices she's almost dead.

"Why are you arresting her," he asks the policemen as he shows him his documents introducing: 'Mischa Rasputnis, member of the OGPU.'

Scanning the official papers, the officer stands to attention and salutes, though it is hard for him to believe that this young-looking, civilian-dressed man in front of him is a commissar and a secret agent combating foreign-inspired terrorism.

"She's mad with hunger," declares the trooper. "She was eating the flesh of her child. That's what fellow passengers told me. They said they buried the child quite a ways back."

"What are you saying? Are you sure?" Mischa questions.

"Look at her, salivating at the mouth. She barely can talk," says the policeman.

"хлеб хлеб" "(bread, bread)," whispers the woman prisoner in a scratchy voice. "Please comrade, help me."

The starving woman is hauled away by two arriving policemen.

"What's going to happen to her," Mischa asks the guard.

"She'll be liquidated."

Mischa doesn't object. "Like the government says," he tells the guard, "we can't have people practicing cannibalism."

•

Even in the noisy waiting room, Mischa manages to doze off and dreams. A woman appears before him. He doesn't know her name. Ah yes, it's that old woman in the train depot. She haunts him to the very depths of his mind. He tries to remove her from his dream. He can't.

He awakes and recalls the woman again. *Is this what a proud Soviet wife has come to be? She could be one of my sisters, or my mother.*

He boards the train and once it pulls out of the station, he again wants to sleep. He's lucky. He has an empty seat next to him. He can stretch out. "We just might get there on time," he thinks as he falls into a deep sleep.

Later, coming out of his trance, he notices, with half-open eyes, the train has halted in the middle of a huge wheat field, just outside Vinnitsa. Looking out the window, he spots an endless line of stopped trucks on a road. The passengers wear exhausted expressions on their pale faces, which are covered with dust. Their children are asleep in the laps of their weary and impoverished parents. They are being deported to Siberia for refusing to turn over their grain.

Mischa has no idea when the train will continue. Restless, he disembarks and stands by his rail car where he observes his fellow passengers throwing scraps and pieces of bread out of the train windows. He sees men and women and children - a whole village - walking in the field along the tracks searching for crusts of bread. Watching families eating grass and acorns, he imagines he hears a huge roar of hundreds rising from a nearby village. Even a tough soldier like Mischa cringes from fright from their howl of starvation.

Those screams. I'm shaking. This policy is inhumane, insane.

At that very moment, Mischa watches an officer, with a red armband on his sleeve, corral a family on the tracks and motions to them to get into the truck. They carry all their possessions in string-tied bundles and a few old suitcases. But they are dressed decently. This husband, wife, teenage son and daughter apparently had to walk out from the town to get on the train when it shot by the rail station at Vinnitsa. It's the daughter that gets his attention.

"Move. Damn it. Get into the truck with the kulaks, you Jews," yells the local policeman to the family. "Quickly. Trying to escape, are you? We're not letting anyone out of the country," he adds in a sharp voice.

"We're not kulaks. We're from Zboriv. We're not leaving Russia. Just going to Odessa to visit my wife's sick mother. Look at our tickets and papers. We couldn't get aboard in the station. We were told to come out here," says the head of the family, avoiding the reference to their being Jewish.

"I don't care what you were told. You look like bourgeois enemies to me."

"Just a minute officer," says Mischa, interrupting, "I know this family. I'll take them on the train."

"And who are you," shouts the officer indignantly. "Protecting some rich *zhids* (Russian anti-Semitic slur)?"

"Commissar Mischa Rasputnis, OGPU," he replies, emphasizing the title 'Commissar.' He shows the officer his papers, and declares: "This family is going to Odessa where I'm stationed. I'll be responsible for them. Besides comrade, in our Soviet society, under the wise leadership of Comrade Stalin, we don't slander any group."

"Yes, comrade. You're correct," sneers the cop who turns to the family and instructs them: "Go with the commissar."

Mischa escorts the astonished family onto the train. He gets them settled. He doesn't ask them their name. They thank him, profusely. Even the teenage daughter shakes his hand. They sense his aloofness, however. Yet, for the first time, as a commissar, he's risked his life for someone, including, threatening the 'protection of his title.'

"I can't stay here," he tells them. "Unfortunately, you're on your own."

"We understand. Thank you."

He informs them he's going back to his compartment which happens to be the last car on the train. He bids them a safe journey. Heading back to his seat, he mutters to himself.

"I can't get involved. I saved the family. I did a good deed. Enough. Besides, Comrade Stalin knows what he's doing. Since he and the Party have this policy against the kulaks and the bourgeois, our job must be to obey."

•

For a while, it's a clear run for the Kiev-Odessa-line, even though the train rattles and shakes. About an hour from Odessa, the train is halted again in the middle of an empty field. Passengers are told not to disembark. Gazing out the window, Mischa sees that heavily armed Red Army units are boarding and dragging out some passengers from each rail car. A few moments later, the train lurches forward and stops. Now gazing out the window, Mischa sees the painful faces of the family he rescued in Vinnitsa. They're climbing up into the truck. Mischa notices the girl is missing.

"Oh my," he whispers to himself. *"I've got to...*

But doesn't move. He doesn't look at them. He doesn't want to see their faces. He knows they're doomed. But he wonders: *"What happened to the daughter?"*

Putting his elbows on his knees, his hands holding the sides of his face, he looks down to the floor. He admits to himself, he tried to save them, but not hard enough.

I'm letting them down. Besides being outranked, these army officers will want to know why I'm protecting kulaks, or worse yet, rich people, and Jews. Have to watch out for myself or I'll end up in Siberia. The only way you can stay alive these days is by looking the other way.

And with that, he looks outside again. They're gone. Sadly, he remembers what his sister, Klara, used to say, *"Their luck ran out."*

As he continues to justify his action, the blond, lanky, teenage girl, the daughter, slinks stealthily into the narrow space between his body and the back of the train chair in front of him, and plops right down into the empty seat next to him. She wipes her tearful eyes.

He touches her arm to calm her down. "If the soldiers come by," he whispers to her, "don't say a word. I'll do all the talking. Act as if I'm your uncle. If they ask, show them your papers. Just tell them we're going to see your ailing grandmother in Odessa."

The girl nods, takes a handkerchief out of her small haversack and wipes her frightened eyes. She tells him in a whisper her name. "Slava, Slava Abelevskaya." He's sure she's in some form of shock, that lost-look of which he saw so frequently in the eyes of the wounded on the battlefields of Siberia. Or is it her seductive eyes that move him.

How her parents got her to separate from them and run to me, I'll never know.

As it happens, when the soldiers arrive in his car, they look at his papers. He motions to Slava and says, "She's my niece." They don't bother waking the girl. They salute and move on.

Then a new thought plagues him. "It's only natural," he says to himself, responding to sad thoughts about his daughter, Klara, now a teenager, whom he gave away for adoption, even though she's younger than this Slava, who's about sixteen. The incidents with the kulaks, the arrested family only slightly penetrate his conscience. He can't see that the lack of humanity shown to these people causes cracks in his Communist belief system. At least, not yet.

•

Mischa can tell he's getting close to home. A final burst of speed and the train plunges into Odessa and soon crawls into the station. He forgets the family and the kulaks and even the teenager. He's filled with nostalgia. Images of childhood penetrate his mind, the city's tastes and smells that he left a dozen years ago, including the fishy smell of the Black Sea off the Odessa Steps. His job will be to organize the port of Odessa as he did in Vladivostok. If war comes, everything must be ready, so the country can increase the ability to export and import arms.

But he's puzzled about one thing. He's been instructed by an official, Alyosha Kovalchenko, a leader of the Comintern. The Communist International, which advocates world Communism, to study Spanish. He figures that Kovalchenko needs to enlist people to fight for Communist revolutions throughout the world. Perhaps Spain is the next battlefield.

On arrival in the station, a cold wind whistles up and down the platform. As he and Slava leave the train and melt into the stream of people exiting into the bitter cold weather outside, he imagines he hears the raucous cries of news vendors: "The prodigal son returns."

That's me. And that's my welcome to Odessa on the Black Sea.

But before he reports to OGPU headquarters, he takes Slava to her grandmother's apartment. When the old lady hears the news of her family's arrest, she breaks down and screams, bringing in a rush of neighbors. Mischa calms everyone. He's a commissar. They listen. A few hours later, he is ready to leave. Saying goodbye to Slava, he advises, "Don't lose hope. I'll try and get them out."

With a dazed look in her eyes, she answers, "Thank you," and closes the door. He's moved. Something about her reminds him of Basya.

Mischa reports to the OGPU and then checks into the elegant Londonskaya Hotel, located near the Odessa Steps. He'll be here a few days, until he's assigned permanent quarters. Thoughts of Slava fade away. He doubts he'll ever see her again. He takes a bath, dresses, and like the detective he aspires to be, begins to search for the whereabouts of one, Basya Abramskaya, still the special one.

•

Chapter 14. Odessa, 1932.
MISCHA.
"Mischa Searches for Basya."

•

"When I am dead, bury me In my beloved Ukraine."
Taras Shevchenko "Zapovit" (MyTestament) 1845.

•

Next day, a stranger approaches Mischa in front of the Londonskaya Hotel.

"You're originally from Odessa. Aren't you."

"Yes. A long time ago."

"Family?"

"They're gone."

"So what are you doing here?"

"Working."

"When were you here last?"

"After our glorious Soviet Socialist Revolution."

"Exciting times, yes?"

"No. Too much killing. Lost a lot of comrades."

"Too bad."

•

Once again, Mischa constantly thinks of himself as being on a hunt - a cold-crime case needing to be solved. His goal remains to catch Basya - in this case, a good person, an innocent.

As a political propaganda officer, Mischa often travels from Odessa to Moscow for briefings by the OGPU. There, he stops at the Bureau of Missing Persons. He has access to files that could lead him to the whereabouts of Basya Abramskaya. He gives the official of the files, the name of another case and gains entrance to an off-limits room. He searches documents. He's discreet. Nothing turns up.

He can't seem to find her in Odessa, either. He goes to the apartment building where she lived. The family had moved and there was no forwarding address. Not since the end of the civil war has anyone heard about her. That was nearly a dozen years ago.

One morning, he knocks on the door of another aunt and uncle, whom, Basya said, resided in Odessa. But they had passed away. He seeks out some school chums who might have been in contact with her but they shed no light.

One friend, Annika, who resided in a nearby apartment block, had received a note from Basya in the early 1920's from Siberia. "But after that, nothing," she tells a despondent Mischa.

•

A week later, Mischa is called into the office of Comrade Col. Semyon Ignatiev, Mischa's boss. He likes Mischa who at this moment is sitting before him. Comrade Ignatiev has read reports that since his guerrilla days in Siberia, Mischa has an exemplary Party record in Vladivostok where he managed the port. So far, he is respected by the Party bosses in Odessa, for his efficiency in keeping the port humming, and arresting suspicious persons who bad-mouth the regime. Above all, he is loyal.

Looking up before him, the commissar decides he must deal with Mischa in a tough manner. "As your superior, Comrade Rasputnis, I must warn you to stop putting your nose in matters that don't concern you. Specifically, seeking information on one, Basya Abramskaya who's on an important mission. Don't do it again," the commissar warns harshly.

"But Comrade Ignatiev. I was never told about this."

"That's impossible," answers Commissar Ignatiev, realizing that Mischa's answer is plausible, what with the vast unmanageable bureaucracy of the secret police. *They obviously didn't tell Mischa to stay away from her. The bunglers. But I can't admit that.*

"Well, now you know. Don't do it anymore," he says like an admonishing parent.

"Yes, Comrade Ignatiev."

"Keep up the good work in the port. You may go now."

•

Returning to his office above the harbor and looking out on the Black Sea that late fall afternoon, Mischa was stunned by the order. No wonder he could never find her. Not only did they fail to give him any information as to Basya's whereabouts, but now they were officially banning him from contacting her. As he sat there, he realized that something was very clear. He was going to have to defy the Soviet state and the Party. And that was very risky.

Basya! Where are you.? Don't worry, love. I'll find you.

•

A few months after his rebuke from Commissar Ignatiev, Mischa gets a tip from a sailor off a Bulgarian ship. The sailor advises Mischa, "An elderly Tarter, kind of a shady character, helps out-of-towners find missing persons. He can be found in the market. His name is 'Uncle Ayaz.'"

Mischa knows he's disobeying an order. *No matter. I must. I'm not going to give it a second thought.*

He doesn't. But before contacting the Tartar, he does check police files. No record on "Uncle Ayaz."

The next day, Mischa, unusually dressed as a civilian, enters the market place where he stops at the outdoor stand selling vodka.

He waits.

An hour later, a man, obviously a Tartar, dressed in traditional wide trousers, a shirt tucked in, enters the market. He wears a long and wide belt, a vest, a jacket, a long coat, leather boots and a *tubeteika*, a low, brown hat made of sheepskin. He's alone.

Mischa thinks that for some reason he knows the Tartar who, now leaning against a post, possesses a funereal pallor as if something dreadful had happened to him.

"Maybe. Just maybe…" he thinks as he approaches the older man and asks the question he's been offering up since he got to Odessa, "Do you know a Basya Abramskaya?"

"I don't remember the name," says the bearded one. "If she was in the Party, she probably stayed at the commune where a lady friend of mine is one of the managers."

"Where is this commune?"

"Let's see now if I can remember the name," he says, fidgeting. "You know comrade, things are bad. Can't even afford food. 'Trouble with farmers,' they say. Kulaks. By the way, comrade, I make a few extra rubles helping… You know what I mean."

"How much?" interrupts Mischa.

"Fifty rubles."

He knows it's wrong. He could get in trouble offering what amounts to a bribe. But a lead is a lead and when it comes to Basya.

"Here is my friend's address," Uncle Ayaz stutters, as he writes the address on a piece of paper. "Ask for Ludmilla. Tell her Uncle Ayaz sent you."

Mischa hands over the money to the Tarter. He gives the address and directions to Mischa and says goodbye. Mischa follows instructions down winding streets and narrow alleyways with laundry-strung courtyards. He reaches a wooden building at the city's edge. Through the window, he spots a woman dressed in a long, peasant dress. She carries a dirty dish towel in her hands. Her name is Ludmilla and she's standing behind the counter in the office of the commune.

"Who?" Ludmilla questions in a loud voice.

"Basya Abramskaya," he answers. Like he did with Uncle Ayaz, Mischa does not volunteer that he is a member of the OGPU.

The woman pulls out the leather-bound register book from behind the counter and skims the pages of the volume.

"She stayed here alright. In the beginning of the year. They were here for a week." When Mischa presses her for more information, she responds, "I don't know where she went. Kind of closed-mouth. Except the friend who was with her. Now that woman was pretty talkative." Ludmilla studies Mischa intently. "The friend told me that this Abramskaya lady was trying to find an ex-boyfriend, named 'Mischa.' Nothing more. They left suddenly. But I remembered the name 'Mischa,' because my son's name is 'Mischa.'"

"Really," says Mischa, trying to keep a straight face and not blurt out that his name is Mischa, too. He's not interested in blowing his identity. He really wants to hug the woman, but he dare not. Instead, he takes out a fifty ruble note and hands it to Ludmilla. Despite self-righteous Communist indoctrination, Mischa realizes money talks. A bribe will keep her talking, even though it could get him in trouble. But he'll do anything to find Basya.

"Do you know where they were going?"

"Not really. Except out of the country. I once spied a foreign passport when she opened her bag to pay for refreshments. But I didn't ask any questions." "

Thanks," she says, waving the fifty ruble note in front of her as she examines it. "With all the food shortages, this will come in handy. What did you say your name was?"

Mischa grimaces. Elated at hearing something about Basya, he walks away without answering her. He tries to digest all he's heard. *She's looking for me. She must still have feelings for me or she wouldn't be in Odessa searching. Maybe she'll hear I'm here now. Maybe she'll come back. She may be out of the country. But where?"*

He's so excited and deep in thought that he does not check the surroundings around him. But others who are observing the scene from across the street, spot the exchange of money.

Minutes later in a deserted street, a blow to his head interrupts his pleasant thoughts of closing in on Basya. When Mischa wakes up hours later in a vacant hut on the other side of town, his head throbs. He's been whacked with an iron instrument. His body's sore from being dragged. He tries to get up. His money and wallet are gone, as is the only photo of Basya he possessed. He doesn't report the incident to the police. He can't involve them. The police would want to know why he was in that neighborhood. He can't confess he's looking for Basya. They're forbidden to see each other. He ponders what to do next.

Basya had to be taking a big risk. Actually, she should have chosen her girlfriend more wisely. A talker. Thank goodness she made that mistake. I may never have known she's alive. There's still hope. I have to find out where she went after leaving Odessa. How can I do that?"

•

That night, he dreams he's back playing soccer in Odessa. Knocked down by a sneaky opponent who trips him, he struggles to get up. Coach Ivan Hoyer in his usual inspiring voice is yelling, "Forwards move up." Mischa, rising slowly, in a minute gets a ball pass from a teammate, and shoots the white soccer ball into the net. The announcer yells, "Goal!" A whistle blows. The game is over. The crowd roars. He embraces Basya. "Nothing can stop us from being together now," he tells her.

He wakes up. He tries to hold onto the embrace. *"It's a sign. Go for it. Find her."*

But it's only a dream.

It's no dream, however, when he is summoned to meet Comrade Commissar Ignatiev.

"I won't cover for you. I'm not going to warn you again, Comrade Rasputnis." He paused before continuing, "Stop snooping around for information on Basya Abramskaya." He gets in Mischa's face. "Going to the market in town here, speaking to what I might call riff-raff, bribing them for knowledge of the whereabouts of Comrade Abramskaya. She's on a delicate, diplomatic mission. Don't do it again," rails the Commissar, pounding the table in front of him, causing tough-minded Mischa to flinch. But he kept quiet and listened.

"You better mend your ways or next time, I'll have you shot. Is that clear?"

"Yes, Comrade Ignatiev," Mischa replies, staring straight into the angry eyes of his chief.

"Now get out," yells the commissar. "You're lucky to be alive."

•

Unbelievable. What kind of diplomatic job must she be doing to get them so angry that they're ready to shoot me. I'm not going to stop. But I really have to be careful. I wonder who ratted on me? Uncle Ayaz or the lady?

For the first time since the battles on the Trans-Siberian railway, he's frightened.

Basya, What happened to you?

•

Mischa wallows in Odessa, the city of his birth, for four long years. He had arrived with great expectations. Despite the euphoria of hearing that Basya is looking for him, it all morphs into an illusion. As time passes, this love affair becomes a doomed romance. On any given day, he thinks he sees her across the road, so he crosses the street and follows a woman until she stops and faces him. It isn't her. It gets so bad, that sometimes at night, he thinks of Basya as he tries to fall asleep. Then, he'd move back in time to imagine he's with his wife, Olga.

Then came the Spanish fascists threatening the leftist government of Spain. Mischa recognized that Russia now had a fight on its hands. Moscow would have to aid the Republic to defeat the rebels aided by Hitler and Mussolini. He had a feeling he might be sent to Madrid.

He's correct. One morning, in September, 1936, Mischa gazed out of his second- floor apartment at Varnenska St., Number 71D, in Odessa. Overnight, the sea's whipped-up wolf-like winds that inflict a shiver in his bones. A messenger knocks. Opening the door, Mischa's handed an envelope. He's being reassigned to Spain. The assignment will pole vault him into the Spanish Civil War, the forerunner of World War II, the most destructive conflagration in history.

"I've seen too much war. But I have to heed my country's call," he says to himself, a day later. Donning his black leather jacket, he grabs his old, neatly packed suitcase and is about to leave his well-kept, furnished, but small apartment. He stops and sits on his suitcase.

What I'm doing?. This is nothing but superstition. Like a peasant, I'm a victim of that Russian custom that says, by sitting on my packed bag before a long trip, I'll be lucky in my journey.

On September 26, he and other volunteers are transported to the city of Feodosia in the Crimea in the Black Sea, where they board the

Spanish ship, *Campeche.* The ship is conveying ammunition to the Spanish Republic to quell a rebellion that's thrown the nation into a civil war engulfing all of Spain.

It is an uneventful journey. The vessel zig-zags to avoid detection by the German and Italian navies who have joined the Spanish fascists. Eight days after leaving Feodosia, the *Campeche* berths in the Spanish port of Cartagena. Hundreds of screaming civilians gather at the pier. Soldiers, sailors, old men and women, fathers, mothers, children, greet their saviors.

"Viva la Rosie!" they yell, as they watch six English howitzers, 6,000 shells, 240 grenade launchers, 100,000 grenades, 20,362 rifles and seven million rounds of ammo, being unloaded.

After the shouts, however, comes the grim thought that danger looms on the horizon.

"What's happening in the war?" Mischa asks an officer who understands his poor Spanish.

"The fascists are poised to take Madrid."

"They'll never succeed," responds Mischa. "They must be stopped. This is no time for celebration. Back to work," he says sternly. "The very life of the Republic is at stake."

When the Soviet munitions are finally off the ship, Mischa's thoughts leap ahead. *I must get to Madrid. I'm sure I'll be walking into an abyss.*

●

Chapter 15. Madrid, 1936.
MISCHA.
"And then came the Spanish Fascists! Mischa joins the Fight."

•

The Spanish civil war, 1936-39, a salient event in Spanish history, was the forerunner of World War II. A military uprising, led by Generalissimo Francisco Franco and supported by Nazi Germany and Fascist Italy, erupted against the legitimate government of the Republic of Spain. The civil war turned out to be a battle for the soul of Europe. Spain became the front line against fascism and the battle dominated the headlines around the world. More than 40,000 volunteers, mostly signed up by the Communists, arrived in Spain to fight the fascists. Among them, men and women from the U.S. The most noted volunteers were the several thousand strong American-unit known as the 'Lincoln Brigade.' The Soviet Union was the only major nation that sold arms to the Republic as well as dispatching more than two thousand advisors, including NKVD agents, of which Mischa Rasputnis was one. As Mischa would discover, the USSR would extract a considerable price in return for its aid.

•

It is a chilly Sunday morning, October 11, 1936. A weak fall sun shines down on a 35-year-old, wiry Mischa Rasputnis standing on the Gran Via. He has dreamt about the magnificent thoroughfare in the city ever since the functionaries in the Comintern instructed him to study Spanish.

"Ah, Madrid," he remembered someone saying, "your very name makes me salivate." Maybe his longing to be here had something to do with learning Spanish and reading about the wonders of the Iberian Peninsula. Now, he just wants to wander around and forge an immediate bond with the capital. He moves with a bounce in his steps through the warren of streets and twisting alleys. He carries his small suitcase containing several changes of clothes and a few books. He has five hundred *pesetas* in his pocket which the NKVD, (The People's Commissariat for Internal Affairs), successor to the OGPU, gave him. It is not a huge sum, but enough to get around. He passes deserted side streets and senses the oppressive silence broken by the distant rumble of enemy artillery which frequently causes him to wince.

Even on a Sunday morning, he eyes the *madrileños* taking their morning *paseo* on the wide boulevard. Church bells are silent. There is no church going these days in this anti-clerical Red city, fighting for its life against Franco's battle-tested Moorish troops encircling the capital.

Right now, he's on his way to the Hotel Florida to find legendary Mikhail Koltsov, top Soviet agent and Stalin's special envoy to Spain. As the city turns dark, grey and gloomy, Mischa enters the Hotel Florida where he discovers the establishment is crowded with a strange assortment of characters among the many foreign guests of the hotel - including, photographers, airmen, refugees, ambulance drivers, and Communists from all over the world. This is the hangout of the world's press corps, as well as the haunt of American celebrities.

Showing his credentials at the front desk, he checks in and quickly gets a room. Not on the top floor, but on the side of the building which unfortunately faces the heights where the enemy is positioned. Fascist shells aimed at the Telefonica, the Republic's communications center, often veer into the hotel.

"Comrade Koltsov won't be back until near midnight," a clerk tells him.

Mischa will have to wait. But he's not upset, for he keeps repeating, "Madrid is a city of much beauty," and that includes the women. Except that in Spanish society, they are watched.

•

The evening of his first day in Madrid comes quickly. The blackout begins.

So what does a virile, Russian bachelor do in a strange city? He either gets drunk or finds a woman, or both. And in this war-time capital, that's not difficult.

"As much as you love Odessa, don't think of being homesick," he tells himself. "Don't put yourself in such a mood. Be as happy as a young man looking for a girl."

A woman. That's what I need. Manual, the sailor on the Campeche, told me of that bar on the Gran Via which caters to foreigners. 'Ask for Luciana,' he said.

Next stop, the cabaret. Luciana turns out to be a plump, older, peroxide blonde. Hailing a taxi, she takes him to an apartment which is empty except for one room which is replete with a bed, a night table, and a bowl of soapy water. No words. No foreplay. No love. No endearing words. No kisses. She just disrobes and lies on her back. He feels her soft belly under his weight. They go right at it. He smiles. It goes quickly.

Afterwards, she informs him a taxi is stationed at the corner. He pays her and leaves and in the taxi. On the way back to the hotel, he thinks of Basya.

•

The next day, having heard that Koltsov might have gone to the Majestic Hotel, Mischa decides to walk over there to find him. Walking cautiously close to buildings, he realizes it's been a while since he was in combat back in Russia. *Sixteen years to be exact. This one's going to get rough. These days we have aerial bombardment. I don't think I'll ever forget that gun battle on the Trans-Siberian when I almost lost it. That won't happen again.*

As he gets closer to the hotel, fascist shelling increases. Boom! That explosion makes him duck into a nearby doorway, but as he does so, he bumps into a soldier dressed in a strange outfit. He's wearing a khaki shirt and green pants. The helmet resembles a tin-wheel cap.

Maybe, he's a volunteer from England, Canada or America. Micha ponders as another ear-drum-breaking, blast startles him and the pair fall to the ground.

Maybe the stranger has just arrived in Spain to fight Franco.

"Greetings Comrade," Mischa says in Spanish to the soldier.

No reply from the ruddy, round-faced tall foreigner with brown hair and piercing eyes.

Then, *"Sprichst du Deutsch?"* asks Mischa.

"Bissel," answers the man, mispronouncing the word *'bissel.'*

"Doesn't sound like real German," thinks Mischa. "There's an accent in the word that makes it sound different. Ah! It has the ring of Yiddish. A Jew in Spain? The land of the Inquisition and expulsion. Not likely. Few Jews live here. This soldier must be a member of the *International Brigade* formed by our Comintern."

Mischa is ready to continue when the man interrupts him:

Ich spreche kein Deutsch. Sprechen Sie Englisch?

"English? Yes."

"Good. I don't speak German," the soldier replies in English.

"But you have a *Yiddish* accent?"

"I try and fake German with *Yiddish* which everyone knows is a jargon of German. Many of my Jewish comrades will be able to use *Yiddish* to communicate with volunteers from other countries who speak German."

"Fake. What is fake?" Mischa asks.

"Fake? To cheat. To make it sound real," answers the American. "Sometimes the false story works and sometimes it doesn't."

"By the way, are you a Communist, comrade? Where are you from?" Mischa asks in a puzzling tone, knowing full well that the fighter might have been recruited by the Comintern.

"Yes," replies the soldier, adding, "I'm an American, and a good Communist."

Smiling, Mischa remembers the Americans during the Russian civil war. He observed the 'Yanks' as they were called. They were tall and strong. Even those out of shape could pass for soldiers. They didn't show signs of hunger. Nor did their eyes display fear or despair.

"As the English say," quips Mischa out loud to his newly found comrade: "You Yanks are jolly lads. You possess a fully-equipped military. But why are you here in Spain?"

"To fight the rebels," answers the soldier. "Our battle is here. But it's not just Franco. Our battle is against Hitler. We know what he is doing to my people. He's beating up on Jews in Germany. And he's aiding the rebels. If he and Mussolini win, the world will sink into barbarism and blood."

"That's our battle, too, against Hitler," answers Mischa, not mentioning Jews as the American did. "We're advisors from the Soviet Union. We fight fascism, including Franco and his renegades, and anyone who's against the working class."

The shelling has stopped, so the two find a nearby bench, and with the all-clear sounded, the American offers Mischa a cigarette and says: "My name is 'Michael.'"

"I'm Mischa. Glad to meet you," he replies, extending his hand to this American who warmly returns the gesture in a hearty manner and hands over a cigarette.

"I am with an International Brigade," continues Michael, explaining what Mischa already had figured out. But he's polite and allows the American to go on. "Ours is known as the Lincoln Battalion. More Americans will be coming over. We expect several thousand. They're good men, many unemployed sailors or longshoremen. Three-quarters of them are members of the Communist Party. Half are Jews."

"Comrade, "interrupts Mischa. "Unfortunately, I've got to go. We must meet again."

"Me, too," answers Michael. "I have to be back at headquarters."

"I am staying at the Hotel Florida. If you need me, call. And which unit will you be in?"

"They haven't arrived yet, but I will be with staff officers of the Lincoln Brigade."

Both wave as they separate. Both are excited about the meeting. Mischa may have found an American asset, valuable in the struggle for Russia to further strengthen the revolutionary cause against capitalist America, even though President Roosevelt recognized the USSR in 1933.

Mischa will check him out and exploit the unspoken yearnings, rage, and ideals of the American for Communism in order to get him to pass on secret information.

As for Michael, he's enamored to meet a Russian comrade, though he doesn't know that Mischa is an NKVD agent.

•

The next day, Wednesday, October 13, Mischa uses every means possible to meet Koltsov. Finally, after many messages and calls, he is ushered into the leader's room.

"Welcome, Comrade," says Koltsov, taking off his glasses to polish them. "As you've heard, I'm sure, I can't see without the damn things. You know, Comrade Rasputnis, if they ever shoot me, I'll ask them not to take off my glasses." Seeing Mischa smile at his joke, Comrade Koltsov pauses to study him. "Just arrived in Madrid, have you?"

"Yes, Comrade Koltsov."

"Good. Let's get down to business. I've read your plans. You have free reign to roam the country, go where you want, wherever it's necessary to advance our Communist cause. Officially, you're a Commissar assigned to the Spanish Communist Party and the military. If the government gives you a hard time, let me know. Here's plenty of money for anything you need," he says, handing him a large wrapped-up package. "What you do with the money is up to you. But you must account for every expenditure."

Of course, Comrade Koltsov."

•

What did Mischa Rasputnis do with that money? As an agent of the NKVD which replaced the OGPU, his job is to build membership in the Communist Party of Spain (PCE). He bribes, buys favors, pays loyal agents. He's good at it. He's a born organizer. He wins people over with a smile. He mobilizes masses for mass meetings. He pens pamphlets and articles. He builds the Party's numbers by 250,000 from a paltry 30,000, a feat Moscow appreciates.

While Stalin has warned them to stay undercover, that is not possible all the time. The day after his meeting with Koltsov, for instance. Mischa leads a march of several hundred local Communist volunteers to defend Madrid in the beginning of the fascist siege.

I can't believe it. The cheering crowds. And they're waving red handkerchiefs in our direction. Men, women and children applauding us. And they're singing the international,' Arise ye workers from your slumbers. Arise ye prisoners of want.'

"To the barricades," he shouts, repeating the battle cry of Madrid, "*No pasarant. (They shall not pass)*. The fascists are at our gates. The Republic is in danger."

•

Chapter 16. Madrid, 1936.
MISCHA AND BASYA.
"Mischa Follows a Lead regarding Basya's Location."

•

A few days after his meeting with Koltsov and his work at the University strengthening Madrid's defense, Mischa travels on the afternoon of Saturday, October 16, to the outskirts of the capital. He is to give a talk to the Czechoslovakian contingent of the International Brigade, known as The Thomas Masaryk Battalion.

Getting out of the military-assigned car, he cuts a fine figure: a blanket rolled over his shoulder, a black leather coat that keeps him warm, a sidearm attached on his belt. He finds his way to the local headquarters where he converses with one of the Czech officers who's a liaison to the Soviets. But in the middle of the discussion, the Czech is called away and he's left alone.

As the afternoon darkens, Mischa, left to his own devices, begins looking around a nearby army parking lot. Spotting what appears to be an attractive woman accompanied by several soldiers, he walks towards the group and nearly reaches the end of the lot by the road. One of the troops he recognizes is the American, Michael, whom he met back in the capital, and who's taking a picture of the lady, apparently a visiting dignitary. But they quickly move further away. He barely makes out the features of the woman. However, there's something about her movements that draw him closer. Obviously, she's important. Everyone's catering to her as she's ushered to a private car.

Revving up the vehicle's engine, the driver moves the vehicle forward, slowly at first, then turns and increases speed as it heads in Mischa's direction. Since the car is coming right at him and since he's intrigued, he steps aside and waits for it to pass so he can glimpse the lady. As the automobile speeds by, Mischa stares in amazement. He can feel his heart suddenly beating faster.

"No, it can't be," he gasps and chases the auto as if he's running to a house fire to rescue a child trapped inside. However, it's useless. The car's already at a distance. "Stop!" he shouts as he desperately waves his hands in the air for the vehicle to stop. But driver and passenger don't hear or see him.

"Damn it, Basya. Stop! It's you. I know it's you," he shouts, still chasing the disappearing car.

A nearby soldier tries to bar his way. Mischa pushes him aside.

No matter. Driver and passenger are gone. The rising car dust swirling in its wake and dirtying his uniform.

He feels his emotions rising, just as they did in Madrid and the many battles in Siberia. No thoughts. Just pursue, attack, kill, go on. He wants to continue, but he stops, bends over, puts his hands on his knees to catch his breath.

He's sure she didn't see him. He walks back and locates Michael. As pleased as they are to see each other, Mischa doesn't hang on pleasantries:

"The lady who just left in the car, what's her name?"

"Tatiana Kovacova. She's a Slovak. A diplomat. She works in the Czechoslovakian Foreign Ministry. She's on a goodwill mission from Prague to visit her country's soldiers fighting for the Republic. She'd be what one calls, a 'morale booster.' A good looker, too. She goes from base to base and talks to her countrymen. I was her liaison for the day."

Damn, Mischa thinks. *It's her. That name. It must be her diplomatic name.*

"Sorry, Comrade Michael. My mistake," murmurs Mischa as he slouches away, but manages to ask this time, in a low, calm, official voice, "Do you know where they're going next and where they're staying?"

"Madrid. They're probably stopping at Hotel Florida, in Madrid, where all the big shots stay."

"Good," responds Mischa, thinking he can follow the car and catch up to her in the capital. But then it dawns on him, he can't get back until evening, as the relief car is coming to pick him up at seven o'clock. But with communications cut off in some places, it's lucky if he'll get back tonight. So, he goes ahead and gives his scheduled talk to army officers on how the war will be won by the Spanish Republic.

After my presentation, I better arrange to get that picture Michael took of her before she got into the car.

The relief car doesn't show up until morning. Driving back to Madrid, Mischa can't help but think about his and Basya's ugly parting in Yekaterinburg. *I'm haunted about that and I have to change it. The only way to do that is find her and tell her I regret the incident.*

•

Mischa didn't return to Madrid until mid-morning, the next day, Sunday, October, 1917. He hastens to the Hotel Florida's front desk. Showing his ID, he asks nonchalantly:

"Comrade. Do you have a Tatiana Kovacova here? What room number is she in?"

"We did. But she checked out early this morning. She went on to Valencia."

"Valencia? How long a drive is that?"

"Normally, four or five hours, if you're lucky. But in wartime, who knows"?

"Did she leave a forwarding address?"

"Yes. The Caro Hotel."

"Thank you."

Am I going to Valencia? he asks himself, answering his own question, with a resounding *'Yes!'* Trying not to get too excited about anything anymore, he realizes, however, there are always roadblocks in life which have to be solved. In this case, friendly Republic troops on the Madrid-Valencia road who will slow him down with demands for papers, and rightly so.

A thought flashes in his mind. *Maybe I should call ahead of time to the hotel and leave a message that I'm coming. No. Why would I do that? She's likely to try to avoid me. She'll resist and maybe even reject me. I'll surprise her. That's it. To win, I'll have to wind myself up. I can do it, roadblocks or not.*

Pulling his weight as a Soviet operative, he commandeers a car from a nearby military garage, gets the mechanic to be his driver, stops at Republic headquarters, signs up a guard to ride shotgun in the vehicle, and shops for some provisions. All in a few hours!

"Rank helps," he says to himself. He then notifies Koltsov's office that he's going to Valencia. Preparations are underway to prepare that city to become the capital of Spain, as Madrid is being threatened, and he wants to see how much progress is being made. He knows they won't question his reason for traveling there. Anyway, he believes, Koltsov's office doesn't know of the restraint put on him from seeing or communicating with Basya.

That day at noon, he and two comrades find themselves driving along perilous mountain roads, sometimes at an excessive speed of sixty miles an hour, through charming towns and villages. Fortunately, they sail through roadblocks, mainly because Mischa Rasputnis has proper credentials and the Red star on his cap reduces suspicion. Drawing closer to Valencia, however, anxious thoughts envelope him. It's like he's walking into a minefield.

What's going to happen to Basya and me? Two ghosts meeting after sixteen years. Who knows if she'll take me back.

Finally, he turns off his negativity. He inhales the sweet aroma of oranges and almonds. "A few Republic army roadblocks to pass through and we'll be there," he says excitedly to himself. He wishes this was late spring when there are fiestas that celebrate the end of winter with firecrackers. Driving into the center of the city, he remembers that Valencia is the fireworks capital of Europe, which causes him to smirk. "That's one thing we don't need -fireworks to light up the sky. We already have fascist bombs destroying Spanish cities."

Moving toward the hotel, he notices the endless cobblestone streets and pretty squares, replete with boutiques, galleries, and taverns, untouched by war, unlike Madrid. An intense feeling comes over him. Everything about the landscape of Valencia suggested romance.

The car stops in front of the Caro Hotel. He proceeds with the first phase of his plan of which he has given much thought. He doesn't think it's wise to rush right in and say, "Hi, Basya. Here I am. You remember me, the boy who loved you and still does. No that won't work," he reflects. *I'm first going to reconnoiter the area, like a scout. I'll spot her from afar. I'll follow her and try to find the right moment to approach her, especially when no one is around. Better that way.*

Entering the hotel, he feels his heart beating. He heads to the front desk to talk to the hotel manager, who immediately informs him, "They're not here."

"What! I don't believe that," Mischa says, his voice rising.

"They got here. But they didn't even check in. They left immediately for the port."

"Tell me you're kidding," says Mischa.

"Something about fearing the fascists were going to break through and the shipping company didn't want their vessel to get caught in the harbor, so they were departing right away."

"Again, I don't believe you," Mischa says, pounding the counter. "Franco's nowhere near here, I ought to know," he says, pointing to the Red Star on his hat. His eyes blaze at the clerk whose face tightens as he backs away from Mischa who's up on his toes, about to lunge at the clerk.

"There was nothing I could do sir," whimpers the clerk, as he tries to calm Mischa.

"How long ago did they leave for the harbor," demands Mischa, his voice so loud that he draws anxious attention from guests in the lounge off the reception area.

"A few hours ago. But I'm sure...."

Mischa's out the door and into the car. "To the port," he commands. The screeching wheels outside at first alarm the clerk, though now he exhales and relaxes somewhat.

"I missed her. I missed her. She's gone again," was all Mischa could think as he and his two comrades stare at a ship, far off on the horizon.

Standing at a port walkway, he can only utter: "I missed her by a couple of hours."

And then at that very moment, he hears a woman scream nearby as members of the militia drag a man away, throw him into a car, and drive away.

The woman runs up to Mischa.

"Commissar. Please save my husband. He's innocent."

He pushes her away and yells out, "Senora. Senora. At this moment of tragedy in my life, you're bothering me about a traitor. Get her out of here."

His two comrades push away the screaming woman.

•

Chapter 17. Moscow, 1936.
MISCHA.
"They won't be able to see their Ears."

•

In years to come, Mischa Rasputnis would tell everyone that during the Spanish Civil War, he witnessed the Battle for Madrid in 1936. True, he helped organize the resistance, but he didn't remain in the city to observe the full brunt of the fascist attack which raged on at the end of October and into November of that year. Where did Mischa go when the battle began?

On October 20, Mischa is summoned to the Hotel Florida's front desk where he is told to go immediately to Comrade Koltsov's suite.

Moments later:

"Total secrecy. Not a word now, during or after the operation," Koltsov demands of all the commissars present. "Never talk to anyone about this mission. We're transferring a very large portion of the gold amassed over centuries by the Spanish crown from Inca and Aztec treasure to our *Gosbank,* our central bank in Moscow. We're doing this so it doesn't fall into the hands of the Franco fascists, or Hitler, and Mussolini."

In a hushed voice, he went on to tell the group:

"Spain has one of the biggest gold stocks in the world. We convinced the Madrid government to give us that treasure for safekeeping. The money is to be used in exchange for the arms we're shipping them. A windfall for us."

Up to now, silence has pervaded the large, smoke-filled room of battle-weary Russians who are beginning to wonder why they are in Spain, anyway. Koltsov's explanation elicits smiles and sighs of awe, because they realize that the success of this mission will alleviate an already harsh economic situation for families throughout the USSR, their own included.

Looking directly at Mischa, Koltsov informs him that he will be organizing the shipment of over 500 tons of Spanish gold to Moscow. "The value comes to over $US 500 million. Make sure there are no leaks to the press."

•

As dawn breaks over the besieged Spanish city the morning after the meeting with Koltsov, Mischa packs his small suitcase, goes down to the front of the hotel, and is picked up by an army vehicle. He is driven to a boarded-up warehouse on the outskirts of town. He and other NKVD officers, chosen by Koltsov, team up with Spanish soldiers and begin loading boxes of gold onto military trucks which will convoy the heavy metal to the Spanish port, Cartagena.

"Treat each box as if it contains dynamite. That's how dangerous it is, if you drop it. Careful now!" Mischa commands the workers. Over and over again, Mischa and Spanish officials count the boxes of gold and match it to their inventory list. He writes in his notebook that out of the 10,000 boxes, corresponding to approximately 560 tons of gold, only 7,800 boxes of gold will sail to Russia. Apparently, the remainder were sent elsewhere, mostly to France. He surmises that 100 boxes may have vanished from the warehouses before he and his fellow Russians got involved in this transfer venture.

My men and I can't be punished for that, he figures.

•

Overnight, while German and Italian bombers raid the blacked-out city, the Spanish laborers, under the watchful eye of armed soldiers and police, load the gold boxes, one by one onto the army trucks waiting to drive to the old and stately Madrid Atocha Railway Station.

After the trucks are loaded, the military vehicles line up in convey formation and head for the train station which the Spanish police have closed to train and passenger traffic. They stop vehicular traffic on streets approaching the station and the Plaza del Emperador Carlos V.

Inside, the station platforms are covered by a glass and steel roof in the form of an inverted hull, with a height of about 160 feet. Mischa's men place the boxes into the rail cars for transfer to the capital of world Communism, Moscow, USSR.

"Let's just hope that we first make it to Cartagena. That's a scary six hours away. We leave at midnight," Mischa tells fellow comrade, Boris Volkov.

"I don't know about you," Boris replies, "but this trip is going to be a most tense train ride of my life. One mishap and we'll all be shot at dawn."

•

"The gold train," as Mischa begins to call it, is about to leave. Before departure, he places two guards to stand on every platform between each railcar.

"Hold on tight," he tells his guards.

At exactly midnight, the train, belching black smoke, lurches forward and chugs out of the station. Rocking and swaying, it heads to Cartagena and as it moves to its destination, Mischa is lost in thought: *It's not every day that one country picks up the gold reserves of another country to store in its treasury vaults! I hope this transfer's not a heist. No. Can't be. Not us Soviets.*

•

After the gold train leaves, Mischa paces up and down the aisles of each car. He walks between rows of boxes, making sure all are secure. He checks on the guards. The seats have been removed. The cars look strange: Boxes, without passengers.

The locomotive keeps a steady pace, though at two o'clock in the morning, there's a jolt and the train grounds to a halt as the engineer toots three times, a danger signal.

Mischa jumps up, pulls out his revolver from its holster and rushes up to the locomotive. He looks out through the engine's side window.

"Damn it. There's a lonely donkey-cart on the tracks and it's full of large boulders."

Silence. Only the murmuring of the train is heard in the few minutes that have passed.

Mischa can see that the engineer's frightened.

If he pushes the cart head on, the stones will fall on the tracks and make matters worse. We don't want to sit here that long and become sitting ducks, even though we're ready for anything, Mischa thinks. Beads of sweat break out on his forehead and force him to come up with a plan.

Got to act quickly. I'll send a dozen soldiers out to remove the stones from the cart. I'll get others to take up positions alongside the rail cars. Using the train as cover, the troops will be prepared to fire if a fascist unit chances upon the train. He adds an important calculation to his plan. *Everything depends on how long it takes us. Wouldn't you know it, no moon.*

He barks his order to his men who slowly begin to remove the stones. Not only is it taking longer than he thought, but they have to light a few torches so they don't trip over the tracks and injure themselves because they can't see the ground.

He tells Boris, "The light from the torches and the delay increases our chance to be discovered."

"Agreed, Comrade Rasputnis. But what can we do, except keep reminding our soldiers, to move carefully but faster. Just hope the enemy can't see this far."

Finally, they push the cart out of the way..

Thank goodness, it turns out to be nothing. But we lost over an hour and soon the sun will come up, Mischa thinks.

Once again, the front engine, which continues to spew out smoke and steam, begins to haul the closed cars filled with the precious treasure through the Spanish countryside. Suddenly as dawn breaks and the sun rises, Mischa spies an enemy plane in the sky. "It's one of the new, Nazi Messerschmitt fighter planes," he shouts. knowing full well that the airplane is part of the Condor Division of German aircraft, armored cars and anti-aircraft equipment given to Franco.

As he did in Russia, Mischa outfitted and camouflaged two flatbed railcars and mounted anti-aircraft guns manned by Red Army gunners on them. One such car was behind the engine, the other near the back of the train.

The train's defenders have no time to lose. The German fighter pilot, wanting to get a better look at his target, drops down and in so doing turns the craft into a space above the rail cars, but parallel to the train and when it does that, the machine guns on the two flatbeds open fire. The Messerschmitt is hit and bursts into a ball of flames and crashes into the hard, Spanish earth. The flames light up the dismal, dark sky and the red and orange fireballs can be seen for miles. The soldiers on the train roar their approval. "Good job." The engineer shouts, gleefully, "we got the Nazi bastard."

"We did it. Now Comrade engineer, let's go as fast as you can," encourages Mischa. "Obviously, the fascists can see the smoke and send planes. We have to make up for lost time."

•

The battle is over. The Nazi plane is history. For a while the soldiers scan the sky to see if another plane is coming. It isn't. Believing they're in the clear, they relax. Some sit on the boxes and close their eyes. All except the engineer. He has a bad feeling about the route ahead, especially a final bridge which must be crossed on the journey to the port. He wonders if he should remind Mischa that fascist guerrillas also possess good bridge blowers, even though there's no intelligence that the Francoists are in the area.

An hour later, the engineer sees the bridge ahead. Slowing down, he stops the train before the long span which hangs above a deep ravine. When Mischa comes forward, the engineer explains his feelings.

"I think we should check the bridge," he tells Mischa who agrees and sends several sappers who spend an hour meticulously touching, crawling on their knees, and looking over the span for wires as best they can.

He paces back and forth between cars. He keeps looking at his watch. He sits down and tries to close his eyes for a brief snooze after a night of little sleep. "Everything depends on those sappers," he believes. He steels himself against the anxiety that has sprung to action, like a saw cutting into a tree bark. Minutes tick away, until an hour has passed. "It's the damn wait," he repeatedly mutters to himself.

Finally, the sappers don't observe anything unusual and give the conductor the go-head as they board the train.

"Full throttle it is," the engineer commands himself.

A burst of speed and the train whips across the span. As the last car clears the structure, a loud explosion hurls massive concrete blocks into the air. Crumbling boulders and steel girders disappear into the deep ravine below. A soft murmur is heard throughout the train. Shaken, shocked, no one says a word, though their minds remind them, as if they didn't know, how lucky they are. No one, except Mischa, asks why the sappers didn't spot the explosive devices, and most importantly, why the bridge blew after the train crossed over. Some nervously stand up in amazement. Others bow their heads, and some cross themselves. In stressful moments, even anti-religious Communists find God. Not Mischa. In this situation, he gives the order to a subordinate for the two sappers who failed to discover the dynamite charges, to be shot when they reach Cartagena. Mischa Rasputnis is a commissar.

•

Once in the rail station in Cartagena on October 22, the vehicles truck the $518 million cargo to the harbor. Everything is running late. Mischa notices that four small Soviet freighters are tied up along separate docks and waiting for the gold. They are the *Kine, Kursk, Neva,* and *Volgoles.* He watches nervously, as stevedores, under heavy guard, unload the secret cargo and carry it slowly on board the docked ships waiting to sail to Odessa and then by rail, to Moscow.

Mischa thunders at the Spanish workers to hasten the unloading which will take a night or two because they must work under darkness to put the boxes of ingots aboard the ships. Each crate contains thousands of cloth sacks tied shut with twine. The sacks are the normal form in which national banks hold gold. These thousands of sacks contain an estimated 60 million coins: Lire, florins, pesos, escudos, pesetas.

Mischa sleeps during the day. At night, he circles the docks. He checks anything suspicious. Randomly, he examines credentials of workers whose eyes bulge with fear when they see him.

One night, he sees two stevedores who are tipsy. He hastens over to the truck as the two of them, snickering from the effects of liquor, are unloading a large and heavy box.

"I don't believe it. They've dropped the box. The lid is cracked open. They're looking inside. Their mouths are open, like they've never seen gold before. Their eyes are literally popping out of their heads. They're beginning to look around. They see me. They freeze in fear."

Fortunately, four of Mischa's men, who heard the box tumble to the pavement, ran to the scene. Two of the soldiers close the box, nail it down, pick it up, and get it on board the ship.

"You two, take the two Spaniards to Comrade Pyotr Polyakov, head of security," Mischa says in Russian to two NKVD guards. "He'll know what to do with them."

Fifteen minutes later, two shots ring out in the loading area. Other Spanish dock workers weren't near the scene and didn't learn what was in the boxes. They realized now, however, they better not drop a box. They take off their berets and bow their heads.

"It couldn't be helped. Our work has to be kept secret. Eventually, human nature being what it is, the two Spaniards would talk. We acted correctly," Mischa tells his agents.

Finally, on October 25, Mischa boards the Neva, one of three vessels setting sail. He's told the Kursk can't depart because of technical problems. It'll depart several days later. A security team is left behind. The ships arrive in Odessa on November 2. Mischa relinquishes his authority to the top command of the NKVD. A ton of steel has lifted from his shoulders.

"I can relax now. Done with my responsibility. Most importantly, I'm away from war. If I have any free time before we get to Moscow, I can walk around the city which always brings me joy. My city no longer, but it is nice to be here. Can't say that I'm not homesick."

And then comes the order. Immediate unloading of the ship. Unbelievable what happens next. He watches in amazement as he sees who is unloading the precious cargo from the vessel. Not your usual stevedores, or even regular troops, but for security, only high-ranking officers from various Soviet secret police units. Each one, a captain or major, or colonel, carries a box of gold on their back, and loads it into railway cars which will carry the treasure to Moscow.

On the train ride to the capital, an NKVD officer, David Sebshevich, tells Mischa, "You know comrade, if all the boxes of gold back there on the wharfs of Odessa were to be placed in Red Square, they'd cover up the huge plaza."

Arriving in Moscow on November 5, Mischa watches an honor guard accompany the Spanish reception committee which meets the shipment. The treasure is moved to the State Depository for Valuables *(Goskhran)*. He observes the shipment is received as a deposit, by bank officials, as well as representatives of the Spanish government, the Bank of Spain, and Soviet officials. The fortune is carried in by soldiers and stored inside the bank.

Since Mischa helped to supervise the transfer of the gold, he's invited to the Kremlin banquet hosted by Comrade Stalin to celebrate the arrival of the precious metal. He stands proudly in a newly-issued, dress uniform. In a few minutes, the words of Comrade Stalin will deal a death blow to the spirit of the achievement. In an off-the-cuff remark to the gathering, Stalin declares, "The Spaniards will never see their gold again, just as they don't see their ears."

Hearing this, Mischa is furious: *"That expression regarding 'ears' is based on a Russian proverb. It figures. Comrade Stalin is systematically swindling Spain out of several hundred million dollars by rescuing their gold and then tricking them into paying inflated prices for needed arms deliveries. They're dying and we're cheating them. Logically, how can this be?"*

"But we Communists don't believe in logic. Comrade Stalin and the Party are always right. I must obey," he utters, somewhat unconvincingly. He doesn't realize that even slightly questioning Communist ideology, creates doubt. The crack in his blind faith in the Communist Party widens a little more towards disillusionment. *Does the Party and Comrade Stalin always follow the correct policy? Does the end justify the means?"* Now, Mischa is not sure.

•

Chapter 18. Barcelona, 1938.
MISCHA.
"The Lincolns' Farewell."

•

There's a valley in Spain called Jarama.
It's a place that we all know too well.
For 'tis there that we wasted our manhood
And most of our old age as well."

(Sung to the tune of "Red River Valley").

•

In mid-November 1936, Mischa's ship, sailing from Odessa, returns to Spain where his first task is to re-establish contact with his asset, Michael Rapaport. Michael is now fighting with the Lincoln Brigade and wants to help the Communist cause in any way he can.

Be nice to see how these Yanks fight now.

•

While he was away, Madrid was saved; the nationalists were checked. But the Spanish Republic fighters failed to make the city "the grave of fascism" as the Communist slogan demanded. Historians will say that this failure would be their downfall. Still, Madrid's victory enormously enhances Soviet prestige around the world.

But then, a surprise fascist attack on February 6, 1937, shocks the Republic's high command. The Nationalists press forward to cross the Jarama River, south of the capital, in order to sever the Madrid-Valencia highway. They plan to strike toward the northeast to cut the road off from the port of Valencia. The highway is the lifeline which Madrid depends on to be supplied with guns, ammunition, and food. It's the very road on which Mischa passed a year ago in his failed attempt to find Basya in Valencia.

•

For Mischa now, the normally hour-long drive from Madrid to the Republic's location on the Jarama River took more than a half-day as the road was clogged with army trucks full of soldiers moving into battle. All he would remember from this trip was riding in a Russian truck and following army vehicles for many freezing hours on a pot-hole road towards the battle. He was eager to re-establish contact with the American.

Moving up to the line, he could see that this once peaceful valley had turned into hell. He could hear the whining of the shells exploding over the battle area. He feels fear beginning to overtake his body, as his truck pulls into Lincoln Battalion's headquarters where he's told the group, including Michael, is engaged in fierce combat.

An officer explains, "We attacked the fascists a few days ago right through those olive groves down there. But their machine guns stopped us in our tracks." He shakes his head in disbelief. "Our machine guns didn't work. We lost twenty men and forty were wounded. And now four days later, we're at it again. Take my binoculars and you'll see what's going on."

Mischa couldn't spot Michael, and Michael, not far away, does not turn around to see Mischa standing at the top of the slope. No matter. The battle's on. The four-hundred-fifty Lincolns are getting hammered.

At that moment down below, Michael and his men, lying flat on their stomachs, are gnawing and clawing the rocky soil, each trying to dig a hole as enemy fire is halting them in their tracks.

Michael's yelling. "Where's the damn Spanish artillery to soften up enemy positions, especially those machine guns."

"We have no air cover. No airplanes to strafe the enemy. No artillery either," says his adjutant. "Look. Over there. At the bottom of that hill. That Spanish battalion that was to move forward with us, side by side. They're meeting heavy machine-gun fire."

"Oh my," says Michael. "Our Spaniards are pulling back. The Nationalists have our trenches in sight. We've got to retreat," Michael commands.

"But we can't, sir. Crazy, as it all sounds, a messenger has just arrived. High command insists we attack. No matter what."

"Attack at all costs? That's suicide," yells Michael. "The minute we get up, we'll be stopped by heavy enemy fire. Our machine guns are broken. We have bullets that don't even fit our guns."

Michael was correct. They never got promised rapid firing guns. It was a disastrous day with motor shells falling among, and stretcher bearers being shot. But they must follow the order to attack. Michael manages to cry out. Jumping up and waving his hand forward, he notices his men follow blindly.

These men of the Lincoln Brigade, composed of American former students and seamen from Brooklyn have no military training, so while estimates vary, one hundred twenty are killed and one hundred seventy Lincolns are wounded. Other International Brigade units suffer heavy losses. Nevertheless, the battle on February 17 ends in a stalemate. The rebels are halted despite the fact that the Lincoln commander, Robert Merriman, is wounded. At the same time, the Nationalists drive to cut the Madrid-Valencia road has begun to stall due to the murderous defense put up by the Lincolns. The integrity of the Madrid - Valencia Road is maintained.

•

Later, in the regrouping area, Mischa assures Michael. "You fought gallantly. It's not your fault that nothing went well. The Lincolns had to pay a terrible price in helping the other International Brigades engage the enemy."

"Well, thank goodness I lived through that skirmish," Michael replies.

"Glad you're safe," says Mischa, keeping up his ingratiating manner. "Is there anything I can do for you?"

Michael, not wanting to anger his fellow Communist, tries to explain as diplomatically as possible, that his comrades are equipped with seventeen different types of firearms, four kinds of ammo, and no helmets. "Sometimes we had to move forward without bullets," he says. "That's no way to fight a war."

He goes on to hint that some Soviet weapons are barely usable, that other pieces of equipment from Soviet ships, such as German grenade launchers are obsolete. He shares that some of the American rifles that the Russian government got rid of by giving them to the Republic, were produced in 1860 and originally pawned off to the Czar. Michael doesn't come up with a laundry list, but he pleads for more arms.

"I'll see what I can do," Mischa tells him reassuringly, realizing again that his country was shortchanging the Spaniards.

•

Sharing a bottle of vodka that Mischa secretly acquired from Koltsov's aide de camp, he and Michael began to throw back one gulp after another. The vodka stimulates them to talk about America.

"I'd like to visit America someday in an official capacity," Mischa tells Michael. "I have family there. I could see how they live in a capitalist country."

"That would be nice," agrees Michael.

•

On the way back to Madrid the next day, Mischa keeps going over one word in his mind: shortchanging. "What is my country becoming?" he whispers to himself. He doesn't answer his own question.

•

In late fall of 1938, Mischa and Michael meet in Barcelona, the two-thousand-year-old city on the northeast coast of Spain, and a major port to receive Soviet aid.

"A nightmare, it was, that battle of the Ebro River this past summer," were the first words Michael uttered at the meeting in a café on the Las Ramblas boulevard, full of International Brigade troops back from the front. "We lost thirty thousand men in the Ebro attack."

"I realize that," sighs Mischa. "I was here in Barcelona. I recall how the results of the Ebro battle were bawled out by newsboys.

"With that loss," says Michael, "the war was over. But if there's one thing I've learned in Spain, capitalism is finished. You see what the workers in Spain have done. They've taken over hundreds of factories from the bourgeois. We're going to do the same in America."

Hearing this Communist line sprouting from his protégé, Mischa agrees. He leans forward and whispers, "Michael, speaking about the defeat of capitalism, you can help us."

"How's that?"

"We want to send organizers to rouse Americans in the Communist battle. We try to get our people into the United States to bring about the Revolution. But your immigration officers stop us. We smuggle a few in. But we need American passports. You can help the cause."

"How?"

"If an American dies on the battlefield and you can get us his passport, or, you can steal a passport, we'll pay you for each one."

"Money? I don't want money. Are you kidding? Do you think I believe in the rot of capitalism? Offering me money is what Americans do." He pauses. "No comrade. I'm with you. It's my duty."

•

On a freezing night, several weeks later, in a small café near the Soviet Mission in Barcelona, Michael Rapaport hands over five passports of deceased Americans, the beginning of many deliveries. He receives no money, only a handshake and a raised, hand-fist salute from his Soviet Commissar, Mischa Rasputnis. Mischa is well-aware that in the last two years of the war, his fellow Communists had successfully penetrated the Spanish government. Had the Republic won, he and his comrades would have installed a dictatorship.

•

Years later, Michael would read in an American newspaper that some five hundred eighty American volunteers in Spain would report lost passports to the State Department. The Soviets would use them for their own purposes. The stolen passports would play a significant role in history after Mischa and NKVD agents in Spain dispatched the passports to Moscow. Russian bearers would enter the United States as citizens. One of these documents, stolen perhaps by Michael, ended up in the hands of one Catalan, Ramon Mercader, who, on August 21, 1940, in Mexico, killed former Bolshevik and Soviet revolutionary, Leon Trotsky, Stalin's most hated enemy,

•

At the end of that meeting with Mischa, when Michael passed him the passports, both men got up from the table, hugged, and again gave a clenched fist, farewell-salute. A driving rain slapped the café's windows when finally, their voices were heard again.

"Goodbye, Comrade Mischa"

"Goodbye, Comrade Michael. We shall meet again."

A few days later, Michael crosses the Spanish border into France. His personality has changed from his overwhelming self-centered outlook. He's withdrawn, hangs back. His body has changed. He looks gaunt and hungry. His eyes, once sparkling, are cold. Though lucky to be alive, he cannot hide his fear. His left-hand shakes. He watches silently as the Spanish carabiniers, with patent leather, Bonaparte hats and shot guns on their backs, stand on one side. On the other side, French soldiers, with the famous kepi hat, check passports. He fills out papers, boards a train to Le Havre, sails to the United States, and never looks back. He can only repeat day after day, *"A noble effort of men in Spain to govern themselves has perished."*

•

Shortly after Michael leaves Spain, Mischa Rasputnis departs for Paris. Feeling the beating in Spain deeply and personally, Mischa knows that the Republic has been defeated by Franco, Hitler, and Mussolini, as well as by the complicity of the British, French, and American governments because of their policy of non-intervention and arms embargo on the Republic. But he's distraught about another matter. He has learned that many of his Russian comrades who were such valiant fighters and tireless workers, who served so well the Republic's cause, had been executed or disappeared in the Stalin purges when they returned to the Soviet Union. They knew too much and had seen life in the West. Does the same fate await him? He'll know soon enough.

He realized he could be executed. *"I have no choice,"* he thought to himself. *"The French wouldn't willingly let a Soviet official cross over unless he was seeking asylum and why would I do that. That's desertion. I'm loyal. I love my Soviet homeland. No! I'll take my chances."*

Boarding a train to Paris, he connects to the Nord Express for Moscow. Luckily, the train operates with sleeping and dining cars. He eats decent food and has no trouble at all falling asleep at night. The hum of the train wheels makes it easy to dream that after his express train bursts into Moscow, he'll be sent back to work in his hometown, Odessa. Or so, he believes.

•

Chapter 19. Prague, 1939.
BASYA.
"Goodbye Czechoslovakia."

•

On September 20, 1938, Great Britain and France formally
asked Czechoslovakia to cede part of its territory to Germany.
By doing so, the two betrayed Prague and appeased Hitler.
Then, at the end of September, 1938, Germany, Italy, Great
Britain, and France signed the infamous Munich Pact, by
which Czechoslovakia was dismembered and forced to
surrender its Sudetenland region to Nazi Germany. Six
months later, in March, 1939, the Germans grabbed the rest
of Czechoslovakia. Now, the world saw the pact to be what
it was all the time, appeasement of expansionist totalitarian
states, such as Germany, Italy, and Japan. In September,
1939, the world went to war.

Several months after the announcement of the disastrous Munich
Pact in the fall of 1938, a striking and elegantly dressed female
diplomat walks out the main entrance of the Czechoslovak Ministry
of Foreign Affairs. It is located in the majestic, baroque Czernin
Palace, just above the historic Prague Castle. She slowly heads toward
the car waiting to take her to the airport outside Prague for a flight to
London via Lisbon. She doesn't turn around for a last look.

For the last decade, the woman has been a Soviet spy within the
Czech foreign office. She loves her job in her adopted country, even
though she spies on it and often favors policies not in its best interest.
Her working conditions in the Czêrnín Palace enhance her lifestyle.
The building is one of the most classical structures in Prague, a castle
which dates back to the Habsburgs in the 1660s.

The woman's name is Tatiana Kovacova, also known as Basya
Abramskaya, age thirty-eight. She's part of a group beginning the
advance work for the soon-to-be exiled Czechoslovakian government
headquarters in London. The date is January 8, 1939.

Czech intelligence has discovered that the German dictator, Adolph
Hitler, after marching into the Sudetenland as a result of the Munich
pact, may send tanks and troops in the spring, to gobble up what's
left of Czechoslovakia. The foreign office has kept the evacuation plan
secret for fear of sending the country into panic mode.

Tatiana stops and waits for her aide to place her two small satchels in the back seat of the vehicle. Most of her belongings will be shipped by train through France and then by boat across to London. Keeping a close eye on her baggage, she stands respectfully until the aide finally opens the door for her to enter the car.

Pausing for a moment before getting in, she turns and shakes his hand. She smiles and with her other hand, gently places it over his, and calmly says, "Good bye and good luck, Anton."

"The same to you. Do take care of yourself, Tatiana Kovacova. The rest of the group is already at the airport." He then adds, "I'm sure we burned all the papers in your office."

"Good. Please, Anton, nothing should remain with my name on any piece of paper, especially the emigre dossier. If the Germans find that special document, people will die."

"Don't worry, I'll handle everything," he says, opening the door of the limousine.

I'm sure you will," she answers, as she enters the car. Seeing her seated, he closes the door as she rolls down the window half way, to hear Anton say, "Bon Voyage. Have a good flight to London."

The vehicle pulls away and heads for the gate. Then, and only then, does she finally turn and take a last look at the Palace which she entered as a civil servant about ten years ago.

Sitting in the cushioned back seat of the limo, the cool winter air, the hum of the engine, the early morning-hour drowsiness, lull her into closing her eyes and nodding off.

A half-hour later, she's awoken by the noise of an airplane's propellers circling like tall fans at maximum speed on a passenger plane poised for takeoff. Her flight will leave in two hours.

"Madam Kovacova," says the voice of the driver, Bronislav. "We're here."

"Thank you. Could you be so kind as to bring my suitcases to the airport café?"

"Yes. Of course," the driver answers, eagerly.

•

Few passengers occupy the café. Not many passengers are waiting for a flight to Lisbon and London. Not many Czechoslovakians are aware that the Germans actually will strike in a few months and swallow up the rest of the country.

After instructing the driver, Bronislav, to wait for a moment, she spots her diplomatic group and tells her colleagues she wants to get an espresso and read the morning papers. "Would you excuse me?"

"Of course," they answer. "We've already had our coffee. See you on board the flight."

On her way back to the cafe, she picks up a newspaper. Glaring headlines.

"Madrid Expected to Fall to Franco"

Not a surprise. Everyone knows a fascist victory was coming. If Mischa was in Spain, I'm sure he got out. Moscow wouldn't leave anyone behind to be caught by the fascists, she thinks, as she reaches her corner table in the café. She thanks and dismisses the driver who has placed the two small satchels, one of which has a red ribbon fastened to the handle, under the table by her chair. She has plenty of time to order a coffee and continue to read the article.

•

"Good morning, Consul Kovacova," greets a middle-aged man who, standing before her, waits for Tatiana to motion to him to sit across from her. He is not carrying any luggage. She rises and greets him with a smile on her face. He gazes into her eyes, and kisses her on both cheeks in the European way.

"Anatoly Abramov, how good it is to see you."

"Same here," answers the Soviet diplomat stationed in Prague. Over the years, especially in the Yamagata case, he has worked with Tatiana on various projects and has become her mentor. Happily married, he never strays from his wife. He considers himself a Russian romantic.

She's a capable diplomat and the foreign services should be proud to have her, he thinks.

"I came to say goodbye," he whispers, while adroitly pinning a corsage on her dress.

Anatoly and the people at the Soviet Embassy know that Tatiana's code name is her real name, *Basya*. She's their asset in the Czech Foreign Office, though she usually never reports or contacts them directly, or discusses her work with them, other than matters which deal with Czech-Soviet relations. While Prague and Moscow are on good terms, each side spies on the other. That's why in this case, Anatoly took no chances on being followed in setting out to meet Tatiana. His driver, using vehicle twists and turns in the city, managed to dodge surveillance. The car arrived at the airport, unnoticed.

"You've served us well. I'm returning to Russia soon. I'll be reassigned," Anatoly says resignedly. "I hope we'll meet again. If you ever get to Moscow, call on me, for anything. I'll help you."

"I will," she answers sincerely. "Good luck. Anatoly." And then, just like it was a spur of the moment thing, but obviously percolating for a very long time in the recess of her mind she asks, "Please, do me a favor," she says. But before she could get the rest of the words out of her mouth, she realizes she's making a mistake for which they both can be shot. And yet, maybe because he's not NKVD secret police, but a member of the diplomatic corps, she says to herself, *"I'll risk it,"* even though she is bound not to contact anyone regarding Mischa.

"What is it?" he asks as she leans over and whispers in his ear.

"His name is Commissar Mischa Rasputnis, NKVD, Lubyanka, Moscow. Tell him, 'Basya sends regards.' That's all. He's a high school friend. Please try to find him."

Anatoly smiles and is ready to assure her he will, when an announcement is made.

"Flight to Lisbon. Passengers will please board."

"Goodbye, Anatoly."

They both stand and shake hands. Basya picks up one satchel, leaving the one with the red ribbon behind. She heads to the gate and joins her group for the flight to Lisbon and London.

Anatoly waits until she's gone, gets up, walks out, carrying the satchel with a red ribbon. He enters his waiting car. What he and Soviet intelligence will discover is that Tatiana, through Anatoly, has passed to the Red Army, copies of lists of Czech military installations. Three months later, the Germans will occupy these military posts. In six years, however, the conquering Russian military, armed with the lists they obtained from Prague in 1939, will overwhelm the Nazis defending those positions in 1945.

Boarding the plane, Tatiana sits back as the aircraft climbs into the clouds. She looks down at the country she has come to love.

•

Six hours later:

"Tatiana. Look. The White Cliffs of Dover, the coast of England," says a colleague, Ivonka Bezek.

"Yes. London's beckoning," she replies, happily.

And then, almost as if she had forgotten, she whispers to herself:

"Mischa. My love. Where are you? Will I ever see you again?"

As the British Airways flight from Lisbon follows the Thames River over England, Tatiana turns, and with her face crowding the window, smiles as she observes the mighty tributary below. The plane twists over a landscape of arterial roads and railway lines until in the distance stand the Tower of London, St. Paul's Cathedral, Houses of Parliament, and Big Ben.

From the moment the aircraft touches down on the small, grass airfield of the Great West Aerodrome, southeast of the hamlet of Heathrow, London will cast a spell over Tatiana, even though her job again, will entail spying on the people she would come to admire.

•

Chapter 20. London, 1939.
BASYA.
"Danger Lurks."

•

After the Nazis marched into Prague and thus occupied all of Czechoslovakia, England, recognizing the perfidy of the Germans, increased manufacturing of armaments. All through the first part of 1939, MI5, British secret service, were on the lookout for radio transmissions of all kinds. At the same time, it not only watched Communists in Britain as it had done for years, but its secret service kept an eye on Czechs who fled to England because the British recognized that after the Munich Pact, the Czechoslovakian government-in-exile in London, was moving closer to the Soviet Union. Tatiana Kovacova had to be careful.

•

After Tatiana and fellow Czech diplomats began settling in their new Embassy home, at 9 Grosvenor Square, in London, a new protocol was instituted. "Embassy and consular officials must remember that they are now guests in a foreign country," said their welcoming document.

"We no longer rule the roost. This is not our homeland. It's exile," stressed their security memo. In blunt terms, the memorandum reminded them they could be under surveillance. There is always a possibility that someone is tailing them from the British MI5. It doesn't let up in monitoring and cracking down on espionage from foreign states.

Basya didn't need this warning, even though she might have to get involved with social relationships to serve her undercover work, until she could establish herself. As in Prague she has to watch when transmitting radio messages to the Center. She has learned how to protect her clandestine, shortwave operations, including concealing her wireless equipment in a Communist safe house's kitchen cabinet not far from the Embassy.

Always cognizant of her surroundings, Tatiana avoided surveillance. She knew how to dodge a stalker. Go here. Go there. Get in a taxi. Stop the taxi. Get out in the middle of the road. Go up the stairs. Go down the stairs. Seconds before a door closes in the London tube car, jump up and beat the door-closing. Then, change trains at the next station.

●

One day, a half-year after her arrival in London, Tatiana was shopping in the womenswear section of Harrods department store when she felt someone was staring at her. Without moving her head, her laser-beam eyes focus on a woman whom she has never seen at the far end of the very aisle where Tatiana's standing. Not sure if the woman in question notices her, she does an immediate about-face, and without looking, crashes into a thin woman who's coming straight at her. Tatiana grabs onto a mannequin which holds her up as it leans against a table full of lady's blouses. Now getting hold of herself, she observes that the woman she had spotted originally was approaching her and shouting out in an excited, loud voice:

"Basya Abramskaya? Is that you? From Zhitomer, Ukraine?"

Heads turn.

"What are you doing in London? Haven't seen you in ages," continues the stranger.

"Pardon me, madam."

"Who are you? I don't know you," says Basya trying to deflect the stares of the shoppers around her, caused by this tall and big-boned woman.

"Don't you remember me? I'm your cousin by marriage. I'm Sonya Kuznetsova, Lev Kuznetsov's cousin." She presses on, "You must remember me. I met you in Zhitomir. Terrible time. It was after the pogroms and the family losses. I managed to get out of our cursed Ukraine. Been here for twenty years. I work for the British Scientific Commission."

The words 'British Scientific Commission,' set off alarm bells in Basya's gathering- intelligence brain.

"Oh yes. Now I remember," answers Basya, adding, "Do you have time? Let's have a cup of tea across the street. Too many people here listening in."

"Yes. Let's do that," replies Sonya.

●

"But tell me. Do you live here or are you visiting? Working? Where're you staying?" asks Sonya, as they indulge in tea and crumpets.

Basya thinks twice. Fortunately, she has a prepared spiel.

"I'm a professor at the London School of Economics where I teach Russian."

"What about you? Are you married?"

"I never married. I guess I was too picky. And I lost all ties with Russia. I hear things are pretty bad there. Are you remarried?" asks Sonya.

"No. I was married to Lev. He will be my only husband," responds Tatiana in a funereal, but determined voice."

"I understand. Listen, Basya." She pauses before continuing hurriedly, "I have to scoot along now. But let's meet for tea again. Today is Wednesday. Can't do it tomorrow. Let's make it Friday, at four in the afternoon, at the Claridge Hotel." She insists. "Do say yes. It would be nice to have a new friend in London, and a relative to boot."

"Of course," says Basya smiling. "Four o'clock it is. The Claridge. See you then."

And with that, Sonya walks away, leaving Basya no choice but to get in touch with her Soviet handler in London, Sergei Gorin. She feels no particular warmth for this cousin-in-law. She barley knows her. She actually thought she was rather loud.

The next day is hot and summery. London's gardens, now in full bloom, counter the gloom that surrounds the city as it prepares for war. Hitler threatens the Free City of Danzig, then in a customs union with Poland. Rumors circulate in the press that the German foreign minister, Joachim von Ribbentrop has just flown to Moscow, an ominous sign indeed between two avowed enemies. If the Germans and Soviets actually did get together, the consequences would be dire for the democracies in Europe. The balance of power on the continent would change dramatically. Besides, Britain and France have given a pledge to Poland to come to her aid if attacked by the Nazis."

For her clandestine meeting with Sergey, Tatiana takes several buses, each going in different directions. She makes sure she's not being followed.

At the entrance in Green Park, she hears the newsboys bellowing what sounds like a joke. "Red Russia signs pact with Nazi Germany." Stunned, she can think of nothing else as she makes her way into the park.

"How could he? How could Comrade Stalin do such a thing and join the fascists, " she thinks, especially after what the Nazis did to her beloved

Czechoslovakia. *Well, at least I'll hear an explanation from Sergey.* A few minutes later, she spots a man fashionably dressed and sitting alone on a bench. He's reading the *Times of London* and is proud indeed that he, too, has eluded British surveillance by getting on and off various tube lines. Tatiana sits down next to him. This was the first time they met in this park. They never meet in the same place twice.

Sergey is short, stocky, his broad shoulders support a no-neck, egg-shaped head. This morning, he wears a fine-tailored, black suit, a white shirt, a conservative blue tie, black shoes, and a handkerchief in his lapel pocket. Taking off his bowler hat, he appears quite the dandy.

Exchanging pleasantries, Sergey, with a faint smile on his face, leans forward and in a nervous, almost stuttering voice, declares, "Greetings, Comrade Tatiana Kovacova. You heard the news, no doubt?"

Tatiana, speechless, nods, her facial expression showing displeasure.

"Comrade Stalin is pulling back so the imperialist powers will tear each other apart in what we're calling the 'second imperialist war.'"

Not a sigh or gasp, not a blink or sudden cough or swallow, comes from Tatiana. Her thoughts are somewhere else. They have been shaken by Moscow's perfidy in signing up alongside the fascists whom the Kremlin has been attacking for over a decade, even if the excuse is to buy time to further build up Soviet armed forces.

She could see that Sergey was defending the pact because he automatically backs everything the Party does. *"In this case it's disgusting,"* she thinks to herself.

Anyway Tatiana, that's enough on that subject. What's on your mind?"

After an explanation and description of Sonya and her shout out, as well as the place and time of their coming up Friday tea-time meeting, Tatiana emphasized that the woman works for the British Scientific Commission.

"Good. Stay with her. Get to know her. We may have an asset here," replied Sergey.

They part.

•

"Finally, got a good thing going here and in such a short time since I arrived from Prague. And here I was worried about Sonya recognizing me and that she might blow my cover. Now I can work on her. She leaves the park, making sure no one's following her.

•

Entering revolving doors at the Claridge Hotel on Friday, Tatiana is seated at what appears to be at first glance, a prestigious table in the middle of the dining room composed of a bourgeois clientele.

Our diplomat from the Czech Embassy smiles with delight at the beautifully decorated table, fine jade and white striped china, a variety of finger sandwiches, and two empty champagne glasses set out before her. Even good Communists from time to time like to bask in luxury. Handed the menu by the maître-'d, she notes that it boasts twenty-four loose-leaf teas, including regional English, rare blends and herbal infusions. She can't wait to taste the foie gras sandwiches on white bread.

At the next table, a woman and her son are enjoying cake. "Eat your 'chocolate *gateau,*' the mother tells her son who is dressed in well-pressed short pants and a shirt with lace collar. The youngster seems to be unhappy with his variation of the Little Lord Fauntleroy suit, but he's ready to pounce on the delicacy before him.

Two businessmen, discussing getting in on the arms deal, exchange views: "Did you hear that the PM has ordered an increase in war production."

From another table come the words, "I hear they're going to install rationing. My goodness. You'd think war's coming tomorrow."

"Hear the news. The Soviets entered a pact with the Nazis," one diplomat tells another at a nearby table. His associate stares at his guest uncomprehendingly.

Sonya enters the dining room. For the next hour, the two engage in small talk. Nostalgia reigns in their discussion. Life as it was back in Ukraine. "Life is good," says Sonya. "Except this dreadful talk of war and now I hear the Reds are signing a treaty with Hitler. My. My. My."

After an hour of chit-chat, Sonya pays the check. The two kiss each other goodbye. Tatiana promises to call Sonya now that she has her telephone number. They assure each other they'll meet again. Tatiana is beginning to like Sonya. "She's not all that bad."

•

A few days later, Tatiana receives a radio message from the Center in Moscow. "Sonya Kuznetsova is not in London, but has been reunited with her family in the motherland."

The Center did not go into details as to how they kidnapped Sonya and it wasn't Tatiana's business to ask. But she remembers in spy school that a fellow student told her what secret police services do in similar cases: "They grab the person involved, drug him or her, and then smuggle the victim onto a Soviet freighter to Murmansk. Once in port, they hustle them onto a freight train moving across the Soviet Union to, let us say, the Dneprovsky gulag camp near Magadan, where prisoners wake up."

Stunned by the news, Tatiana says to herself. "They might as well have killed her rather than send her back. It's obvious she's going to Siberia. Oh my," she says, picking up her cup of morning tea. After a few minutes of silence, she gets up and looks at the park below her window:

"I'm responsible for that happening to Sonya. Not even the fact that Sonya worked for the British Scientific Commission mattered.

But then like all good Communist agents, she returns, for the moment, to the official line:

Even as good a source that Sonya could have been for me, I guess it wasn't worth the risk having her walk around the streets of London, knowing that if she discovered that I was engaged with the Russians, she could blow my cover.

That night, Basya can't fall asleep. Stuck fast and cracking like cement in a brick wall, the unthinkable thought that Stalin and the Revolution are failing her and the people of Russia, keeps her up most of the night. It is the beginning of insomnia.

•

At the same time that Tatiana continues to have negative thoughts about Stalin's perfidy with joining the Nazis and gobbling up half of Poland, Mischa Rasputnis arrived in Moscow from Spain. He treks through a changed capital. He can't believe his eyes. Tall buildings, heavy traffic with deafening noise, newly-installed traffic lights, large crowds walking along the sidewalk of Tverskoy Blvd. Besides all this change, it is obvious that sprawling Moscow, with its Party institutions and government buildings, still functions as the brains of the Soviet Union.

Back on Russian soil, he recalls the days he spent with Basya in Yekaterinburg. But his dreams that night are not about her in Yekaterinburg, where they split up nor in Moscow. Night after night, he dreams of the sunflower fields of the Ukraine, near Odessa where they first met. "Where are you?" he cries out in his sleep. Suddenly, he sees her romping through flowery fields, her hair waving in the air. She shouts with glee, "I found you! I found you!" He instantly goes to hug her, but she's gone, like gone forever.

A few days later, Mischa's summoned to Red Army headquarters. What he doesn't know is that his life has been saved from being arrested by the NKVD because Alyosha Kovalchenko, the official in the Comintern who dispatched his protégé to Spain, realizes that like other Spanish civil war Russian veterans, Stalin's purges could eliminate Mischa. So Alyosha hid Mischa's Spanish Republic service file in his offices 'dead files.' Still, not taking any chances and to prevent having Mischa falling into the clutches of the NKVD, he suggests to the Red Army that they send him to the Russian Far East where he served during the civil war. The military agrees.

•

"I'm to go where?" he questions in an almost breathless voice, after being handed an envelope by a Red Army officer.

"Khalkhin Gol," says the sullen official facing him.

"Khalkhin Gol," repeats Mischa. He wants to spit the words in the officer's face, but he controls himself. Outwardly, he doesn't react, only offers an expected question: "Where's that?"

"Mongolia."

"The word 'never,' forms on his lips and is ready to be blasted at the official. But he dare not. He can only rebuke the officer in his mind:

So far away. I spent years in Siberia. Who in his right mind would want to travel through Siberia again to reach Mongolia, of all places? What kind of bureaucrat would dispatch an employee, or even an agent there, a third time?

Instead he says, "Thank you, comrade, I will return to the Far East. When do I leave?"

"Immediately," says the official. "You're to go there to serve for the good of Russia."

Mischa walks outside into an early spring breeze. He says goodbye to Moscow.

Again, they're sending me to a deep grave: Mongolia. Not pleasant. But I'm alive and I'm now a Battalion Commissar Senior Lieutenant, with the task of educating troops, and improving their sprit de corps. I know I'm being selfish, but if only Basya could be out here in Siberia, as tough a life as that is, we'd be together at last.

Like most people, he abhorred loneliness.

•

PART 2
"The War Years."

Chapter 21. Khalkhin Gol, 1939.
Mischa.
"The Small War that changed World War II's Trajectory."

•

As Mischa's train scurries through Asian Russia, events in this isolated part of the world will prove that a military skirmish can spark a fire which grows into a roaring blaze. Within weeks, Japan and the USSR fight a four-month undeclared war along the Mongolian-Manchurian border. Not since the Russo-Japanese War in 1904, have these two countries engaged in a fight little known in the outside world, even decades later, as Khalkhin Gol in Russian and Nomonhan in Japanese. Mischa is a witness to this flareup. He will fight in the conflict that will alter the course of World War II. After their defeat, in 1939, the Japanese will give up on fighting Russia over Siberia and turn their attention to Southeast Asia and the South Pacific where they come into conflict with Britain and the United States, the latter at Pearl Harbor on December 7, 1941.

•

On May 11, 1939, early risers in Tokyo, Japan, woke up to a red rising sun which they view as always possessing the color, red. But Asians in other countries interpret the "rising red sun," as a bad omen, a sign of death, especially since Imperial Japan's military, particularly its navy, champions the culture of war.

Be that as it may, on this particular day, the sunshine features a flaming red color even in far-off Mongolia as a unit of Mongolian horsemen crosses the Khalkhin Gol River, (aka Halha River), to graze their horses in fresh pastures. Japan, which occupied Manchuria in 1931, considered that river to be the international boundary between the Russian vassal state of the Mongolia People's Republic, and the Japanese puppet state of Manchukuo, also called Manchuria.

While the exact location of the border is of no consequence to the nomadic Mongols, who have lived in the area thousands of years and who follow their herds back and forth across the river for centuries, the elite Japanese Kwantung Army disagrees. Their army quickly drives the Mongolians back across the Halha which, Tokyo maintains, is the border. The Russians and Mongolians counter with armed force to push the Japanese back across the line and then some, arguing that the border does not follow the Halha, but stands at a line roughly parallel to it, some ten to twelve miles east of the river, near the hamlet of Nomonhan.

By the end of May, after sporadic fighting between the two armies, both sides prepare for further engagement.

•

"It's a damn wasteland," mutters Battalion Commissar Mischa Rasputnis, as he walks through the main gate of the Red Army military outpost at Tamsag Bulak, eighty miles west of Khalkhin Gol. It's June 1, 1939. His eyes sting with fatigue, his body aches, his mind hammered by bleak thoughts.

The Primorski krai around Vladivostok was heaven compared to this. Nothing survives here. Only flat, sandy plains and grasslands stretching on and on. A few short scrub pines and low shrubs, and flatland pasture.

But scouting around the area one afternoon, Mischa does come up with something positive:

This open area lends itself to tank country. We can hurl massive tank formations into battle on this desolate stretch of disputed frontier.

Wiping the sweat off his brow with a blue-and-white, work-handkerchief which he takes from his back-pocket, he mentally curses the weather. He remembers he read that temperatures could jump to above 100 degrees (F) during the day and to frigid weather, accompanied by dense fog and freezing temperatures at night.

•

Mischa enjoys his work with the men on the base, especially as a political instructor.

I should have been a teacher. I love the vibes from the troops. Maybe that's my calling.

So, for the next few weeks, he turns his attention to political indoctrination and the enforcement of Party loyalty among the troops. He tells them, "Japan must be stopped in its aggression toward the Soviet Union and our ally, Outer Mongolia."

June moves into July and July into August. Both sides fail to budge the other. They each bring up reinforcements poised for battle.

After every political session, Mischa and his men stand and shout, "Long live the Revolution. Long live Comrade Stalin." Leading these slogans, he feels he's not alone in war.

But one night, in this stark slice of the earth, he inserts himself into the world of love. He dreams he's with a woman in a bathhouse. He's sure it isn't a stranger. Even though her face is blurred, he knows it's her. "Basya's with me."

•

As a political officer, Mischa learns of the major Russian attack-date a day earlier. On the dark, chilly night of August 19, 1939, Mischa watches in amazement how Red Army troops prepare to cross the Halha River into the expanded Soviet enclave on the east bank.

"Bravo," he shouts out loud. His first time in a long time in a major battle and he's exhilarated.

"Look at them go. Our troops and vehicles are all moving forward."

Finally, Mischa's unit is summoned. Each one, given a shot of vodka, moves into the attack. He jumps aboard a D-8 light armored car which is used in reconnaissance. His vehicle follows advancing units. He feels good sitting in this particular vehicle because he rode in a similar one several times in the Spanish Civil War. This time he'll be on the winning side as the Reds are advancing toward the enemy and pursuing him like a lion pursues a fleeing deer.

"Hurrah," he shouts gleefully. As far as his eyes can see, he's watching Soviet forces chase the opponent. He feels a curious ecstasy grip him as the car weaves to avoid mortar shells causing mounds of dirt, dust, and smoke to fly above him.

Some soldiers with sub-machine guns, running alongside the car, are so hyped-up that they cry out, "kill the Emperor-worshiping savages."

As the morning wears on, Soviet artillery fire continues. Riders in Mischa's car include the driver, a guard, and a radio man who's reporting positions back to command headquarters.

Sometimes, Japanese stragglers in front of the advancing Russians turn and fire on them. Luckily, young Igor, the guard wielding a tommy-gun, drops the enemy with accuracy. Though Igor's methods are effective, it does not stop Japanese machine gun fire opening up again and again, their bullets smashing into the dry grazelands and raising large puffs of dust. Then, silence after Red soldiers hurl dozens of grenades at the enemy gun emplacements.

Later that first morning, as they halt in a wide, open field, two Russian soldiers approach them. One wears a blood-stained bandage around his head. Limping, this soldier, holding his leg with his hand, is being helped by a fellow soldier, with a carbine over his shoulder. Acting as a medic, the trooper has torn open the injured one's pants leg. He saw that dark blood ran down the soldier's white leg. The helpful soldier then inspected the wound and tore a piece of his shirt and applied it as a tourniquet.

As much as the injured Russian is trying to put on a brave face, it's obvious he's in pain. His face is pale and from time to time, he puts his hand on his head. He's breathing heavily, though he attempts to grin. His face's white. His lips tremble. Mischa can see he's tall with thin shoulders. His eyes are small and his mouth is tight and sharp.

"Comrades, this soldier has been wounded and needs to get to the field hospital," yells the trooper aiding the wounded man.

"We have to keep going," says the radio man. "Orders."

"Comrades. Let's see if we can save a life to fight another day," chimes in Mischa.

At this point, the radio operator interrupts again. "Comrade Commissar Rasputnis. I have to get permission to abort our course."

In this case, Comrade, I'm the authority. We're going to take him back. Besides, our advancing troops are way ahead of us."

"Yes, Comrade Commissar."

Getting the wounded man into the car is not easy. Seconds seem like years. They have to lift him gently, and make sure his head does not hit anything. He's barely conscious, but manages to growl.

"What's your name, comrade," Mischa asks the soldier.

"Sergeant Ivan Dimitriovich Dudin."

"Dudin. Did you say Dudin," Mischa retorts excitedly. "Are you the son of Dimitri Abramovich Dudin."

"Yes," mumbles Ivan Dimitriovich Dudin. "He's my father"

"I know him. We served together. Please tell me, he's alive?" asks Mischa, shaken up. "I haven't heard anything about him in a long time. We worked the trains together in Siberia in 1918 and then he disappeared after being thrown from the train, probably, by the conductor. We did catch up a year later in Yekaterinburg," explains Mischa, not mentioning the tiff they had on the battlefield.

"Yes, he is alive," answers the son.

"Thank goodness! Don't talk," says Mischa. "We'll talk later."

The young Dimitri agrees with a muffled answer that sounds like, "yes."

Mischa takes a liking to the young man. He observes the soldier's long nose and bright oval brown eyes come through, even though his face turns even paler, highlighting frightened eyes. He agrees that the soldier and radio man can remain where they are as they are behind fellow Russian troops.

"The driver will take me and the wounded man back to the field hospital and we'll come back to get you, if you haven't joined another unit. Won't take long," says Mischa.

Within minutes, the driver turns the vehicle around and heads to the medical unit as Mischa remembers days with Dimitri on the Trans-Siberian. *Here, in this forsaken land, I'm rushing Dimitri's son to a field hospital. Thank goodness, he's alive. I personally will help to ensure the medical people are on top of this case.*

Arriving at the field hospital, medics rush out and remove the infantryman from the car.

"Take good care of him," says Mischa in a commanding voice to the hospital medical officer. "I'll be back later to visit him. If you transfer him, let me know."

"Yes, Comrade Officer."

Walking away, Mischa's relieved that Dimitri, the elder, is alive.

"Hope the son makes it. Not only must he live, but he must tell me about his father," he thinks as he returns to the battlefield. The meeting with young Dimitri had relieved the stress of battle; it had brought him back to the exciting but fulfilling days of the revolution.

•

The end of the battle was never in doubt, though it lasted about a week. Soviet forces pierced the Japanese main defense line. Armored brigades looped around behind the Japanese, a classic double envelopment. When Red armed winged formations linked up at Nomonhan Village, the Kwantung Army was trapped.

Events move fast for Mischa. He realizes he's simply a cog in the vast Soviet Army, but buoyed by a great Russian victory which turns out to be Japan's worst defeat in its recent history.

On August 31, Zhukov declares the disputed territory between the Halha river and the boundary line running through Nomonhan to be cleared of the Japanese. The curse of the defeat of the Russo-Japanese War in 1904 is lifted, as Mischa views Red Army soldiers stomping on a Japanese military flag, a red ball with sixteen red rays, the emblem of the rising sun.

•

A few days later, Mischa's ordered to head to his new assignment in Vladivostok. Before his transfer, he visits Ivan Dimitriovich Dudin now in the camp hospital. Color has come back into the soldier's face

Now that he's healing, he's more talkative.

"What happened to your father after he left Siberia," Mischa asks Dimitri. "The last I heard, he had disappeared again. I hate to ask, but did he go over to the...."

"Please, Comrade Rasputnis," interrupts Dimitri. "Never. My father remains a steadfast Communist. He's secretly assigned to a young Chinese group, victims of the Japanese attack on China two years ago. He's working with the Chinese Communist Party in their revolution," Dimitri says politely, not giving the impression he's talking back to a high-ranking Commissar.

He pauses before changing the subject. "Comrade Rasputnis, I think my father told me that one of the persons he liked very much was your sister. Is that so?" he asks, thinking he could get on the good side of Mischa. But it backfired when the latter answered sarcastically.

"I didn't know too much about my sister Klara's love life. For a while, I guess, he was with her. It's known to the Party that she went to Canada or America. The Party forgives."

"Yes, Comrade Rasputnis. It does."

"Where is your father now?"

"I don't know exactly. But he moves in and around China, as it fights Japan. I heard my father has moved on to be an adviser to Chairman Mao Tso-tung, head of the Chinese Communist Party."

"I see. And may I ask about your mother?"

"My mother was killed by the Whites in Harbin shortly after I was born."

"So sorry. We've all lost someone," responds Mischa.

For a few moments, neither talk. The silence is broken by Mischa.

"I must be going. I'm being shipped out. I leave tomorrow for Vladivostok."

"Thanks for coming, Comrade Rasputnis, Dimitri says, his voice breaking: "Good luck."

Early the next morning, Mischa leaves behind the Khalkhin Gol battlefield, a vast graveyard of military equipment and a place where many men had been killed and wounded.

•

Chapter 22. London, 1939.
Basya.
"London Fling."

•

Meanwhile, Basya, aka Tatiana Kovacova, is adjusting to her new surroundings in London. She digs into the daily, diplomatic briefs in various departments of the exiled Czechoslovakian government. Her Czech higher-ups have no idea that behind their backs, she's continuing her undercover work of passing vital information relating to the exiled Czech government to her bosses in Moscow. After all, she has absorbed a dozen years of experience as an undercover Soviet intelligence officer who has proven herself. Her spying goes undetected.

To Tatiana, London, the capital of the British Empire, and a huge metropolis compared to the small city of Prague presents new challenges. She memorizes drop-off locations for photographed copies of intelligence documents, as well as safe spots to meet fellow agents.

At the same time, more and more Czech pilots and former army personnel, smarting from the loss of their homeland, cross over from Prague and elsewhere to London. When they arrive, Tatiana organizes housing assignments for these patriots who immediately sign up with the Royal Air Force (RAF). She loves her assignment working with the new volunteers, as well as being around those flyers. Many of them fit the romantic, movie characterization of the time, tall, dark, and handsome. Sure enough, one of those dashing aviators will enter her life.

•

On a grey, dismal January, 1940 afternoon in London, which grows only greyer and damper as the day wears on, Czech military attaché, Col. Anton Novotny hosts a reception in London for his country's pilots who fled to England to battle the Nazis.

Standing in the reception receiving line in a third-floor, mirrored hall in the Czech Embassy is Tatiana Kovacova, who, along with attaché Col. Novotny, welcomes the guests. After everyone enters the ballroom, the two circulate among the officers and, as is custom, engage in conversation, acquaint themselves with new pilots, keep the chatter going, and urge pilots to refresh themselves with drinks, including a Czech, Pilsner-type beer and English tea sandwiches.

A short while into the reception, Tatiana, always at home and energized among a group of men, hears a booming laugh which immediately draws her attention. She turns to see a young, RAF officer expressively relating what appears to be an air battle. His hands are moving up and down in the form of a mythical fighter plane crashing downward, dropping its bombs, and rocketing upward into the clouds as an imaginary train explodes down below in a fireball seen for miles.

As she draws closer to the officer in question, their eyes lock. They're immediately enamored with each other. He's tall and strong, with wavy, blond hair, a narrow face, that gives off a gracious smile offered up to the good-looking woman standing in front of him. Blushing, her eyes brighten and the corners of her mouth curve slightly upward. She turns away; he goes back to his story-telling.

Without drawing attention to herself, or for that matter, stopping to chat with other servicemen, she walks back to Col. Novotny. She utters not a word, but moves her head toward the group surrounding the young RAF officer, and signals to the colonel, she'd like to meet the pilot. The colonel waits until the young man finishes telling his adventurous story, takes Tatiana's elbow and deftly guides her to the flyer.

"Lt. Arno Novak, meet Tatiana Kovacova, our consul and liaison to embassies."

"How do you do, Lt. Novak. Welcome," Tatiana says warmly, which leads to a soft interjection from Col. Novotny.

"The lieutenant here was just telling the men how he got to London. An amazing story, you see. Working with newcomers from our homeland as you do, Tatiana, you'll appreciate his tale. Lt .Novak, why don't you tell Tatiana your exploits?"

"You're too kind, Colonel."

"I'm all ears," insists Tatiana."

"Not a problem. Always ready for the opportunity to tell it, especially to someone so charming," he replies to Tatiana, who, despite her usual diplomatic expressionless face, blushes again.

Meanwhile, Col. Nivotny, seeing that he has accomplished his introduction, says, "Sorry folks. Excuse me. Must greet a foreign dignitary," adding politely and taking leave of the pair who now alone, momentarily stare at each other.

"Consul, if you wouldn't mind, why don't we talk after the reception. Let's say over a drink or a cup of tea," says Lt. Novak in an inviting voice.

"Tea would be great. There's a quiet place down the road. The Old City Tea House."

I know it well."

"After the party then?"

"Yes, of course. See you soon."

•

An hour later, Lt. Novak and Tatiana leave the party together and saunter over to the chic tea-room near the Embassy. Despite the fact that the notorious London fog, with its low visibility, wraps around her like an octopus who has snared a hapless swimmer, she's pleased as punch, that someone, especially one with a handsome face and muscular body, accompanies her.

Entering the café, the two are ushered to a round table featuring straight back chairs, and a checkered tablecloth which hosts a small vase of flowers. Exchanging pleasantries, they pick up the menu, the tableaux of which offers a variety of teas and homemade scones. The afternoon tea-time crowd has not yet arrived, so they can talk without having to raise their voices.

No one, but Tatiana hears him recount his odyssey to freedom, though the waiter eavesdrops from time to time when he brings them fresh tea. Tatiana, her voice parched from talking for several hours at the reception, listens intently to the pilot with shiny, blue eyes and dark wavy hair. She leans forward and eagerly awaits a story of a flight to safety by a man who, as he begins, changes his demeanor from a bright face to a wrinkled countenance.

"He speaks calmly, telling her that on the night German troops roared into Prague in March, he hitched a ride with a friend to Brno. "There was no use going back to the air base. The government had made it clear we wouldn't fight a Nazi invasion. Since I was a pilot I had a valid passport, even if it had the term 'military' on it."

At this point, Arno stops for a moment and takes a sip of tea.

"What happened then?" Tatiana asks eagerly.

"Simple. I went to the train station and I requested a one-way ticket to Bratislava."

"He gave it to you, I'm sure," interrupted Tatiana.

"Wait. Not yet. The price was thirty *koruna*. I was shocked. I didn't think I'd need that much. I only had twenty-seven koruna. Then, I did something I've never done. I begged."

Arno recounted the event, "'I'm afraid I don't have that amount. I'm short three *koruna*. Perhaps you'll still let me have a ticket? It's not a big sum. I need to get to Bratislava. Death in the family and I left the house in a hurry.'"

"I am afraid I can't do that, sir."

"Please. It'd be a good deed on your part and I'd be forever grateful."

"Well, you'll have to go and speak to my supervisor over there."

"When I looked in the direction he was pointing, I saw a German officer with two police officers. "Thanks anyway,' I said, turning away."

"'Wait,'" said a woman behind me. 'I couldn't help but overheat you. Here's the money for the ticket, sir,' she said, pushing in front of me, and handing a fiver to the agent."

"'You don't have to do that,' I said. Really, just to be polite."

"'That's okay. I'm religious,'" she said, crossing herself. 'You must be at that funeral.'"

"I gave the ticket seller my twenty-seven koruna, plus her five, took the two koruna change and the ticket. I thanked her and went to the gate where I boarded the crowded train to Bratislava.

At this point, Arno stops in his story, for the waiter pours more tea into their half-finished cups. The scones are untouched

"I'm not sure I'd be here today if not for that woman."

Tatiana could see Arno was having trouble going on. So she took his hand, held it in hers for a moment, and in a comforting tone, she says. "Let's get to the scones and tea."

While they drank, he regained his composure and informed her how the trip generally went okay after that, with few mishaps, as well as how Czech consular officials aided him in his quest to get to freedom.

"Fini, That's it. Here I am," he said and stopped talking.

"Yes. You ought to thank God you're alive. You're very lucky," says Tatiana, her bright eyes shining. "You did what you had to do. You took risks."

"Nothing new. I take a risk every time I get into that plane," he says thoughtfully. "It would be nice to tour our temporary city together," adds Arno in an inviting voice.

"Yes. Agreed. I've been wanting to do more of that for a long time."

"Fine. I'll call you."

"Yes. Do that, please."

"Well. I have to get back to the base. Nice talking to you," he says.

"And I've got to return to the Embassy," she replies, heading out the door.

I'm sure he'll call. He'd better. I need a fling. Besides, he's a source for

information which I can report to the Center. They like when I cavort with the enemy.

•

Holding hands like teenagers.   Touring like honeymooners. Stopping often like lovers do to embrace in the middle of a crowded shopping street, Arno and Tatiana explore every nook and cranny of the huge metropolis. They saunter down wide avenues and circle squares. They ride double-decker buses to learn their routes. Arm-in-arm, they window-shop in Regent Street, in the West End. They visit Westminster Abbey, Trafalgar Square.

Doing the sites is better with someone, she muses. *What good is looking at Big Ben if you can't hold someone's hand?* She's so happy sightseeing with an admirer that she even snares a couple of passes to Parliament.

On Whitehall Road, the couple dodge red omnibuses swinging down from Charring Cross, some bound for Waterloo Bridge, or Victoria, or Chelsea.

Even though he's training to integrate into RAF flight procedures, Arno manages to get two nights off a week during the first four months of 1940, the so-called "phony war," when neither the Allies nor Germans are moving from their dug-in battle lines.

•

Meanwhile, Tatiana suspects that he has another girlfriend. She needles him about it.

"I do," he admits.   "I fell in love with her the moment I was introduced," he says laughing. "I was captivated by her sheer beauty. She was slimly built with a beautifully proportioned body and graceful curves just where they should be."

"You can't have two lovers. Who is she?" Tatiana frowns.

"My Spitfire, the fighter plane. Mark my words, she'll become a flying legend," he says giving Tatiana a big hug.

•

The couple are comfortable with each other. She needs company. When she's alone, she fights anxiety, an anxiety caused in part by living in a large metropolis such as London. This cold-minded, Anglo-Saxon city, like any huge city, can overwhelm a person who has no friends, no relatives, no parents. She often compares London to her former, friendlier Slavic surroundings. In many ways, Arno reminds her of Mischa: tall, broad shouldered, protective. Arno's ready to take risks, a quality she admires. She realizes she doesn't think of Mischa much these days.

•

My God. Being with Tatiana is like first love. I'm into it and I love it. She's wonderful. A Czech, no less. Beautiful. Lovely body. Intelligent. Who could ask for anything more. I need someone like that. But we need privacy to do our thing. I've got to find what the Canadian fliers in my squad call, 'a pad'. A hotel room is expensive. Besides, it's distasteful."

Luck seems to follow Arno wherever he goes. He obtains a hideaway from a British mechanic, Bill Randall, who works nights at the airbase.

"I have a small two-room flat in Kensington, in a house with a private entrance," explains Bill. "I work nights at the base. You can have the place between eight o'clock in the evening and five in the morning, except Monday and Tuesday when I'm off."

He outlines some rules:

"No loud noise. No playing the wireless. Even though I know you're in the room when I'm at work, put on the small light in the foyer-window when you're there. So, if I get off early, I'll realize that the apartment's in use."

He then adds, "Bring your own food - third shelf down in the icebox is yours. Bring your own linen and towels. That'll be thirty quid a month, payable in advance."

"Accepted, sight unseen," says Arno. "Here's the money. What's the address?"

The bedroom itself is non-descript, not much to look at. That doesn't matter to the couple. They are only there at night when they're free from their jobs. What counts is privacy. A metal framed bed stands along one wall, while a chest of drawers and small desk occupy the other. In one corner to the left of the window, is a wall-hung sink. Sgt. Randall keeps the rooms clean. The loo is off the sitting room. The latter possesses a loveseat, a single wooden chair, and a settee. They don't care about the furnishings - they're not there to live in, only to make love.

•

And then it happens. "The Battle of France is over. The Battle of Britain" is about to begin. The first Nazi bombs drop out of the sky over London one black night in late August, 1940, and the heavy German bombing, known as *"the Blitz,"* begins. The real crunch comes on September 7, 1940, when London becomes Hitler's target. Night after night, Tatiana witnesses German wave after wave of bombers over the city. The nightly wail of the siren with the searchlights lighting up the sky above the capital. The sight of barrage balloons frightens off enemy bombers, while the exploding anti-aircraft shells thud down to earth. The stacks of Nazi bombs dive down on a war-weary city, constantly bombed and numbed by explosions.

Day after day, Arno, who's in a frontline squadron, runs out to the grassy airport field. He climbs up and jumps into the cockpit of his plane, and like a bold eagle, rises to the sky to meet the German invaders who are stretching RAF capacity to the limit. He becomes a hero, a flying ace, one of the best foreign fighter pilots to bag over a dozen enemy planes, in September alone.

•

One fall Monday, the weather was so bad, that Arno was given a two-day pass off the base, a chance for Arno and Tatiana to bed down. On the second night, an air raid siren goes off and Tatiana gets up from the bed and pulls back the blackout curtains blocking out any light. Searchlights track enemy bombers and sometimes follow them down.

"Arno! Come here! Quick! Look, a plane is faltering. Staggering out of formation. My goodness it's coming down. Bravo, we got one."

Arno, who's groggy, quickly jumps up. "It's a Heinkel. Crashing."

"I can see it. You men are giving their lives to defend us."

"Come, get away from the window, Tatiana. I know it's awesome to watch. But the Luftwaffe's wearing us down. We're weary. Our nerves are taunt to the breaking-point."

"I believe you."

"Like I said. Better move away, or we'll have one of those air raid wardens on our backs."

No sooner were his words uttered than a whistle sounded from below.

"You up there. Go to the shelter in the Underground. Now. That's an order."

•

A year later, June 22, 1941, to be exact, in the middle of the night, Tatiana's awakened by the panicky voice of a colleague shouting into the telephone:

"Tatiana. Come to the office now. The Nazis have invaded Russia."

'What's that? I can't hear you. Repeat it," says Basya in a faltering voice.

"The Nazis have invaded Russia," the woman in the Embassy repeats. Silence.

"Tatiana. Are you alright?"

"I'll be right over," she replies, hanging up and muttering: *"Mischa wherever you are, I hope you'll be safe."*

Chapter 23. Vladivostok, 1941.
MISCHA.
"Mischa Finds a New Love."

•

Commissar Mischa Rasputnis is now back in Vladivostok as head of port security. He has heard rumors that there was a network of criminal prison and political punishment labor camps that were set up throughout eastern Russia in the 1920's and grew in the 1930s. He shrugged off the idea that horrible conditions existed and if they did, it was necessary for the success of the Revolution. Known as the *Gulag,* an acronym (used from 1930) for *(Glavnoye Upravleniye Lagerei)* or Main Camp Administration, the Soviet labor-camp system took peasants, criminals, kulaks, counter-revolutionaries, and forced them to dig for gold and process timber which could be traded abroad. Most prisoners were deliberately worked to death or murdered. With no drugs or proper care, Russian Jewish poet Osip Mandelstam died in Vtotaya Rechka, near Vladivostok, in December 1938, paranoid and raving. It would take a visitor to shake Mischa's self-denial of this horrendous crime.

•

In the late summer of 1941, several months after Basya bleated out a murmur of fear from London for the safety of her ex-lover as the German horde swept over the Ukraine and deep into Russia, Mischa Rasputnis sluggishly walks up from the docks of the Soviet naval base in Vladivostok. He's going for lunch at the communal cafeteria where he takes all his meals.

Strong winds off the Pacific Ocean and under a weak high-noon sun, whip his tall frame.

Mischa, who at age forty still maintains a young-looking face and strong body, is fantasizing that Basya, totally naked, is waiting for him in his apartment.

"That's impossible and you know it," he says to himself.

He stops and looks around. He wonders if anyone is watching him. He continues his line of thought: *Am I deluding myself that these illusions are all that's left of Basya's love? How long can I wait for her. Maybe if I get married, it would be easier, though I'm not sure pining for her would ever end, even if I was in the arms of a beautiful wife."*

As for Basya, Mischa figured she fled Prague when the Nazis took over, but he didn't know she ended up in London. He's been living on a planet in the Russian Far East. Despite the Nazi attack, however, Siberia is peaceful. War is thousands of miles away to the West. The Kremlin has ordered Mischa to tighten security and increase vigilance around its Pacific fleet docked in Vladivostok. He constantly tours the docks, consults with staff officers, urges his men to carefully check each freighter entering and leaving. Frequently, his subordinates pick up suspected stevedores and sailors smuggling in luxury goods or slacking on the job. No trial needed; they're disposed of or immediately sent to prison. Although the Japanese were soundly defeated at Khalkhin Gol, they remain prime targets for surveillance, for Tokyo could launch an attack on the USSR.

•

One windy day in September, 1941, Mischa, again daydreaming as he heads to the communal cafeteria, believes he hears Basya's voice whispering 'hello' in his ear. Entering the hall, which usually serves up boring food, especially in wartime, he approaches the serving counter with his head slightly down. Holding his tray, he lifts his half-closed eyes up to see his choices on the menu board. Today there is only one: sardines and cabbage. As he is about to receive his portion from the server, he fixes his eyes onto those of the woman dishing out the food. He almost drops the tray. On her part, the woman continues holding the ladle suspended in the air. She's staring at the man in front of her.

Seconds pass until he smiles, relaxes, and holds the tray steady. Regaining his composure, he says: "Hello Slava. Good to see you here."

"I also, comrade commissar," she says with a welcoming smile, as she places bits of sardines and cabbage on his plate along with two slices of black bread and tea. He smiles.

•

My goodness. Slava, the teenager. I met her on the train from Kiev to Odessa. The daughter of the Jewish family I tried to save. She's now a grown woman. He felt his emotions rising, just as they did when he first met his late wife, Olga in Moscow, or when he first spied Basya in Odessa and even when he saved Slava nine years ago on the rail tracks in the Ukraine.

She came to his apartment that night. Except for work, they spent the next days together, most of it in bed. For a while, he thought he was in love again, and so did she. War does that to people. It makes them fall into situations, especially when they are lonely, as these two were. They might never find themselves together during normal times, especially in Stalin's Russia where he is a Party official and she is the daughter of parents who are "enemies of the people." As it is, he's in danger, just talking to her. But it's wartime and those civilian restrictions are less harsh. He decides to take the risk, since she could bring him satisfaction and happiness, even if it was infatuation. It had been so long since he was with a woman, a woman, that is, whom he found young, beautiful, with soft baby-like skin, and above all, for whom he cared.

They try to be discreet. At night, walking in the gardens, they take in the chilly, night air. They talk about the war and the gulag, though she does most of the talking, in part because she and her family had been so wronged. She felt that the cover he had given her in order to save her would last forever. He would help her again and again, especially since she notices how attentive he remains in waiting on her and in making love. She could tell he enjoyed her.

Slava's story touched him. Yet, because he rescued her and protected her, he knew she was his for the taking. That bothered him. She was fifteen years younger than him.

•

One late afternoon, when he came home from an assignment off shore, he was sweaty and smelly from having to go down into the hold of a tanker loaded with fish. Because of his rank, the Party installed a shower room in his quarters. When he opened the door to the apartment, he could hear the shower water running. He stood for a moment, hesitating. But he realized he couldn't wait and went to the room, and opened the shower door. Her naked back and buttocks were facing him. She quickly turned around. The sight of her small upward breasts and her dark grey pubic hair aroused him. She blushed and gasped a slight sigh of objection to being disturbed. No words. They went at it, as their sighs of joy echoed the shower's rushing water.

For the two of them, they were the best of days and they passed quickly. He had a young girlfriend. She had a muscular, mature man. They knew it wouldn't last. It was a matter of time. But she did manage to share with him another traumatic experience that fractured her life:

"One night, the NKVD came to my grandmother's place in Odessa and took me away, They said, I was 'the daughter of arrested kulaks.' I would have

to join my family in the Gulag. Everyone knew that being sent to the camps was a death sentence. They piled us into trucks and took us to the rail station. Because they were afraid some might run away, they forced us to kneel alongside the train. You knew if you got up, they'd shoot to kill. We were locked up in cattle cars, the windows were barred. The embarrassment of relieving ourselves in a hole in the car was bad enough, but it was the lack of food, especially the lack of water that tormented us. On top of that, during the journey, they gave us salty fish to eat, frozen bread, and water in the form of ice. The heavy smells in the cars were unbearable. Two women in our car slit their throats with broken glass. Their bodies were dumped in a field. Day after day, we were shunted here and there. After a month of hell, we reached Vladivostok. There, they informed me my parents had died. Because Russia was fighting for survival, however, they were releasing some prisoners from the Gulag into independent, criminal groups to fight the Nazis. First, they sent me to a labor force here in Vladivostok. Once they felt I was rehabilitated, they sent me to a crash course in nursing,"

He kissed her and tried to comfort her. They never talked about the subject again.

At times when he was with her, he thought of Basya and felt guilty. Slava had made him happy. He wondered if his relationship with Basya was doomed. As conflicted as he was, he knew that if Basya showed up at any moment, he'd leave Slava and run to Basya's side. Meantime, he and Slava liked each other. At the same time, the Red Army was reeling from horrific losses. The Germans were at the gates of Moscow. The government needed medics and nurses. So, they finally sent Slava to a local advanced training course. In early October, 1941, she was transferred to Moscow.

Slava blew kisses at him from the window of her train compartment. He returned them and smiled as the train jolted away. His only thought as he left the station: *Slava, just like Olga and Basya, comes into my life and quickly leaves. Is this what my life comes down to?*

•

One day, Mischa receives a cable. A Red Army nurse unit writes it's sad to report that Slava Abelevskaya was killed attempting to reach a wounded soldier during the battle of Bryansk, near Moscow. Slava had named Mischa as next of kin. Tears well in his eyes when he reads the telegram. He wipes his eyes and goes outside. He thinks about Slava. He tells himself that some things are better forgotten. He begins to wonder again if Basya is alive.

•

Chapter 24. Moscow, 1943.
BASYA AND MISCHA.
"Basya and Mischa secretly reunite in Wartime Moscow."

•

After living in Siberia for many years, Mischa Rasputnis has learned, as have all Russians, that "there is no bad weather, only the wrong clothes for it."

•

In December 1943, Soviet diplomat, Anatoly Abramov, now a high-ranking Soviet official in the ministry of foreign affairs, glances over a confidential communique listing the members of the Czecho-slovakian delegation coming from London to Moscow in a few weeks to sign a friendship treaty between the Czechs-in-exile and the Kremlin. Scanning the list, he suddenly fixes his eyes on the name, "Tatiana Kovacova. "Oh my," utters Anatoly guiltily, remembering that upon his return to Moscow from Prague in 1939, he didn't follow through to get a message to a Mischa Rasputnis.

He never told Mischa that Tatiana sends regards and that she is in good health. First, he rationalized, it was too risky. The NKVD, at that time, was carrying out Stalin's order to purge thousands. Second, with the Nazi attack on the Soviet Union in 1941, there wasn't time to look up someone's boyfriend.

I never did deliver her message to Tatiana's friend. I can make up for it now. Threat of purges is almost non-existent, and we've beaten back the Germans. Besides, I like that woman. She's an asset to the homeland. Risks her life. Let's give her a little joy?

Brazenly, he knows he's taking a chance, even though he's risen on the ministry ladder of power. As he sees it, even fear has its limits for a romantic Communist like himself. As a trusted official, he easily obtains from the NKVD, Mischa's address in Vladivostok and sends a cable.

"Your friend, Tatiana Kovacova will arrive in Moscow from London on December 10. Stopping at Metropol Hotel. Let me know if you're coming to Moscow. Anatoly Abramov. Deputy Ministry of Foreign Affairs."

•

Two days before the treaty signing date set for December 12, Tatiana Kovacova finds herself a passenger on a British airliner military plane to Moscow. She's part of a Czechoslovakian government-in-exile delegation, headed by President Edvard Benes, to sign a pact calling for "mutual respect of sovereignty and non-interference in internal affairs."

The flight, which has British fighter escort to the Russian border, is so smooth that Basya, soon after takeoff, falls asleep, only to be interrupted by two female Czechs, sitting in the row behind her, loudly discussing their love life. Nearing the end of their babble, one of the ladies forcefully declares: "You never know how a thing is going to turn out."

The words are like a dagger piercing Tatiana's heart, mirroring her situation. The ladies are not discussing her - she knows that. They're divulging the love affair of the Embassy's press officer whose fiancé has broken off their engagement.

But Tatiana takes it personally. A discussion of romantic breakup inevitably brings Mischa to mind. Sitting up, she wishes she wouldn't be plagued by thoughts of him. *That relationship died a long time ago. I'm about to land in Russia and I don't even know where he is. Even if I did, the NKVD would stop me from meeting him. They've warned me. 'Don't pose in any photo-taking. Somebody might recognize you. We don't want anyone to say that's Basya from Odessa and then the Czechs realize you're a Russian.'*

Looking out the window, and seeing the fluffy white clouds, broke her train of thought. And then: *Besides, I have a new boyfriend, Arno. The last time I saw Mischa was twenty-three years ago; teenagers we were."*

•

As for Mischa, he didn't know what to think regarding the news that Basya was going to be in Moscow. All he knew was that he longed for her. But he never heard of Anatoly Abramov. Who is he? Maybe this is a trick. Re-reading the message and then doing a little research with his own NKVD friends, he discovers Anatoly is a legitimate, high-ranking government official in the foreign office. In fact, he is a deputy minister.

Mischa is beside himself. He can't concentrate on work. His emotional temperature rises.

The next day, returning to his apartment, he closes the door, grabs a shot glass from the cabinet, pours vodka into it, gulps the fiery liquid and has another. Downed with one swallow and warmed by the burning jolt of the clear liquid, he starts pacing the floor.

If two people are made for each other, no matter the distance or time lapse, the relationship will survive.

A moment later: *Calm down. She's not here in Vladivostok. How in hell am I going to get to Moscow. Even if I do get there, how am I going to see her. They'll watch her constantly. This is insane! Must get to Moscow. I know what I'll do.*

Mischa leaves the apartment and goes to his office telegraph room.

He doesn't go through local channels, but instead types out a cable directly to his Moscow superior in Harbor Security, Abrasha Volkov, whom he knows has taken a liking to him. He explains he has difficulty dealing with the American sailors off ships bringing in locomotives for the Red Army transportation teams supplying arms to Russian troops in the West. He smiles, for there is some truth in his statement which he's sure will help his request.

"Despite our regulations" he points out, "the Americans talk to our people, infecting them with capitalist poison." He knows how to pour it on to his old-fashioned, Bolshevik commander who has survived the purges. "I don't think we can deal with such a sensitive issue over the phone or in a communique. We don't want an incident with the Americans, our Allies in our war to defeat fascism. We should have a plan and discuss this in person," writes Mischa convincingly.

A gamble on his part. Would it work? He had to try. *This can land me in the Lubyanka where I'll get a bullet in the back of my head. What else is new? I must be in love with her.*

The wait for clearance is one of the hardest in his life.

"God, get me there. Please," begs Mischa silently, realizing that he's doing something he hasn't done for over thirty years. He's praying. He hasn't sought God's help in the battles of the civil war; or in Madrid or at Khalkhin Gol. *"I'm a good Communist and here I'm seeking God's help for a love affair. Happens. Just don't tell my comrades."*

The next day approval comes. He's asked to liaise with the same Anatoly Abramov who cabled him about Tatiana's arrival. Anatoly, they say, is obviously interested in Mischa's views on the Americans. Knowing the regulations, he believes the NKVD in the capital won't know he's coming to town, only Harbor Security. And Harbor Security, because of Anatoly approving the visit, has no reason to report to the NKVD that Mischa is coming to Moscow.

A few days later, he hitches a ride on a supply plane to the capital. He never bothers to thank God.

●

Hearing from Abrasha Volkov in Harbor Security that Mischa is arriving on December 9, Anatoly contacts the NKVD and tells them that he's working on the Czech visit and will be able to keep close tabs on one, Tatiana Kovacova, whose providing his Foreign Office, with secret information. They approve his request. He's not worried about the couple being traitors because they are meeting with each other, he just wants them to be without harassment, especially Tatiana, who has a job to do supplying him with intelligence on the Prague delegation. To do that, she should be comfortable in her work. He believes it's a good deed to help people fall in love, and he is fond of Tatiana. The two lovers, however, will have to be careful.

•

Landing in the capital, Mischa is welcomed with snow. Bundling up in this bitter cold Russian winter, he goes directly to the iconic Metropol Hotel on Theatre Square, near the Kremlin, located in the heart of the capital, the preferred stomping ground for foreign dignitaries. He asks for Nikita Lebedev, a long-time employee and night manager. Mischa knows him from civil war days. Whenever Mischa comes to Moscow, he visits Nikita. They down a few shots of vodka in the elegant hotel bar which boasts an American jazz band.

"Comrade Rasputnis. I can see from your face something's bothering you. How can I help you?" questions Nikita Lebedev.

"I've got a problem. I need your help. I have a friend in the Czech delegation coming tomorrow. Her name is Tatiana Kovacova. We're not supposed to be together. That's why I can't stay here. I'll be at my Aunt Inna's communal apartment. I'll just be another soldier meeting with Harbor Security and I'll have some leave time."

He then adds "Nikita? Could you...? Let me put it this way. I want to spend some private time with Tatiana. I just can't walk in the front door of the hotel. I'll be spotted. Then, there's the key lady on each floor recording every time a guest leaves and returns to their room. If the ladies spot me going to her room, it's the Gulag for me or even worse."

"Not if the key lady doesn't see you," rejoins Nikita. "Do you think I'm going to let the State stand in the way of true love. I'll help you." What he says next surprises Mischa. "A fellow from the foreign affairs ministry, Anatoly, contacted me. It seems he's interested in helping you meet your girlfriend. Don't worry, you're in good hands, comrade. I'll get her a private room. Here's what you do when you want to visit her..."

Nikita finishes giving him instructions. Mischa smiles.

"I'm not going to let you down."

He doesn't.

•

Two nights later, Nikita Lebedev opens the door of Room 315 in the Metropol Hotel. The room is registered in the name of Czechoslovakian delegate, Tatiana Kovacova, who is now out for the evening. Nikita motions to Mischa Rasputnis to enter the dark room and when he does, Nikita, having put on the lights, closes the door and leaves. He called the key lady moments before the two men arrived on the floor, giving her orders to come down for a short break. He'd watch the floor for her. No one on the floor saw the two men arrive, or the departure of Nikita.

For several hours since the moment he entered Tatiana's room early that evening, Mischa sits in a comfortable armchair in a corner of the room. He has positioned the chair so that anyone entering could not see him when the door opens.

Convincing her that all that happened was my fault, shouldn't be hard. We'll both know she's had a drinking problem which I'm sure she's over now, especially in her job. I'll apologize. She'll like that. I hope it's not too late. What if she has a husband, children? What if she rejects me out of hand? What if,…What if…" he mumbles to himself, as he gets up and removes the wire from the monitoring device in the chandelier.

•

Earlier on that evening, while Mischa is pondering whether he will have a future with Tatiana Kovacova, the latter, a member of the Czech delegation to Moscow, is being chauffeured to a palace in the tall and mighty fortress, known as the Kremlin, the heart of Mother Russia. She and the delegates, riding in plush limousines, are silent as they observe that they are moving along under a full moon illuminating red flags emblazoned with the Soviet insignias of the hammer and sickle. The banners are waving atop the ancient iconic red walls and towers of the Kremlin, the headquarters of mighty and powerful Communist Russia, founded by Vladimir Lenin who now lies in state in a mausoleum in adjacent Red Square.

But the fortress itself does not just display raw power. It also exhibits archaic beauty, with its swallow-tail battlements and soaring towers. Its palaces and churches are resplendent with golden spires and domes, in some places rising more than sixty feet above the surrounding land.

Red Army guards, shouldering rifles, raise the barriers at the guard gate. Others offer up a snappy salute to welcome the leader of the Czechs in exile, President Edvard Benes, and his entourage. Tatiana is overwhelmed by this ceremonial gesture as she enters the mythological Valhalla where the Bolshevik czar, Comrade Joseph Vissarionovich Stalin, the voshd, (the leader), has his office surrounded by thirteen-foot thick walls and high vaulted ceilings.

As the delegates drive down the broad avenues in the Kremlin, they notice they're in the bowels of a citadel where it's dark, gloomy, and sinister, historically a true mirror of the czars and dictators that ruled Russia. Finally, they are ushered into a large banquet hall adorned with brightly-lit chandeliers, Persian rugs, flower arrangements, portraits of Marx and Lenin. Guided to the receiving line, Tatiana realizes she is about to meet the most powerful men in the Soviet Union. Dressed in business suits and Red Army uniforms with flashy medals, these moguls wait to snare their unsuspecting guests with propaganda and trickery. The British warned President Benes not to enter the lion's den. As a Soviet spy, Tatiana is glad he didn't listen.

Noticing the receiving line is moving, she becomes nervous. She feels the bile rising to her throat. This never happened before. She'd like a glass of water. Maybe she should leave, feign illness, go to the bathroom, and skip the receiving line. Too late. There he is, Papa Kalinin. He is better known as President Mikhail Kalinin, the formal head of the Soviet state, a mild-mannered, former peasant with round spectacles, goatee beard and droopy moustache. He smiles; she smiles. He says a few gratuitous words. She moves on.

Tatiana can see President Benes is standing next to Premier Stalin. The two are obviously talking politics. Czech Ambassador to Moscow, Zdenek Fierlinger, is doing the introduction honors. Tatiana's palms are sweaty. Stalin is dressed in his brown Party tunic, his trousers pressed for the occasion. He's short and has a pock-marked face with a prickly moustache. She notices his left arm is slightly shorter than the other, the result of a childhood accident. He has thick, low hair, but with some white patches of grey, caused undoubtedly by the stress of the war. His almost Oriental, and his feline eyes, at times, honey colored, grab her. She looks at him with smiling eyes. She knows eyes can talk and she flashes her rapturous smile as well. In England, upon meeting royalty, she would curtsy. Not the Communist way. She's drawn into the spell of this extraordinary personality, a personality, which carries people away and is utterly impossible to resist. They shake hands. Both utter a few diplomatic niceties. She nods at this messianic hero and moves on to Vyacheslav Molotov, minister of foreign affairs, and then Marshal Kliment Voroshilov, member of the State Defense Committee. No one lets on they know of her work, even if they do.

After the receiving line, Tatiana, relieved, hobnobs with the Russians attending the banquet. She works the room; she's good at it. They know nothing about her being a Soviet spy. Only Anatoly knows, but he's careful to wait to contact her. In a brief exchange, she promises to brief him tomorrow on the Czech reaction after the treaty signing.

Suddenly, her mind is taken off exchanging information as she turns to the kitchen entrance and spots young, beautiful women balancing mountains of food, such as, beetroot soup, cured meats, eels in cream sauce, beef tongue with horseradish sauce, ravioli stuffed with veal and pork sausage, not to mention the roasted pate dumplings, the salad bowls of gherkins marinated in maple syrup, and hors-d'oeuvres dishes brimming with caviar.

"My goodness, my colleagues act as if they have never eaten before. They're gobbling up all the hors d'oeuvres," she says to herself. "I can't blame them with austerity in London. Here, they are wined and dined at dinner tables."

The white-clad waiters keep the vodka flowing. That's the way Russian celebratory meals go. She notices a few of her colleagues are already tipsy. For several hours, the Soviets keep the toasts coming over a dozen courses, a complete orgy piled on the table - more fish, and even a small suckling pig.

The evening ends with more toasts, a diplomatic tone in all of them: Friendship and cooperation. Defeat fascism. Toast after toast 'to the war effort' and 'to the heroes of Stalingrad,' 'to the Czech partisans.' And finally, there is a final toast 'to our coming new treaty.'

After the toasts, Stalin asks his friends to indulge him in a movie on the preparedness of the Red Army in 1938 and the prowess of Soviet soldiers. Silence descends in the room. Many remember the dark days in November 1941. They turn their faces toward the direction of Red Square where, on an open-air platform on Lenin's mausoleum, Stalin waved to the Red Army troops as they marched through Red Square and straight off to the front. She doesn't know it yet, but those reserve troops were brought here by trains from Siberia organized by Mischa Rasputnis, the former boyfriend of the spy now sitting amongst them, Tatiana Kovacova.

After the movie, the Czechoslovakians, awe-stricken, leave the Kremlin. Most of them tell each other, what a great evening it was, an evening which made them forget the war raging only several hundred miles away.

Tatiana fantasizes she is Cinderella at the ball. Only, unlike the mythical princess, that first night after meeting Prince Charming,

Tatiana doesn't know it, but she's about to reunite with another prince. But for this moment, as the limousines pull away and until they reach the Metropol, Stalin is the mythical Prince and Tatiana, the Princess.

•

The room is dark when Tatiana enters later that night. "What a night this has been," she whispers to herself, as she puts on the lamp by the door. Immediately, her keen sense of smell inhales a male scent, though the room is empty. Turning, she closes the door, bolts it and swings around to scan the room once more, and she comes upon him.

"You," she gasps.

He smiles, putting his finger to his lips and softly intones: "shhh."

Neither party says a word. They just stare at each other. He thinks his heart misses a beat.

"What are you doing here? How dare you come here," she says, agitated. "You threw me out, you bastard. Go and don't come back or I'll tell the key lady to call the guards."

"Basya, let's not have a scene. Let me explain," he says convincingly. "I've chased you all over Russia," a sentence which startles her. "I've just come all the way from Vladivostok to see you. I'm not supposed to be here and could get in a lot of trouble. What happened in Yekaterinburg is my fault. I've regretted every minute of every day of every year since then. I never stopped loving you. I'm sorry. Give me another chance."

She looks directly at him. He's older with a little wider girth. A few more wrinkles on his forehead, and the beginning of the greying of his hair. But still, that strong, handsome face.

"I grant you I had a drinking problem," she admits truthfully. "Ironically it ended after I left you and got to Moscow. But you should have consoled me. Instead....."

"I agree. I didn't," he says, wanting to say how badly she behaved in the tavern, but not willing to mention it verbally. He holds back. "Look, I only have a few days here. Let's start all over as if it was that first morning in Yekaterinburg when we were reunited. No more running away," he says quietly. He smiles at her, having noticed from the first moment when she put on the light, she was still good looking.

"You've got to be joking," she says. "You owe me a big apology."

"You're right. I do. I apologize. I was wrong," realizing he better say that if he wants her. He smiles and once again, that engaging smile of his begins to melt away her anger.

I'm still attracted to him.

"We were young then," he says

His comment hurts her. "I couldn't help it. I lost everything. I needed revenge, even against myself for giving up my baby."

"But you're cured," he says, not reminding her of the raucous tavern scene. But somehow by the look on his face, she knew what he was thinking.

"I don't remember exactly what happened that night in the tavern. And I'm sorry for that. I guess I just couldn't handle it," she repeats. "What happened?" she says in a serious tone.

Stunned, Mischa is silent for a moment, and then, taking a chance in telling the truth, he says, "You got on a table, bared your chest and danced to the cheers of the crowd."

"No! I don't believe it," she says, pursing her lips.

"Yes."

"No wonder you were angry with me. How could I have done something like that? Maybe I should be the one to apologize."

"No need for that," he says convincingly, shutting out any indication he's patronizing her. "But we can start over and put it behind us. I know you're hurt, but…,"

"Okay," she says and cuts him off. Getting up, she moves toward him. He puts his arms around her and kisses her on the mouth. She presses her body against his.

He takes her hand. She doesn't resist. He kisses her fingers and feels the warmth. He leans over plants a kiss on her forehead and then again on her lips.

•

Later, they talk.

"Love conquers everything," he says, slightly shivering and lying next to her naked body. The blanket gives them some warmth in the room which is cold despite being in the Metropol.

At the same time, she pinches his arm to see if what they just had together was real.

"Mischa. You shouldn't fight with me anymore. We should do this, instead," she adds, as she cuddles closer. He, in turn, softly caresses her face with gentle strokes and, in the dead of a Moscow winter night, draws the blankets tighter around them.

•

Next morning, back in front of the Kremlin for the ceremonial signing of the "Treaty of Friendship, Mutual Assistance, and Post-War Cooperation between the USSR and Czechoslovakia," stands Tatiana Kovacova who has spent the night partying and love-making in her room. Despite the eye-shadow and heavy makeup, she looks exhausted; her eyes are blood-shot, her face slightly wan, like a student who has burned the midnight oil studying for exams.

The spokesman for the host nation, calls out: "The treaty ceremony is about to begin. Please take your seats." The Czech and Russian delegations move to the cushioned chairs that are lined up facing the large French-renaissance, antique signing table. Flags of the two nations drape each side of the table. Tatiana is assigned a seat on the aisle on the Czech side in the second row.

All eyes are on the leaders sitting down to affix their signatures to the documents: Molotov, Soviet foreign minister, and Czech President Benes.

Tatiana, with her up-close view of the ceremony, notices that the Russian leaders Stalin, Voroshilov, and Kalinin stand behind Molotov and Benes. They are grinning with cat-like expressions on their faces, telegraphing to those in the know that they have just snared the Czech mouse and are holding it in their claws.

The opening remarks begin in serious, monotone voices.

Within a few minutes, Jiri, Tatiana's young colleague in the Czech foreign office who is sitting next to her, is shocked and terrified or concerned? He sees Tatiana's head drooping down onto her chest. Fortunately, all eyes are on the interpreters now reading the short document. Careful not to wake her in such a way as to cause her to mutter indiscreet sounds of surprise at being touched while in slumber, he leans over and whispers in her ear, "Tatiana, stay awake."

Opening her weary eyes, she smiles embarrassingly. She whispers "thanks," realizing she dozed off as she daydreamed about Mischa and the night they spent together.

Jiri's not suspicious as to why she's nodding off. He assumes she's exhausted because of the banquet lasting late into the night. How could he know she was up until dawn with her lover.

Her head droops again. Jiri is quick. This time, he touches her arm. She smiles, assuring him with a grimace, it won't happen again.

The program proceeds, she realizes the die is cast. The seeds are sewn for a Communist takeover of Czechoslovakia after the war. Despite the idealistic words in some of the articles, such as "the principles of mutual respect for Czech independence and sovereignty," as well as "non-interference in the internal affairs of each other," the Czechs are obliged to collaborate with Moscow in every respect, including economic and military matters. "Parties will not engage or conclude any alliances and not take part in any coalition directed against the other…"

Tatiana is convinced that the Czechs, with their naïve trust of the Russians, have subordinated themselves to the Soviet Union by allowing Communist Party members living in the USSR during the war, to enter the cabinet in Prague after Germany surrenders.

Everyone stands and applauds, including Stalin and Benes and their top officials. The room is abuzz. Champaign toasts. Clicking of glasses. Circulating, Tatiana bumps into Anatoly and discreetly tells him that President Benes is pleased with the conversations he had with Stalin.

"Get some sleep; you look exhausted," Anatoly says with a straight face, though he doesn't hear her say, "I agree. I've got to get back to the hotel room and get to bed."

•

Chapter 25. Moscow, 1943.
BASYA AND MISCHA.
"A Night at the Bolshoi. Walking in Snowy Alleyways."

•

On the third night of their stay in Moscow, Tatiana and her fellow diplomats, except maybe President Benes, were not thinking of Soviet-Czech relations. They were on their way across Theater Square to the famous world theater, the Bolshoi, to see Rimski-Korsakov's opera, the Snow Maiden.

Walking across Theatre Square, they could see the Bolshoi was lit up from portico to portico.

"It's really exciting to be here," remarked Jiri to Tatiana. "The highlight of our trip, this cultural icon in the land of icons."

Finally seated and anxiously waiting for the curtain to go up, Tatiana scans the audience and as she does so, the lights flicker on and off. Right before her eyes, people get up from their seats and applaud madly. At first, she couldn't figure what was going on and then she realized, Comrade Stalin, unexpectedly, had entered the government box seats where President Benes had been welcomed earlier. Later, she would remember that during the intermission, the leaders would continue their discussions in one of the government lounges.

After the opera, the Czechs were thrilled by the performance. To continue the aura of entertainment and royalty, they eagerly return to the Metropol which they know sets the standard in its city for luxury and service. Its magnificent decor includes immense candelabras, oversized lights, heavy furniture, marble staircases, and red carpets. As guests, they enjoy the atmosphere of uniformed bellhops in the lobby and silver service in the restaurant, which includes a great circular pool with lights and rather proletarian-looking fishes. They have heard that the luxury décor was installed by the Soviet government to impress foreign dignitaries. Of course, the Kremlin added the secret police who come in search of loose-lipped Westerners or compromised Russians.

•

Amidst this opulence and the watchful eyes, Mischa and Basya make love in a room on an upper floor. Mischa didn't have to climb walls to see her. He didn't have to sneak into a house to hold her. He didn't have to meet her in a seedy hotel room. He just has Nikita escort him into the building through a delivery entrance, take an elevator by himself to the third floor, and walk past the empty chair of the key lady who was suddenly called away from her post minutes before Mischa arrives on the floor. He goes to Room 315 a prized room with its twenty-foot high ceilings, according to the hotel brochure. The brochure points out that onlookers can look out the room's tall window every November seventh and observe Red Army regiments march toward Red Square, on the anniversary of the Bolshevik Revolution. At the present moment, Mischa knocks three times, enters, and removes the monitoring device in the chandelier, as he had done the previous night. When he leaves Basya, he puts the listening device back on. The key lady again is not at her desk. Nikita makes sure of that.

•

"Basya, love," says Mischa in her room the night after the opera: "Why is the Party making us go through hoops to be together. It's not fair. The war is looking good for us. Our victory at Stalingrad earlier this year, the big tank victory at Kursk in July, and the soon-to-be American and British invasion of France, means we're going to crush the Germans."

She agrees. On her part, she tells Mischa that after the war, "we

Communists are going to implement our plan to subvert Czechoslovakia and bring it into our orbit."

Throughout the two days, neither of them really rail against the ignominies of the Stalin regime, while the war against Nazism is proceeding. "The only thing that matters now is the fight against the German fascists and victory," he stresses.

•

"For now, I'm going back with the exiled Czech government back to London, and then after the war, to Prague. You'll come to Czechoslovakia."

"Just like that."

"You got here. You're capable of doing anything. You're a planner if there ever was one. And to think you never even went to spy school."

"This time, it wasn't me. It was your friend, Anatoly, and my friend, Nikita."

"Well. Maybe. We learned there are people who will help us."

"You never know who can rat on you, however," he says convincingly. "Russia is a country of spies and secret agents and a nation that wallows in distrust."

"That's true."

•

That night, the two make a vow. They don't swear on a prayer book. He just gets down on one knee and proposes.

"Will you marry me?" he asks, and while he can't give her a ring, he gives her a locket he has carried around with him. It was his mother's.

"Yes." she says, her eyes gleaming as her smile widens. He could see excitement in those eyes.

"Our wedding will be after the war," he promises.

"Yes," she says again and embraces him.

"Now, thankfully, we have something permanent."

"I guess we're going to see a lot of each other."

"You're fixed in my heart now. It's sealed. We'll be together when I rise in the morning and go to sleep at night."

They embrace again.

At five in the morning. Mischa, ecstatic, leaves the Metropol. They're engaged.

Basya hangs up her dress, puts on her nightgown and crawls under the quilt covers. It's another winter night in Moscow.

•

No formal events are scheduled the next day. In the evening, Anatoly comes to the hotel and tells the hotel security guard at the front door that he'll be escorting Tatiana on a walk. He figures if he does that, they won't alert the state security guards. Anatoly has clearance to meet with foreigners at the Metropol or escort them outside.

Undaunted, he brings Tatiana to an artist's gallery on Arbat Street, about twenty minutes from the hotel.

"I'll say goodbye now. In ten minutes, you'll meet Mischa in front of that art supply store across the street."

For the next ten minutes, Tatiana walks up and down the street, darting into one store and going out the exit in the back. She is alert and can tell if the same person is appearing behind her more than once. There were few cars on the street and a vehicle never appeared twice. No alarm bells have gone off in her head; she's sure no one's following her. She goes back to where she's to meet Mischa. Greeting each other, Tatiana tells Mischa that Anatoly will pick him up at his aunt's apartment quarters at seven o'clock in the morning. Not a good idea for either Mischa or Anatoly to be seen together in and around the hotel.

Walking along the Arbat, Mischa and Basya spot a drunk banging on the hood of a parked car. It's obvious the two passengers sitting inside the vehicle are frightened.

"I should go over there and collar him," says Mischa angrily.

"That's all you need," remarks Basya. "Let's get out of here. Two policemen are approaching."

The couple walks several blocks away. This time, they enter a gallery.

"Drinking's a big problem in our country. It continues even in wartime. I stopped, but the country will never change," emphasizes Basya.

"Basya. It's our last night together until who knows when. Let's not talk about politics or serious matters. Let's talk about us, especially here, I might add, under a starry Moscow night."

Indeed, it was a beautiful Moscow evening, with the bright, silvery moon leading the way for this couple in what is usually war-darkened Moscow. They begin their walk back to the hotel. Everything is calm. Hand in hand, the two traverse the snowy streets. They don't talk much. It's as if there's no need to rehash how they are to prepare for the future.

But they do discuss Anatoly and how he helped make them happy. The only answer the couple could come up with regarding his aid was that he was a Russian romantic who liked Mischa and Basya, and with Nikita, had devised a plan allowing them to be together.

Nearing the hotel, Mischa whispers. "I'll never forget these few days." He hugs her.

And then come the final words - the end of any further meeting, the inevitable split.

"I can't go into the hotel and we shouldn't say goodbye in front of the security guards."

He plants a kiss on her inviting lips and whispers "I love you." She repeats the words.

Another long kiss.

"I'll be watching you until you get into the hotel. Okay?"

He walks with her to about a hundred feet of the building which is across the boulevard from where they're standing. They stop.

Throwing caution to the wind, they stand and kiss again. And then he turns and begins to walk away and every few seconds, looks over his shoulder to see if she's okay.

She's about to cross the boulevard when, from behind a snowbank, a disheveled man rushes her.

Mischa blinks. He can't believe it. A drunk is sidling up to her and attacking her. She's down. Mischa runs as he never ran before. His fiancé is being molested!

Basya struggles with the assailant and shouts for help.

The hotel guards see what's going on.

But Mischa is there first, and now he can see the drunk's face, sporting long, unkempt hair, a huge pug nose plastered on a face that resembles a boxer.

A very hard blow to the man's back of the neck, and the goon is down and out.

Mischa lifts her up.

"Go," she says, panting. "I'm okay. No incident. Please. You don't want to be seen or questioned. Go now. Get out of here," she demands, raising her voice.

He runs away and disappears from the scene. A few minutes later the hotel guards arrive.

"That soldier got away," one of the guards says. "Who was that soldier? Do you know him? We saw him accost the drunk."

"Never saw him before in my life. You saved me, Comrades. I am so grateful," she repeats. "You did it all. It's all over. Forget about it."

"We didn't do anything. That soldier did it."

"Well it doesn't matter. It's over now, officer." Then more sternly she says, "I am a Czech diplomat. We don't want an international incident, now do we?"

"You're right. I'll just tell my superior, Comrade Nikita Lebedev."

"Yes. Of course. You do that," she says, as she sees a hotel security car drive up, pick up the drunk and haul him away.

Having been told about an incident outside the hotel, Nikita comes over to console her. The incident in the police report will be buried in the files of hundreds of drunks attacking innocent people that night in wartime Moscow. There is no mention that the victim was a diplomat.

Getting on the elevator to her room, she thinks,

"Once again, Mischa saved my life. My protector."

•

"Thank goodness the plane is leaving in the morning," says Mischa, still hiding across the boulevard, under a tree. Knowing that Basya is in the hotel, he slinks back into the shadows and begins his walk to Aunt Nina's. His hand is swollen. He will have to ice it.

•

"I want to be invited to the wedding someday," says Anatoly to Mischa, the next morning as he drives Mischa to the military air base for his flight back to Vladivostok. As far as the NKVD knows he's in the port city. That's what the record says.

•

As for Mischa Rasputnis, he is beside himself with joy. On the flight across Siberia, he realizes that the euphoria might soon disappear. But things are more formal. Still, how is he going to get closer to Basya after the war? Will they reconnect again.? "What a life. I wonder if we will ever consummate our love," he says as the plane circles Vladivostok, the city on the moon.

•

Several days later, Tatiana spends the evening talking to Anatoly in the hotel's luxurious restaurant, the Boyarsky, with its elegant decor, vaulted ceilings, and dark red walls. As they toast, the vodka warms them. Their dinner consists of a bowl of black caviar, cabbage soup, steak, fried potatoes, cheese, and two bottles of wine.

Watching the water spouting up from the iconic fountain in the middle of the dining area, she briefs him on President Benes favorable conclusions regarding the meeting. "He told me, 'We came to a complete agreement about everything.'" Adding her perspective, she notes, "He got his two main objectives - restoration of the pre-war frontiers and expulsion of the minorities."

Tatiana also recounted the incident with the drunk.

"You're lucky," Anatoly says nervously as he checks the dining room.

"Without you and Nikita," she says, 'Mischa and I wouldn't have been together."

•

What Tatiana and Anatoly did not notice as they dined in the Boyarsky, was that on the other side of the room, sat Dimitri Abramovich Dudin, Mischa's comrade during the Civil War. Though he observes other foreign guests, he is fixated on this couple, so much so that he even gets up and walks past them to get a better look at the lady and catch her voice. Having survived the purges, he has gained a reputation of ferreting out numerous foreign envoys who act as spies. Reassigned to Moscow after a stint in China, he possesses a good memory. He can recall everyone from a past surveillance. Something about the woman attracts him. That high forehead. He stares at her; his eyes glued at the long face, all the time racking his brain. *Who is she and where did I see her?*

And then he remembers. *Basya. That was her name. Mischa's girlfriend. He kept showing me her picture in Yekaterinburg. He didn't just glance at the photo. He stared at it all the time. Maybe I'm on to something. What is she doing here? And why is she with Anatoly Abramov who's high up in the foreign office and has powerful connections in the NKVD?*

Dimitri waits until the couple leaves. He approaches the night manager, Nikita. Flashing his NKVD card, he asks: "Who's that stunning woman who had dinner with Minister Abramov?"

"She's a diplomat with the Czech delegation. Her name is Tatiana Kovacova."

•

Going to Lubyanka that very night, Dimitri, with access to the most secret files, discovers that Tatiana is in fact a Soviet spy. Buried deep in the file lies a memo that Tatiana, aka Basya Abramskaya, should not be in touch with Mischa Rasputnis or any ordinary citizen in order to protect her from being recognized as Russian and not a native Czech, as she pretends to be. She can be with a Soviet diplomat in London or a Soviet representative in any country. That's her job.

Dinner with Anatoly is correct, Dimitri realizes. What Dimitri didn't know was that Nikita had not reported the incident of the Red Army soldier and the drunk to the police, so Dimitri had no reason to believe that Mischa was in the capital. Stymied for the moment, he put the matter aside. Yet in the days ahead, he felt intuitively that Mischa had been around. *If he was, I would have nailed him. I'll catch him, yet,* he vows. *That argument I had with Mischa during that civil war still rankles me. He also could have helped me with my relationship with his sister, Klara, and he didn't.*

Boarding the aircraft next morning for the flight to London, Tatiana wonders if she and Mischa ever will be together. "Maybe with war's end. And when will that be?" she asks herself. "Who knows? Yet, every day that passes means it's a day closer to the end of the war," she adds as she looks down for the last time at the cupolas and golden domes of Moscow, not knowing that henceforth NKVD surveillance on her and Mischa will be increased as recommended by agent Dimitri Abramovich Dudin.

•

Chapter 26. London, 1945.
BASYA.
"The War Ends."

•

They had become engaged and that changed their lives. Mischa Rasputnis was no longer just Basya's boyfriend or lover. He was her fiancé.

In Moscow, she had inhaled the symbols of a wife-to-be: His profession of love, the crowning moment of his placing his mother's heirloom locket around her neck, and his saving her from a brutal attack by a drunkard. Those actions, symbolizing the love of her protector, turned her into a woman happily looking forward to being united in matrimony. Her fellow workers in the embassy caught on immediately.

"Tatiana, since Moscow, you're acting differently. You're smiling as before the war. Not so crabby."

"Maybe you met someone there. That's it. You found a beau?"

"Who's your Prince Charming now?"

"Thought you had an RAF lover? Did you dump him?"

The questions were endless. "Nonsense," she retorted angrily, thinking she had to squelch suspicions that she had met someone in Russia. She didn't need Czech security getting suspicious about her. She made sure she didn't give further encouragement to the rumors and the matter died down: "It must have been a one-night stand," her girlfriends thought. Which proved of course, that having been a diplomat for about twenty years or so, Tatiana knew a thing or two about masking true feelings. She was in love. But she didn't know how or when they would consummate the marriage. That was not up to her or Mischa. *War events would have to decide the outcome.*

Her first task was to break her relationship with Arno. How could she even think of going to bed with the Czech pilot now that she was engaged to Mischa. The problem, however, was he had become a source and she was a Soviet spy. *Easier said than done to get rid of him. He has no idea about Mischa and me. He's giving me good information on Czech attitudes in the armed forces toward the Soviet Union, as well as news of the Czech civilian population filtering to England. I have to keep....*

Changes came sooner than she expected regarding the pain of offering herself up to Arno.

•

A few weeks after her return from Moscow, Bill Randall, the landlord of Arno's hideaway flat was transferred to the day shift at the airfield and took back his apartment.

While Tatiana was in Russia, Arno lost a lot of money in card games with some American GI sharks. With limited funds, he was reluctant to spend more money on a hotel room, even if it was for a tryst with Tatiana. And then, coming back from a sortie over France to an airport in the south of England, the wheels on Arno's plane malfunctioned and his plane came in for a belly crash. They pulled him out before flames engulfed the aircraft, but he suffered a broken arm and leg and back injury. He was rushed to the hospital.

•

Several weeks after the accident, Basya traveled by bus to the hospital in Brighton on a Saturday morning to visit Arno. Her plan was to sleep over Saturday night in the nearby somnolent village's bed-and-breakfast. She'd return to London on Sunday evening. What started out as an every-weekend visit, morphed into every other weekend. On one occasion, he revealed what he knew about the forthcoming Allied landing in Normandy. She sent the information to the Center. She was still serving the Motherland.

Yet, she could tell that Arno sensed she wasn't as warm to him as before the trip to Russia. She had to keep her informer sexually happy. The curtains around each bed in his hospital room were drawn and his roommate in the other side of the room was so medicated that he was asleep most of the time. When the nurse left the room,

Basya kissed and hugged Arno and even put her hand under the blanket. He was so happy, he squelched the sounds of sexual satisfaction, so his mate in the other bed wouldn't hear him in case he was awake. Sometimes, she crawled under the covers with him and they did it quickly.

"As long as I'm in this business, I'll have to use my body," she rationalized. Unlike the dozen years ago when she first arrived in Czechoslovakia, however, she realized she had to try to stop what was still sleazy behavior. But how?

At the end of one visit, Arno reports new enhancements to the Spitfire fighter which she quickly transmits to Moscow. She's praised by the Center.

•

During the war, she and Arno felt no matter what they did, they wouldn't die. Nor did they fear death which always hovered over them. Who knew if their luck would hold?

Some days after the Allied landing in France on D-Day, June 6, 1944, Tatiana paid a visit to Arno. After she returned to her room that night, she heard a loud and hideous noise. Looking out the window, she sighted a burning aircraft flying low over the roof of the house. Another and another, all of them coming in low.

"Never saw anything like it," she exclaims to herself. "They're all flying in the same direction, at the same height, the same hideous racket - and all toward London. My goodness, Hitler is firing rockets at Britain."

The next day, reading about the missiles in the newspaper, Tatiana notices that one writer comments, "Hitler's malevolent flying bombs are aptly named 'doodle-bugs.' The V1 rockets are being launched in formidable numbers without respite and with the object of causing infinite disaster to London, as well as serious damage to the morale of the civilian population." The article describes the robot bomb as a rocket with a 20-ft-wide wingspan, 15-ft.-long, weighing two tons and going four hundred miles an hour. It was hard to defend.

•

Later that month, Basya and a fellow Embassy worker, Adela, attend a nearby cinema. A break from the dark chilling air of gloom caused by the rockets.

After the movie, the two head back to the Embassy.

"I can hear one of those buzz bombs even if it is ten miles away. I just pray it doesn't cut out and fall on me," Adela tells Tatiana, adding:

"Please let them go farther and fall on somebody else. I know that sounds terrible. But I don't want it to happen to me. It's like seeing a big rat poised to leap on you. You're horrified. All you can do is pray."

Seconds later, Adela mutters. "By George! There's one out there now. I hear it coming."

"Better start praying," Tatiana says coldly.

"That woman must have ice water in her veins," thinks Adela. Grabbing Tatiana's sleeve, she yells, "Here we go again."

Tatiana's friend's bulging eyes frighten her. "Each Londoner has a bomb marked for them," she thinks stoically. "I just don't want to meet mine," she adds, staring up at the sky and trying not to imagine chaos, pain, and death.

"Let's get to the Embassy. There's an underground shelter. We can make it," declares Adela, in a panicky voice. "Oh my God. Look back there. I can see a couple heading toward us. Tatiana, one can drop down any second. Duck."

"Not yet," answers Tatiana. "The noise of the buzz bomb hasn't quit. When that happens, we'll have twelve seconds to take cover. Get closer to the building."

"I hear the sputtering roar. It's closer," cries Adela.

The noise cuts out. Adela screams.

"Get in that doorway over there," yells Tatiana, knowing it's going to explode on impact with the ground. She grabs the girl by the arm and pushes her into the building entrance. They automatically duck down on the floor. That's when they hear a loud explosion and the shattering of stones and bricks. Soon the dust and smoke clears. Coming outside moments later, they see that the rocket lifted the nearby building off its foundations into a heap of stones.

Silence in the street.

"That was close," Tatiana says to a stunned Adela.

Suddenly, they hear a few more explosions further down the way.

"The Embassy! the Embassy!" Tatiana shouts. "I hope those bastards didn't hit it."

They wait a few minutes and then begin running. In fifteen minutes, they spot yet another site of partial rubble and smoke, caused by the pilotless airplanes. They stare at the extensively damaged Embassy building. Firemen and civil defense workers are looking for survivors in a cavity formed by a large pile of broken bricks and wooden planks.

A staff member comes over and tells them fortunately nobody was inside. "We believe we all got to a shelter in time. Thank God."

•

"Somebody is protecting me," thinks Tatiana. *"Not Mischa. He's too far away. Luck."* Unlike her fiancé, however, she doesn't even think that maybe, it's God.

•

Meanwhile, Arno healed and was transferred to an Allied base in France. She kept up the love affair by mail, writing and receiving romantic notes. She dismissed any thoughts of the romance they had before she went to Moscow.

Tatiana's work becomes easier. Russia stands alongside Britain and the United States in the war against Hitler. As a result, many consider it patriotic to praise the Soviet Union, and unwittingly, advance the cause of Communism.

Finally, the worst war in human history draws to a close. Londoners began to spruce up their public housing, private homes, and shop fronts. Soon, her everyday vision of London's bridges, spires, and towers, the crowded streets, will disappear and she'll be gone.

"Victory in Europe Day" arrives on May 8, 1945. A day later, the Red Army enters Prague. On May 10th, Tatiana returns to Czechoslovakia with the government-in-exile.

A week earlier, Arno had sent her a note that he is scheduled to go back to Brighton for a final medical exam and then fly directly to Prague to help re-establish the Czech air force. "Will meet you in Prague," he wrote. "Can't wait."

But Arno never shows up in Prague. Inquiries back to the Czech Embassy in London, are for naught. One day, word comes that Arno Novak signed on with a foreign domestic airline. They don't know, however, which one or for what country. There is no evidence of foul play.

She can't believe he would leave her without saying a word. But, as far as she is concerned, ever since she reunited with Mischa in Moscow, her affair with Arno ended. He's long gone from her mind. It's all so humorous. *We both agreed we're not in a permanent relationship. Nevertheless, the bastard didn't even say goodbye. I feel jilted. I guess that's human.*

And then a minute later she catches herself.

What was I thinking? I should be happy as hell. I'm free of him. My thoughts should be only on Mischa. Oh, if I could only communicate with him.

•

Meanwhile, thousands of miles away, on the other side of the moon, nearly two years after he saw Basya in Moscow in 1943, Mischa Rasputnis sits on a bench in a quiet spot high up on the mountain overlooking Vladivostok. Blocking out everything around him, he realizes that unlike millions of his fellow citizens, he survived the war unscathed, because he worked in the non-combat zone of Siberia. He only engaged in battle during the last Soviet campaign of World War II, when the Red Army overran the Japanese army in Manchuria in a fifteen-day war in August, 1945. He stayed on in Manchuria to help remove a huge amount of Japanese war booty and turn it over to the Chinese Communists who already were fighting Chiang-Kai-shek's Nationalists.

After Moscow, I'm sure, as in the past, war drives the narrative of my and Basya's volatile life. As long as they won't allow me to be with her, they've got me by the balls. For our sake, once again, he pauses, *I've got to get out of this city at the edge of the world. I can't do my work. I smoke a lot. I drink more. I walk slower. I overwork. I stay late at the office.*

He jumps up: *"No. Not me, comrades,"* he shouts, knowing no-one can hear him. He gets into his American-made jeep, part of the U.S. war aid to Russia, and quickly drives down the hill to his office in the port. Picking up official stationary, he applies for a transfer, and sends the request via diplomatic pouch to Moscow.

I'm stuck on the moon. Please bring me back down to earth.

Two weeks later, his transfer papers arrive. He knows it's a reassignment by the brown envelope. Opening it, he can't believe what he sees. Since there's no one in the office, he mumbles out loud: "There must be some mistake. Are they out of their minds? Why would they send a Jew there? He'll be prejudiced. Makes no sense, though it's closer to Prague and my loved one."

Again, he looks at the document dated November, 15, 1945. The words are the same.

"Report to Moscow Institute of Languages for a combined foreign office study-language program in Hebrew to prepare you for your eventual assignment in PALESTINE."

•

While Mischa is preparing to relocate in 1945, Basya remains ensconced in the foreign office in Prague working with pro-Red labor leaders and police officials to help the Communist Party infiltrate the democratic elected government of Czechoslovakia. She watches the Communist takeover of East European nations: Poland, Hungary, East Germany, Bulgaria, Romania - all totally under the Kremlin's control. Democratic Czechoslovakia will be next.

•

Then, she suffers a personal loss. The Soviet Embassy in Prague receives word of her parents' deaths, and secretly informs her. They died in a Nazi roundup and were shot as hostages for a guerrilla attack on a German army barracks. When Basya left them in 1927, she used a cover story of going to Australia. They didn't believe her. Devastated, she mourns their loss.

"I'll avenge them," she repeats over and over again. "Just as I avenged my daughter's life and relatives on the Whites." Interestingly, her vengeance will be meted out in an unbelievable way. She'll help the Jewish people restore their homeland in Palestine.

•

One day at the end of November, 1947, just about the same time that the United Nations General Assembly calls for the partition of Palestine into Arab and Jewish states, Tatiana is summoned to the deputy foreign minister, Vladimir Clementis' office.

"Please take this top-secret dossier to the anteroom. Study it. Read it carefully. Do not photograph or copy any page. Do not take any notes. Commit everything to memory. This may come as a shock to you, but we're giving you a new assignment," says Clementis. "You'll be working on an arms agreement which we're planning to enter into with the Jews in Palestine. In a few months, you'll be going to Tel Aviv to supervise our arms shipments to the Jews which will bring in needed-millions of U.S. dollars to our treasury. Your job will be to liaise with Haganah, the Jews' underground defense army in the British Mandate, soon to be its official army. Our arms must be delivered without a problem."

Clementis hands her the dossier marked, *"Top Secret,"* and bears the title, *"Selling Weapons to the Jews in Palestine."* Reading the dossier, she gets the point: "Czechoslovakia, with Stalin's approval, supports a Jewish state in Palestine in its struggle with the Arabs, though it opposes Zionism. The USSR agrees to supply arms to the Jews because it seeks to remove the British in the Middle East and end its stay there, thus leaving a vacuum which we will enter."

I have a big job ahead of me, a thought which prompts Basya to think, Maybe being in Palestine will bring me closer to Mischa. Since Moscow, where we became engaged, the longing for something we both couldn't ever have, is over. *Maybe now it's reachable. Mischa, help me. I love you, and you love me. We'll find a way.*

She could not know when she left for Palestine in early 1948, that her lover, Mischa Rasputnis, was already there, having arrived in the late spring of 1947. Both their lives would change dramatically.

•

Chapter 27. Tel Aviv, 1948.
BASYA.
"Tatiana works with Haganah.
Supervises Czech Arms Delivery."

•

Several months later, Tatiana Kovacova boards the famed Orient Express in Paris for the three-thousand-mile-journey to Tel Aviv, translated from the Hebrew as, "Hill of Spring." The thundering train races through the Balkans to Istanbul, with a change-over in Konya and then by boat to Aleppo and Beirut. She arrives in Tel Aviv where she inhales the smells of the fresh sea which inspires her to harness every ounce of determination and ability to make sure the arms transfer goes well. She has no idea Mischa is in the same small country she now inhabits.

•

Tatiana finds a studio apartment in Geula Street, just off Allenby Road, near the Czech mission in the bustling all-Jewish city of Tel Aviv. It is next to the ancient port of Jaffa on the Mediterranean coastline. She contacts members of Haganah. She knows very little Hebrew, but many in the city, because of the presence of the British who hold a League of Nations mandate over Palestine, speak English. At the same time, she's in touch with Prague and can send reports back via a diplomatic pouch in the Czech mission. However, she prefers to work secretly behind the scenes, away from her fellow diplomats, most of whom are not told she's in the country.

She has installed a short-wave radio in her bedroom closet. She can send and receive coded messages to the Moscow Center via her radio transmitter. She also can use old-fashioned techniques, such as sending letters by mail to Moscow with a few pages in invisible ink.

At first, Tatiana does not take to her new city. Even a Communist can get accustomed to a more elegant life-style in cities like Prague and London, despite post-war austerity. She doesn't mind living alone; she has done so all her life. But she misses Prague's fairy tale beauty. None of this compensates for her spacious, well-furnished apartment near the Moldau.

One night in early March, 1948, Tatiana is listening to the underground Haganah radio station, *Kol HaHaganah,* (the Voice of Haganah), broadcasting from Tel Aviv. She hears the newscaster report how the Communist Party in Prague used intrigue and deception in taking over Czechoslovakia.

The broadcast continues:

"Many observers believe," according to the announcer, "the Reds yesterday murdered the architect of aid to Israel, Foreign Minister Jan Masaryk."

The news erupts all over the world into one of the most momentous events in post-war Europe. It triggers one of the most notorious and unsolved political assassinations of the twentieth century - unsolved because even decades later, no one could be sure whether the death of Jan Masaryk was murder or suicide.

At sunrise, on the morning of March 10, according to news reports, Masaryk's body, clad in blue silk pajamas, was found lying spread-eagled in the courtyard of the Ministry of Foreign Affair, just below his apartment bathroom window three stories up. The Czech government told the nation he committed suicide. Even a close confidante insisted he had killed himself.

Most Czechs, however, believed he was murdered by the Communists and their Russian allies through defenestration,- the action of throwing someone out of a window.- a centuries-old Prague style of execution. Others felt he committed suicide in protest of the Communist takeover, or because many of his friends turned on him for giving in and joining the Communist government which had just seized the country.

When she hears the news, Tatiana stands outside on her balcony, looks out at the sea. Tears come to her eyes. *That good, decent man was a father figure to me.*

That night, she cries herself to sleep. In the morning, she goes over to the Czech mission, which she has rarely entered since her arrival in the country a month ago. Mourners, mourners and more mourners - survivors of the Holocaust, Czechs natives, children of

Czech parents, arrive at the building. One by one, they pile into the
mission and sign the memory book. She writes: "I loved him. May
he rest in peace and his memory be a blessing. Basya Abramskaya."

Walking home, she realizes the death of Masaryk confirms her
suspicions regarding the Party: *"The Center has thwarted my being with
my love. It signed a pact with Hitler. It deported Sonya. It killed Masaryk.
I have to cut the umbilical cord. Enough. Oh, if only Mischa were here."*

The next morning, Wednesday, March 31, 1948, dawns as a cool,
cloudy morning. Skies are a mixture of dull, blue and white. There
is no sun. Tatiana awakens to loud knocks on her door. Opening it
reveals a young man, his face crowned with reddish brown hair and
brown eyes, his face sporting a handlebar-moustache. He's dressed
in blue overalls and a short sleeve blue shirt.

"I'm Isaac," he says. "Please come with me. We're starting
"Operation Balak." A short while later, he leads her outside. After
helping her into the front of his pickup truck, he gets in and guides
the vehicle to the outskirts of Tel Aviv. Proceeding south onto the
coastal road, he drives south, for an hour until he reaches a secret
landing spot, which turns out to be a makeshift airfield at the village
of Beit Daras, located twenty miles northeast of Gaza. For centuries,
the village served as a part of a mail route from Cairo to Damascus.
A shipment of Czech arms is to arrive at that airstrip that night.

Tatiana doesn't know Hebrew, but Isaac speaks English and Slovak.
He learned English from the British and Czech from his parents who
were from Bratislava. Growing up as Zionists, his mother and father
came to Palestine to help build the Jewish homeland. Tatiana's quiet
the whole time as he tells her that as a kibbutznik, (member of a
kibbutz, collective farm), he and his friends are fighting for the land
itself. He's proud he's a farmer - farmers know the value of their
nation's soil.

Tatiana's job is to check the inventory and make sure that the arms
transfer goes well. Czech arms are Israel's only source of weaponry,
as the United States had cut off supplying weapons to the region last
year. She's worried the British might discover the location and seize
the shipment. She knows the plane took off earlier in the day from
Europe. Before its arrival, Arab guards were silenced and crude oil
torches were brought to outline the runway. The flight is part of
the Israeli Operation Balak, the code name taken from the Biblical
story, referencing Numbers 22.2 in which Moabite King Balak, son
of Tsippor, (which means bird), was dissuaded from attacking the

Israelites by the prophet Balaam. Darkness makes it perfect for a secret landing on the narrow runway.

Haganah men wait impatiently alongside the airfield for their lifeline from the sky. Finally hearing the hum of aircraft engines, they fire the oil on the torches creating a path for the incoming American cargo plane coming in off the sea.

"My God, all that work. I hope we make it," she says to herself. At that every moment, the heavy drone of an airplane is heard. Descending, the plane touches down on the miserly runway and comes to a halt.

Amazed, she watches young Army lads, mere teens, dart out to the plane's door and begin unloading two hundred rifles, forty MG-thirty-four machine guns and one-hundred-fifty thousand bullets, and place them on trucks. The operation takes eighty minutes. Everyone smiles. Another arms shipment by sea later that month proves decisive. David Ben-Gurion, Israel's first prime minister, soon declares, "Without these weapons, we wouldn't have survived the war."

Driving back to Tel Aviv, their vehicle is stopped at a British checkpoint. A soldier peers through the car window and asks for their documents. Receiving them, he notices that Tatiana is Czech, and says, "What're you doing with this kike. Hitler should've killed them all."

Tatiana snaps. She gets out of the car, walks up to the soldier, and slaps his face. He's about to hit her back, but stops when she flashes before him the page in her passport that shows her diplomat status. "I'm a Jew, too," she adds. "Now if you don't get out of the way, I'll..."

Smarting from her blow, the guard says: "Get the hell out of here." He waves them on.

"I didn't know you were Jewish," says Isaac.

"I'm not," she lies."

"Then, why....?"

"Shh. Please don't say anything more."

•

PART 3
"Reunited Forever."

Chapter 28. Tel Aviv, 1948.
MISCHA AND BASYA.
"Basya and Mischa are Reunited Again."

•

**No sooner had the devastating World War II ended in 1945,
when a new undeclared, cold war erupted between the Soviet
Union and the United States, a war that launched the world
into a state of terror, technological advancement, and made
Mischa and Basya Russian warriors in espionage. The political
rivalry and tension between the two superpowers, known
as The Cold War, involved their respective allies, members
either of western or eastern blocs. Each side sought to gain
dominance over newly independent states, at first in Europe,
and then Africa and Asia, including Palestine and China.**

•

Wwhat chance meeting, task, or opportunity could cause Mischa
and Basya to meet in the same small country? Would they pick
up the relationship as if it was yesterday in Moscow when he last held
her in his arms and they agreed to get married.

Would it be God's will or destiny?

•

On a warm, June afternoon in 1948, as the new state of Israel fights
for its survival against seven invading Arab armies from as far away
as Iraq, a Kremlin diplomat, a covert Russian intelligence operative,
sits in a seaside café in Tel Aviv, sipping Turkish coffee. Even if Mischa
Rasputnis never forgot that he was Jewish, which he didn't, he realized
he can't pick up a gun and help defend the Jewish homeland like he
would like.

•

Mischa had been assigned to the Soviet mission in Jerusalem upon
arrival in Palestine, in May 1947. Good fortune looked down on him
shortly afterwards, when he discovered that his long-lost daughter,
whom he had given up for adoption shortly after she was born during
the Russian civil war, was living in Tel Aviv with her husband, Volya,
and two children. Despite the guilt and the bitterness built up over
the years, father and daughter had met and had begun healing the
deep wounds of separation which the Center in Moscow was aware of

and had not lifted a finger to stop. In fact, the foreign office approved this relationship. It would be good for Mischa to have a family in Palestine.

In early 1948, Mischa had moved to Tel Aviv because of heavy fighting in the holy city. He took a two-room apartment in the Keter Dan Hotel, though it was unusual for a member of the Russian mission to have quarters outside the official rezidentura of the Soviet diplomatic corps. But in the month of June that year, the Soviet embassy did not exist, so Mischa conducts consular business from 10 am to 12 noon, and from 2 pm to 4 pm in one of the rooms of his two-room hotel suite. The other room serves as his bedroom. For now, Mischa is the top Soviet diplomat in the city. This will change when the Soviet ambassador and staff arrive in Tel Aviv, the war-time capital of about 200,000 residents.

Meanwhile, the title, People's Commissar, has been dropped for the designation, Minister, a title which had not yet come through for Mischa. He remained unaware that Basya Abramskaya, the love of his life, walks the same city streets. Stationed in Israel for over a year, he's still consumed by thoughts of the woman he has not seen since they became engaged in Moscow five years ago, as she was in London and then Prague and he was languishing thousands of miles away in Vladivostok. And the intelligence services ban on their contacting each other was still in effect. Even with this prohibition, he's reminded of her by unintentional remarks of fellow diplomats. Not intended for him personally, his colleagues' innocent comments sting nevertheless. It often happens to those who have lost or have been torn away from a loved one - a mention of a certain city, a book, a song, a photo.

What causes Mischa deep pause is someone simply mentioning Prague or London. That sets him off. So, when an aide in the foreign office urges Mischa to keep an eye on Czechoslovak diplomats and advisors in Tel Aviv and to double check that the Soviet-backed Czech arms shipments are getting through to the Israelis, he listens. And when the same Kremlin spokesperson informs Mischa that an intelligence briefing at the Czech mission will be held on June 15 regarding the Czech arms deal for Israel and encourages Mischa to attend, he jumps at the opportunity and records the date in his diary. He writes a note to the Czech mission that he'll be present at the meeting and to please add him to the guest list.

Just by being in the Czech mission, I'll be closer to Basya. Who knows, she

*might even be here in Israel. What an insane thought. It's such a small country,
I'd have heard of her or bumped into her already. If she's here, she might show up
at the meeting. The Czechs are dealing with the Israelis on our behalf.*

Throughout their quixotic relationship, everything had been
so secret. The pair rarely flouted the rules. Both of them had
excellent records in their espionage work and Czechoslovakia was
no longer independent - it was a Communist satellite. About this
time, the Center felt the couple could now collaborate. A Cold War
exists between the U.S. and the USSR and the Kremlin needs all its
intelligence resources it can get. The problem is that the Center did
not inform Mischa or Basya that they were lifting restrictions against
them seeing each other.

●

Despite his misgivings that nothing he didn't know already would
come out of the briefing, Mischa was excited to have an official excuse
for going to the Czech mission. He could work the crowd and maybe,
just maybe, hear about Basya. Like many single, middle-aged men,
he realized that, though he was set in his ways, time was running out
regarding marriage. *It's 1948 and I'm almost fifty. Even though we're
engaged, I could end up a bachelor.*

He gets up from the table, pays the bill, and begins walking toward
the Czech mission. He needs something else to focus on and once
again his thoughts of Basya remind him of the obstacle that has kept
them apart - the Party.

Thoughts of his life in the Party rankled him.

*To think I've been a zealot all my life for Communism. I believed I was a
builder of socialism. But the Party is not always right. Did not Stalin make
a pact with Hitler?*

He stops for a moment to look in the window of a popular book
store. But he doesn't linger. He has always been punctual. He
continues walking and thinking about Stalin:

*What about the disasters of the first months of the war? Our army was
poorly equipped, only partially mobilized and generally unprepared. Many
saw the German attack coming, except Stalin. We lost millions because of
his blunders. Yes, we finally won the Great Patriotic War. However, purges,
including new ones against the Jews, are resurfacing. Always the Jews."*

These thoughts lead him to his personal life. *The Party - the one
measure of my whole life - has failed me. Something changed. I can't lead a
life with my loved one. The Party has ruined our relationship.*

As the thought ran through his mind, he was startled and stopped in his tracks right there on busy Baron de Rothschild Boulevard. He had a determined look on his face.

I've made up my mind. I know what I have to do. Break away. Disassociate myself from…I can't even say that word, I have to….. One thing for sure, I can't do anything until I'm reunited with Basya,

He picks up his walking pace and heads toward the meeting, happy at least that he is now free of doubts.

•

Entering the hall in the Czech mission, he sits in the back row. The Center doesn't want him to give the impression that the Russians are involved in supplying arms to Jews, though the Kremlin approved the sale. The meeting has been designated as an East European briefing, superfluous for the foreign office which is aware of every action of Communist satellites. But it's best to go through the motions, the satellite nations' diplomats will feel important.

As the group awaits the opening of the meeting, Mischa spots an issue of the English-language newspaper, the Jerusalem Post, resting on a nearby chair. Since no one's reading the paper and there's time to kill, he picks it up and notes that Israelis are fighting off the Arab invaders. He's so engrossed in the article that he fails to see that time has gone by quickly, and that the main speaker has not come out to speak

"Late already," he concludes as he impatiently checks his watch. "Maybe I should go. I'll give it ten more minutes."

And where is the speaker? An aide comes out and tells the restless audience that the person giving the arms-deal report has been in the field all day checking on a clandestine shipment. "The work goes on," says aide, Mira Dmitrievna Brezovskaya. "Our speaker has just arrived. We'll start soon."

Mira returns to the waiting room of the guest speaker.

"Comrade Tatiana Kovacova. Would you like to see the invitation list?"

"Sure. Maybe I know some of them," she says, lifting up her tea cup, taking a sip and putting it down as she reads the guest list. She starts at the top of the page: "Afrim Ajeti from Albania; Nandor Kovacs, from Hungary; Jan Wojcik, Poland," and then, a name on the list almost blinds her. She blinks twice: "Mischa Rasputnis, USSR."

"Oh, my God," Tatiana says in a loud voice.

Shocked that a Communist leader invokes the name of God, Mira notices that Tatiana has closed her eyes and is holding her hands together and upright. She is smiling and getting excited, so much so that she knocks over the tea cup sending it crashing to the floor. The hot liquid pours over the paper with the list of names, causing the handwritten ink to begin to wash away, including the one that obviously is a problem for her.

"Sorry. I can't believe I did that," says Tatiana, picking up a piece of the broken cup and a napkin to soak up the water. She flashes a smile, which causes Mira to think, *"if you are so shook up that you spilled a cup of tea, why are you smiling?"*

"No problem, Comrade. I'll clean it up," says Mira. "You didn't spill it on your dress, so don't worry." Studying her, she adds, "Did you see someone on the list who shouldn't be here. If so, I'll have the person removed."

"No. No. It's okay," Tatiana stammers, inhaling and exhaling somewhat more than normal.

She doesn't tell Mira, but she hasn't felt this way since the day Mischa Rasputnis met her in Moscow.

"He's in the audience. Unbelievable," she repeats to herself, and as she does so, she becomes frightened, realizing that she can't show such a crowd of top officials that she knows him. These Communists, unlike her lower status delegation from Czechoslovakia, are higher up, some even secret police personnel. The Center warned her about contacting friends or relatives, which she occasionally disregarded. She's sure he'll react when he sees her. *No way can I let him be shocked when I walk out in front of the audience. Someone will notice his facial expression or even loud sounds. They'll be suspicious.*

Although Tatiana barely knows Mira, she feels she has to take a chance to get a message to Mischa that she, Basya, is here, so he won't react in a compromising way.

"Comrade Mira, I need your help."

"Of course, Comrade Tatiana, what can I do for you?"

"I want you to deliver a note for me, a private note, to one of our fellow diplomats in the meeting room, if he's actually there. He's on the list."

"Sure. To whom?"

"To Mischa Rasputnis," she utters in a raspy voice, barely getting out the name.

"Mischa Rasputnis," says Mira, somewhat astonished. "You know him?"

"Yes," she says with a faraway look. "We were once on a mission together."

A woman knows when another woman speaks about a lover. Their eyes glisten, a smile comes over their face, and their voice cracks. Mira is sure Tatiana has a lover in the audience and it's Mischa Rasputnis.

"Do you have a pen and paper?" asks Tatiana.

"Yes. I'll bring it."

After Mira returns, Tatiana writes a message, seals the envelope and hands it over. "Please," says Tatiana. "Get this message to Comrade Rasputnis before I speak. Ask for a reply."

"Sure," says Mira, a better actor at hiding emotion. She knows there's more to this story.

"Mira, do you know him?"

"I've seen him around the mission."

Tatiana hands the message to Mira who can't break the envelope's seal, but will watch the face of the recipient, as he opens it and reads the note.

"Comrade Rasputnis. Our speaker wants me to hand you this note. I need a reply," says Mira.

"Of course," answers Mischa, not suspecting anything amiss.

Mischa opens the letter and reads.

"Please try not to react to this as you read on. Definitely not in front of Mira. It's me. Basya. Please, don't come over to me and say anything. Tomorrow, meet me at the Brooklyn Ice Cream Bar. On Dizengoff, at four o'clock in the afternoon. Come alone. Not one word to Mira or anyone. Destroy this note as soon as possible. I love you, Basya."

Too late. Even though he was trained to mask his feelings with a diplomatic smile or frown, he can't control his emotions after he reads the letter from the very person he has longed to see and hold again in his arms. He smiles. *She wrote, 'I love you.'*

No, he doesn't look around the room for her. Finally, he looks at Mira with a straight face. He wonders if Mira has caught on? He's sure she has.

"Tell Comrade Kovacova, I agree. Thanks for bringing me the note," he stays to Mira and folding the paper, he puts it into his side pants pocket. "Also, tell the comrade speaker I appreciate the message." and with that, he turns away.

Meanwhile, back in the waiting room, Tatiana paces the floor. Doubt. Maybe she shouldn't have sent the letter. No, it was the right thing to do. She doesn't know what she would have done had she spotted him from the lecture podium. *What would he'd have done if he hadn't received the note? Stand up and wave from the audience? Walk up to me? Run to my side? Chances are he wouldn't have blown our cover. But I can't rely on conjecture now, can I?*

Tatiana walks out onto the stage. At first, she doesn't see him. She purposely wants to avoid eye contact, but she can't help it. She smiles at the warm welcome. The audience claps and she claps back in the Russian way, and that gives her reason to scan the room until their eyes meet. It's as if she had just seen him yesterday.

Mischa believes that that first glance of a person is the one that counts to the onlooker regarding the future of the relationship. No exception here. "She's beautiful, her face, her smile, just as she was in Moscow; a bit more mature, mind you," he says to himself, avoiding using the word, 'age.' "She hasn't changed much in five years. She still has that youthful figure," he notes as he scans her curvaceous body.

In the next hour, he studiously avoids making eye contact with her. He's all ears. Actually, he sits in disbelief. He never thought of her giving a speech. The young woman he knew as Basya Abramskaya, stands before him as an articulate, polished and urbane senior Czechoslovak diplomat explaining the Communist bloc's attempt to plant satellite 'republics' in the Middle East, a theater of the Cold War.

The lecture continues.

"Regarding the Czechs and the arms to the Jews," she explains, "we crave foreign currency. The Jews are good customers, and they pay in badly needed U.S. dollars. We guarantee the supply, spare parts, and know-how, as well as a speedy delivery. Don't think we're not charging high prices for these arms. We are. They're willing to pay, because the guns and planes are essential to their survival. Our supplies to them will enable them to win the war."

He has to be careful. No eye-contact. No approaching her. Wait. He already knew most of what she said. Afterwards at the reception, he mingled with the audience, stealing some quick looks at her, and at the same time avoiding her.

On her part, she pleads with her frightened eyes: "Don't come close!"

He submits. But he learned, oh so long ago, how to make a dead drop. He takes out his notebook and writes on a page, "See you soon. Love you, too."

On his way out, he surreptitiously hands it to her.

He walks back to the hotel, taking a short detour to the Brooklyn Ice Cream Bar. He wants to view the location of tomorrow's rendezvous. He knows he'll have a hard time sleeping that night. Yet, even in the midst of darkness, he's excited and yearns for the morning when he can finally see her. He's happy.

•

The next day, Mischa leaves his room early. He has to make sure he's not being followed. He tries a few evasive tricks, like jumping on a Number 4 bus for a few blocks. Descending, he stops at a kiosk, drinks a soda, ducks into a café, and then darts out the back door. He doesn't think he's being tailed, so he enters a nearby hotel and makes a reservation for the night.

Naturally, he arrives at the American-run, ice cream establishment ahead of time. He hangs around the periphery of the serving window which even in the afternoon draws a crowd.

Then he sees her.

Their eyes meet. Smiling, he holds back his joyous tears.

"I wondered if I'd ever see you again. Let's find a place where we can talk?" He also really wants to say, "I rented a hotel room." But it doesn't sound right. His mind flashes back to when this love affair started at the Odessa railroad station.

After sitting down, Basya surprises him. "We should move to another café."

"Why the mystery?"

"The world knows me as a Czech diplomat," she says, emphasizing the word 'Czech.' "I might have been followed. We have to keep this meeting secret."

But they don't get up. They don't talk. They don't hold hands. They don't hug. They don't kiss. Each think, *I could get a bullet to the back of the head for this.*

After a few minutes, the reunited couple look at each other with glowing eyes.

"The hell with protocol," he says emotionally. "Forget another café."

"Let's go," she says.

They walk quickly down the dark street, kissing as if each kiss is the last on earth.

Ten minutes later, they open the door to the hotel room.

In minutes, each is spent from hurried sex. They didn't even take time to shut the lights.

"I never stopped loving you."

"Me, too," she answers smiling. "I guess you missed me?

"Kiss me."

He kisses her again.

Between the times they took each other, they related various escapades.

Suddenly, a change. Silent worried eyes.

"What is it?" she asks.

"Let's defect," he whispers so quietly, she barely hears him.

After he repeats it, she shudders. "Are you crazy? Impossible. You know what will happen if you're caught. The reach of the NKVD is long. They never let you out. They'll be after you the rest of your life."

"Nothing's impossible," he says, but gives her a sign with his eyes as if he's casing the room by moving his head up and down and sideways. She gets the signal to desist from talking about this. The room could be bugged. He then reaches for a bottle of vodka he obtained from the night clerk. Sitting on the edge of the bed, each raise a shot glass.

" За твоё здоровье! To your health! To us," he says, smiling.

She smiles back.

He points to his lips and silently mouths two new words: "To freedom!"

Staring at each other, they realize they're ideological turncoats. No longer torn from each other by Party loyalty nor bound by its decisions. It's now all about them. If only they can bring it about. If they fail, they're dead.

"We shouldn't meet for several weeks. I'll contact you," she says, quietly. Final exchanges of 'I love you' a final embrace, and Basya Abramskaya leaves the hotel, Mischa Rasputnis departs ten minutes later.

•

Chapter 29. Tel Aviv, 1948.
MISCHA AND BASYA.
"Basya and Mischa Question the Party."

•

"…and suddenly everything became clear to him," attributed to a story by Anton Chekhov.

•

Finally, official word comes from Moscow Center that Mischa and Basya can be together. Since they are stationed in Israel, they can work side-by-side, so to speak. The instruction is music to their ears.

In the following days, Mischa walks around in a daze; Basya's name on his lips. He relates to her, whether working or daydreaming. He's like the teenager he was back in Odessa when he first met her. She causes him to hum Russian love songs. She puts a smile on his face. She's responsible for the lift in his gait. She gives him energy and determination to rise in the morning and face the world. Living in the same city, the two develop a stronger relationship, stronger than the sex that had served as an anchor for their staying together during those long years of separation. Now that they can be together, they frequent cafes and movie houses.

•

On a Sunday morning in June, a work day in Israel, they meet in a seafront café on the Tel Aviv beachfront.

The café employee notices that the couple seems to be in a dream of their own. They sip their coffee served up to them by a waitress at the Keter Dan Hotel cafe located at the intersection of Hayarkon and David Frischmann streets. The four-story hotel sits comfortably along the palm tree laden beachfront drive, named for the small river, Hayarkon, located in the north of the city.

"I'm glad I'm here and not in Jerusalem," Basya says. "At least in Tel Aviv, some buses run and some cafes and stores are open on the Sabbath," Basya tells Mischa after the waitress leaves.

"We're lucky, Basya. I'm not sure if I believe in God, so it must be fate. I shouldn't even be here." he utters, telling her that two months ago Moscow had ordered him back to Russia in the middle of May. "I already boarded the damn ship to Odessa. But for no fault of mine…"

She cuts him off.

"What happened? Why would they do that, especially when you

agreed to depart?"

"You know better than to ask why the Center acts as it does," he replies by way of explanation, somewhat harshly, but not directed at her.

"The Party unwittingly saved me from death by its impulsiveness. That terrible day, for instance, the twentieth of May, was the day I was to return to Moscow and possibly face death in the new Stalin purges." He pauses to contain his emotions. "On that very same day, my daughter, Klara, whom I was reunited with just a year ago here in Israel, was killed during an Egyptian bomb attack in Tel Aviv. I was there when it happened. May she rest in peace."

Again, he pauses. "I couldn't even go to the funeral. I had no choice but to return to Russia with Igor, my assistant, as ordered. But then Moscow realized at the last minute that they had made a mistake to have me leave and now wanted to keep me here to analyze British intentions."

Basya nods and he continues, "The Kremlin's suspicious of the British. Someone with experience is needed here. I had the contacts and I'm one of the few in our delegation that speaks Hebrew." Mischa shakes his head. "The irony is that that cable from Moscow, informing the ship captain to put me back down on the dock, saved me from Stalin's purges."

Right before her eyes, he looks away and she can see a few tears forming.

"Can't help it. It's too hard," he repeats over and over again. "I know I can't bring my daughter back. I don't even see my grandkids. My son-in-law and the children moved to a kibbutz, Kfar Blum, in the north. And to think I would have missed you if I had sailed. Fate or God is playing with me. Bad, then good. What's ahead for us.?"

She holds his hand. It comforts him.

"So quiet out there on the water" he says, now in a relaxed tone. "You can barely hear the rocking of the sea."

He's unaware, for the moment, that a small piper cub plane takes off from nearby Sde Dov, the Tel Aviv airstrip that purports to be an airport. The plane hugs the shoreline and then heads south over the blue Mediterranean on another bombing run against Egyptian armed forces now halted in the Negev. The Egyptians recently failed in their initial thrust into the new Jewish state and their drive to Tel Aviv was aborted.

After a few minutes of silence, Mischa exclaims: "Look. The vendors are out hawking already. Better take our morning walk before the crowds arrive."

Rising, he gently takes Basya's hand which she gives to him gladly. Whenever they walk on the beach, they hold hands. And so, this middle-age man and his middle-age-love exit the café and inhale the fresh smells of the morning's salty air infusing them with a quicker step. The sand crunches under their feet, even as it makes them stumble a little, so they hold onto each other as a feeling of happiness comes over them.

As Mischa and Basya tread along the soft warm beach, they are getting to know each other, the little things that one notices about a lover. He's impatient. She's extremely punctual. He ponders. She's impulsive. Neither talks about former spouses or love affairs. No confessions of guilt. They both suffer the loss of a child.

As they walk, she recalls the night they were reunited. He mentioned the unspeakable word, "defect." Over the years, she, too, had been immersed in Red jargon. After her time in London, she began to see that the dictatorship of the proletariat had become the dictatorship of Stalin. What shook her on a personal level, was the abduction of Lev's cousin, Sonya Kuznetsov in London, and the murder of Jan Masaryk, in Prague.

"They didn't have to do it. They already controlled the government," she whispers.

"Do what?"

"Kill Masaryk."

"I know how you feel. Having the same trouble understanding their actions."

She pauses and stares out into space, before continuing: "I love my country Russia and the human values of Communism which not only overthrew the Czar but turned Russia from an agrarian backwater to an industrial power." She stops before saying with determination, "But those values have been squashed by leader Stalin. Life isn't worth anything. Mischa. We have to get out."

"I agree."

"You have an in with Israeli intelligence. Maybe you can find out about transportation out of here, someway, somehow?" She encourages, "Keep at it, Mischa."

"I'll work at it, Basya. We'll escape."

•

Chapter 30. Tel Aviv, 1948.
MISCHA AND BASYA.
*"The'Altelana' Ship Brings the Israeli War
to Mischa's Doorstep."*

•

On May 14, 1948, the British mandate over Palestine expired and a Jewish state, Israel, was established. Warfare broke out between the new nation and seven Arab states. Israel badly needed arms to hold the Arabs at bay. A month after independence, a violent confrontation would take place on the beach of Tel Aviv between the newly created Israel Defense Forces, (IDF), aka Haganah, against the nationalist Irgun Zvai Leumi (IZL). That clash caused a near civil war between two Jewish armies vying for control of the new nation. Organized by the Irgun, an American LST, now named the Altalena, loaded with a huge cargo of French arms and crammed with about 1,000 Jewish refugees, sailed from Port-de-Bouc, near Marseille, and beached at a village known as Kfar Vitkin, near Netanya, north of Tel Aviv. Insisting on one united army, the Government of Israel demanded that the arms be handed over to its Haganah force. Irgun refused. Mischa would have a front row-seat as the battle unfolded.

•

He had heard love-making in the morning was the best. It sure was, he confirmed to himself, on this beautiful sunshine morning in Tel Aviv, an hour after he and Basya returned from the beach. His body was fatigued with pleasure, though usually, the sexual energy unleashed would soon power him in what was to be an exciting day, this June 21, 1948.

"I'm going to that press conference at eleven o'clock regarding a ship called the *Altalena*," she says, putting on her sandals. "I have to deal with anything involving arms coming into Israel."

"If you don't go to that meeting, our absence will be noted. Comrade Stalin disapproves of Russians and Czechs socializing. He goes so far as to forbid Soviet citizens to marry foreigners, even from a socialist bloc country! How about that?"

"But what they don't know, can't hurt them as my mother used to say," replies Basya.

Wrong, love. Big Brother is always watching you. Stalin knows and hears everything," were the last words he said to her as she hurried down the steps of the Keter Dan Hotel. He couldn't wait to be with her again. He didn't yet know it, but he wouldn't have time, however, to make love or even get adequate sleep in the next few days. The blue and white waves washing ashore would cast up a ship whose story will remain forever on the pages of Israel's history - *The Altalena*.

•

"What happened to that Irgun ship? Did it breach the shore up the coast at the village of Kfar Vitkin yesterday?" he wonders, standing in the shower as the water, warming his firm shoulders and dripping down over his muscular body, gives him pause for thought. His mind ponders his report to the foreign office, as well as various leads for his forthcoming newspaper article. It's amazing what magnificent ideas for stories he conjures up under a hot shower.

When not in diplomatic attire, he dresses like an Israeli. He slides into his khaki pants, dons his usual short-sleeve blue shirt - the shirt of the working class, puts on his sandals and hastens out of the room. He hurries down the steps to the Keter Dan Hotel reception which is now full of United Nations representatives observing an imposed truce between Arabs and Jews.

"Any calls for me?" he asks the anxious clerk.

"Nothing yet, sir."

After pacing the lobby floor for a few minutes, he steps out doors to scan the beach to see if there is any military preparations or movement in front or behind the hotel. He notes the usual morning rush - People scurrying to work, Dan and Egged company buses weaving in and out of light traffic, bleary-eyed residents stopping off at their favorite sidewalk café emitting the smells of Turkish coffee into the air. And far away, rising out of the sand dunes and desert in the east past the river Jordan, a bright, red hot, blazing June sun.

Turning back to the hotel, Mischa wonders if Igor got up to Kfar Vitkin. *"Maybe he'll call?"* he thinks to himself. *"He's great in situations like this, usually on top of things."*

Since the day Mischa arrived in the Holy Land back in early spring of 1947, Igor has served him well, "though, as an assistant, he sometimes can be exasperating, offering too many details and not getting straight to the point." No matter. Although Mischa likes Igor, he has been careful never to divulge his feelings about some of the mistakes of the Kremlin.

For now, however, Mischa can't be bothered with these thoughts. He barely has time to light up a cigarette when the hotel employee knocks on his door and tells him there's a telephone call from an Igor Riasanovsky.

"The ship's off shore at Kfar Vitkin," are the first words out of Igor's mouth.

"I heard that. What else's new?" he barks into the phone.

"What did you say?" shouts Igor who apparently has a bad connection, or can't hear because of intermittent shooting in the background.

"I said, what else is new?" yells Mischa, moderating his voice after absorbing his assistant's explanation that the head of the new Israeli government, David Ben-Gurion, has ordered the ship, *Altalena,* to be surrounded by Haganah troops taking up positions on shore, and to be shadowed by two naval gunboats, should the LST try to break out to sea. "After they began to unload the cargo, Haganah gave Irgun ten minutes to surrender the ship or be fired upon."

"What happened then?" asks Mischa.

"A firefight broke out on the Kfar Vitkin beach. I'm not clear which side started it, although I did see Israeli soldiers firing machine guns and raking the beach area occupied by Irgun fighters.

At the same time, those Israeli Navy corvettes I told you about, well, they, too, opened fire on the *Altalena.* Anyway, that skirmish didn't last long."

"Any casualties?" asks Mischa.

"Six Irgun members and two IDF soldiers, dead. But wait, the worse is still to come." Igor continues hurriedly, "Menachem Begin has boarded the ship and wants to take it to Tel Aviv. I'm told he thinks the public in Tel Aviv will be more sympathetic to taking in the arms for their own sons and daughters who're fighting with few guns." He takes a breath. "There's going to be a clash," says Igor. "Bullets will fly."

"Thanks. I'll be on the lookout for this Altalena."

•

Mischa didn't have long to wait.

Hours later, in the middle of the night of June 21, The *Altalena* arrives. The roar of heavy engine motors reverberates throughout the neighborhood, as it hits the beach at top speed and runs aground about five hundred feet off the Tel Aviv shoreline at the end of David Frischmann Street, almost on Mischa's doorstep. The dim street lamps outline the ship's bulk in the dark night.

As Mischa waits patiently to see what's going to happen next, he refreshes his mind regarding the Kremlin view on the situation.

"Both Haganah and Irgun will each demand that the ammunition be handed over to them. That fight could lead to civil war, the last thing Moscow wants. The Soviet government believes that kind of conflict will give the British an excuse to come back to Palestine and all our work will be for naught," he says to himself, adding. "We're on Haganah's side."

•

By mid-morning on June 22, Tel Aviv is in a frenzy. Begin's loyal adherents have arrived in trucks from the surrounding area. In opposition, are Haganah troops who have taken up positions on the shore and in the buildings near Mischa's hotel.

Going back downstairs, Mischa finds a few Haganah soldiers just outside the lobby door. He introduces himself to the officer in charge, Yitzhak Peres. Mischa informs him he is a Soviet diplomat and a journalist for the Pravda newspaper. He flashes his ID. Not only is Yitzhak nonplussed, but he hollers at Mischa to get back into the hotel.

"I'm not going anywhere," Mischa's ready to say, when a volley of gunshots is unleashed by both Haganah and Irgun. It is then that Mischa spots a launch being lowered from the *Altalena*. The smaller craft is so close that he can count a dozen men on board who hover around explosive crates. Gunfire erupts from shore and sea, and the launch returns to the LST.

"I must get closer," Mischa shouts out loudly in English, a language he knows many Israelis speak and understand.

"You're going nowhere, mister," yells brash Yitzhak, whose hands are raised upward and palms toward Mischa, signaling the diplomat to halt.

"I'm an officer in the Red Army," declares Mischa, in a commanding voice.

"Congratulations. But this is not Russia. Here you're under my command," declares Yitzhak planting his feet firmly and standing up tall to the Soviet man. A group of soldiers loyal to the government nervously gather around the two in the doorway.

"Okay," says Mischa with a fake smile. "You win."

A soldier breaks into the conversation, "I just heard that by a seven-to-two vote, the government instructed Irgun to surrender the *Altalena,* especially since there's a ceasefire in effect and that Begin has ordered his men not to fire even if they're fired upon."

At that moment, Mischa and the others hear a voice booming out to civilians hovering in the distance. Menachem Begin's speaking on a bull horn.

"People of Tel Aviv, we of the Irgun have brought your arms to fight the enemy, but the government is denying them to you. For God's sake, help us unload these arms which are for our common defense. If there are differences among us, let us reason together."

"Don't anybody move," commands Yitzhak, stepping out and looking up and down the street. "I can see everyone's staying put. But get all those civilian bystanders who are watching over there to step back," he tells a few of his men who, ducking down, move away.

"Here comes a second launch. Let's get down to the beach, men, commands Yitzhak. Turning to Mischa, he says, "Comrade officer, you stay here. And that's an order. That all I need is for a Red Army officer to get killed on my watch."

Mischa observes them move forward and fire at the barge.

"Now, all hell will break loose," he says. "If Irgun fires back, they could easily hit me. What the hell? I'm not staying here. I'm getting closer," he says with bravado. "Now's a good time, as Begin's people are unloading more of the cargo and that Yitzhak is nowhere in sight."

Up and crouching down and at the same time, hearing more gunfire from behind, he takes cover in the sand behind a dumpster, a few feet in from the road. Turning his head, he notices more Haganah forces race to fortified positions in nearby buildings, from whence they fire onto shore and ship. He hears screams from the water, as *Altalena* sailors leap into the surf, trying to avoid the bullets fired from the beach, some of which hit the dumpster with their call of death. Ping! Ping! Ping!

The skirmish doesn't last long. "Haganah is negotiating with Irgun," Mischa observes, peering around the huge container in front of him. "That won't get them very far. Only force will do." He hears an officer on his right, telling his men to fire another barrage onto the *Altalena.* At that very moment, he watches Haganah move an antique cannon near the beach boardwalk. "They're firing it. One, two, three cannon shells." The shots are splashing down near the LST. "Here comes the fourth from that decrepit artillery piece. Bravo," he yells after that shell slams into the *Altalena,* and penetrates the ship's hull, igniting a blazing fire in the cargo hold. Smoke bellows from the portholes.

He observes Haganah troops on the beach are firing again, spraying the ship's decks. The ship's captain is flaying his arms. Crewmen are racing below to open water valves. There's no chance in the world they'll be able to extinguish the blaze. The captain commands, 'Abandon ship!' Irgun fighters are leaping into the water to swim ashore.

Mischa notices The *Altalena* is in flames. Thousands of exploding bullets in crates are turning the LST into a burning pyre. All is gone. *Altalena's* flaming hulk sinks. Its firearms, tanks, and anti-aircraft guns spill into the sea.

"It's a black day for Israel. Jew fighting Jew," says Mischa watching the smoke bellow from the blazing ship. "I must get out of here before that loud-mouth Israeli officer returns."

He gets up and races back to the hotel. Within minutes, he's writing his story for Pravda:

"Total deaths in the twenty-four-hour standoff at Kfar Vitkin and Tel Aviv: Sixteen Irgun fighters were killed and of these, six at Kfar Vitkin and ten in Tel Aviv. Three IDF soldiers were killed, two at Kfar Vitkin and one in Tel Aviv. Force against the Irgun was necessary. However, Begin refused to ignite a civil war. Now disbanded, his units have been interspersed into one, united Israeli army, now known as the Israel Defense Forces, (IDF)."

Unlike other reporters, Mischa sends his story on a secure line to Moscow via a teletype machine in an office on Ben-Yehuda Street. He's pleased. He makes the early edition of Pravda.

•

Chapter 31. Tel Aviv, 1948.
MISCHA AND BASYA.
"Mischa Bumps into Michael, Spanish Civil War Veteran"

•

On a sunny day in early fall of 1948, Mischa and Basya are seated inside the Casit, a cafe on Dizengoff Street, and are sipping steamy, bitter Turkish coffee from small cups. From time to time, he leans over and plants a kiss on Basya's rose-colored inviting lips. They chose this spot to observe the passing scene. No longer separated, it's now easier to lure Israeli civilian and army leaders into their net. That's their job.

Few pedestrians notice the pair. No-one, that is, except the one person who sees them is a senior citizen, a spy for the Soviet secret police. To the casual onlooker, she's an old lady walking down the street with a large purse in one hand and a small umbrella in the other.

Mischa pays no attention to the secret watcher and even if he did, he wouldn't recognize her as being in the employ of his own government. Even though the Center had given permission for the two to work together, it had no qualms about keeping an eye on them.

Anyone looking would see that they were gazing at the calm sea and then back to scanning the headlines of the morning paper. But they were deep in thought, focused on every passerby.

Suddenly, Mischa, jumping up from his chair, tells Basya, "I'll be right back." Before she can ask what's happening, he twists and turns through the maze of rows of café tables and chairs, until he catches up with a man on the sidewalk. Basya sees Mischa stopping the startled pedestrian and uttering a few words which she can't hear. Recognizing each other, the two give a perfunctory hug and then, smiling like friends who have not seen each other for many years, they return to the table that Mischa so hastily vacated.

"I know you from somewhere," Basya says, greeting the guest with a welcoming smile. "Please join us. What'll you have?"

"I'm fine."

"Basya, this is Michael Rapaport," Mischa says, this time speaking English. "A good American. Sympathetic to our cause. At least you once were. Right, Michael?"

"Correct," replies the short and stocky muscular man, who, bristling, adds, "But no longer."

Mischa doesn't react. Instead, he says, "You've put on weight. You're not the old scarecrow I met in Barcelona in 'thirty-eight' after the battle of the Ebro in Spain."

"How could I ever forget it?" answers Michael whose head is adorned with a fresh crew cut. "Black days after that fight. We were defeated. We were ghosts. And there you were, my rescuer."

"Yes, Michael. You will always be my good comrade."

"I'm your friend, Mischa, not your comrade," he says meaningfully before continuing. "The cause in Spain was just, although I didn't agree with the Republic with its firing squads, execution, and church burnings. We didn't have to ape the fascists." He looks at Mischa, adding, "Your NKVD people did just that. They imprisoned and killed anarchists in the POUM, the left-wing splinter group of Trotskyites.

The Communist goal in Spain had escalated to the point where you didn't want a Republic, but a Communist dictatorship." He finishes angrily, "Now you guys are up to your old tricks, subverting governments throughout the world."

"If it wasn't for us and Czechoslovakian arms, where would you Zionists be today," " Mischa retorts harshly, raising his voice. He would like to openly agree with Michael regarding Spain and post-war Europe, but then, he'd blow his cover. He realized Michael spoke the truth.

"Yes, while they persecute Jews back home and bar emigration," counters Michael.

"Gentlemen, no arguments. We're all friends," chimes in Basya, diplomatically as ever. "Michael, I'm a Czech diplomat and as one, I visited Spain. Now I remember where we met. It was outside of Madrid. You were a press officer and I was visiting Czech volunteers."

"Right," says Michael. "In thirty-seven."

"How's your Hebrew?" asks Mischa, picking up on Basya's changing the subject.

"Not great," replies Michael. "Been here a while. I managed, even if I break my teeth on the language, as the Israelis say."

"It's so good to see you. You're still my friend, though we see political matters differently. Much has happened," says Mischa warmly.

"Would love to sit and reminisce, Mischa. But I can't. I must get home. I'm catching a bus at the Central Station."

"Where are you going?"

"Kibbutz Kfar Blum, in the Upper Galilee."

"Oh," says Mischa, stunned, though trying not to give away he knows the place very well. His son-in-law, Volya, and grandchildren, Dora and Uri, went there after his daughter Klara was killed. But it's prudent for everyone that he doesn't disclose to Michael that his very own family lives there.

"You know the place?" asks Michael.

"Yes, I've heard of it. But I've never been there," he says. "I understand it's unique. A lot of Americans and English are there."

"That's correct," answers Michael, honored that someone knows about his home. "In the old days, it was called 'Kibbutz Anglo-Balti.' There are a lot of Lithuanian Jews, too."

Suddenly, the conversation stalls. Nobody breaks the silence, until Michael says:

"I want to catch up, Mischa. Really, I do. But I must be off. Come visit us in Kfar Blum. But if you can't, I come to Tel Aviv pretty often."

"I'm sure we'll meet again," says Mischa. "I know where to reach you. Here's my card."

Michael bids Basya farewell and has another bear hug for Mischa. He is lost in thought: *That woman really was the Czech diplomat I met in Spain. Mischa moved mountains to catch up with her. He chased her all the way to Valencia. Unlucky that day. I heard he missed her by a few hours. But he sure was persistent. Actually, I'm happy for the guy.*

A few minutes after Michael left, Basya tells Mischa: "Got to run, love. Talk later."

"Basya," says Mischa, frowning. "Don't tell a soul about our encounter with Michael."

"I won't. But my dear, it's not necessary to say that. They already know."

"How's that?"

"See that man at the end of the bar with his nose in that Russian language newspaper." As he looks, she adds, "Guess who he is? It's written all over his forehead in capital letters, 'NKVD." She shrugs. "And here I thought you know all your friends. Bye, my love." Basya blows a kiss as she slips away.

Stalin is watching our every move. They're everywhere. No escaping them. Nowhere to hide. When they want you, they'll come for you, Mischa thinks.

"*Dasvidaniya,*" Mischa says loudly, facing the secret agent as he gets up, pays the check and waves brazenly at the man reading the Russian paper. The agent, realizing his cover is blown, frowns.

•

Basya caught up again with Mischa in the late afternoon. For a while now, she felt she would soon have to relate a piece of news that usually excites a couple and makes them think of their future even more.

Basya felt guilty about not telling Mischa she's pregnant. She had a good excuse, she rationalized. She simply wasn't sure as her menstrual periods had always been slightly irregular. But her last menstrual period was June 15 and she missed it in July and August. It was now September.

Standing in front of the mirror one morning, she noted that her breasts were getting fuller and her abdomen seemed slightly larger. Beside all that, she didn't need the mirror to tell her she had been peeing frequently. She heard of a Dr. Chaim Beitan.

"Don't worry about your age. We have women in their late forties having children all the time. Stay with your normal routine. As a precaution, avoid strenuous activity. No need for me or your husband to pamper you. You'll be fine. Take good care of yourself," were his parting words at the end of the examination.

Basya didn't want Mischa to be burdened with the added responsibility of a child, especially here in Israel, with the work the two of them were doing. Besides, his mind had to be clear so that he could come up with an escape plan to extricate them from the jaws of the death penalty waiting for them back in Russia. She would keep the secret until a propitious moment presented itself.

That line of thought, however, didn't last long. She knew that his daughter had been killed in an Egyptian bomb attack last year in the war with the Arabs. She thought that his feelings, raw with grief over losing his daughter perhaps could be assuaged by another chance to be a father. For that to happen, they had to get to the West. No matter how she looked at it, she knew she had to tell him. He would have discovered it just by looking at her soon-to-be, very pregnant body.

The next day over breakfast of fruit and *labana,* as well as toast smeared with honey, and a plate of fresh vegetables, came words repeated thousands of times by others.

Mischa. I've got something to tell you."

"Go ahead."

"I'm pregnant."

He didn't know what to say. A woman, whom he loved very much, was telling him he was going to be a father.

His first reaction was a big smile and an exclamation. "Wonderful! I thought you looked like you were glowing more than ever. He took her into his arms and hugged her delicately. He had hoped that someday they would have a child, a daughter. Yes, a daughter, a thought which he kept to himself. A child would make him young again, and if it was a girl, and Basya agreed, they would name their child after his late daughter, Klara. Which led him to think of Klara, his sister. Maybe he would find his sister if he ever got to the United States, though the resentment of her being chosen over him to find their father, Gershon, lingered. If it was a boy, he would leave the name up to Basya. She knew her father was dead. Mischa didn't know if his father, was alive. Gershon had left thirty-five years ago for the United States and Mischa had never heard from him or his sisters who who had followed him. He knew his mother had died in a fire in Odessa at the end of the Civil War.

"Mischa. I'm so excited and yet I'm afraid. A child at my age!"

"Shh. Don't jinx it. Let's not give it a *"kein ayin hara"* ('*no evil eye*' *in Yiddish/Hebrew).*

She's amazed at his using an old Jewish saying, he, of all people, a Soviet man.

"People might say," he continues, "this is not the time to have a child, especially during what could be another war in the Middle East. But I think it couldn't have happened at a better time. Maybe it's a sign we're lucky and showing us a new life is coming. Is it possible, a dream come true?"

He stops, and then asks, "When does our little one arrive?"

"Next March, according to the doctor I saw," she says. "With a child on the way, we have to get out of here and to the West for the baby's and our sake."

•

Chapter 32. Tel Aviv, 1948.
MISCHA AND BASYA.
"Mischa Solves Security Problems at Soviet Mission."

•

A few months after meeting Michael, Mischa is summoned to a security committee meeting in the rezidentura. He is early so he decides to kill some time by waiting across the street on a bench and enjoying the weather.

It is a day unlike the usual November cool day in Tel Aviv when the thermometer sinks into the fifties. But in the afternoon, the temperature climbs to seventy-four degrees Fahrenheit. He realizes that the sea behind him remains calm and that some residents, taking advantage of the warm air, jump into the cool waters and ride the foamy waves. He stares at the Gat Rimon, one of small hotels fronting Hayarkon Street. He notices the flags of the United States and the USSR blowing in the ocean breeze, a sight that always causes him to snicker.

I can't get over it, he thinks. *We're foes of the Americans. Yet, both ours and their diplomatic delegations are housed, not only in the same hotel, but on the same floor. Two of the most powerful nations on earth, thrown together in one building. Humorous it is to see representatives of both countries bumping into each other in the hallway during the day and proffering up a polite, diplomatic nod at the same time that the Cold War is heating up.*

As he reflected on this situation, he realized that in the final analysis, both parties want to influence Israel. *That's why I was sent here by the foreign office.*

Mischa's job prompted him to choose the Gan Rimon as the headquarters for the Russian diplomats. He had to have it ready for Soviet Minister Pavel I. Yershov, who arrived in the summer. The American heading the United States Mission is James G. McDonald who had checked into the hotel a few days after the Soviet diplomat.

At first, Mischa was embarrassed when he discovered that the Americans had selected the very same accommodations. But, he realized, there was just no other choice. Hotel space was scarce in crowded Tel Aviv because of the war. The United Nations truce observers grabbed all available rooms in the better hotels.

From the start, Mischa and his fellow diplomats recognize that Yershov is a tight-ass boss. He insists that the Soviet staff reside in the rezidentura. And so, Mischa has to give up his hotel suite in the Keter Dan and move to the Gat Rimon where his new home consists of a tiny, corner, stark room, with no view of the sea. He's on the same floor as the Americans; their rooms are located at the other end of a long, carpeted hall. His room barely handles a cot, a small bureau, a washstand, and a hidden bath. There is no toilet. He has to use the facility down the hall. Still on a nice day, he can walk to Basya's apartment on Geula Street.

•

At one weekly meeting, attended by several security officers, Minister Yershov voices deep concern that his agents are not able to gather intelligence because they can't break away from American or Israeli surveillance.

"We have to shake those following us," the Soviet chief diplomat tells his staff. "We can't leave the building without being watched"

"I have a plan to stop the Americans and Israelis from following us, at least one time," Mischa explains.

"I'm all ears, Comrade Rasputnis," says Yershov.

"Confuse them," Mischa declares.

"How's that?"

"Simple," he begins "We gather our entire delegation - a dozen or so of our staff - in one group, standing shoulder-to-shoulder in the lobby. We walk out the front door, keeping together in a single unit and then quickly scatter in all directions." He continues enthusiastically, "Some walk away. Some bike. Some run. Some enter limos and drive off in different directions."

"What happens then?" asks Yershov.

"The other side's men won't have adequate numbers to cover us all. Some of us will get through. Those who escape the dragnet will be free of enemy hounds. Neither the Americans, nor the Israelis, will know where we've gone."

•

A few days later, Mischa is summoned to Yershov's office where he is commended for planning and executing 'Operation Breakout,' which was a great espionage success. "I have reported your accomplishment to Moscow," Yershov informs Mischa

"Thank you, Comrade Minister," Mischa says, and leaves the rezidentura to meet Basya.

"Yershov is happy with me. That means he doesn't suspect us," he tells Basya.

•

One day, at the end of 1948, however, Minister Yershov asks Mischa, "Where did you meet Comrade Tatiana Kovacova?"

"Where diplomats usually meet each other, Comrade minister. We met at one of those official meetings when she briefed us on the Czech arms deal to Israel."

"Of course," rejoins Yershov. "In our job, we must attend meetings and diplomatic receptions. You never know what a useful piece of information an inquisitive ear can pick up."

"Yes, Comrade Yershov."

"Comrade Stalin, in his infinite wisdom, wants to slow down the arms shipments to Israel. The Israelis are leaning too much on the Americans." He pauses and stares intently at Mischa. "We have traitors among us, such as Tito of Yugoslavia" And then he adds, "Give my best to Comrade Kovacova."

Walking out, Mischa is concerned. *What's that all about?*

•

Mischa never imagined his handler in the Kremlin, Alyosha Kovalchenko, head of the Cominform, the successor to the Comintern, is thinking of moving Mischa to China to aid the Communists battling the Nationalists. Well-supplied by Russia, Communist Mao Tse-tung's army poses a moral threat to Chiang Kai-shek's weary regime, which was crippled by the war with Japan.

This is not a rash decision for Alyosha. Mischa had proven himself adaptable and reliable on every assignment. What ensured the transfer was that Mischa had spent many years in the Russian Far

East where he came into contact with Chinese Communist leaders. However, Moscow can't send him as a diplomat to Shanghai, because the Nationalists are in power and don't recognize the USSR which backs their enemy, the Communists. Mischa would be an 'illegal,' a spy, and if something goes wrong, Moscow can't protect him. But the Cominform can turn him into a White Russian émigré who ended up in Palestine as a businessman and hates Communists.

Alyosha sees the benefit of Mischa having an English-speaking wife to accompany him to fit the appearance of a businessman. Hearing about the Czech female spy and her finesse in infiltrating the upper echelons of government to Moscow's benefit while in Prague and London, Alyosha chooses Tatiana to accompany Mischa. He and the diplomats as well as Red underground leaders know of their liaison and the fact that she is pregnant. Their working together is paying off for Soviet intelligence. Why not keep them a formal team?

A month after his meeting with Yershov during which the minister asked Mischa about Basya, the couple is shocked by orders from Moscow commanding them to leave for China. Dr. Beitan gives Basya permission to fly, even though she's nearing the end of her pregnancy. A week later, an Air France flight lands them in Shanghai, a gaudy city of crowded streets of beggars, pimps, gamblers, and opium smugglers. The two sense everyone awaits the arrival of the conquering Chinese Communist army which already has conquered Northern China.

•

Chapter 33. Shanghai, 1949.
MISCHA AND BASYA.
"Working Together in Shanghai"

•

Mischa and Basya learned from briefings that in 1945, the Chinese had emerged from eight years of brutal Japanese aggression and occupation during World War II. When the war ended, the long-smoldering civil war between the American-backed Nationalists and the Soviet-allied Communists, reignited. By late 1947, the United States had lost confidence in the Nationalist leader, Generalissimo Chiang Kai-shek. A year later, at the end of 1948, the Communists were gathering in northern China, and would soon move south across the Yangtze River and into Shanghai. Leading the Communists is a Hunan province peasant, Mao Tse-tung, popularly known as Chairman Mao, a revolutionary and a believer in Marxism-Leninism.

•

I don't want to be in China. Damn it. Why now? Basya and I could have maybe made it to the West from Israel. Never from here. This posting is a bad dream? thinks Mischa on a bleak and dark night, a few days after he and very pregnant Basya arrived in Shanghai in early January, 1949.

Walking the city streets, in the damp cold of the Shanghai winter, Mischa notices the avenues, usually bustling with vendors and crowds of people, are deserted at night. He recognizes he's just another sad foreigner slinking along in the shadows of Nanking Road, a small glint of fear in his eyes. He'd like it to appear as if he's out on a leisurely walk. But he remembers his driver, Shen, informing him, "If you see a dead body, turn around and go the other way."

Alone, he stops now and then to gaze at a store front window. His head moves ever so slightly. His eyes dart here and there to see if he's being followed, a habit among intelligence officers. Cabaret dancers and textile workers lol about. They are White Russians who, after the 1918 Revolution, filtered into the city and worked in cabarets and bordellos, some as sex companions for the rich in this beating heart of China.

The night air has done him good. He's ready for bed. Tomorrow is his first assignment. Basya will remain in the hotel. Her pregnant condition means that she can't go with Mischa on this special mission. She's due in a couple of months.

As dawn breaks on a misty, cold winter morning on the Bund, the most famous street in the most famous city in China, noisy crowds already are out on the maddening streets, replete with order-taking kiosks, indoor and outdoor shops and luxury hotels. It's 6:37 a.m. in Shanghai, five thousand miles from Moscow. At this very moment in the city's centuries-long history, Mischa Rasputnis escorts Basya to the breakfast room, kisses her goodbye and walks out of the famous Cathay Hotel, known to the British as 'The Claridge's of the Far East.' He had read that the pyramid- shaped copper roof of the ten-story hotel was the showplace of Victor Sassoon, one of Shanghai's most prominent Jewish businessmen.

Moving onto the *Bund*, a Hindi word referring to an embanked thoroughfare along a river, he and his Chinese comrade, Shen, observe the powerful institutions of the major commercial houses and the hulking neoclassical bank buildings. They take in the swarm of thousands of people in tattered clothing moving briskly on crowded pavements. Not far away is Shanghai's Chinese sections of dilapidated shacks and squalid tenements reeking of raw sewage and general decay.

As the rays of the rising sun appear in the east, these two early risers scurry out of the way of rickshaws, pedicabs, bicycles, cars, carts, trucks, and electric trams. The duo joins the moving crowd and focuses on one thing only - completing today's job, for they recognize that bankers and industrialists in Shanghai, the "hotbed of capitalism," are a doomed class.

How do they know this? They are Communist agents and their brothers, the Chinese Reds, are coming.

The pair's only exchanged words as they enter a parked vehicle and drive off are, "Let's go. We've got work to do." No one pays any attention as they get into their car.

•

Four blocks into their assignment, Mischa realizes something's amiss.

"Damn it. I forgot the envelope."

"You what!"

"I forgot the envelope."

"Are you sure?"

"Yes. I left it in the drawer in the hotel room. We must go back. Turn around and return to the hotel, please. I never did anything like this before."

"Good thing we left early. We've got time. It'll take only five minutes or so," says Shen.

Swinging around, the car darts in and out of voluminous traffic and reaches the hotel.

Despite their calm exteriors, the thought that this assignment in Shanghai may be botched races through their minds.

The car screeches to a halt. Mischa opens the door and stands alongside the vehicle, surveying the street behind the hotel. He counts. 'One, two three, four, …nineteen, twenty…twenty-eight, twenty-nine, thirty."

Never be in a rush and never appear flustered or self-conscious remains part of his chameleon-like discipline. He doesn't want to act like any traveler who forgot his pajamas on a bathroom door hook, or his watch on a bathroom sink, or his passport in a night-table drawer and thus attract attention to himself.

Still, the deafening noise over the babel of Shanghai, reminds him he must move quickly. Taking measured steps, he ventures onto the curving walkway back of the hotel. He forges his way through the rush of pedestrian traffic.

"Look out," he yells to a young girl, barefoot in her sandals and covered in a slightly torn jacket. She's moving in front of him, but doesn't see a truck barreling down on her.

Throwing his arms around her, he quickly pulls her out of the way.

"You could have been killed," he shouts in Russian, shocked at himself for screaming at the child. It is so out of character for this man who, in middle age, is now described as affable and reserved and whose voice is generally kind.

The girl, frightened by the man's foreign-language warning, ignores the threat of being run down by the vehicle. She only knows that some foreigner is molesting her; his arms still encircling her trim body. Her only thought is that she's being groped by a European, though not a Britisher.

She snarls and curses him. Her throaty voice bellows vulgar, guttural-toned Chinese words, words that would cause a sailor to blush as she untangles herself from the grasp of her rescuer and safely crosses the street.

Watching all this with amusement, stands Shen, who leans against the car as his keen, almond-like eyes scan the street. Any other intelligence agent would think that this muscular man would have headed right to the hotel and not bothered about a young Chinese girl about to be killed in a horrific accident.

Mischa realizes he must reach the room before the maids clean it, find the envelope, and turn it over to his Communist cohorts. Its contents are military maps and a passport belonging to an American, Kevin Armstrong, whose drowned body was found in the river last week.

The back entrance of the hotel is empty and the guard looking away, is standing and talking on the phone. Slipping past the clerk and taking a single step on the back staircase up to the second floor, Mischa stares into the panicky eyes of a youth hurrying down the steps. The teenager pushes Mischa out of the way and causes him to fall backwards and land on his side on the ground floor. But as he slips, Mischa reaches out and grabs the extended leg of his assailant, causing him to fall to the floor. As his attacker begins to rise, Mischa, within seconds, jumps up, lands a hard blow with his fist on the attacker's head. The boy falls onto the floor and slips into unconsciousness.

Mischa searches the prostrate youth, spies an envelope in the inside pocket of his suit jacket, and lifts it out. The envelope turns out to be the one he left behind.

He gets up, stops, and with his finger over his lips, says goodbye to the shocked watchman. He hands him an English twenty-pound note. The guard nods. Mischa bows and walks into the lobby where he spies Basya in the dining room, still eating breakfast. *She's safe, thank goodness.* He hurries out of the hotel and walks out into the crowded street.

"Got it," he says, breathing heavily and having trouble recalling the last time he was in a fight. Not bad for an old man, a thought which encourages him for future battles.

•

"What a relief. Mission back on track. How could I be so careless on our first assignment," mutters Mischa, somewhat embarrassed.

"It happens," says Shen, his sallow skin and hollow cheeks making him less conspicuous in a crowd.

"For sure," Mischa says, frowning, as he tells Shen to proceed. "Let's go. We have a date to keep."

•

After a half hour drive, they arrive at an abandoned warehouse on an empty wharf. It is unusually quiet. The lifeless-dock reminds them that the Chinese civil war is approaching Shanghai and it's coming on fast. In the distance, they spot Nationalist soldiers unloading sandbags from trucks to build up machine gun nests. Despite Nationalist assurances that the Red horde will never reach this Asian city, the populace whispers, "Mao is on the march."

•

Exiting the car and walking toward the warehouse, Mischa can't believe what he sees. Dressed in Western suits and ties, bourgeois men are taking wads of cash out of their briefcases and handing them to officials. In turn, the recipients shamelessly grab the money and give the civilians fake exit visas allowing them to get to British Hong Kong and avoid falling into Communist hands.

Standing outside the door are some workers and hangers-on. Mischa and Shen pass through and walk upstairs to a balcony built around the building's four sides with offices representing various shipping lines. They stop at the door whose company sign says, "Shanghai Express."

At first, no words are exchanged between Mischa and the Chinese clerk behind the counter. Boldly, the clerk says to Mischa, "What did you do for Chiang today?"

"I brought food to the troops," came Mischa's reply to the password, *Chiang*, which was a reference, in this case, to the enemy, General Chiang Kai-shek and his Nationalist Army. That army occupies Shanghai, for now.

Mischa, his hands sweating, gives up the envelope. He's glad that the ordeal is over.

The clerk takes the envelope. He doesn't open it, even though they both know the maps inside show the location of the gap into Chinese Nationalist lines on the Yangtze river into which Communist forces can penetrate and achieve ultimate victory in the city.

"Well done, Comrade! Well done! We just couldn't trust anyone else to deliver this. We had to have loyal Communist agents do it," says the clerk. "As you can see outside, many leaders of the Chinese Nationalist Party as well as rich civilians are fleeing even before the fighting begins. Believe me, thousands of civilians will follow."

Mischa and Shen smile. "That's a good sign," they say. "Victory is ours." They turn and walk out and head back to their car. They drive toward the imposing skyline of the Shanghai Bund. Shen drops Mischa off at the spot where one sees the Huangpu River flow right through the city. No wonder, they think the name, Shanghai, means above the sea.

The chaos of the waterfront is hard to believe - Huge wooden junks, with high sterns adorn the river with colorful, painted dragons, phoenixes, and other symbols calling for prosperity, good health, long life, and other blessings. Large ocean liners and freighters dock near the waterfront. Launches and sampans move alongside cargo ships. Here again, at the docks, Mischa spots barges loaded with cotton waiting to be unloaded. The problem is that these huge cotton bales have already been ruined by hundreds of women, risking arrest, who have stolen large globs of raw cotton to resell - their only source of a livelihood. What's left is being unloaded by dockworkers who lift the remaining cotton bales with carrying poles.

As Mischa walks toward the hotel, the smells of Asia surround him. The aromas of seasoned noodles and Szechuan spices laced with chilis waft into the smoky air. Stallholders won't let passersby forget that the city stokes the appetite for the exotic, even in wartime.

Mischa is greeted by the doorman at the Cathay Hotel, near the Hong Kong and Shanghai Bank building. Facing the Bund, the hotel is considered the best address in the Far East.

Minutes later, he enters the hotel dining room with its fine linen tables and sterling silver cutlery. Waiters dressed in black and white, are standing at attention. Basya's waiting for him. He joins her. The couple fits in. They are flushed with money, much needed during these days of high inflation. And she plays the part perfectly. She often goes out of the hotel and returns after a shopping spree with hat and shoe boxes. At times, she waits patiently in the cocktail lounge for her businessman husband.

"Glad you made it back okay," Basya repeats several times.

"Yes," he answers quietly. "We're going to start spending more time in our safe house on the Huangpu River. It's not far from the Shanghai Longhua Airport. We may have to get there quickly one day." He explains the residence has two floors, two large rooms, a kitchen on the main floor, and a staircase leading up to a second floor. In between the two floors is a railed balcony with Venetian blinds running up to the ceiling. The rooms cannot be seen from the outside. Shen occupies one of the upstairs rooms. A room downstairs serves as their bedroom and off that, is a small room for the expected baby.

Basya gets the message. Here in the hotel, they are business people. When they are in their safe house, they're underground agents and provocateurs. The house on the river stands alone on the street. There are no neighbors - only a few vegetable gardens surround it.

•

Usually, they separate after breakfast and spend the day at the port, supposedly checking on cotton shipments. But actually, they're observing arms shipments arriving in the harbor for the Nationalists. They meet in the evening for drinks in the hotel bar, empty at this time of day.

"Do we have time here together or have you heard that they're going to send you back," Mischa asks one evening, noticing Basya's face tighten a bit, indicating she's hiding something.

"Mischa, I'm scared, I've been warned by a colleague who knows of our mission. After our assignment here, they'll ship you home." More emotional now, she asks, "What are we going to do? We can't let this happen after all we've been through." Tears well in her eyes. His eyes open wide in an unbelieving stare. His thoughts race and hushed words follow.

"Maybe my time has come. A huge Stalin purge similar to the one of the 1930s' is underway again in Russia. Luck saved me before. Can I count on that again?" He stops. "Is our plan to escape...,." he pauses once more, "dead? No matter if I stay or run, they'll come after me." He takes her soft hand and squeezes it gently. He's lost in thought. "Let's go to the room."

Basya agrees. *"Hopefully,* she thinks, *"He'll formulate a new plan. He knows how to survive. He showed that when he rescued me in the rail station."*

"Think Mischa," she whispers. "Make an escape plan. I want to wake up one morning and not have to go out on an assignment that terrifies me." She is again emotional. "Let's stop this double life. There is no honor anymore to be a Communist spy. After all these years of dedication, obedience, and service to the Party, we deserve to live like normal people, especially with a baby coming."

That night, they sleep in each other's arms. Their sleep is uneven. Though their lives are now more intertwined than before, the question remains in their minds.

Will we make it to the West?

•

Chapter 34. Shanghai, 1949.
BASYA.
"The Birth of a Daughter"

•

Among the thousands of Jews who managed to escape Nazi Germany in the 1930's after Hitler came to power, were those who headed to Shanghai. Shanghai became the port of last resort for safety. The city remained one of the few municipalities in the world that would admit Jews fleeing Germany without a visa. All you needed was the price of the boat ticket to get there. Basya would fabricate the story that her parents did just that. She would explain that after the Japanese bombed Pearl Harbor and America entered the war, the men from Tokyo rounded up Jews, including her family, and kept them in a one square mile area where she, with her mother and father, resided. She was proud, she said, that she learned English in the ghetto.

•

Shortly after their arrival in Shanghai at the beginning of the year, Basya visits Russian doctor, Nikolaev Rodchenko, the gynecologist at Renji Hospital, a university hospital affiliated with the Shanghai Jiao Tong University School of Medicine. The 300-bed hospital is the first Western hospital in Shanghai and boasts an excellent gynecological department headed by Dr. Rodchenko. Though born in Russia, the doctor emigrated to China as a young man after the Russian Revolution and is not tainted as a Communist sympathizer.

In their first exchange, Basya uses her diplomatic skills to convince Dr. Rodchenko that she is accompanying her husband, an exiled Russian émigré, now businessman, who, like the good doctor, hates the Communists.

Basya has grown bigger and moans of back pain. After examining her, the doctor advises her to see him regularly. He explains that she'll be due by the end of March. He does not see any particular problem, though he notes that being in her forties, she might have difficulties.

Basya likes Dr. Rodchenko. He's short, stout, with wavy, long white hair combed back. She trusts him.

"Come to me if you have any problems, especially heartburn, cramps, back pain and, for sure, depression."

"Doctor," she asks hesitatingly, "am I physically fit to have this child?"

"Yes. Especially if you take care of yourself."

"I hope I can. For our sake and the sake of our child."

Leaving the doctor's office, she isn't sure he's correct. The mental and physical toll of the last few months in China have had some effect, especially stress over watching Mischa conduct undercover work.

•

One cool, late night in March, Basya awakens in their safe-house around midnight in terrible pain. Though the night's cool, she's sweating. Her face, hands, and ankles hurt. She doesn't need to arouse Mischa - he's a very light sleeper, a condition acquired by long years in military-intelligence. He knows she's up. She was tossing and turning. As he looks at her, she moans.

"Mischa! How much more can I take of this pain?"

Coming over to sit on her side of the bed, he holds her hand and tries to comfort her.

"Take it easy," he says, patting her gently on her back. "I'm going to wake Shen up to take us to the hospital. Let's not take a chance."

"No. Not yet. But it'll be soon."

As the night deepens, the pain gets worse. But she manages to doze off again.

He looks up at the ceiling. "Brace yourself, Mischa. This is not going to be easy."

•

A few hours go by.

"How often are the contractions coming?" asks Shen who has been a medic assigned to the American army during World War II. In the countryside he assisted in a few births.

"Every quarter of an hour."

"How long do they last?"

"About thirty to forty seconds. They were mild around midnight, but now they seem to be somewhat irregular and coming on stronger and more frequently. Basya feels terrible. Her lower back aches and it's getting tight in her pelvic area."

•

Mischa had taken all precautions to be ready for the time of delivery. He helped Basya pack a small suitcase of a night gown, toiletries, and two baby outfits, one blue and one pink.

Walking out the door into the lonely hours of the early morning, Basya manages to stand, though she appears very weak. At that moment, she stops and sees water leaking down under the tip of her nightgown, forming a tiny puddle on the porch floor.

"Don't worry. Everything is going to be okay," says Mischa. But he and Shen have difficulty helping her into the backseat of the car. Mischa tries to calm her. "We'll be there soon." His voice is hoarse and she can tell he's nervous. His hands twitch slightly.

•

"I'm going to be a father," he says to himself as they reach the hospital. "Hope it's a girl." The car turns into the hospital driveway and he hurries out of the car. He beckons to a nurse who happens to be standing outside the entrance and smoking a cigarette. When she looks into the backseat window, she knows exactly what to do. In minutes, the hospital staff transfers Basya to a gurney and whisks her inside the hospital. He feels angst when an attendant tells him, "Unfortunately, you'll have a long wait."

Rushed to the delivery room, Basya lets out a hellish scream. It's so loud that in one explosive contraction the baby is born moments later.

Mischa never hears the scream which even startles veteran doctors and nurses, witnesses to thousands of births. In the waiting room, he paces the floor. He hopes the doctor will come out soon. No one tells him of the birth.

All our lives we believed that in many cases our survival has been dictated by fate. At least that's what I thought. But I wonder, maybe there is a God.

"I must keep my eye on that exit door," he utters to himself. "Let me welcome the obstetrician when he walks in with the good news of my newly-born." He waits and waits, feeling depressed. Thoughts of the past years rush by, like an incoming ocean tide.

Olga's death, the civil war, battles, rendezvous and separation from Basya. Fear of the gulag, escape, adjusting to a new country. Now this. It could be a difficult childbirth with the increased possibility of complications due to her age. My wife could - God forbid - die!

And then, Dr. Rodchenko waddles out. Mischa has met him once when the gynecologist examined Basya. The two men got along splendidly since both were exiles from the Motherland and anti-Communist, at least that's what Mischa imparted and the doctor believed him. Dr. Rodchenko looks different now. He takes off his face mask and brushes his hair back in a gesture that indicates this has not been an easy delivery. Mischa notices he's not smiling. With years of experience on the battlefield, Mischa can tell the first instant when a messenger stands before him, whether that messenger brings good or bad news.

Noticing beads of sweat on the doctor's forehead and upper lip, Mischa watches him wiping his face. He tries to put on a happy countenance. Seeing the doctor up close, Mischa's sure it's going to be bad news.

Dr. Rodchenko. explains that in spite of the new-born girl being a few weeks early, the infant is doing well. She weighs almost eight-and-a-half pounds. "Your wife, on the other hand," continues the doctor," has sustained an extensive laceration and has lost a large amount of blood. We'll be taking her back to the operating room shortly to repair the laceration and reduce the amount of bleeding."

"That sounds serious."

"Serious, it is," grimaces the doctor. "During surgery, Basya had a convulsion and her blood pressure, in spite of the blood loss, is still high. He explains that this was toxemia of pregnancy, but with the medication that they were giving her, they expected her to improve within the next two days, now that the baby had been delivered.

"I understand," says Mischa.

"We will do all we can to save her," mutters the doctor, not going into more detail than necessary.

Mischa realizes the doctor has flashed him a warning.

•

He had received danger signs all his life. He remembered them: the NKVD's command to stop pursuing Basya. Or the time he drove to Valencia in Spain, supposedly to check the city's readiness for battle, but really to find Basya. Or when, in 1943, he invented an excuse to go to Moscow to see her. He ignored the risks. Whenever he was in danger, especially on the battlefield, he always believed he'd survive. This threat, however, frightens him.

As the lights in the waiting room begin to dim, he thinks. *I know one never gets all one wants in life. All I want is to be with Basya and the baby.*

Others might have cried. He didn't. He just sat there in a trance. Then he did something totally out-of-character for him, he closed his eyes and prayed. "God, let her live. Please."

•

He couldn't go home, - no one was there. So, he wandered the halls of the hospital, or went outside for fresh air or got a bite to eat in the canteen. But most of the time, he sat in the room and held Basya's hand. He put on a good act. In the next few days, in order to lift Basya's spirits, Mischa expresses joy as the father of a healthy, baby girl. He tells

Basya the doctor says they're both going to be okay. Comforted, Basya tries to sleep.

One night, seeing that she's finally sleeping, he leaves the room. Standing against the wall, he again prays quietly, but anxiously. *We finally made it together, and now this. God forbid. What if…. What am I going to do without her? If only she'll live.*

The birth of his daughter that first day was the happiest day in his life. It wasn't his first, but he hadn't been there when his first daughter, Klara was born. This time, this birth allowed him to enjoy having a newborn, an experience that brings one joy in life. He smiles. He stands at the nursery window where this tough once Soviet commissar, still a secret agent, giggles, and brags to everyone, "Isn't she beautiful?"

"Lovely," they say. He doesn't say that his wife's in danger. He doesn't want sympathy. He doesn't notice the wide smile and joy of other parents and grandparents looking through the pane glass window onto their newborn children and grandchildren.

"Who does she look like?" he asks the nurses.

"Like your wife. She's beautiful."

•

Over the next few days, Basya's blood pressure improves. But she remains anemic and develops a fever. Dr. Rodchenko considers giving her a blood transfusion. He already began penicillin injections, which he got from the American Embassy. It's obvious to him that Basya has developed a serious infection and when the penicillin has no effect, he decides to add a newer antibiotic, known as tetracycline which he again obtains from the Embassy where the doctor, a strong supporter of Chiang, has friends on the staff.

On the third day of her hospitalization, Mischa's worries increase. Without getting obnoxious, he keeps reminding the doctor of the urgency of the case. Dr. Rodchenko is not unsympathetic, but he has many patients. He's only one of a few staff obstetricians.

When her condition does not improve, he and several other staff doctors decide to give her a blood transfusion. It doesn't work.

"We're doing everything we can," was the message Mischa receives from the doctor via the duty nurse the next day. The cold reply again stirs his worst fears. *"It is unthinkable,"* he says to himself.

Sitting in the waiting room, his thoughts take him back to Odessa. He remembers what his sister, Klara, said when someone died: " *'Their luck ran out.' It was that simple.*" He pushes that thought aside. *That may be, but this is not the way it's supposed to happen. The baby is healthy and they all live happily ever after.*

The loss of others, especially to his parents, was easier. If someone was sick, a special prayer for a speedy recovery would be said in the synagogue. He can't remember the name of the prayer. At this point, he can't rely on luck or even fate. He needs something more and increasingly, he believes it's spiritual.

•

One morning, Rabbi Chaim Lipshutz, who has been in China for many years at the *Ohel Moishe Synagogue,* visits the ward. He calls his trips to the hospital, *'bichur cholim,'* the good deed of visiting the sick. He stops at the foot of the bed of another patient in the room. The rabbi smiles - that's all he does. The woman smiles back as if to say, "your presence comforts me."

Then the rabbi stops at Basya's bed. Basya's asleep. Mischa is sitting on a nearby chair. He rises, rubs his eyes, and tries to stand up straight. He shakes the rabbi's hand and motions that they go outside into the hall. He tells the rabbi he's a businessman who, though he fought in the Red Army during the war, deserted, and is a sympathizer of the Chinese Nationalists. He then proceeds to tell the rabbi of Basya's poor prognosis. He asks the rabbi if he can say a special prayer for her.

"Yes. Of course."

And then he asks the rabbi, the question of the ages.

"Why us?"

The rabbi smiles. His wise eyes put Mischa at ease.

"Let me tell you about Moses who, as you know, led the Jewish people out of Egypt and finally was set to enter the Promised Land. At every turn during the entire journey of forty years, Moses listens to *Hashem* (God) and struggles to keep his people in line as they surmount every obstacle. He always receives Hashem's approval in the form of 'Yes.' Only once did Moses disobey Hashem. He took his staff and struck the rock to get water without Hashem's permission. Therefore, Moses had to be punished. When Moses beseeched Hashem to allow him to enter the Land of Israel, Hashem said, 'No.' Moses died on Mount Nebo."

"I don't know your story. But I bet when you fought in the War, Hashem said, 'Yes.' When you survived the Holocaust, Hashem said, 'Yes.' When you deserted to China, he protected you. The same with your wife. All her life. Hashem said, 'Yes,' whenever she found herself in dangerous situations. He protected her. Now, she's ill. We'll have to see whether Hashem answers, 'Yes' or 'No'"

•

A day later, in desperation, Dr. Rodchenko and colleagues contact a consultant at Huadong Hospital, a teaching hospital in Shanghai. He suggests that they try a newer form of tetracycline, Aureomycin. One of the doctors at the hospital was a colleague of Dr. Benjamin Minge Duggar, the inventor of Aureomycin and was doing some of the basic clinical research which afforded him a supply of the new drug. A member of the hospital staff arranges to transfer a supply of Aureomycin for Basya. Within hours, the new medicine is injected. Then begins a long twenty-four hour wait to see if the drug works.

Mischa waits in the room. He holds Basya's hand. "Be strong," he urges. She dozes off.

The next day, Dr. Rodchenko enters the room, with a smile on his face.

"She's out of danger. We're monitoring her. Hopefully, she'll go home in a few days."

"Thank you so much," says Mischa as he vigorously shakes Dr. Rodchenko's hand.

•

Eager to leave, Basya obeys the medical staff. Two days later, aided by a nurse, she gets up and, for exercise, walks up and down in the hall. She breast-feeds the baby as Mischa sits by her bedside. Overjoyed with the birth of a daughter, they promise they'll never tell this child of their Communist undercover work. Never. They have named her, Klara, after Mischa's daughter.

A few days later, Mischa notices Basya's swollen pallor has disappeared. He kisses her.

On discharge day, Mischa and Basya, accompanied by a nurse who carries infant Klara, walk out of the hospital to their waiting car. As he turns for a final look at the building where his wife was spared, Mischa says, with a smile on his face and a few tears forming in his eyes:

"You know, Basya, God said, 'Yes.'"

•

Meanwhile, the Chinese Civil War intensifies in April, 1949. Shanghai is poised for revolution. Mischa and Basya hunker down with their newborn in their safe-house near Longhua Airport.

"It's a good spot and no one will suspect us. If things get rough, we can stay here and avoid surveillance. We fit in. Besides, we have Shen with us." Mischa tells Basya one day when they're in the sitting room. "You know. I've taken Shen for granted," says Basya. "Never asked. What's his story?"

"Back in nineteen-twenty-seven," answers Mischa, "the Chinese Communists had been instructed by Stalin to work with their rival Chiang Kai-shek. Only Chiang tried to eradicate the new Chinese Communist Party and attack Shanghai's workers who had gone on strike. Russian Communist agents in China supported the worker's uprising which backfired and ended in the violent suppression of the Communist Party of China, (CPC)."

He stops. He goes to the door. Basya can see he's checking to make sure no one can hear him, even in his own house. Not discovering anyone nearby, he continues. But this time, his eyes narrow and his lips purse.

"Since his strike-call failed, Stalin recalled his operatives. As in Spain, he ordered those Russian agents jailed or shot. Shen still hates Chiang for causing the hunger and poverty of China and killing thousands of his comrades. But he blames Stalin for the death of his deported friends. I'm sure he'll protect us, even if we defect."

"I see," interrupts Basya. "Let's hope we don't have to chance that," she says, not realizing that Shen, with his sharp eyes, clever smile, and loyalty, will protect them.

•

While Shen watches over them, Mischa is organizing resistance to the Nationalists. Mao's army, renamed the People's Liberation Army, has swept across north China. It captured Beijing earlier in the year. On April 24, the Nationalist capital, Nanjing, falls to the Reds. Mao is ready to pounce on Shanghai.

•

In May, Mischa's routine and underground work increase. He provides Moscow with a steady stream of information on Nationalist troop movements, command structures and weaponry. He sends the information by radio which he has hidden in the safe house. The transmitter's powerful enough for the Soviet receiving station in his former base in Vladivostok.

But he's perplexed?

"Why is it that in Israel, I felt more comfortable working with Jews than Communists here? He senses he's becoming enamored with the Zionists. *They're fighting for their future. They're young and excited like we were in the*

days of the Revolution. They're revolutionists." Pausing for a moment, he smiles and thinks to himself: *"Basya and I should join them. What the Party has done to the Jews is really bad. They took away our culture and made us into second-class citizens. They label us rootless cosmopolitans. There's no future for us in Russia."*

•

Meanwhile, the possibility of getting out of China and to the West will increase in the days ahead when Basya, clever in the art of being another person, is ordered by the Center to go out into the field again. The Center expects it, even though she's just had a baby. Shen hires a Chinese nurse, Milling, whom he has checked out and is loyal to him, to take care of the infant, Klara. This move frees up Basya to once again put her spy talents to good use.

If Mischa and Basya are to succeed in their espionage task, she must find a local job that will give her access to information. For that, she needs a new cover. Her new forged documents state she has been in China since nineteen thirty-eight when, fleeing from Hitler, she and her parents settled as refugees in Shanghai.

After a few interviews, she obtained a position in a commissary, known as a PX, on an American army post in Shanghai. The PX serves as a retail store that sells Army surplus equipment and provisions to military personnel. The supply store hires her as a sales clerk; she knows English.

Having secured the job, Basya's in a position to meet American servicemen, especially pilots. She picks up tidbits of intelligence to help Mischa and his Communist underground which sabotages the city's infrastructure allowing Red troops eventually to enter with few losses.

Events move quickly. "Shanghai will not hold for more than five days." Mischa messages the Kremlin, noting, "American ships are evacuating their diplomats, a sign that defeat may loom for the defenders." He witnesses the Nationalists proclaim martial law throughout the city as their troops search for suspected Communists. Executions multiply.

•

During this time, Mischa saved Shen's life. One night he and Shen, with three of their guerrilla comrades, entered an abandoned garage in the outskirts of the city. They had walked through the main floor where they saw a hydraulic lift was up with a windowless car with bullet holes on its door panel. One of the guerrillas shouted,

"Clear." But Mischa, looking ahead into the hall's office, spied a lone gunman rise up and aim his rifle at the group. Instinctively, he pulled Shen down and they both fell to the floor. A shot from the gunman erupts and flies past the pair. But one of the other guerrillas who entered with Mischa and Shen, fires his pistol and kills the enemy. Later, Shen, never one to show emotion, pulls Mischa aside, and says, "Whatever happens, I'll support you and stand with you. I give you my word."

"Me, too. Comrade."

They bow to each other.

•

Chapter 35. Shanghai, 1949.
BASYA.
"Enter Arno and International Airlines"

•

One of the first major international crisis of the post-World War II, Cold War period resulted in the Berlin Airlift. The consequences of that event would play a huge part in the defection of Mischa and Basya. In May, 1948, the Soviets shut down rail and road deliveries to Western suppliers who were bringing in food and supplies to the sectors of Berlin under Western control. Moscow had hoped to isolate West Berlin, so the Communists could take over the entire city. Now, the Americans began to fly in food and medical aid. That operation foiled the Soviet attempt. Moscow backed down. One of the airlines flying supplies into the former German capital was International Airlines. With that experience under its belt, International Airlines would go on to enter the refugee transfer business.

•

Mischa and Basya, Russian Communist agents assigned to aid their Red Chinese comrades, often are congratulated by their Chinese Communist friends for their help. What the Chinese don't know, however, is that despite the couple's success in bringing victory to their Chinese compatriots, Mischa and Basya could face the death penalty when they return home to Russia. That's why the two feel they must overachieve to enhance their value. With an axe hanging over their heads, the pair must find some group which will help them escape to the West. Little do they know that help will come from a city they don't recognize. Seattle in the American state of Washington.

•

Thousands of miles away in Seattle, Washington, Bill Worley, president of International Airlines, leaves his office for a brief stroll around the city's airport terminal. Stepping outside, he hears the loud noise of a plane racing down the runway. The blasting sound still gives him chills - he's been in love with airport noises all his life.

Thank God, dad brought me here as a young kid to watch the planes take off and land. He'd lift me up to the top of the fence to see the aircraft climbing up into the wild blue yonder.

Now, Worley needs fresh air to clear the statistical mush in his overwrought brain. He must make a fateful decision and resolve the problem that faces him and his company:

What to do with recently acquired war surplus DC-4 and DC-6 aircraft?

He must utilize his new fleet to the maximum for his fledgling group to survive. He knows he can take advantage of fast-growing tension between the West and the Communist bloc, in the new Cold War; as well as, move the airline more into freight and low-cost, passenger-charter service. All he has to do is to convert a few more DC-4s to civilian aircraft to carry passenger-cargo. He and his staff begin to contact aviation fuel providers in Asia, to set up a network of handling agents who could coordinate and provide the charter flights the local-service they need at major international airports. Thus is born the new International Airlines Transfer Program.

Worley realizes that the Chinese civil war looms as another chance to market his aircraft. Many foreign firms will be moving their offices from Shanghai to Hong Kong as part of their foreign divestment, following the expected Communist victory.

Being somewhat altruistic, more than the usual corporate, profit-hungry corporate heads around the country, Worley sees the enormous flow of refugees in Europe and Asia as a humanitarian obligation to help those displaced persons escape grave danger. In 1949, 900,000 Jewish refugees need transportation to Israel and the West. Worley has a market.

With a plan now in place to expand his airline in the Far East, Worley hires George McKibben to manage his Asian operations. McKibben, a career pilot and a former RAF member, had signed up with Britain's air forces in 1938 before World War II. He was shot down and captured by the Japanese during the British debacle at Singapore. He makes a striking figure. Tall, muscular, and a hard-drinking Dubliner, he survived a brutal Japanese POW camp in the Malaysian peninsula. At war's end, he wandered around the Far East until Worley hired him.

As an experienced combat flyer with the RAF, McKibben went right to work. His first task was to gather around him a group of fearless pilots. Partial to former RAF lads like himself, he'd hire them on the spot. One lucky man to be interviewed early in May, 1949, is a Czechoslovak national, Arno Novak, who's between assignments and looking for a job. He tells McKibben that after Germany surrendered in May, 1945, he wanted no part of what he saw as the beginning of a Communist resurgence that would engulf his homeland. So, he flew to the Far East to fight the Japanese. Because of his service in the RAF, he became a British citizen. He's hired immediately.

What Arno didn't tell McKibbin, however, was that it was a spur of the moment decision that brought him to Asia. Waiting at an airbase near London for transportation to Prague, he heard British Command Headquarters needed pilots to fly cargo to the Pacific to be used against Japan, then still putting up a fight. So he signed up. He had made up his mind not to continue the relationship with his girlfriend, Tatiana, now in Prague. The war in the Pacific was soon over, but he remained in the area. He had fallen in love with mystic Asia.

McKibben and International Airways offer Novak his first assignment: Transfer Shanghai Jewish refugees, whom the Japanese imprisoned in a ghetto during the war, to the newly-created State of Israel. He eagerly accepts. Worley and McKibbin are overjoyed they have someone reliable to pilot the Jewish transfer and continue the airline's activity in the Far East.

•

On a warm, spring morning in war-torn Shanghai, days after Arno is hired by International Airlines, Basya Abramskaya wakes up, dresses quickly, gobbles down breakfast, and exits her residence. She made sure her child is okay and properly attended to by the nurse, Milling, before she walks several blocks to her new job in the PX. It's a good job for her - near home and not stressful.

Hanging her coat up in the closet and tidying up a bit after her walk from her house, she takes her post behind the counter. She can sit much of the day. Two fellow clerks are busy manipulating their chopsticks into a bowl of fish and rice and then smacking their lips as they wash down the food with hot tea. The PX doors haven't opened yet. Looking around the large hall, she feels uneasy as always, knowing another boring day looms ahead. After all, she's dealing with what she calls young, chewing-gum, senseless, and brainless American pilots, from whom she can pick up bits of intelligence vital to the Communist cause.

Moments later, the store doors open and soldiers, sailors, marines, airmen, and their raucous Chinese guests rush in.   Later that morning, Milling brings Klara to the PX to be hugged by her mother. As she puts the baby back in the British-designed perambulator, she feels that a pair of owl-like eyes are boring into her body. Glancing here and there, she notices nothing out of the ordinary, other than the increasing bustle of morning business. She's convinced, however, that someone is looking at her, now that Milling has taken the baby back to the house.

At that moment, a pair of strong, male hands grabs her from behind around her waist.

"Hey," she yells."

Anyone watching this scene, might look askance at what is taking place, and perceive some harm is being done to a lady right in front of their eyes. But Shanghai is a violent city. Scenes like this occur every day. Basya, however, is no docile servant. She turns and, recognizing her assailant, slaps his face so hard that the shocked man releases his grip, reels back against the counter, and holds his painful right cheek.

"That's for not contacting me and not telling me that you're going to take a powder."

Not forgetting where she's standing amidst Americans and Chinese, she realizes she shouldn't have spoken Czech which sounds like Russian. But she throws caution to the wind and follows it up with one of the most notorious, curse words in the holy Russian tongue, *"May you go back to your mother's…"*

He looks at her in disbelief and breaks out into a nervous laugh, a not-unusual reaction among those who see a loved one act out of character and use foul language in striking back.

"Can't we go outside? I'd like to explain," he says, excited to have discovered her, but smarting from her blow.

Standing in a little garden just on the other side of the building, Basya, regaining her composure, exclaims in English. "You look good, suntanned as if you just came off a beach vacation. But how did you get to China?"

"Is that all you can say," laughs Arno. Not wanting to attract further attention even in Shanghai, he dare not get too close to her. But he does have the courage to ask:

"Found someone else, have you?"

She nods. "Yes. I'm in love with someone else. My long-lost boyfriend.

I found him by accident. I didn't know he was alive."

"Congratulations. I saw the baby when the maid was here."

She nods again, remembering that this man was nothing but a long-ago fantasy. She puts on a wan face. She stares at him and signals she's not adverse to hurting him again, and wants him to go away quickly. But she realizes she's antagonizing him and that's not good. He could blow her cover and tell the authorities his ex-girlfriend, a former Czechoslovak diplomat, is now a Communist agent.

"Once doubt is woven into a blanket, the fabric rips apart," she recalls an old saying.

He looks at her for a moment and then says calmly, "I missed you. Believe me. When I saw you just now, it was like my whole mind and body changed. I couldn't believe it. I instantly thought we could pick it up again. But now I see you're a mother."

"Look Arno," she replies harshly, "We both moved on. I want you to go away and never come back."

"Move on, have we. You bet. When I saw the Communists were going to take over Eastern Europe, including our own country, I fled. I want no part of the Reds."

Basya can only frown. She can't admit that she, too, can't stand the Party.

"Besides," he continues, "I longed to get back into the air. I'm a good fighter pilot. I've got a gift. I can scan the skies, take it all in. I know how long I have to do something and then do it. Very few people have that skill. When I got out here, I did some combat flying in the Malayan states until the Japs surrendered. Stayed in the force, until earlier this year, when I picked up this new gig."

"What's that?"

"I'm a pilot for International Airlines. We're now flying stateless Jewish refugees out of Shanghai to Tel Aviv. Before the Japanese attack on Pearl Harbor, Shanghai played host to a bustling Jewish community of more than 20,000. After the war, many went to Australia, the United States, and other places. About six to seven thousand Jews remain. It's time for them to get out. The war is over and the civil war here has intensified. The Chinese, both the Nationalists and Communists, will let them depart."

"Sounds amazing," she says with interest. "Go on."

"After we take them out, we land in Israel and discharge them. From there, we go to Cyprus, or Amsterdam, and lay over and then return to Shanghai. I got here just in time to help the Jews. We're doing so well that the Israelis may ask us to fly Yemenite Jews, out of danger. We're going to pick up the Yemenite Jews in Aden. Tel Aviv calls it *"Operation Magic Carpet."* We're getting the job, because we know the route from Yemen to Israel"

Basya is stunned. She can't believe what she's hearing. Right before her eyes, in the shape of her old boyfriend, she's discovered a path to freedom. *"Mischa and I can leave with the Jewish refugees"* is the thought now mobilizing her brain. Her face lights up. She's sure he's very upset. She hopes she hasn't alienated him completely. She smiles at him. After all, they did live together for a few years. She blushes as she thinks of those intimate hours.

But that's the past. Besides, he's changed. In London, he had charm, no longer. Maybe it's the war. Back then we liked each other. But it was a fling. I have Mischa and my baby now.

But Arno, who's been lonely, too, continues to move the conversation, not letting her talk. He's suspicious about something that doesn't make any sense: *Why is Tatiana in Shanghai and not in Prague.*

"Tell me Tatiana, how did you get to Shanghai? How did you come to work for the Americans in a PX when you're a Czech diplomat," he questions with a puzzled look.

She recognizes at once that he's figured it out. She knows it's a gamble, but she proceeds to tell him that she was sent to the Czech embassy in Tel Aviv and then to China with her long-lost boyfriend, whom she now reveals is Russian.

"I'm on loan to the Soviets who are aiding the Communist Party in China."

He frowns. He wants to tell her, he can't see her anymore because of her Communist connection. He wants no part of Commies. He starts to get up to leave.

She grabs his hand and says, "Wait!"

"No, I can't. I have to get back."

Since she and Mischa are desperate and knowing Arno's view on Communism, she offers up a convincing argument by spilling out that they want to defect.

"Arno, please. We've got to get out of China. I don't want to raise my baby here. The Soviets will kill us, whether we stay here or return to Russia. Arno, help us. It's hard for you, I know. My boyfriend, and all that. But he, too, wants to defect. He's had it with them. It will be a great thing if we get to the West because we'll tell all. I plead with you, help us."

"I don't know what to say. It's all so shocking," he says, and for a few moments he's silent. "I may be able to help you, even though I don't know why I should after that swat in the face."

"I'm sorry."

Just then, a round of Communist mortar fire hits nearby. They duck.

"Your Commie friends are getting closer. They'll be here in a few days. I'll try. You'll hear from me. You're lucky the airline I work for is flying the Jews out soon. The date is May 31st. Mark it down. Maybe I can get them to squeeze you on the flight. He's Jewish, too, yes?"

""Yes. Of course. Oh, Arno, if only you could."

"Let's see what happens. Where are you staying?"

"Near Longhua airport. We have a courtyard house on the Huangpu River," she reveals as she writes the address on a piece of paper. She doesn't tell him that Mischa has luxurious digs at the Cathay which, because of the Communist advance, he rarely uses. Better not to be with a group of foreigners residing in a well-known hotel where the Nationalists can pick you up.

He puts the paper in his pocket and plants a kiss on her forehead.

She lets him.

He walks away.

The date is May 22, 1949.

Returning to the airline office, Arno reflects on his meeting with Tatiana. Though he has not seen her for several years, and though he left her, he's muddled.

I made a mistake. If only I had met her first instead of her Communist friend. I really should help them. But I can't fly them out on my own. I need to tell McKibben. He'll agree. Getting two defecting Soviet agents on my flight will be a feather in our cap with the Yanks.

•

McKibben sits in his office, feet up on his desk, and utters approval to Arno's plan.

"Russski operatives. That would be something. Risky. If it gets out that we aided the West in an espionage matter, the Chinese Communists, who look like they're going to win this war, will be pissed as hell," explains McKibben.

"I agree," replies Arno.

"The Reds could scuttle our whole operation," continues McKibben. "Remember, we have a contract with Israel and the American Jewish Joint Distribution Committee to fly the Jews out of here to Tel Aviv. That's money in our coffers."

"What do you suggest?"

"I have an idea," replies McKibben leaning forward with a smile on his face:

"There's an Israeli here in Shanghai, Yaakov Namir. He's from their new intelligence organization. He's watching over the operation to transport the Jews. Here's his card. Let him make the arrangements. We'll fly them out. But he's got to put them on the plane. That way, the Chinese Reds can't blame us. We'll deny we knew anything about it."

•

Arno and Yaakov Namir arrange to meet late that afternoon at The New Shanghai Tea House on Nanjing Road. He easily spots the Israeli as there are not many foreigners left in this Shanghai neighborhood. Most have fled, taking so much with them that trucks loaded with foreigner's luggage jam the harbor's dock area.

Yaakov is one of the Jewish state's top organizers, ostensibly working for the Jewish Agency which handles what the Zionists call, The Ingathering of the Exiles. The Agency is bringing in Jews from all over the world, especially from Arab countries. That's why he serves as the Agency's liaison to International Airlines. He's well-trained. He's a member of *Shabak,* also known as Shin Bet. He came to Shanghai early in 1949, as part of the Israeli effort in counter-intelligence.

At the meeting, Yaakov is fascinated with the plan to fly two Communist agents out of China and turn them over to the Americans. *Our counterparts in the United States. will love us for this package.*

Arno asks Yaakov if it is okay to set up a meeting to meet Mischa.

"I'll meet your guy," Yaakov responds. "But in the meantime, as you can appreciate, I have to consult my people in Tel Aviv. While we're trying to stay neutral between the United States and the Soviet Union in this Cold War atmosphere, I believe our future lies with the Americans and the West."

Both Yaakov and Arno know that while they make plans, God, chance, or their government's leaders can change their arrangements.

•

Meanwhile, Mischa has to be careful. Keeping discipline in Shanghai, the Nationalist police continue to put on drumhead trials to accused black marketeers and suspected Communist agents, even though the Communist assault on Shanghai begins that very date on May 23. The Communist underground says they'll let the Jewish refugee flight go if they take the city, but Yaakov knows it's not a guarantee.

A day later, Tuesday, May 24, thousands of Nationalist troops appear on the Bund to make a last stand against the Reds, though top municipal officials have fled. Sand-bagged sentry posts are set up at main intersections and armored cars rumble through the streets. Fleeing Chinese civilians, carrying what possessions they can on their backs, choke all the exit roads.

Next day, Wednesday May 25, the skies are clear. Mao's unstoppable forces launch their invasion of the city. The Bund is empty, as if a tornado has swept through it, dispersing its human population to the four winds. The conquering troops reach the main business district.

Actually, Shanghai isn't really taken over by the PLA. It is conquered by municipal workers. Mischa has labored for months within the Communist underground network and the trade union movement. He provided them with assignments to take over municipal buildings.

Early Thursday, May 26, Red General Chen Yi first troops, clad in green uniforms, move further into Shanghai from the south and southwest. After breaching the wooden palisade that so ineffectually rings the city, the Reds advance.

Fighting continues as the American military men and government advisors speed away, leaving the Nationalists to fend on their own. Chiang's troops put up little resistance. They flee.

By Friday, May 27, it's all over. The city changes hands without a battle. The transfer of ruling the city takes place without a hitch. Chinese Communists soon will conquer all of the Middle Kingdom, and in six decades will become a global power.

•

"There's an organization flying Jewish refugees to Israel of all places," Basya whispers to Mischa, on Saturday, May 28, the morning after the Reds took over the city. "We can get out," she adds as they walk in a park near the Cathay Hotel.

"Just like that, huh. Sounds too good to be true."

"But it is true. I have it all figured out. I approached Arno, my old boyfriend in London who showed up. I asked him to put us on the flight. He's anti-Communist. He'll do it."

"Yes. But we're Soviet agents. Our officials here will know we fled and NKVD will easily figure out that we got out with the Jews. They'll pick us up in Tel Aviv when we land," says Mischa, also feeling a stab of jealousy about an old boyfriend of Basya.

"Maybe. But I know Arno will save us and Klara," says Basya. She doesn't want to remind herself or Mischa that thirty years ago, she left a daughter behind and lost her.

"He wants you to meet with this Israeli, Yaakov Namir of the Jewish Agency. Arno's setting up that meeting. See if it's good for us. Nothing to lose. For sure, we won't be able to get off the plane in Israel. The flight is on May 31.

"I'll speak to him," says Mischa, still feeling jealous. But then he thought of his own encounter with Slava.

"Incidentally," she chimes in, "we got a message from Nanking addressed to you. It looked official, so I opened it. Says that a Dimitri Abramovich Dudin is coming tomorrow night, Monday, May 30th, and wants to meet with us."

"You're kidding. Dimitri. My old comrade from the Civil War," he says excitedly. "You met him once in Yekaterinburg."

"I don't remember. I don't like to recall anything about my stay there. Besides, look at you. You'd think boss Molotov is calling on you."

"He is by way of Dimitri. I told you I helped save his son. Thank goodness. And now Dimitri, the father, actually is arriving," says Mischa, lowering his voice.

"What if Dimitri isn't like us," she questions. "What if he never changed. It could complicate matters."

"No matter. We're not going to tell him. Anyway, I know how to talk to him. Nothing to be afraid of," he says convincingly.

"Glad you feel that way" she answers, wondering why Mischa's excited over a Soviet agent joining them at this time. Not a good sign. "What's Dimitri up to?"

"Incidentally," Mischa explains, "the last time I heard about him, he was in Harbin. He remained in the Far East but soon joined the NKVD. I heard he was back in China. Why worry? He's probably coming to help our cause. The Center doesn't know we want out."

"Still, unusual," she says.

Later that same day, Saturday, May 28, a pedicab pulls off the Bund onto a side street. It proceeds to one of the most congested areas of the city, usually so crowded that it's hard to identify a single face in the sea of pedestrians buying and chatting in the alleyways. Not today. Not even cooking on street stoves. Residents are staying indoors. The Reds have taken over.

Mischa descends from the cab and instructs the driver to return in an hour. Entering the deserted passage, he can't locate the alley guard. There is nobody around. He gets to the Half Moon Tea House and walks through the eating area to the kitchen and out the back into a flowery courtyard. Yaakov Namir is sitting at a table. Mischa smiles and shakes hands with him. They order a dinner of noodles and chicken, and then begin plotting a Soviet defection.

"We'll get you on the flight from here," says Yaakov in a hushed tone. "But we can't let you off in Israel. Too dangerous. We'll fly you to the Americans in Amsterdam. Do you agree?"

"Agreed," answers Mischa. "That's just what we want."

"But Mischa, what happens if the Americans won't take you in Amsterdam?"

"Are you kidding? With what we know, why wouldn't they? There's a 'Cold War' on."

"Okay. But after Amsterdam, you're on your own. Meanwhile, let's go over some security matters." He draws a few diagrams of the plane in a notebook he carries. The two sit and talk for a while. Concluding, they shake hands. Yaakov uses a Yiddish word, *"gemacht"* (done) to seal the deal. Mischa smiles. They return to their cabs and leave in opposite directions.

•

"Hope it works out. What if Yaakov turns us over to the local Reds to gain favor. But we have no choice. It's the Israelis or death in Moscow," Mischa says to himself.

•

"We better succeed, or I and the State of Israel are in deep trouble," thinks Yaakov.

•

Chapter 36. Shanghai, 1949.
MISCHA AND BASYA.
"Comrade Dimitri calls on Mischa and Basya."

•

For the last six years, Dimitri Abramovich Dudin increasingly has begun to think like a hardened criminal. He is a person who has mercilessly murdered innocent people. He doesn't feel queasy about a new assignment to cut short the life of a comrade in arms, one who trusted him like a brother, who watched over him and even went looking for him when he was believed dead. But Dimitri recoils every time he thinks of the time after the battle along the rail tracks when Mischa berated him in front of the troops with his sarcastic utterance of 'fun and games.' Moreover, he has grown to resent that Mischa never helped him in making his sister, Klara. go for him. When they parted after the Civil War, Dimitri's anger toward Mischa increased. Spurned by Klara, it makes it easier now for Dimitri to eliminate Mischa's girlfriend. *"Why should he have a lover. I don't."*

A friend or relative who knew Dimitri back in Russia would observe that he is now rather thin, his face gaunt with a sickly yellow pallor. His cheeks are covered with pockmarks, and his long hair, though still combed back in the Polish style, has thinned out. Now his cold tiger-colored eyes, which once shined with enthusiasm, are now colorless and are covered with big, blue rings.

Dimitri has lived a life of wretchedness. It shows in his mean, bullying look. For a few years, he kicked around the Far East, mostly in Manchuria. After Mischa's sister, Klara, left Harbin, he and friend, Osip Rabinovich, stayed behind. They lived off the land by harassing and threatening White Russian emigres with extortion of their families back home or in other lands. It was a con game that paid off handsomely, until he re-joined the NKVD and spent some time in Moscow during the Great Patriotic War. That's when he spotted Basya in the Metropol. After the Moscow stint, he returned to the Far East. He accepted any assignment with the same passion he displayed in the Russian civil war three decades ago, and that included orders from the Center to kill anyone, including friends and relatives.

•

Now that he was in Red-occupied Nanjing, the Center in Moscow could call him on a secure phone line. And they did.

"Dimitri.   You're to go to Shanghai and eliminate Mischa Rasputnis and his lady friend, Tatiana Kovacova, also known as Basya Abramskaya. Our agents here in Moscow, have discovered that Rasputnis was mysteriously transferred from Israel to China when he should have been sent back home and put away. Heads have rolled," the NKVD indicated in its message to Dimitri, adding, "the culprit Alyosha Kovalchenko of the Cominform, and others, were executed a month ago for participating in a plot to kill Comrade Stalin."

"This assignment is serious, as is every killing of traitors to the working class. Rasputnis is to be taken out for harboring Trotskyite thoughts and selling out to the West."

Dimitri is so brainwashed that he cannot see that Stalin, as in the civil car in Spain, is about to murder his agents in China. They know too much of the workings of the former Comintern and the new Cominform. Their usefulness is over.

•

Meanwhile, Dimitri's Chinese Communist comrades have taken over Shanghai, so he can now travel from Nanjing which he has made as his base, even though he'll have to drive over rutted roads. Checkpoints will slow his progress, turning a half-day journey into a long day's drive. No matter - he will make an appointment with his unsuspecting intended victims for Monday, May 30. He doesn't know it, but it is the day before Mischa and Basya's flight from Shanghai.

Accompanying Dimitri is the driver, Gleb Federeov, an NKVD operative. As they begin their journey, Dimitri tells Gleb, "Looking forward to this hit."

"I am, too. I was off-duty for a while."

"What happened?"

"Gallstones. But I'm fine now."

"Good."

•

Early Sunday morning, May 29, the day before Dimitri is scheduled to leave Nanjing, Mischa and Basya realize they face a huge dilemma. The three of them can't board the plane with their passports. Because the Jewish refugees are stateless, the couple, who are posing as Jewish refugees, needs a temporary Chinese exit visa to depart. The only way for these two agents to get the visa is to obtain forgeries. To do that, they must disclose to Shen they plan to leave with Jewish refugees on Tuesday, May 31. He can help them obtain the documents.

"Now you know," Mischa tells Shen.

"I'll help you. Pay a visit to Sam Wo, the forger," Shen tells Mischa. "You go. Take your daughter, Klara. They have to take her picture. I'll meet you there."

•

On Sunday afternoon, May 29, Mischa and Basya board a pedicab. Milling, carrying the baby, hails another. They proceed through alleyways, known as hutongs. That the crowds are back out on the streets can be seen as the cabs squeak as they progress inch by inch through masses of residents and shoppers who block the way. Finally, the cabs push through an alleyway entrance which runs off a busy avenue, replete with small shops located in the commercial district about five miles from their house. The pedicab drivers stop at a nondescript two-story house whose ground floor contains a communal tap to wash rice and do laundry, a procedure which makes the ground slick with water. Because of this, they are careful how they get out of their conveyances.

Shen's waiting for them in front of the building. He rings the bell twice and a woman answers and shows the group up to the stairs leading to the second floor. Like similar houses in the neighborhood, the rooms are small and every inch of space is accounted for. Several tables are positioned in one room, and include two typewriters on one side of the table and blotting paper on the other. Different-size bottles full of chemicals and various inks stand on another counter. Each of the tables has sliding shelves installed underneath them, that way, it's possible to dry out a large number of documents. The operators of this establishment have placed fixed paintings to the wall, behind which they carved out shelves so they can hide false documents waiting to be picked up. If the police or strangers wander upstairs, they won't see hidden papers. They keep the paintings up, because under Red rule, their work remains illegal. Many Shanghainese want new passes, so they can travel to their former homes, or to those of relatives in Nationalist-occupied territory. The crew here can produce new passports or visas as genuine as if they came from the government printing office. This illegal installation is aptly called the 'House of Forgers,' and its inhabitants churn out passports like water crashing down a waterfall.

The group Mischa, Basya and Shan, Milling and baby Klara, don't spend too much time in the facility. They all have their pictures taken. Klara doesn't cry. They fill out forms: date of birth, weight, height, color of eyes and hair. This information is needed for new documents to be used in their planned escape which is duly noted for Tuesday, May 31. Provided with new names, they sign the papers: Ilse and Heinrich Rosenberg, as well as daughter, Klara. They put aside their original identification cards for the moment.

When they're done, Shan whisks them back to their quarters where their suitcases already are packed and hidden in a closet. After their documents are picked up later on Monday, May 30, all that is left for them to do on the day of departure, is to get into the taxi that Shen, their devoted assistant, will hire. He'll accompany them to the airport. Milling will remain at home.

Back in the residence, Basya says, "Shen now knows everything."

"He'll be loyal to us. I feel it."

"How can you be so sure?"

"I'm not. But we don't have a choice."

She turns away.

•

The plan may be set, but Shen realizes that hastily drawn escape routes usually are flawed. What he doesn't know is that a Chinese Communist espionage unit has planted a spy in the 'House of Forgers.'

•

At lunchtime, Monday, May 30, the day after Mischa and Basya's stopped at the forgers' facility, the staff goes out to eat at nearby food stands. A worker, Bao Wang, who is the only one who stays behind at the noon break to watch over the facility, serves as a Communist police spy. Every day, he goes to one of the tables and checks on the previous day's work orders. Today is no exception. He notices three documents with Russian names, Mischa Rasputnis and Basya Abramskaya changed to Ilse and Heinrich Rosenberg, plus a child, Klara, born in China. He recognizes their former names, as he met them at PLA office, but was out when they returned to this office to obtain their forged documents. The date for the exit visa is May 31. He writes the names and departure date on a card and walks down the steps and hands it to a messenger.

"Take this to our comrades at PLA headquarters. They should know about these traitors trying to defect. They'll know what to do with them."

As the courier departs, Bao smiles. Patting himself on the shoulder, he begins sweeping the floor. By tomorrow, he'll forget about these three visas and check for other violators.

Meanwhile, several miles from the PLA barracks, Dimitri and Gleb are riding in a captured American Army car heading to the barracks where they must report their arrival in Shanghai. At a major intersection, Gleb, the driver stops the car and screams!

"The pain! It's excruciating," he yells as he holds the right side of his stomach. "You better drive," he shouts, his face thrown into contortions.

"What is it?"

Gallstone attack. It's back."

"Okay. Go sit in the back seat where you can stretch out."

•

Arriving at PLA headquarters, Dimitri calls for a medical assistant to come out with him to see the patient.

"Yes. He's got gallstones," agrees the aide moments later. "We have to take him to the hospital. I'll call an ambulance."

Twenty minutes later, as the orderlies pick up Gelb's stretcher, Dimitri bends down and reassures him: "You'll live."

Gleb waves goodbye.

Another soldier, who was told Dimitri has arrived, walks over to the ambulance.

"Comrade Dimitri. Here is a communique for you and the new Soviet Consulate. It's been in our stacked-up outgoing file and I just noticed it. I was going to get it over to the Consulate, but now that you're here, I'll give it to you."

Dimitri reads the note. His intended victims have obtained exit visas to leave China.

"I'll take care of this," he informs the PLA official.

"Thanks. Sorry it sat here so long. But we've got much to do."

"No problem. So long," replies Dimitri.

Now, I really have to hurry, even if Gleb is out of the picture. I can't wait.

"Take good care of him," Dimitri instructs the medic. "I've got a job to do." He thanks the PLA soldier and returns to the car.

So, they're preparing to fly the coop, are they?

•

A few hours later, Dimitri knocks on the door of Mischa and Basya's residence and is admitted to the premises by the maid.

"Mischa."

"Dimitri"

They bear hug.

Dimitri observes that no-one is sitting in the large receiving room. The balcony is clear. Not seeing or hearing anyone upstairs on the second floor, he enters the dining room.

"Mischa, your work has become well-known."

"Thank you. I am a Bolshevik and that's what Bolsheviks do."

Basya, who's standing by, smiles in admiration, although she knows they're acting.

"Dimitri, please meet Basya."

Noticing Basya holding the child, Dimitri smiles and says, "Congratulations."

She thanks him with a wan smile, though in his presence she immediately feels fear.

"Might I just say that your photo - the one that Mischa always showed me in Yekaterinburg back in nineteen-nineteen - does not do you justice, Basya."

"Let's drink to that," interrupts Mischa. We are so happy, comrade.

Time for a toast. You know us Russians - we love vodka like cats love milk."

"Here's to our reunion and our child, Klara," toasts Mischa who, for the first time, notices Dimitri's haggard eyes and shallow complexion. Hearing Mischa say the baby's name as Klara, the name of Mischa's sister as well as his sought-after girlfriend, the guest feels he has to say something and utters, "The great Stalin will save us," he toasts, raising his glass to Basya and adding to his own dour countenance, a provocative smile.

When Dimitri turns back to Mischa, Basya winces.

In one gulp, the vodka, burning their throats, is downed. Patting each other on the shoulder, they again toast and munch *zakuski* which Basya puts out on the table, having squirreled it away since arrival in China. She watches with approval as Milling, who took little Klara back to her room a while ago, now brings in various courses and skillfully serves the men. At the same time, Basya doesn't know what to make of the fact that after the toast, Dimitri rarely looks at her.

There are more drinks as Dimitri and Mischa reminisce, though, she notices Mischa is sweating.

"I know you searched for me after that conductor threw me off the train," Dimitri reminds Mischa. "I appreciate that. I recuperated. Never found the bastard. But as you know, I did meet up with your sister, after you and I met in Siberia. By the way, how is Klara?" he asks Mischa in a nonchalant manner that a former lover uses when inquiring about an old girlfriend.

"I have no idea," responds Mischa glumly.

"I pleaded with your sister to stay with us in Manchuria. But she kept repeating she had to find her father whom she knew was in America, or was it, Canada? Even then, she wasn't like us. Her only purpose in life seemed to be to locate him, so much so that she didn't even go to Palestine with a fellow who had become her boyfriend. She was tempted, I know. He was one of those Zionist idealists, conceited, self-assured," says Dimitri, smirking. "They'd make a good pair. She had his main character trait: Aggressive."

Mischa's stunned somewhat at Dimitri's description of his sister, Klara. But doesn't want to start anything, so he reluctantly agrees. "You're right," replies Mischa with a checked smile. "But some women are like that sometimes," he snickers, adding, "Not my love here, of course who's one of us. We'll probably get married soon."

"Yes. Of course. But how did you know your sister Klara is dead.

Jews don't name a newborn after someone unless they're sure the loved ones are deceased."

"No. Not the Klara you're thinking about. We named the baby after my late daughter who was killed last year in a bombing raid in the Israeli war. Her name was Klara, too."

"Oh. Sorry to hear that."

"I didn't tell too many people."

As the conversation continues, it dawns on Mischa that even in the short while that Dimitri has been with them, he never mentioned his son.

"You know I met your son at Khalkin Gol?"

"I heard."

"He was wounded, you know."

"I heard," Dimitri repeats again, showing some anger.

"Mischa, I don't talk about him. I disowned him just before the Great Patriotic War. He refused to apply for officers' school. I told him he's a shirker, and not acting like my son. The Army needs officers, not just foot soldiers. I said I'd never speak to him again. And I haven't."

"But he's so proud of you - he told me so."

"Inconsequential. Let's not talk about it anymore. I would rather eat, if you don't mind."

"But of course," says Mischa, smiling faintly.

Milling then serves up three bowls of dumpling soup, followed by crispy chili beef and pork, steamed sea bass, chicken wings, egg fried rice, and hoisin wraps and wintery rolls.

After dessert and tea, they again reminisce about events in their lives. At first, they are like two old soldiers recalling adventures together in a forgotten war. How they rode the railway together as guards, for example. They joke. They laugh. For good reason, they don't bring up the argument they had during the skirmish off the railway. And like Russians at a party, they down more shots of vodka.

During the next few rounds of imbibing in which Basya takes no part, she realizes that Dimitri probably was the Red agent whom her late husband, Lev, pushed off the train. She could see now that he probably was drunk on the train and that Lev was in the clear. "I don't trust this one," she says to herself, reinforcing her earlier suspicion.

Neither Mischa nor Basya indicate anything that hints at their planned departure in the morning . Nor does Dimitri give away his intentions and plans. Trained agents know how to act - a non-committal face, just like the poker player holding a flush. Dimitri even mocks a few minor Soviet leaders to hide his real intentions to strike at his opponents.

The minutes tick by. The clock moves forward, very slowly.

Despite his uneasiness with Dimitri regarding his feelings toward his son, Mischa tells Dimitri about the civil war in Spain. He believes he can unburden himself with Dimitri with whom on those frightening train rides in Siberia, they often confided in each other.

"With all due respect, why did the *Voshd* (Stalin) eliminate good comrades who fought so hard for the Party in Spain. Stalin went on to sign a pact with Hitler, the very same Nazi leader he denounced for years."

"I disagree. Stalin bought Russia time to strengthen our forces before the war. Besides," Dimitri adds in rebuttal, "be careful. Those words you are uttering are treasonous."

A lull in the conversation. Quiet. Embarrassment. Nervous eyes scanning the room.

Mischa breaks the silence as he calmly asks:

"Dimitri Let's get down to business. Why are you here? Something special?"

"To kill you both," he says, his eyes cold and steely, a demonic expression on his face. Gritting his teeth, he draws a revolver from under his belt which he points at his hosts. Recoiling, Mischa and Basya stand against the wall. Mischa gasps slightly. He realizes he can't draw his revolver on his belt as Dimitri's gun is aimed right at him. His eyes grow narrow and seem to bulge with fright. Frozen, he glares at Dimitri and tries to steel himself further. But as he does so, his hands shake. He can feel his heart thumping. Words don't come out. His only thought is that he, Basya and the baby, were so close to escaping. *So close and now this.*

Basya, her face ashen, her lips pursed, her eyes terrified, freezes. She wants to scream, but can't. Sounds get stuck in her throat. She wants to tell Mischa something, but she's unable to utter a word.

"Why Dimitri? Why?" mumbles Mischa hoarsely: "How can you? We were so close. Put down that gun."

"The Party. You see..." shouts Dimitri, his face growing darker.

Silence.

Then, a loud noise from the blast of a gun. A familiar pop. One shot. One bullet. Dimitri instantly falls to the ground, dead.

Mischa is rattled. He stares at the dead man, blood oozing out of his head onto the tile floor. He has seen lifeless bodies on battlefields. This is just one more.

Basya barely gets words out. Her sentences are garbled, stuck in her throat. Her face is still dark and pale. "Who fired the shot," she finally asks.

"Shen. He has eyes in the back of his head."

A few minutes later, Shen appears, a revolver in his hand. He's followed by Milling who remains silent, stares at the dead body and returns to the kitchen.

"I knew that you two are leaving tomorrow," declares Shen. "I was suspicious of a Russian, coming here a day before your flight. I worried the same thing would happen to you as occurred to my friends back in twenty-seven when those agents were murdered by the Kremlin."

He stops talking. He looks at his lifeless victim on the floor.

"Watching the agent enter the house, I went up to the balcony and hid behind the bamboo screen in order to keep an eye on events below. I hoped the Russian could not see my two black eyes between the tiny spaces in the screen. When Dimitri pulled the gun out, I quietly moved the screen and grabbed my weapon, and in seconds, fired at the assassin."

•

Even days later, Mischa would recall three simultaneous noises: the quick clickety of the bullet, a faint gasp, followed by the thud of a body hitting the floor. Mischa shook his head in amazement. Basya would only remember the shriveled body.

After wiping off the blood from the floor with the aid of Milling, and getting rid of the bloodstained rug, Shen manages quick remedies to the situation. He removes belongings in the victim's clothes. He goes outside and spotting Dimitri's vehicle, he sends word with a messenger for three friends to come to the house with their car. After an hour - it's now dark outside - the group arrives and wraps the body in a large rug, carries it outside and places it in Dimitri's car trunk. A driver is assigned to Dimitri's car. The two automobiles drive to Suzhou Creek where it meets the Huangpu River. Upon arrival, they are forced to wait in the vehicle because a group of Communist sympathizers caught a Nationalist soldier. A full moon gives Shen's crew light to watch the angry crowd decapitate the trooper's head and place his severed skull in a carved-out hole in the nearby wall, leaving the mutilated remains on the ground to fester.

Finally, the crowd disperses and with night closing in, Shen and his friends begin their gruesome task. Nervously checking surroundings, they shoo away the wild dogs who are waiting to feast on the dead soldier's body which lies in a pit. Then the men drive the car with the corpse in the trunk a short distance to the river bank and push the car into the water. As they watch the vehicle sink, they avoid looking at the soldier's dead head staring at them from the wall.

•

After Shen's men finish, they leave the scene in the second car. Shen notices a shrunken silver moon witnessed the grotesque acts and sighs. *You'd think the moon would move, after seeing this crime scene. Yet, it lingers over Shanghai, anticipating more bloodshed.*

In a few days, the soldier's skull is removed from the wall. Only the nearby patched-up shanties will stand over the sunken watery grave. The car will not be found for months.

At about the same time that Shen and his band ditch Dimitri's car, Leonid Krymov, a hardened Soviet counter intelligence agent, just arrived in Shanghai, woke up from a bad dream. Realizing he hasn't recently heard from Mischa and Basya whom he knew from training when they all were in Yekaterinburg, and now again in Shanghai, he sends himself a mental note to contact them in the morning before dozing off again.

•

Chapter 37. Shanghai, 1949.
MISCHA AND BASYA.
"Mischa and Basya elude Police on the Way to the Airport."

•

At seven o'clock the morning of Tuesday, May 31, 1949, Shen obtains one of the few taxis running in the city. It is a near impossible feat, when one considers the city has just been conquered by a Communist regime that has zero tolerance for private enterprise, like ownership of a taxi.

A couple approach the hired cab. The man limps as he uses his cane with dexterity. A woman who's obviously his wife, sporting a fake gold wedding band, walks alone. She's carrying a baby in her hands. Shan carries the suitcases, one per passenger allowed, according to International Airlines.

Shen places the bags in the trunk of the taxi. Taking the front passenger seat, he instructs the driver to take them to *Ohel Moishe*

Synagogue on Ward Road, in the Tilanqiao historic area of Hongkew. From there, they'll go with the Jewish refugees by bus to the airport.

The driver nods, pulls into traffic and drives slowly. There's no time for an accident. No horn blowing. No passing other vehicles. Nice and slow. The driver now glances at his passengers through the rearview mirror. While he notices no shaking hands among his guests, he does observe fearful eyes and expressions of alertness. Years of training and experience driving a taxi, trains a cabbie for moments like this. He knows he's carrying precious cargo.

"With this move, our fortune will change. Bad luck can't last forever," says Mischa.

Basya doesn't respond.

Along the way to the gathering point for the refugees, the vehicle's occupants look straight ahead. They don't want to glance at the passing scene. This self-inflicted prohibition doesn't work - they can't help but look. Curiosity and external danger cause them to gaze out the window and stare at the dead bodies on the ground.

Mischa's anxious. He knows PLA guards can be sticklers and search everyone. *We're unarmed. If we were to be seized, we'd all be picked up together, Shen included.*

The first challenge looms up ahead as the car reaches a checkpoint. Shen explains to the Communist police, sporting red armbands, that the two in the backseat are Soviet diplomats with their daughter. He shows them their old Kremlin papers. The stone-faced guards look at them, smile, wave to the baby, salute, and immediately lift the barrier to allow them to pass.

At a second checkpoint, a long line of vehicles await inspection. Shen, Mischa, and Basya, again are drawn to look to their right and immediately close their eyes and turn away. The repulsive scene shatters their very souls: A large bicycle cart stuffed with frozen child corpses, with gaping mouths, bulging bellies, and limbs dangling, await transfer inside a temporary morgue. Not even in death, are they allowed to keep their dignity. Mischa and Basya don't say it but they know under different circumstances, it could be their child.

At a third military post, Basya notes a driver abandoned his dead mule alongside the road. Further down, in front of an aid station, she watches an old man slurping down bean and millet gruel into his mouth. This is the Shanghai they are leaving behind, a city of hunger.

"Mischa, I can't take it anymore. This isn't even poverty. This is humanity at its worst. Death made over," she whispers.

"Take a deep breath. We'll get out of this," is the only answer Mischa can give other than the usual platitudes about the horror of war, even the undeclared ones. He remembers the shrunken bodies he saw in the Ukraine famine over a decade and a half ago.

The taxi enters the Hongkew and Yangpu district, with its squalid three-and-four story tenements. The district is known as "Little Vienna." The area once housed the Jewish ghetto. Shen explains that the ghetto was roughly a square mile of old, narrow lanes and dark, cramped alleyways, bordered by Gongping Road on the west, Tongbei Road on the east, Huimin Road on the south, and Zhoujiazui Road on the north.

"You know," says Mischa, "it's fitting that we're escaping from Communist rule to freedom in a synagogue. Jews leaving slavery in Egypt. Let my people go."

Basya's not sure Mischa is serious or making fun. "Not a bad thought."

"Could you believe it," continues Mischa, "twenty-thousand Jews lived in this poor and crowded area for four years during the war. It was known as The Shanghai Ghetto.

"At least they survived," she answers, taking in the teeming street. "Unlike the millions the Nazis murdered in concentration camps. Jews in those prisons couldn't escape."

Arriving at the synagogue, Shen guides them to the front entrance of the building, which boasts a beautiful wood, arch-type entrance. Mischa sees the *mezuzah* on the wall. For the first time, since he was a teenager, he puts his hand on the tin piece, a symbol of a Jewish home, with the prayer *shema yisrael* inside the casement. After he touches it, he puts his fingers to his mouth in an affectionate kiss.

"He's really got it bad. Returning to Judaism," Basya observes, but says nothing.

They enter the hall and mingle with the crowd. These two anxious-looking middle aged parents, with a baby no less, who, having been in China a short time, now have to put on an act, that they are leaving a place they called home. They have to display sad eyes, downcast faces, pursed lips, a troubled look, which isn't hard considering that they're not sure they're going to get out safely. So far, Klara has been quiet.

Meanwhile Mischa and Basya hear mumblings around them. The words shock them.

"Maybe it's a trick."

"Maybe they're taking us to a camp."

"Maybe the Israeli guy is a fake."

Some middle-aged Jews in the synagogue, hunker down with their teenage children. The young ones know nothing of the outside world. They are brothers, sisters, and orphans, excited to be going on a journey, especially on an airplane. The elders are wearing more than a single outfit of clothing, as they could only take a suitcase each. But they could wear more clothes and many of them dress with heavy shirts, sweaters, a vest, jacket and a top coat.

●

"I must leave now," Shen says. "I'll say goodbye."
"We owe you our lives."
"You would have done the same for me."
"Where will you go?"
"I'll try to get to Hong Kong."
"Good idea."
Mischa bows.
Basya bows.
Shen bows.

●

"Hope he makes it," says Basya.
"He will. Yaakov will help him. That's one thing about the Israelis. They don't leave their wounded or dead behind. Neither do the Chinese, who suffered under Japanese brutality."
"He better get out fast."
"Agreed."

●

The hall is quiet. Three Red soldiers have entered.
Mischa and Basya move slowly into the center of the crowd. They watch the troopers show Yaakov a photo. He shakes his head and says, "no."
"Wonder whose picture that is?" whispers Basya. "Could it be ours? Have they caught up with us so fast," she adds in a worrisome voice.
"We'll only know when they get to us."
The soldiers start walking through the crowd which parts, leaving a walkway through the room. They stop in front of an elderly couple and flash the photo close to the seniors' faces. The pair shakes their head.
The soldiers then halt in front of Mischa and Basya. The chief officer of the group pounds his fist into his hand and asks Mischa for his papers. The latter quickly obliges by pulling out from an inner jacket pocket his, Basya's, and Klara's forged exit visas and ID cards. The policeman gazes at the papers, looks up into Mischa's non-descript eyes, and glances at Basya who's holding Klara. Mischa knows that if the Communist soldiers

grab them, they'll be turned over to the Soviet consulate. They'd be dead within hours because they know too much. She smiles. She watches the officer flash a picture of Dimitri up into Mischa's line of vision. With his other hand, the policeman raises his two fingers up to his eyes and then points to Mischa's eyes with the end of his fingers.

The message is clear: *"Do you know this man? Did you see this man?"*

Mischa shakes his head, no. He had prepared himself mentally not to react even if the person in the photo is known to him.

The officer hands the exit visas and identification cards back to Mischa, looks around and leaves with his comrades.

"That was quick," whispers Mischa. "Not a good sign. Somebody has put out the word that Dimitri is missing. A lot of Europeans stop off in this neighborhood. It' a good hiding place. Naturally, if someone is missing, they'd look here first."

"Well, if it's any consolation," Basya utters; "at least they're not onto us yet."

"'Yet,' is the correct word. It's only a matter of time, till they realize we're trying to get out."

·

With the departure of the police, loud conversations and sighs of relief erupt.

Groups chat about the new Communist regime:

"I know a thing or two about Bolshevism," voices a Russian emigre.

"Believe me," says an elderly man. "The Chinese will be ruthless in stamping out private owners. They'll turn all farms into collectives. Already, they've started shooting land owners."

One refugee pulls out the Communist paper and reads a sentence from an editorial:

"The day will come when China will repay with interest all the injuries and insults she has suffered at the hands of the European powers."

"Boy, will they ever," comments Mischa, adding: "Mao eventually will disengage from the Soviet Union." And forgetting that he and Basya are traitors to the USSR, he adds, "And all we Soviets did for them. Without the Japanese arms we gave them, they wouldn't have won."

Meanwhile, Yaakov is about to chaperone the group to the waiting buses. He nonchalantly walks over in a restrained manner and greets Mischa and Basya. He doesn't want to give the impression he knows them well.

"Everything's on schedule," he whispers. "Apparently, the cops are looking for a Russian agent and possibly for Shen, too, though he's on his way out. Lucky, they don't know he worked for you. We're helping. God be with him."

"Yes," answers Mischa, staring into Yaakov's tired eyes, and saying with a sigh, "Thank you."

As they wait to board the bus, Mischa says to Basya, "I guess we fit in nicely. Nobody's talking to us. Just as well."

But just as the husband of a middle-aged couple, says *"Sholom Aleichem,"* and extends his hand, the loud speaker blares out:

"Chaverim, (Comrades), we're boarding the buses now."

All rise, grab their suitcases, inch forward, - bumping into fellow passengers.

"Easy. Easy," says a man who turns and declares: "There's plenty of time."

"That's what he thinks," Mischa whispers to Basya.

Basya spots a group of Chinese people standing in the alley across from the synagogue. They live in the nearby, narrow streets. They're staring at the refugees with envy.

Basya looks away as her mind conjures up a thought: *We're leaving and you're staying behind in this squalid neighborhood. Not a good thought to propagate or message.*

People scamper to get on the bus, for the last ride on Chinese soil. Their life will be changed, that is, if they actually get out of the country. They only want to recreate the life they once knew. The time is eleven o'clock in the morning, May 31, 1949.

•

Chapter 38. Shanghai, 1949.
MISCHA AND BASYA.
"Mischa, Basya and Baby Klara escape Shanghai."

•

At the very same time that Mischa and Basya leave their house in Shanghai at seven o'clock, the morning of Tuesday, May 31, Comrade Leonid Krymov sits in his office which just opened as a result of the Communist takeover of the city. Staring out of his window, he watches the morning scene, now subdued somewhat under the new Communist rulers. He has been in the Far East most of his career, having served in Siberia during the Russian Civil War.

Tall, he shoulders a dominant, egg-shaped face resting on broad shoulders that hide an almost invisible neck. Perhaps that's why his assistants fear this total disciplined master who is extremely dedicated to the Communist cause. They refer to him as "the bulldog;" and they don't snicker when they say it.

Leonid arrived at his office this morning in an agitated mood. Somehow, he has the feeling that things aren't going well. And that belief is quickly reinforced when he discovers on his office desk, a message from the Nanjing bureau, that agent Dimitri Abramovich Dudin arrived last evening, with his assistant, Gleb Federeov. The two, the message says, should have contacted him last night. Nanjing, however, does not tell him why Dimitri, known as a hit-man, is coming to Shanghai. Leonid can only surmise that his job was to take out someone within Soviet ranks who has expressed deviationist thoughts. *We do that every so often; lately, more than ever,* he realizes.

The message goes on to say: "Dimitri and Gleb will explain everything, including the accomplishment of this urgent mission when they successfully complete it."

Upset that Nanjing didn't inform him earlier of this happening, Leonid wonders why Dimitri had not called him last night, nor this morning, now that he has arrived in Shanghai. He and Dimitri also go back a long way to training in Yekaterinburg. "Small world," he thinks. "We all ended up in the same place."

Despite being puzzled regarding Dimitri, however, he's not suspicious of foul play. He chalks it up to sloppy, intelligence work. Yet, he believes he better hear soon.

The clock strikes nine o'clock. No word on Dimitri's whereabouts. Leonid's instinct instructs him to start looking for the Nanjing emissaries who should have contacted him by now.

After all, this is my bailiwick, thinks Leonid.

"Maybe I should try to reach Mischa and Basya to locate Dimitri. Maybe Mischa can find him and see what this is all about." He sends a note to Mischa via a member of his staff and asks the messenger to report back to him.

An hour later, at ten o'clock, Leonid realizes that he has neither heard from Dimitri nor from Mischa. Impatient by character, and not one to sit back and let things slide, he calls over to PLA barracks and requests to speak to Chief of Intelligence Zhou. He asks Zhou if he has heard from the Soviet agent Dimitri Dudin. Zhou knows that arriving Russians have to report to the Chinese military since the Communist victory a week ago.

"No. Haven't seen him, nor heard anything. Perhaps my assistant knows something. He'll be back in an hour. Ask for Comrade Huang, of counter-intelligence. We didn't have a chance to talk this morning and I've got to go to a meeting at headquarters. He'll help you."

Angry at the push-off and frustrated by inaction, Leonid decides he cannot wait, so he presses the Chinese official:

"Comrade Zhou. Do you mind if I put out a lookout bulletin of my comrade at your check points, and to area supervisors, to see if anyone comes up with something."

"No. Not at all. Permission granted. And now Comrade Krymov, I really have to depart for my meeting. Comrade Huang will help you. Thank you."

"Goodbye comrade. But please note, we have to find Dimitri - he's one of us," he tells the PLA officer and hangs up. He goes ahead and puts out a bulletin for Dimitri. Fortunately, he has a picture of the Nanjing agent and orders his assistant to take the picture to the PLA so they can distribute it to various checkpoints and public meetings asking if anyone had seen him. The time is 10:30 am.

At 11 o'clock, Leonid, fidgety, believes he must do more regarding Dimitri's disappearance. He follows up with another call to the PLA. This time he reaches counter-intelligence agent assistant, Huang.

"Nobody has seen Comrade Dimitri this morning," answers the Chinese officer on the phone. "But he was here yesterday afternoon with another comrade, Gleb."

"Really," says Leonid, shocked and startled at the revelation.

"We last talked to Dimitri when he arrived at headquarters yesterday. We had to take Comrade Gleb to the hospital. Neither one of them, however, informed us of their mission."

"I don't believe this," Leonid shouts into the phone, his angry voice rising to a crescendo, with pursed lips and an angry frown.

"What hospital is Gelb in? Quickly," he screams into the phone.

"Shanghai Municipal."

Leonid is up from the chair so fast, he doesn't even have time to say to the police officer: "You dummy. Why didn't you call over and tell us our agents were in town. Even worse, you take one of our men to the hospital and you don't notify your Communist ally."

He slams down the phone so hard, it leaps off the cradle and dangles alongside the desk. He puts it back and hastens out the door.

•

A half hour later, at 11: 30 o'clock, Leonid, accompanied by one of his agents, arrives at the hospital and hastens to Gleb's room.

Gleb has remained in pain all night. He has been wondering why Dimitri hasn't visited since they parted yesterday. He's furious. He can't communicate with his Chinese doctor or nurse. Demanding a phone to call Comrade Krymov, whom he knows, the Chinese refuse. They want him to rest. Finally, he's in the process of getting an orderly to take him to the office for a phone call, when Leonid bursts into the room.

"Where's Dimitri?"

"How should I know?"

"Why are you here? Why didn't you call me? What's your mission?"

"Can't you see I'm in terrible pain. We were ordered to kill Mischa Rasputnis and Basya Abramskaya" he mutters in a weakened voice.

Leonid doesn't ask any further questions. He doesn't demand an explanation. He doesn't thank Gleb for his answer. He certainly doesn't console Gleb. He actually pushes Gleb back onto the bed. Fortunately, the patient doesn't fall. The nurse holds him and calls for an aide and the two lift Gleb to a comfortable position. By the time they do this, Leonid is downstairs on the main floor. He shows his badge and credentials from the Chinese Communist government and hauls himself over to an empty desk with a phone. Looking at this watch, he sees it's already 11:45. At that very moment, two Red police enter the room and ask for Krymov.

"We have information, sir, that a Mischa Rasputnis and Basya Abramskaya and their daughter, were carrying forged exit visas which they obtained from a place called "The House of Forgers" The visas are for today.".

"I don't believe this. Such incompetence," thinders Leonid, "again not notifying us."

"Oh my! How could I have forgotten? An International Airways flight with Jewish refugees. It's supposed to leave about this time. Damn. I bet the two traitors are on it," he says, looking at his watch, and then turning to an assistant:

"Get word to the airport to stop the flight. If the plane has left, let me know. Meanwhile, I'll call to warn our people in Tel Aviv to grab the two criminals if they elude us. They should be on that plane, unless this is a trick and they're getting out of the country another way. But I don't think so. Go. I'm going back to the office."

Contacting the Soviet representatives in Israel by phone, however, takes time. Relaying the details of Mischa and Basya's defection to Moscow takes time. Commanding the Soviet embassy in Tel Aviv to make sure the plane, if it lands, is not allowed to take off again, takes time. But then it's done, and Comrade Leonid Krymov walks away, feeling he's in good shape. He has moved quickly and warned everyone, everyone except the Red Chinese air force, who possess only a few planes, but possibly could have scrambled and forced down the airplane. Before he can realize his failure to do that, he's so pleased with himself that he declares:

"I should get a medal for this; those two will die for sure."

And then it dawns on him. "Where's Dimitri?"

•

Meanwhile, a half hour earlier, at about 11:15 o'clock, a bus arrives at the Lunghwa Airport. The refugees aboard are hustled to benches inside a large, empty, terminal waiting room. Armed guards surround the building, on the lookout for die-hard Nationalist remnants who, supporting the old regime, may have gone underground. Because intermittent fighting breaks out now and then outside the center of the city, the guards are not concerned with the refugees.

Two planes are on the tarmac.

"It's too quiet," Mischa says anxiously, realizing that any delay means trouble.

Basya sees Arno coming into the waiting room. Spotting her, he approaches the couple.

"Be polite and thank him profusely," Basya advises Mischa, whom, she's sure, harbors a tinge of jealousy.

"Don't worry," Mischa reassures her.

Basya is shocked when she sees Arno. He looks haggard, unshaven, and flashes tired-eyes. For the last twenty-four hours, he's been working with the ground crew to prepare International's DC-4 plane. She owes him a lot. She wasn't nice to him at the PX and look what he's done for them.

What's going to happen now? she ponders.

Will we get out safely?

Will we arrive safely?

Will the Russians be waiting to grab us at the Tel Aviv airport?

Will the Israelis rat on us and turn us over to Russian agents?"

•

"We have a slight delay. Some paperwork," Arno says nervously as he greets Mischa and Basya in the waiting room. "We're also lucky. It seems when they fled, the Nationalist leaders detonated a massive store of aviation fuel just yonder. Luckily, they forgot one storage tank. There's enough for us. And the Commies patched up some holes on the runway."

"Arno, how can we thank you," says Mischa, offering his hand.

"Don't thank me. Thank her," says Arno with a smile and an accompanying handshake.

"I'll do that. However, we can never repay you for what you've done."

"Not a problem. Just hope we make it. With that said, I better get going. Cheerio." Turning, he blows a kiss to Basya, and heads out toward their plane sitting on the tarmac. As he walks nonchalantly, he spots a Russian T-34 tank, several armed jeeps, and groups of Mao's Red Army units spread out at one end of the airfield.

"Greetings, Ol Chaps. I do hope you'll stay put, so we can get out of here," he wants to walk over to tell them, but doesn't dare.

•

Nearby, Yaakov Namir explains to the refugees he can't go with them on the plane. He must remain in Shanghai to shepherd more flights. "My assistant, Amir Cohen, will accompany you. May God protect you until you safely reach the land of our fathers. Shalom."

"Amen," some refugees answer as they line up and proceed to passport control. Red troops are standing by, their searing eyes searching the faces of anxious passengers. Officials at a table are checking each exit visa and looking into weary faces.

Mischa and Basya hold back the fear. She's keeping her worrisome thoughts inside. Strange, he, a war veteran, feels more anxiety than Basya, the diplomat. He's showing it, with a tremble in his hand. He's sure it harks back to the civil war, cooped up for days in that Nakhodka shed. He wonders how he'll manage in a plane on a five-thousand-mile-flight across Asia.

A soldier stares at the couple's exit visa and the one for the baby. He glares at Mischa for a long time. Neither blink. He smiles at Basya. She smiles back. He blows a kiss to daughter, Klara, who remains asleep. The soldier waves them through.

All the refugees begin to walk out to the plane as the engines are warming up. They want to run as fast as they can and cut the five-minute walk to a single moment. But they know that would arouse the suspicion of the Red guards and maybe halt the flight. Others, like them, must follow in the coming days. And so, they trudge forward with wan smiles.

Basya sees Arno climbing a ladder and entering the aircraft's cockpit. Smiling, he looks out and waves down at them as the couple reaches the air-stair steps. Seated across the aisle from Amir Cohn, Mischa takes the window seat and sees the plane's propellers whirl and the motors begin to race. Basya holds Klara tight to her body. Hearing the motors start up, she bawls. Basya calms the child.

It's now noon, about the same time that Krymov's aide has contacted the airport.

"What's happening Mischa?"

"There's a plane going out ahead of us. It's unmarked. Ah oh," he adds, "Arno better get this plane moving. Two jeeps with mounted artillery guns are headed our way," he says. "One good shot and we're dead in the water," he adds, anxiously. The plane in front of them rolls out toward the runway, makes a sharp left turn and another left turn, and after a slight pause, fires up its engines. Like a cat stalking a mouse, the International Airlines plane, following the lead plane, prepares for takeoff.

"The jeeps haven't reached within firing distance, but the gunners are waving frantically at us," says Mischa, just as the first plane takes off. An artillery shot causes Mischa and Basya to duck as their plane races down the runway and begins to take off. Another canon blast. Some passengers cower; others shudder and many scream. A few put their hands over their ears to block the frightful shouts of impending death. Klara just alternates whines and screams.

And then there is silence in the cabin.

"What's happening," Basya asks again as beads of sweat form on her tall forehead.

He doesn't answer. He holds her hand. His lips seem to be moving. She knows the look and recognizes the movement of his lips. *"He's praying. Just like I used to do, even on the day, when we first met. And look where we are now. Now, he prays and I don't."*

Mischa turns to Basya: "Guess the PLA didn't seem to know which plane to fire on. They went for the first and missed," he says. "But if they get one more shot in, we're dead."

At that moment, the lead jeep, making a sharp turn to avoid a huge pothole on the tarmac, falls into the crevice and is out of action. The second jeep turns sharply and in so doing, can't get its gun around fast enough to fire.

"Too late, you bastards, we're out of here," says Mischa raising his voice so all around him can hear. And then he quiets down. Silent, he can only think: Terrible way to leave China. I hope this, and any other Communist country, is gone from my life forever.

Turning, he notices Basya and Klara have fallen asleep. He closes his eyes. Shanghai disappears behind him.

•

Chapter 39. Shanghai, 1949.
MISCHA AND BASYA.
"Danger in Flight, but They Reach Tel Aviv."

•

O to live free, freer than free;
O to live free as the wind.
-Novgorod folk song.

•

"They're out," Yaakov says to himself, with a sigh of relief, as he heads out the airport terminal door and walks to his car. The driver greets him.

"Cathay Hotel," he tells the driver in a confident voice.

The ride back to the hotel is uneventful, even though he's stopped at a few checkpoints and then waved on because of his diplomatic status. He knows he doesn't have much time. The police probably are onto him, especially since he figures that by now they must know Mischa and Basya are on the plane.

Arriving at the Bund, he exits the car and walks down the wide boulevard. Today, the populace and street merchants are out in full force taking advantage of the opportunity to sell their wares. They realize they'll soon be the target of stringent Communist rules and methods to conduct business.

Entering the Cathay Hotel, now deserted of tourists and business people, Yaakov walks to the reception area and sits down and writes on a piece of notepaper: "Jeanette: Your mother is much better. She's leaving the hospital today. Love, Uncle Joseph." He hands the note to the receptionist, with an instruction to send it as a rush telegram to Mrs. J. Ping, China Imports, 2417 Allenby Street, Tel Aviv, Israel.

Yaakov pays the charges and leaves the building. He's being watched.

•

The International Airlines plane, with a total of sixty passengers and a crew of eight, including two hostesses, has been in the air for several hours. Passengers relax. As for Mischa, his demeanor is quiet. Still, he doesn't underestimate the Soviet secret service whom he's sure is coming after them with a vengeance, no matter where they land.

"I'm sure my Russian bosses here must have notified the Tel Aviv Embassy. The NKVD guys will be at the airport in Israel to greet us," he says to himself as he notices Basya dozing. "I have to keep my fears to myself. No use worrying Basya, though knowing her, she's figured all this out already."

Despite an uneasy sleep, Basya maintains a slight smile on her face. She's comfortable. They're long off the ground. "One thing at a time," her expression seems to indicate.

•

As the DC-4 levels off at 10,000 feet, Mischa and Basya have learned from Arno of several obstacles facing the flight. First, even though they are flying on an American airline, all of the passengers are stateless, without a passport. International Airline officials believe the plane should land, where possible, at an airfield controlled by a nation friendly to the United States. Stateless Jews obviously prefer not to touch down or fly over Muslim countries that refuse to recognize the Jewish state. "Most countries don't distinguish between Jews and Israelis," Arno reminds the couple.

The flight route is set: Over to Hong Kong, Bangkok, Calcutta, Bombay, Aden and finally to Israel.

"In some countries, like Vietnam and Laos, we don't have permission to enter their air space. We'll fly over them anyway. They won't be able to detect us. No radar. Chancy. But we have to do it," Arno declares, adding, "if you hear anti-aircraft shots around you, just keep your head down."

•

With very competent navigation, the flight lands safely at the RAF base in Aden.

Moments later, Arno comes out of the cockpit and walks over to Mischa and Basya.

"So far so good," he says. "Now on to Israel."

"So why the sour face."

Have you forgotten? A weak armistice exists between Israel and the Arab states. The Arabs can shoot us down if we're over their territory," he says coldly. I doubt they would. But I'm going to fly over the middle of the Gulf of Aqaba and make sure I'm equidistant from the Saudi Arabian coast on one side, and Egypt on the other. "

The several hour flight to the airport, located on the northern outskirts of the city of Lod, about twelve miles southeast of Tel Aviv, goes without a hitch. The journey from Shanghai to Tel Aviv, including time in the air, stopovers, refueling, customs clearance, took three days.

Landing, Arno, out of caution, steers the plane to a spot on the tarmac, a hundred yards from the passenger hut, serving as a terminal. He positions the aircraft in such a way that the passenger door is on the far side of the plane. That way, passengers can't be seen from the terminal as they descend the air-stairs.

At that very moment, the cabin erupts with clapping and singing with gusto, the song, *"Shalom Aleichem,"* (a Sabbath welcoming). Mischa and Basya join in. They remember this popular tune from their youth, though they stumble a little over the words.

The Jewish refugees, who have spent years in stateless exile, finally have made it to the Jewish homeland. For them, this is not just another landing; it's the end of the line. Many had never flown before. Their long, pre-war journey to China occurred on an ocean liner. Now, years later, coming off the aircraft and walking around it to get to the makeshift terminal, some celebrate by getting down on their knees and kissing the ground.

Each immigrant receives an Israeli flag and a bottle of water. Many tear up. All the Jew-baiting, pogroms, homelessness, ghettos, are behind them.

"Home at last.

•

All the travelers and crew are off the plane, except Mischa, Basya, and Klara, along with Amir Cohen, the Shin Bet agent. For them, sitting behind the cockpit, it's not over. They wait anxiously. An eerie silence pervades the aircraft. It's like being in a mausoleum with the minutes ticking by like hours, as if one's staring at cold wall vaults.

"What's going on Amir? Why the delay," Mischa asks nervously.

"I don't know. Could be the Russians are at the gate and demanding to come aboard."

Mischa, eyeing the terminal, thinks he spots the familiar faces of Soviet Embassy people behind the roped-off area. A few, it appears even from a distance, are arguing with Israeli officials. He's sure he recognizes his former assistant, Igor Riasanovski.

"Can I borrow your binoculars?" Mischa asks Amir.

Unfortunately, Mischa can't read the lips of the Russian diplomats obviously sent to grab them. But if he could, he would have heard the Soviets shout, "We demand you let us board the plane and search it. We know there are Soviet citizens on board. They're fugitives from justice and wanted for murder. Hand them over."

"You have no jurisdiction here," says Arno, staring into the face of a Russian security agent. "This is an American airline. The Israelis have the say as to who boards planes at their airport. Besides, we don't have passengers with the names you're citing. Check the manifest."

The Russian then turns to the Israeli official who is flanked by an armed guard.

"I order you in the name of the Union of Soviet Socialist Republics, to allow us to search the aircraft. Call your superiors."

The Israeli officials at the airport phone the Minister of Interior in Jerusalem, who in turns calls the Minister of Foreign Affairs, who in turn contacts the Prime Minister. After several hours of deliberation, the Israeli government informs Soviet officials that the laws of the State of Israel forbid airport officials to allow a foreign national to check another foreign country's plane on Israel's sovereign soil. The Prime Minister's office declares the Jewish state must respect the rights of the United States, just as they would the USSR.

During this time, Mischa, Basya, Klara and Amir Cohen sit immobilized. *We knew we were risking our lives. But it's torture; waiting to find out if those bastards will get on this plane and come for us. Maybe we'll never get out of here,* thinks Mischa. He touches his forehead and wipes off beads of sweat. His face is flushed. He doesn't say a word to Basya who's been trying to mollify baby Klara. The infant is screaming her lungs out as babies often do. Even though a few months old, she must sense that there are people outside who want to harm her.

Mischa, his hands beginning to shake slightly, closes his eyes and prays. Finishing a few minutes later, he thinks.

I've been in bad situations before. The gun battle on the Siberian railway. Or the incident with Dimitri. I thought I was finished then. Can I be three times.

But he realizes this time is different: *It's not just me. Or just Basya and me. We've got a daughter. I lost one daughter to war. I'm not about to lose another one. Maybe, just maybe, if they try and board the plane, I can divert their attention. Maybe even make a deal with them, so Basya and Klara can get away. I have to come up with a plan. Supposedly I'm good at that.*

"Basya. I don't mean to frighten you, but...." He's unable to finish the sentence. Pursing his lips, he castigates himself. *I just can't help myself. Need her reassurance.*

"Don't worry Mischa," says Basya staring at him and reading his thoughts. "We'll make it." She takes his hand and holds it tight.

However, a few minutes later, Basya herself, burdened even more with Klara's crying, loses control and yells in a high-pitched voice, "Mischa. I can't take it anymore. Are we ever going to get out? Do something."

Overhearing the conversation, Amir Cohen interrupts them. "Take it easy, both of you. We've got you covered out there. Believe me, we know what we're doing. It's going to be okay," he says in a reassuring voice.

They frown.

●

After the altercation with the Russians, Arno returns with his co-pilot to the parked plane. Impatient, he takes his seat alongside the crew in the cockpit and waits for the Dutch tourist group to board for their flight home. His navigator, sitting behind him, has no outside view. Arno has a clear view out the window on his left side of the aircraft. Just then, coming into view is a baggage cart heading toward the side of the plane, right at the passenger cabin door. The cart is surrounded on all four sides by a tall, thick mesh screen which prevents anyone on the airstrip from seeing into the conveyance. He sees the driver, a member of the airport ground crew, climbing up the ladder to the plane.

What the hell. Something is wrong, he thinks. *No reason for this. Everything's checked and rechecked, including loading the baggage. What's going on?*

"Be right back," Arno tells the navigator and co-pilot. Because of their position in the cockpit, they can't see the passenger entrance. Arno goes out of the cockpit into the cabin. He closes the door behind him. He's armed.

"Bloody hell. What are you doing? Stop! You can't do that," Arno screams as he observes Amir Cohen, the Israeli agent, giving a signal to Mischa and Basya to come back down the aisle and climb down a ladder placed against the now open door of the cabin.

"Yes. We can and we will," comes the firm answer from Amir standing before Arno with a pistol aimed directly at the pilot's heart.

Arno freezes. He notices the ground crew member is also holding a revolver.

"I broke my ass to spirit you out of China and you spit in my face," he yells at Amir, Basya and Mischa. "Is this the way you Jews treat a friend? You people never told me you're grabbing them in Israel," he says, concentrating on Amir's stern eyes. "That wasn't the deal. We're supposed to turn them over to the Americans in Amsterdam. You're betraying us," he says, his eyes blazing with disbelief and anger.

Amir, who's listened calmly to Arno, is not impressed by the pilot's tirade, and snaps back firmly: "Mischa and Basya are valuable to us for our survival and safety of the Jews in Russia. We have to do what we have to do. We're not kidnapping them. They've agreed."

"I don't believe it. "

"He's right," says Basya as she gently hands the baby to Mischa and walks up to Arno. Amir lunges to grab her, fearing Arno will seize her as a hostage. But she's one step ahead of him.

"Mischa and I agreed we had to do this," she says, throwing her arms around Arno and kissing him on the cheek. "What do the Americans say...'there's no free lunch'? There's a price for everything. We have valuable information. For us, we might as well give it to fellow Jews. Israel needs our help now."

Holding her tight, Arno has one last chance to reach for his weapon and hold onto Basya and thus try and foil the operation. *I can't do it. Someone could get hurt. Let 'em go. It's no skin off my ass.* He relaxes.

Basya steps back and blows a final kiss to Arno. She turns and returns to Mischa and the baby. With Amir's gun still trained on him, Arno doesn't try to stop the guard who is the first one to take a few steps down the ladder. He's followed by Basya who hands the child down to the cart driver. They descend safely.

Mischa prepares to follow her, but instead, turns toward Arno,

"Sorry. We were sworn to secrecy. God bless you."

Only after agent Amir again asks Arno to return to the cockpit, does he plead with him to be silent regarding the group now leaving the plane.

Arno heads back to his seat in the cockpit and closes the door behind him.

"What was that all about," asks the navigator.

"Nothing to be concerned about," Arno answers, thinking: *I hope Tatiana will be happy. The Americans are going to be pissed. Fuck the Commies. Who cares about them.*

The Israelis had planned everything to perfection. Amir followed Mischa down the ladder and into the baggage cart where Basya, Mischa, and Klara have been waiting. The mechanic conveys the cart toward a small Quonset away from the terminal. There, stands a black sedan, its motors running, ready to transfer the four passengers to a secret destination away from Tel Aviv.

While the cart carrying the four from the plane moves on the tarmac toward the Quonset hut to get to the car, Mischa breathes a sigh of relief. A slight wind caresses his face. He notices armed Israeli troops posted here and there in strategic places, such as a machine gun nest outside a small hanger. Their eyes are all on the terminal, even though they know the Russians have left. Mischa recalls that meeting he had a week ago with Yaakov Namir in Shanghai in the Half Moon Tea House, where they discussed security matters. At that time, Yaakov pleaded with him:

"Mischa, as I said, we'll get you to the Americans. But did you ever consider that you could be of valuable assistance to the State of Israel. Three million Jews are trapped in the Soviet Union. Both of you know the Soviet and Czech spy system and how we can penetrate it to help our fellow Jews. Mischa, you can help us."

Mischa recalls he responded: "I'll speak to Basya about it."

•

Meanwhile, the Russians realize they're unable to grab the defectors from the plane while it's in Israel. Impossible to pick them up on British-held Cyprus, unless they storm the aircraft. They're not willing to do that. They'll meet the plane in Holland.

As planned, Arno's International Airlines flight refuels in Cyprus and flies on to Amsterdam's Schiphol airport where the Americans also wait for their prize catch.

Even though the Israelis realized Arno may try to stop them, they believed he would remain silent once the group got away. He did. He'd never betray Basya. So, when the Americans cornered Arno in the terminal, he told them that their expected visitors were not on the aircraft. He claimed he had no idea how or when or where they were hijacked or who did it. That's all he revealed. Since his fellow crew members had not seen anything significant at Lod, and since Arno hushed up the two airline hostesses, nothing was disclosed by the crew. The American agents, who couldn't touch Arno as he was British, were so focused on the Soviets, due to the heating up of the Cold War, that they figured the Russians somehow kidnapped Mischa, Basya, and Klara.

Meanwhile, at Schiphol, the Dutch passengers exit the aircraft and go through customs control. The Russians waiting for the opportune moment to snare Mischa and Basya watch the passengers board an airport bus departing for the city's Hotel Terminus. Soviet agents follow the bus. At the hotel, Russian operatives are seen scrutinizing the passengers.

"They're not here. They're gone. Out of the country by now. Blast them," screams the lead Soviet agent. "We've been tricked."

Through diplomatic channels, the American and Soviets accuse each other of snatching the couple. They inform their world-wide spy networks to look for the defectors.

•

A week later, Comrade Leonid Krymov and Comrade Gleb Federeov, are recalled from Shanghai to Moscow. They are never seen or heard of again.

•

Chapter 40. Tel Aviv, 1949.
MISCHA AND BASYA.
"The Defectors and their Happy Family."

•

**"Happy families are all alike;
every unhappy family is unhappy in its own way."
— "Anna Karenina," by Leo Tolstoy.**

•

They feel like fugitives. Three passengers, one an infant, sit in the back seat of the black sedan which drives up to the Lod airport exit which serves as a checkpoint. The driver, Uri Brenner, presents credentials of the passengers, including Amir Cohen. Amir, occupying the front passenger seat, now brandishes a STEN machine gun.

Examining their documents, the Israeli military policeman waves them through. The vehicle picks up speed and heads to the main coastal road which runs from Tel Aviv.

"Where are we going?" Mischa asks the driver.

"Can't tell you. But everything is okay. We'll be there in a few hours," comes the reply.

•

Holding hands, Mischa and Basya don't talk. Driver and guard don't talk. Klara doesn't cry. Silence. No verbal thoughts expressed, only inward ones, especially with Mischa.

We had no choice. We had to trust the Israelis. We've turned our entire lives over to them.

Mischa and Basya doze off. Klara, having had her bottle, sleeps.

The vehicle, sporting window shades which not only block out the burning sun, but shields those inside from preying eyes, heads north toward Haifa, moves northeast to Afula, then northeast to Tiberias, climbs the Galilee Hills, and continues traveling north through Upper Galilee.

Mischa is the first to awaken. He smiles. Looming up ahead is snow-capped Mt. Hermon, ranging between Syria and Lebanon, and towering over the swamp-drained Huleh valley.

Home at last.

Navigating a few turns, the sedan makes a final right onto a dusty, unpaved road leading into Kibbutz Kfar Blum and stops in front of a twelve-foot gate, still standing after the recent Arab-Israel war. The four weary travelers get out of the car. Approaching the gate, four people on the other side of the gate who have been waiting patiently for their arrival, wave to them.

The two Israeli agents open the gate, atop of which is a painted sign that says: *"Bruchim haba'im.* Blessed are those who come."

And then, after Mischa introduces Basya and little Klara, who's settled down and is all smiles, Mischa reminds everyone in a quiet but firm voice, of the missing person, his daughter, whom they all know died last year during the war. He bows his head.

The two officers watch this small group, which includes the four from the kibbutz: Mischa's son-in-law, Volya; his grandchildren, Dora and Uri; and Mischa's American friend from the Spanish Civil War, Michael Rapaport. They explode into jubilation common to family reunions and celebrations all over the world. They hug, kiss, shed tears of joy, laugh, gush with the small talk of a reunited, happy family - all this under the hot Galilee sun and the shadows of the mountains surrounding the valley.

Home at last.

•

Epilogue:
THE RASPUTNIS FAMILY.

•

The arrival of Mischa, Basya, and Klara to Kibbutz Kfar Blum was accepted by the members of the settlement without fanfare. The newcomers were just one more family arriving in the new Jewish state. Only Mischa's son-in-law, Volya, and the American, Michael, knew the couple's story, and they were sworn to secrecy. Granddaughter, Dora, vaguely remembered Mischa when he visited the family the year before in Tel Aviv when her late mother, Klara, was alive; and grandson, Uri, was only an infant. Soon, the children began calling Mischa and Basya by their new Hebraized names, "Uncle Micha'el and "Aunt Batya." Mischa was never introduced to Klara's children as Grandfather, only as uncle, when he first met them in Tel Aviv before Klara died and the name stuck. He was only an uncle. Infant Klara's given name was not changed, although the family adopted a Hebrew last name, Meiri after Mischa and Basya were officially married in a small ceremony in the synagogue in the nearby town of Kiryat Shmona.

Not only were Mischa and Basya thoroughly debriefed by Israeli intelligence a few weeks after arrival, but Mischa became part of the foreign office and the new national intelligence agency, Mossad founded later that year, 1949. Mischa worked in the Russian section. Over the next forty years, he contributed knowledge and analysis of Soviet policy in the Middle East.

Early investigation into the disappearance of Mischa and Basya by the Center in Moscow came to naught. They were convinced the couple were taken by the Americans. They didn't put much stock in the possibility that the couple were in Israel. Still, they did assign Igor Riasanovski, Mischa's former assistant, to look for the defectors in the Jewish state. After a year, Igor, who never carried out the order, cabled back to the Center that a thorough search of the country by his agents, uncovered no trace of them. After serving with Mischa for years, Igor wasn't about to betray his old boss. On their part, the Americans dropped the case. They had other fish to fry, especially in Cold War, active cities, like Vienna and Berlin.

As the months turned into years, Mischa and Basya often would tell each other, "these truly are the best years of our lives." They knew they wouldn't have been alive had it not been for the people who, because of their humanity, aided them: Alyosha, the Comintern official; Anatoly, the Soviet diplomat; Nikita, the Metropol Hotel night manager; Arno, the pilot; Yaakov, the Shin Bet agent; Igor, Mischa's NKVD assistant and Shen, Chinese driver and protector.

One day in 1989, Basya, succumbed to breast cancer, after battling it for several years. She was buried in the Kfar Blum cemetery, a long way from Kosice, Slovakia.

Mischa, sporting wavy silver hair, a little stooped over, but still with a refined face, soldiered on as a widower. The kibbutz sheltered him. His granddaughter, Dora. eventually moved with her husband to a retirement community in Florida. Her brother, Uri, remained in Israel.

•

Two years after Basya's death, the Soviet Empire imploded and with it, the dormant pursuit by the NKVD/KGB for Mischa Rasputnis and Basya Abramskaya. Finally, the Mossad, through its channels with the FBI, informed Mischa that his sister, Klara, was alive and resided in Baltimore, Maryland. Although he never recovered from the shame and hurt he suffered when his sister was chosen to journey to America to find their father in 1917, he desperately wanted to unite what was left of the Rasputnis clan.

In 1992, a year after the fall of Communism, Mischa contacted his sister, Sonya. He wrote that he would like to visit the family in the U.S. Klara, however, forbade Sonya to respond. She still hated him and always believed he, or the soldiers under Mischa's command, had killed her lover in Siberia during the Russian civil war. When his sister, Klara, passed away at age ninety-one, Mischa attended her funeral, without telling his daughter where he was going. That's where he revealed to a nephew, the Rasputnis family story. Two years later, Mischa Gershonovich Rasputnis died in his sleep at the age of ninety-two.

•

Mischa and Basya's daughter, Klara, grew up to become a beautiful, charming, intelligent, young lady. With her thin face and long neck, her well-proportioned body and her infectious smile, young Israelis admired her. Partly because it was a good career path and partly because of patriotism to her homeland, Klara remained in the Israeli army, and worked in the Defense Department. She rose to the rank of Colonel. In 1978, she married Dr. Chaim Shaked, a pediatrician. She and her husband resided in Tel Aviv. They had two daughters: Adele, named after after Basya's mother; and Zahava, named after Mischa's mother, Zlota.

After Mischa's death, young Klara struggled to discover her parents' history. She knew nothing about them. Both Volya and Michael had passed away. Her investigations led nowhere, until one Saturday morning in the summer of 2011, she received a package which contained a book, entitled: *"The Commissar,"* by Consul General in New York, Igor Riasanovsky, of The Russian Federation.

Klara picked up the book, sat down in her reading chair in her seashore home, and over the next few days read the 286-page book from cover to cover, including her father's fight with his sister. She learned about the time that Igor and Mischa worked together in Israel where Mischa lost his first child, Klara Rasputnis Warshawskaya. When the youngest Klara reached the last line of the tome: *"You know Basya, God said, 'yes,'"* she put the novel down and cried. She stared out into space, and reflected on how she had searched for her mother and father's past, and ironically, it arrived on her doorstep in the form of a book by a former NKVD agent. She smiled at her father's picture on the cover; turned and gazed at her parents' wedding photo on the side of her desk. She got up from her chair, went outside into the warm sunshine, and heard the morning birdsong filled with fresh air in the green trees of the nearby woods.

•

A week later, Klara Meiri Shaked, with her husband's and children's consent, drove to the Tel Aviv municipal building, where she signed papers and handed over a birth certificate, affidavits and documents. Soon afterwards, she printed new stationary and social cards. Whenever she was asked: "What is your good name?" she would pull out a card that read: *'Klara Rasputnis Meiri Shaked.*

•

A few months later, Klara Rasputnis Meiri Shaked traveled to Baltimore, in the United States. She went out to the Jewish cemetery and walked to the grave of her father's sister, Klara Rasputnis. Unlike her father, Mischa, who had stood outside the fence at his sister's funeral, his daughter, Klara, walked up to the monument, paid her respects, and in the Jewish tradition of honoring a visitation to a buried loved one or friend, placed a stone on the monument as she was leaving and uttered in Hebrew:

"Now we finally have Shalom Bayit, peace in the family."

•

www.ingramcontent.com/pod-product-compliance
Lightning Source LLC
Chambersburg PA
CBHW051635260626
47170CB00004B/1186